My Boy
Louis Riel

The inside story as told by a Metis relative

Carrie Bouvette-Mason

authorHOUSE®

Parents of the author, Mae Bouvette and Tom Bouvette,
(descendant of the Lagimodiere Clan.)

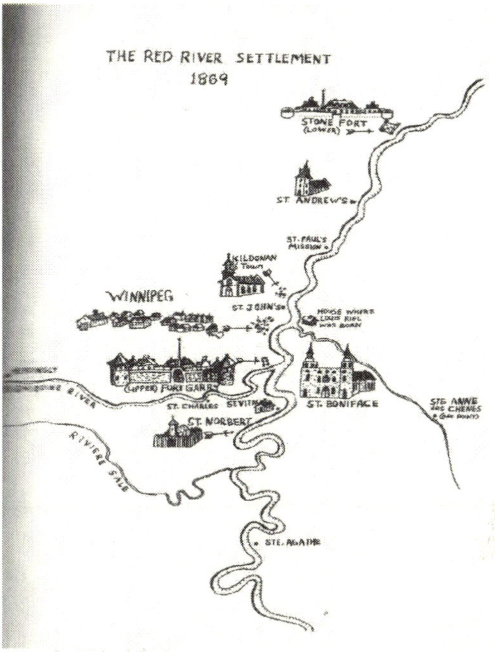

Maps by Michael Siggins

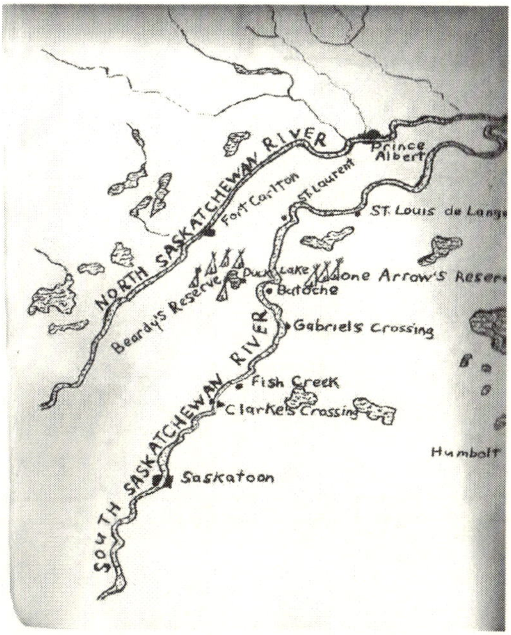

"The Battle of Batoche 1885"

AuthorHouse™
1663 Liberty Drive
Bloomington, IN 47403
www.authorhouse.com
Phone: 1-800-839-8640

Published by AuthorHouse 11/05/2014

ISBN: 978-1-4969-5003-1 (sc)
ISBN: 978-1-4969-5004-8 (hc)
ISBN: 978-1-4969-5002-4 (e)

Library of Congress Control Number: 2014919320

Contents

From the Author's Desk

It all began at a little Catholic parish called St. Vital, in the Settlement of Red River, in what is now Manitoba.

The Louie Riel story has been written many times by some of the finest historical researchers in North America. I swear; I had no idea what I was dealing with.

Most of us have heard the story in Grade six or seven; but somehow, I always felt like there should be more to the story than '…the raving fanatic who led a rebellion against the Canadian government. Then the incredible ending… he was convicted of Treason… and hung for the murder of Thomas Scott. It went right over my head.

Ever since I read "Halfbreed", written by Maria Campbell, I have been toying with the notion of writing. Like Maria, I wanted to contribute to telling 'our' side of the story.

Like I say, the story of Louie Riel had been told over and over by some of the best; but, something was wrong; I could not put a finger on it. They were generous with descriptions; I knew he was handsome; they told of his insanity, his 'triumphs and tragedies', so to speak.

Still, after seven years of researching, at least a dozen versions, my information was overwhelming and I still felt there should be more to this story.

As I continued to accumulate files of research, (7 journals), I began to realize...I had the 'proverbial tiger' by the tail. My three favourite versions: "Strange Empire" by Joseph Kinsey Howard; "Louie Riel", by Maggie Siggins and "Lagimodiere", by Hector Coutu and Terry Lusty, were treasure trove's of information.

I began to feel very intimidated; who did I think I was? I felt that I could never compete with writers of this calibre...but 'God works in mysterious ways, His wonders to perform'.... I entered a contest and out of one hundred and eighty contestants, my work earned me a course in Creative Writing at Banff School of Fine Arts!

My heart soared; my children were thrilled. They stepped in and took over for me in caring for their gravely ill father, who was recovering from a life-saving 'Triple 'A' Surgery'.

The wonderful support and guidance I received in Banff from my fellow students and several published authors, spurred me on.

I enjoyed many quiet and private nights as I sought the will of God out on the balcony of a cozy room in a gorgeous Hotel nestled in the mountains. I felt blessed, after a month of trauma in an Intensive Care Unit, I felt that God really cared what I was going through. Not only did He give me the assurance that my husband would be okay; but, a calmness came over my heart that, '...yes I should write the story of Louie Riel' ; the Creator and my Elders would be with me to guide me as I launched into this monumental undertaking.

I also shook off the idea of competing. I would not be competing; I should consider this as an assignment; another opportunity to give a voice to those who have been wrongly portrayed in history. This would be a chance of a life-time to set the books straight, so to speak.

So, this is my story, the way I see it, from an Aboriginal perspective. It has been seven years of hard work and many tears of frustration, and tears of joy, at times. Louie Riel was coming to life!

I feel like I know Louie Riel, as a good friend…it has been very difficult to finish this book… I hope you all enjoy it!

Note: If you feel like you need insight into his Court proceedings or the massive funeral that was held in the St. Boniface Cathedral, there are some excellent portrayals in my research books that I have previously mentioned.

Acknowledgements

First of all I would like to thank my darling 95 year old mother; for her patience, guidance and encouragement. Secondly I would like to thank my husband Ray (or Teek…the handsome pedal steel guitar player), who provided me with genuine Metis characteristics, humour and at times a generous serving of humble pie.

A special thanks to my children who have been patient with me throughout the long haul, as I slugged my way through the production of this 'phantom' book. I have found it difficult at times to even interact properly as I moved deeper into my research; I am sure they must have needed to tolerate a few blank looks……I love them all dearly. So to Alvin (and Maryanne), Jack (and Dianne), Kathy (and John), Marlene (and Dale), Penny (and Roger), Judy (and Harvey), Rebecca (and Rosco, my deceased son); to Rosco's wonderful twins Georgia and Hayden who reside in Boonah, Queensland Australia, as well as all their Canadian cousins….. please accept Gramma's apologies for forgetting many things, many times. I love you all!

There are many others who have supported me throughout this journey, like Sarah at Blitzprint Publishing, and Delena Barker, my final Editor. Also other Editors like; Marguerite Whiskeyjack, my sister, who found it more important to teach her students, (niche!)' and Carol Simpson, who abandoned me for her sick friends, (the nerve!). Thank you also to my brother George (and Sherry) and to Leo (and Shirley) for the loan of Maggie Siggins's great book.

I would like to send out another thank you to special Elders who have encouraged me like Suzanne Coutu, who gave me written permission to use "Lagimodieres", written by her husband, Hector Coutu with co-writer Terrance Lusty. Thank you to Maria Campbell (author of Half-breed), for her support, and Nellie Carlson, (with Kay Anderson), of Disinherited Generations.

Finally I thank my nephew, Father Cristino Bouvette, who loaned me the precious book of "Strange Empire", by Joseph Kinsey Howard. Above all else, I thank a loving Creator who has stood beside me through all the ups and downs involved with writing this book.

Thank you my readers. Love and Blessings!

Carrie Bouvette Mason

Prologue: Louis Riel, "My Boy"

"My people shall sleep for one hundred years at which time they shall be awakened through the Arts."

Louis Riel, 1885

That gaze........ I have seen that gaze before......

As a self-proclaimed people watcher; anywhere that I can study faces, body language, eyes......

To get to the point, there are all kinds of eyes; sad eyes, happy eyes, busy eyes, penetrating eyes, and eyes that look beyond.....

Such are the eyes of Messrs. Louis Riel Sr., and Louis Riel Jr. They both saw something privileged, and invisible to others.

It is the 'gaze of a visionary'; a familiar look that I grew up seeing in both my Mom and Dad. They shared their visions and worked tirelessly at making them a reality for the First Nations people of this great land.

As I continued to study the life of Louis Riel, I have always been struck by his eyes. In any of his photos.... there it was; that familiar look. Piercing eyes. looking beyond.......

Louis Riel went to his death with a satisfied mind, content that he had forgiven all his accusers, and words of praise flowed from his heart to a Lord who has never let him down.

His vision was for things to come; things that would bring about a series of revolutionary events that would set a new course for the Canadian First Nations people.

The Metis Nation would play a vital role in this series of events beginning with the 1985 inclusion of Metis people into the education budget of Indian Affairs. In the 1986 Annual Report, registration in post secondary institutions hit a record high; it soared to an all time increase of 800%, with the Metis Nation leading the pack!

Since then, increasing numbers of First Nations people have been graduating every year, many of them in the Arts. They can be seen on APTN, the Aboriginal Peoples Television Network, as they appear in a multitude of artistic endeavours, including the practical presentation of daily television.

Where did they all come from? Producers, directors, writers, musicians, dancers, drummer, artists......this is the renaissance prophesied through Louis Riel in 1885!

Discovered amongst the piles of journals, poems and other profound writings of Louis Riel, was the above prophecy.

In 1985, I was blessed to witness the beginnings of this prophecy, as I continued to pursue my degree in Anthropology: Natives of North America, and a Major in English Literature. To my amazement, the halls were sprinkled with aboriginal faces. We formed a Native Student Alliance that met every Friday in the afternoon, and from there it took on a snowball effect to what we are seeing today.

The fulfillment of this prophecy has stirred the hearts of the Canadian Metis Nation. A people who for generations have hanged our heads as grade seven history teachers delivered the shameful events of the Riel Rebellion, influenced by British information.

Over the years, in my career as Executive Director of an Aboriginal Organization, I worked with many people who looked beyond the current situations and news events, to see a vision of hope for the future of my people.

We are beginning to raise our heads and are setting our eyes upon a vision. God help our future generations who are also beginning to look beyond what is today…

***Carrie BouvetteMason,* ©2013**

Chapter One

St. Boniface, Red River: 1857...

A soft breeze is blowing and except for a few high, wispy clouds, the June skies are a clear, calming blue. Louie can smell the old Red River, a few hundred feet away from where he is seated under his 'thinking tree'. It is a familiar smell... a good smell.

It snakes its way along the edge of the old St. Vital property belonging to his Papa, Monsieur Louie Riel Sr. who is adored by Louie, his eldest son. A slight breeze is coming off the old Red River

Louie lifts his little flat-brimmed grey hat from his thick curls; he scratches his head and wipes the sweat from his forehead. The breeze coming off the old Red River is perfect for a hot summer day.

It is late afternoon as Louie shifts his back to a more comfortable position against the bark of his favourite old tree. An occasional scow drifts by, each one carrying a charade of curious cargos.

Louie checks the river traffic from the corner of his eye; if it looks interesting he will tear himself away from his book for a few moments to play one of his river games.

York boats of the Hudson Bay Company and large freight canoes of the Northwest Company are common; they rarely rate a glance.

An old raft drifts by; traditional tamarack* railing surrounds the perimeter of the raft; it provides a secure fence for the transport of animals, children, or whatever might be the freight of the day.

What appears to be a young native mother holding her baby on her lap, rocking gently back and forth, is turning out to be an old Kokum* in a squeaky rocking chair. As the raft draws nearer and drifts quietly by, Louie muses in French… *Not a good guess.* The young bearded man, wearing a tired old cowboy hat, stands like a sentry beside a small heater. In one hand he holds a long pole that rises from the water showing a hand-made rudder; in his teeth he holds a pipe; the other hand wipes the sweat from his brow as he raises the tattered brim of his hat. Small puffs of smoke are swirling around into the air. *He is not so young either; must be the Mooshum*…* Louie thinks in Mechif.

A canvas shelter is stretched across one end over what looks to be a large, stuffed mattress; three small boys are romping on it, "Muh*, mes garçon*, apis*; people are close!"

His gentle mechif* admonition fades into the distance along with the diminishing squeak of the old handmade rocker… as they drift on down the river.

He squints at them from his private vantage point… a comfortable, grassy mound under an old maple tree at the end of a long lane. They cannot see him because of the willows lining the river and the leafy branches hanging over his head… but he can see them… *I wonder if they are enjoying a family trip down the river; or are they so poor they are moving away …or maybe they are going camping with their relations to pick berries.*

Even though his book is in English he is able to think in French. Louie's amusement ends and he goes back to his book.

He leans back to feel the bark of the tree pressing into his shoulder blades once again.

In the background he can hear the laughter of his little sisters, Eulalie and Octavie as they play with Louie Sr.'s old black dog, Ruth. Very faintly Louie can hear the squeak of the old swing as his nine year- old sister Sara pushes their seven year- old sister Marie, gently, back and forth, back and forth; chickens are pecking and clucking peacefully.

Louie is deeply engrossed in a book he has brought home from the Mission at St. Boniface.

He rides his old mare, "Annie", over there to the mission every week or so, to get some schooling; his Papa insists on it. Father LaFloch instructs him when he is there; or, if Father Taché is also away doing parish visits, he is instructed by the nuns.

Soon his beautiful 'Mama' will be calling for help …it is hard to leave his thinking tree; it is his "… *most favourite place in the world"* he tells his Mama.

"It is so quiet and peaceful sitting under dis old tree where I can t'ink and pray… read… or just get h'away and be h'alone for h'awhile." He is thinking in his broken English; his book is an issue from the Hudson Bay Company, the British government of the day. Bishop Taché encourages the three boys, who come for lessons, to learn a bit of English.

"It will help you to manage later, when they get older, my boy." Father Taché speaks in a smooth, sophisticated dialect of French he learned to speak at the Seminary in Montreal. Because Louie's Papa spent three years in the Seminary, preparing for the priesthood, his French is somewhat the same; had he not met the beautiful Julie Lagimodiere, he may have been a priest today.

Julie appears in the doorway, her light cotton skirts held firmly at the waist by a green, striped pinafore*, "Astum,* my boy, sil vous plait*!" she calls out in Mechif, "I am going to make a stew for our evening meal. I will be needing vegetables from the cellar."

As she turns and steps lightly over the door jamb* in her beaded moccassins, a large, green striped bow can be seen hanging from her small waist.* (A larger bow in the back of the dress generally signifies that she is from the middle class.) Louie Sr. is a respected business man and politician in the community, who would be classified as, 'a member of the bourgeoisie'[1].

Julie is using a bit of Mechif today, though she often speaks in Quebec French*[2] to her children; much like her Mama, Marie Ann Lagimodiere.

Now, Julie's mother was born Marie Anne Gaboury, in Maskinonge Quebec. She was married to Jean Baptiste Lagimodiere*[3] April 21st, 1806; he was also born in Quebec; in a busy trading villiage called Three Rivers (or trois Riviere).

Until Jean Baptiste passed away two years ago, they spoke to each other in old French; Julie still finds the Quebec French most comfortable; that is how she was raised. Her Cree and Mechif have been learned from friends and relatives in the community; she has been raised speaking Quebec French.

Most Natives living in the valley speak Mechif. It is the language of the land... a musical blend of French and Cree; the children even speak it as they play.

Julie's handsome husband, Louie Riel Sr. was born at Ile-a-la-Cross, in the Northwest Territories and though he speaks a fine French, he is also quite fluent in several Native languages, due to his years spent as a Voyageur.

While trading with the Cree, Ojibwe, Blackfoot and Sioux, for the fine furs of the west, he needed to be proficient in all languages, as did most of his colleagues.

He has used these languages enough in the presence of young Louie Jr. so that he also has picked up on them, particularly the Cree and Ojibwe, which is commonly used by the Indians who drop by St. Boniface Mission and Fort Garry. They find young Louie to be a friendly face in an unfamiliar place; he greets them quietly in their own language.

When the four little girls see their big brother heading up the lane from his tree they run excitedly into the house, "Louie's coming, Louie's coming!" they squeal.

"Mah*, quiet my girls! You will waken duh babies!" says Papa Louie, as he raises his finger to his mustached lips. He winks at Julie and smiles at his two guests who are in the middle of an intent conversation. Louie does not wish this exchange to be interrupted.

Eulalie runs and hugs Louie's legs as he comes through the screen door.

Twelve year old Louie, acting very grown-up, greets the men who are seated at the large dining room table with his Papa. They are his Papa's good friends, Monsignor Taché and Monsieur Joseph L'Ambitieaux, known only as "Lamito"; from the spelling of Scottish factors working at Hudson Bay Posts.

Louie shakes hands with both men, dark curls bobbing on his forehead as he gives them each a nod. He recalls only raising his hand in a weak wave when they rode their horses up the lane past him, he scarcely acknowledged them; he was deep in his book.

As the sound of hoof-beats faded away, he resumed his reading. A strong feeling of guilt swept over him as he thought to himself, *I know I should have gone to take care of dere horses but I will be sure to fetch dem when dey leave.*

"Greetings Messieurs, I will fetch your horses when you need them." says Louie as he sets himself down by his Papa. Both Louie's thoughts and words have now reverted back to French.

"Well, my boy, your uncle Lamito will likely be camping overnight," Papa Louie informs him. "...he said they would camp if the women take too long shopping and visiting in Fort Garry, tapway,* Lamito?"

They are no relation but in the Metis tradition, 'uncle'or 'auntie' is used rather than addressing an older acquaintance by their first name.

"Oui, mon ami," says Monsieur L"Ambitieaux, with a nod of his wavy graying head.

"Will Pierre be there?" Louie asks his uncle.

"Oui, Lamito's whole gang will be here, I suppose." Papa Louie says, "Now pour us some tea, my boy, sil vous plait."

"Yes," says Lamito, "Pierre and the whole noisy bunch will be here, music and all," he ends with a grin, his grey mustache spreading across his face.

"Aeeee!" yells Louie, as he springs up, both hands on the table, clearing the heavy bench at the back and wearing a big smile as he scurries to pour the tea.

"Settle down now, my boy, and act like a gentleman," says Louie Sr.

"I am sorry Papa, but I get so happy when Pierre comes!" says Louie as he settles back down behind the old table.

The old hand-made dining table is comfortably situated under French windows, which are wide open to let in a slight breeze coming in from the west.

Julie is feeling a bit sluggish from the heat as she returns from a quick trip out to the garden for a handful of small early onions to add to her stew.

She wipes some sweat drops from her small, tanned face using the tip of her long blue apron; a strand of wavy brown hair falls across one eye.

For a young woman who has born seven children and suffered the loss of two of them, Julie is still very beautiful.

The men have resumed their conversation and Louie is sitting up straight soaking in their every word.

"Please Louie, go now and fetch the vegetables, while I watch the girls!" It can be annoying at times when young Louie moves so slow... *If only he would forget about the cares of the adults and pay attention to his chores!* Julie thinks to herself.

She sets the onions over on the utility table next to the tall, kitchen cupboard directly across from the old wood-burning cook-stove. She grabs a sturdy willow basket from among a variety of baskets hanging from a log rafter and hands it to Louie to take down in the cellar for vegetables.

The two older girls, Sara and Marie are now indoors and are playing on a braided rug in the parlor with their little sisters Eulalie and Octavie. Baby brother, Joseph is sleeping in a swing that is suspended from the ceiling above Julie's bed, and little Charlie has been napping on the couch next to a small unlit fireplace at the north end of the house; he is due to awaken anytime.

As hot and tired as she is, Julie still has to smile as she sees her young son sitting spellbound at the table listening intently to his Papa and two other leading politicians from the Red River community.

"You are excused Louie, help your mother now, sil vous plait," says Louie Sr. as he gives Julie his familiar wink.

Young Louie climbs off the wooden bench behind the table and hurries over to the cellar to help his Mama. He needs to get back before he misses something interesting.

There is nothing as exciting as listening to these seasoned politicians. Sometimes, during a lively exchange, the conversation will swell like the old Red River in a raging storm ... then dissipate with a burst of laughter, like the changing weather of the old Red River valley. For a few moments quiet remarks will trickle around the table as they fill their pipes or pour some tea.

There is a fairly lively exchange taking place around the table now and Julie pays no mind to these hot speculations; she has grown up listening to these concerns.

Generally it involves the blatant disregard for Native and Metis issues by government officials... the authority of the time being the Hudson Bay Company.

Lately there has been an ever growing interest in John A. Macdonald, a man of vision and strong ambitions. His influence with policy makers appears primarily to insure support for Upper Canada's wealthiest Corporations. Strangely enough, he conveniently holds positions of influence on most of the governing boards; ...things are getting progressively worse as these people take control.

Julie is informed enough to get a great kick out of some of the pictures drawn by the younger boys who love to make fun of people by sketching their pictures. Some of their depictions of John A. are hilarious; the more that they exaggerate John A.'s hair and nose, the harder their parents laugh.

Most sketches depict John A. as a hard working voyageur or farmer. He is sometimes splattering beads of sweat as he portages over a high river-bank or pulls a plow through lumpy ground, wearing his famous top-hat and 'tails'.

One of the favourite pass-times of the Metis people is to conjure up nick-names for everyone, including the esteemed, John A. Macdonald, who has no use for the Metis people. He once was quoted as saying:

"They are a nuisance and an impediment to economic growth."*[2] Quote Riel Rebellion-1885-Frank Anderson.

One of the favorite nick-names "old Pocket" was introduced by Paul L'Ambitieaux who lives in Montreal. He is married into the Menard family who deal in leather, and is the second eldest son of Monsieur Lamito, sitting here at the table today. He has only used it once but all three men know immediately who he is referring to and they all take the liberty to get as many laughs as possible from the famous line ... picked up by Paul returning from York with the latest news...

"Apparently"... according to a witness, "...the proper and refined John A. was delivering one of his eloquent presentations to a group of stockholders. Suddenly, his "liquid" lunch flew from his mouth with such a force he had only time to open the wide pocket of his fine, long-tailed, red tunic."

As the story goes, ...in his usual gallant form, he immediately made reference to his excellent skills in the game of billiards; then, he carried on with no more than a good laugh from his stockholders. These antics were becoming commonplace so when Paul returned from York with a new name for John A., "Old puke in the pocket", it was very well received! It has been said that, on that notable occasion, Sir John had one opponent question his drunken behavior; his response was, "...it goes to show you that we would rather have a drunk Conservative than a sober Liberal!" ...or so the story goes.

The citizens of the Red River Colony have sensed for many years, the "squeeze" moving in from the east.*

> *[3] This ideology of "ethnic cleansing" is exemplified in "Birth of Western Canada" by George Stanley, pg. 88: Quote from, Canada and the Métis, 1869-1885:
>
> *"... while praising the new dominion for its zealous expansion, he still expressed sympathy for the frustrations of the clergy and the tragic losses of the Indians and the Metis. The tragedy was their doom as a people.*
>
> *The natives had to fail. They were a "primitive peoples" standing against the march of "civilization." At the minimum, they had to be pushed aside to make way for newcomers."* Pg. 88, George Stanley.

Julie is informed enough that she is a faithful support to Louie Sr.; her Papa was a well-known politician, so it is not a matter of ignorance that she pays so little mind to the banter. Having been tutored by the nuns, she is also fairly well read. It is just not her place to get involved.

It would be quicker for Julie to go down in the cellar and get the vegetables but it is an eight foot drop on three narrow steps down into the cellar. The celler was dug fairly deep in order to make shelf space for the preserves, and cold bins for the root vegetables. *I hope I can trust Louie with the children again some day …he means well, he just can't remember to pay attention!* Julie lights the lantern and hands it to Louie.

"I would go down myself if I knew you would not read and would watch the children carefully,"

Soon Louie is handing up her basket filled with potatoes, a few carrots and one medium sized turnip. Flashbacks of that tragic day are trying to press in; …Louie manages to push them away.

Once she has her vegetables up and the cellar door is safely closed with the old rug spread over it, Julie again busies herself around the kitchen and hums a little tune as she works. Humming is a habit with Julie; she doesn't realize the comfortable feeling it brings into the home.

"Merci, my boy, I will watch Charles when he wakens, you may take the girls out to the shade," says Julie.

She recalls the many discussions she and Papa Louie have had concerning Louie's lack of regard for daily mundane chores; …he is generally preoccupied with his latest book, borrowed from the mission.

Some folks think he is lazy but he obeys his parents without question and tries to get back to his books as quickly as possible. He seems to have an insatiable appetite for knowledge.

"Oui,* Mama, only, Papa and Monsieur L'Ambitieux are so very interesting. They are so smart Mama! I wish when I grow up that I shall be smart just like my Papa!"

His Papa has always been a giant in his eyes and today Papa's friends have inspired him with a lively conversation regarding free trade with the U.S. He can sense the pride in their voices as they excitedly recall the 1849 stand-off when they successfully defeated the Hudson Bay's resistance to free trade with the U.S.* [4]

A quote from "Strange Empire" by Joseph Kinsey Howard:

'… and in 1849 the people and the Company had it out. The Company lost … a Metis standing in the doorway (of the courthouse), shouted the news: "Le commerce est libre! Viva la liberté"

The slogan spread like fire across the plains of the Red River, south along the rutted trail to Pembina and St. Paul. The Metis sang and danced; the Yankee traders grinned; the Company of Adventurers had been cut down to size. Enforcement of its monopolistic decrees was never seriously attempted again. One could buy a Red River cart for ten dollars or make one for less, and the trail to St. Paul was open and free.' -Pg. 59, Howard: New York, 1952.

Young Louie has been mesmerized many times by the ambitious discussions between these three articulate speakers. They are actually all seated at Julie's work table having tea and bannock with raspberry jam. What a thrill for young Louie!

"Merci*, my boy, but our talk now is for grown-ups and it is not for a twelve year old boy to worry about. Now take your baby sisters out to play so Mama can fix our meal."

Louie's days are sometimes very busy between caring for his younger siblings and working in the garden. Caring for the two older girls, Sara and Marie, he enjoys. They love to hear him read stories in English, which is one of his greatest pleasures. The two younger ones, Octavie and Eulalie, need to be watched closely if he reads.

Papa reminds him once more…"Now mind they don't go near the canal." Just the mention of the canal stirs up feelings of guilt, fear and foreboding. *There they go again…*tears begin to burn Louie's eyes; once again he must shake off that tragic scene.

He hides his feelings with a cheery reply... "Pardon me Papa, I am twelve and I will be thirteen in October." He pulls at the curls on top of his head as though he is not sure if he may be overstepping his manners.

"Oui, my son, now, awoos!* Take your sisters and watch them close, do not take your book." *'ere we go again; I will be so 'appy to be an h'adult. Louie will no longer be a nuisance...per'aps he shall be a School Master*! No one shall stop him from reading den!*

Glossary.

Footnotes:

1 Bourgeoisie: likely equivalent to the current 'middleclass'
2 Typical Metis humour
3 Those in power viewed Natives as a nuisance to be pushed out of the way of progress.
4 The stand-off of the Metis in 1849 which resulted in a 'Free Trade' victory.

Chapter Two

Riel Gathering, St. Boniface farm: 1857...

As young Louie and his little sisters make their exit, Louie Sr. spreads out a rough sketch of the layout for a grist mill he has designed, a newer version since the last meeting.

His good friend Lamito, is about to support him in his venture. Perhaps he may even get some help from the Catholic Church if the venture will support enough parishioners. The little sawmill is already providing work, from time to time, for several men in the community.

"Mon ami*, do you not see the passion for knowledge in the eyes of your son?" Monsignor Taché watches Louie as he disappears out the door with his little sisters. Louie Sr. looks at his son and winks at the Father in acknowledgment.

Louie has grabbed the hair brush and some ties on his way past the armoire, he remembers to himself ... *both of these little girls prefer the way I braid their hair.* He never gets in a hurry and is always gentle. *Who cares if the braids are a little bit loose*? ...He thinks to himself.

Eulalie looks up at her big brother and tells him in an adorable little French baby talk ... "I like your braids Youie, they don't hurt like Mama's".

Louie is still thinking about the discussion he had to leave. He is having pleasant thoughts. *Now I will be able to hear some of the talk from around that table coming through the open windows.*

"Quiet now, my girls." he whispers, as he grabs a big piece of soft buffalo hide and spreads it on the old heavy work table under the window. It is made of smoothly planed*[1] two inch boards made at his Papa's sawmill. *Solid as a rock…* Louie muses to himself.

He smiles and whispers, "Here you are, my beautiful sisters! Api!* Eulalie first, Tapway, Octavie?" *This old table has held up under the butchering of all kinds of game over the years, so they say,* muses Louie, *I'm sure it will hold up these little girls.*

"Oui my brother, I am the big sister, I will hold the ties for you!" Octavie whispers with a slight lisp added to her French. She is only five and her baby talk is so cute that Louie generally keeps her talking, but not today.

Sara is already busy brushing out her little sister Marie's hair; she is seven, two years younger than Sara. Louie is praying that they do not jabber or he will not hear the men as they speak.

He begins brushing Eulalie's wavy brown hair, it is quite fine and is the color of Julie's, a rich brown with red highlights. He takes his time and brushes ever so gently; only the odd whimper comes from his little sister and even that is muffled, as she sucks her thumb constantly.

He strains his ears to get the gist of what is being said and adjusts to the familiar Mechif dialect used by Lamito. Papa Louie and the Monsignor speak the Quebec dialect as does his Mama, unless in the company of Cree people.

"My friends, I have been feeling discouraged. My dream of providing jobs for half of the community with a woolen mill, or even a grist mill, is fading rapidly. The channel is now complete over to the Seine and the Hudson Bay will still not finance me for the larger wheel…and John A. is of no help.

Our unscrupulous John A. is becoming harder to deal with. If he insists that the Canadian authorities are unable to find money to assist the project, the least they can do is allow me some permits. Someday these things will be the jurisdiction of Manitoba!" He has been fending off threats to shut down the saw-mill, until he has a permit.

"Oiu mon ami, his concerns are for the building of the railroad and we seem to be viewed as nothing more than an obstacle to his plans for progress. We will see what Pierre has to say when they arrive", says Lamito, shaking his head in disgust, "... Pierre and his family will be arriving soon to pick me up for the trip home, or set up camp for the night. Depending how late they are. Our daughter Madeleine and her husband Keiren will also be here soon. Don't forget, my friend, they are also interested in your mills."

"Merci, mon ami, your family has always been a support to us, Lamito. You have grieved with us at the loss of our baby girl, and when we lost our son, you were there for us again. Your boys have been a blessing, my friend; we would never have dug that canal without their help."

The digging of a canal that would bring water all around his property was a massive undertaking. All the L'Ambitieaux boys had spent much of their spare time for two summers digging the canal. Everyone recalls the excitement of digging the final two feet that eventually sent a flow of water from the old Seine River into the thirsty canal that would flow out into the Red River and provide drainage for low lands. There was a big feast and a shindig the day the water broke through!

If the L'Ambitieaux boys were not freighting furs and trade goods out on the rivers they were happy to be at the Riel farm; it was a good excuse to have some of Julie's great cooking.

They looked forward to helping Monsieur Riel set up his mills which would be powered by water wheels or steam. Whenever things began looking hopeless the boys would cheer up "Honcle* Louie with words from Lamito: "It is good for you boys, you need to stay in shape for shooting the rapids, am I right or am I wrong!", a favourite expression of the old voyageurs which would generally bring a response of "Oui, oui." or "Tapway." Both of which meant basically "Yes."

"It has been a pleasure, my friend, God has given us five husky boys and they are not afraid of work."

Lamito is proud of how the boys have turned out. Their mother, Catherine, in her quiet Cree ways, has been a hard worker and has set a good example for her boys. Lamito has trained them all in the ways of trading, trapping, and horse-handling. Above all, he has brought them up in the faith and has taught them all the trade secrets of being a professional Voyageur.

Louie Sr. has made many attempts to get Louie Jr. involved with learning the outdoor skills of the Metis to no avail, he prefers to study and learn under Father Taché and Father La Floch. What little he has learned of the outdoors has been on his trips with his "frére", Pierre L'Ambitieaux who has always allowed Louie to follow him around.

Louie Sr. lowers his voice, "You have all been witness to the disinterest shown by our son, toward the industries of our community. He would rather read a book than to hunt, trap or cut wood ... God forbid that we should ever ask him to run freight in a couple of years, or worse yet, ... train for military service. I swear, he is not lazy or disobedient ...he just has no interest and his heart is not in it. I have no son to work with me."

He runs his fingers through his thick curly hair. "God knows how I have prayed for a son to share my dreams," he says in a throaty whisper, thinking about the handicap of his little son Charles.

Monsignor Taché clears his throat; he has been quietly listening to the two men. They both lean back now to hear what the Father has to say; he is generally quiet but when he has something to say they know that it will be significant.

Monsignor Taché began his commission here in the Red River settlement as a young Priest fresh out of seminary. In a few short years he has won the hearts of most of the community, he is a man of his word.

"I have watched both of you, my friends, I have no intention of directing you in business; however, I may have a suggestion that would be acceptable to all concerned."

He rubs his chin and removes his spectacles … "I also have a dream. You know that I have been supportive to the visions of you all, mes ami." He waves his hand around the table. "We will continue to pursue your dreams and we will accomplish whatever is the will of God, I am sure."

He turns to Louie and fixes his eyes on him. "I will continue to solicit support for your business pursuits from the Government; however, I will pursue support from the Catholic Church even more fervently if you will speak to Madame Julie on my behalf." He clears his throat once more and leans even closer to Louie Sr.

"What I am about to suggest will mean the possible fulfillment of a large portion of your dream. It very well could break the heart of Madame Julie, however."

He leans back in his chair; he can see Julie sweeping off the veranda out front; they will need to be discreet at this time.

"I have no idea what you are talking about, Monsignor!" Louie says trying hard not to show his excitement. "… What are you saying?" Louie leans forward, dropping his voice to a whisper as he remembers Julie out front and young Louie out back, possibly within earshot.

Taché clears his throat once again. "Mon ami, your son is not an average child, he is gifted. We have mentioned his unusual tendencies from time to time. His devotion to our God and the Holy Catholic Church goes much deeper than most other young boys his age."

"Oui, oui, Monsignor, we have seen this many times. He stays behind to pray when we leave the Holy Mass to go home and eat." Louie Sr. is becoming anxious to hear Father Taché's proposal.

Taché loosens his collar, "I am going to suggest that your son be sent off to Seminary in Montreal, one of our faithful patrons from the city is willing to provide scholarships for three of our local boys, I have been praying about this and I have no doubt that your son is an excellent candidate."

"Monsignor, I am overwhelmed! But … please pray for my Julie, she has already suffered the loss of our other son." Louie's voice cracks as he is suddenly overcome with grief.

Julie comes back in the house and the Monsignor lifts his cup to finish his tea. "Merci, Madame Julie, you make a fine cup of tea and your bannock is superb"

"Well, mes ami, I will leave that with you to ponder and bring me your reply when you are ready. I must return to the Mission, our Sisters will have the evening meal cooking, I can hear horses approaching so I will bid you bon soir*," he pushes back his chair.

"Oui, Monsignor, that is the wagons of Pierre and Keiren and their wives, you must stay and eat with us," says Louie Sr., as he stands up looking towards the window.

"Oui, Monsignor. Their wives are excellent cooks, they will be fixing something to add to Julie's meal just as soon as they start a fire," urges Lamito, he has no problem offering the hospitality of his children. It is a Metis tradition to share your food with whoever happens by.

"Merci, merci, mes ami, the Sisters are accustomed to my absence, I will accept your kind offer." The Monsignor fetches his own hat to greet Pierre's entourage who are noisily dismounting from their horses and tying up to the hitching rail out in the yard.

Meanwhile Julie hears the commotion outside. Looking out the window she sees Madeleine driving her shiny black team up the lane. She can see another team turning the bend, right by Louie's tree. His 'favorite place in the world', he always says…he refers to it as, '*je arbre de réfléchir*'*2, *or,* his 'thinking tree'.

Julie squints her eyes as she looks up the lane, it is Joleine driving her two bay mares. They have the flaps closed on their covered wagons to keep the mosquitos out. *Tonight is going to be fun I can see, what a lively family!* Julie is excited to see the company arriving!

"Mon Garçon*! Watch your sisters! Horses are coming!" Julie calls out the window to Louie.

Young Louie appears from behind the house, he is trying to settle his two little sisters down who are both yelling, "Maddie, Maddie!

Madeleine yells out to her team, "Whoa, King, Whoa, Prince!"

She pulls the team up to the side of the house, "Bonjour*, my boy! Your sisters are getting big and very beautiful, Louie!"

"Bon jour*, mes ami!* It is so good to see you and you also Monsieur Keiren!" Louie Jr. says, as he offers his hand to Keiren who gives young Louie a firm hand-shake. At the same time Keiren takes note at just how mannerly he is for his age.

"Greetings me man! Tapway*! Mewasin*and a g'day ta yersef, mon ami!"

Keiren speaks a better Mechif than Louie, even though it is spiced with friendly Irish idioms. He has lived in the valley since Lamito rescued him from the streets of St. Paul, Minnesota at the age of twelve. He is now the husband of Madeleine and the father of their wee son, Bengimen.

"Joleine and Marie are right behind us, with the twins, so we will be setting up camp as soon as we greet your parents, "says Madeleine, the organizer of the clan. She turns to shake the hand of Father Taché "Greetings, Father! We will quickly make a fire and stir up a big batch of fry bannock before you leave. The boys will set up camp in the usual spot out back, Tapway Oncle?" Madeleine inquires.

"The Monsignor is not leaving, my girl. He is staying for supper," says Louie with a grin. There is a community joke that the Priests generally look forward to Metis hospitality.

Keiren has shook hands with all the men coming down the steps of the veranda and Madeleine is giving Julie one of her famous hugs. The little girls are already playing with Louie L'Ambitieux's old black dog "Mooshwa" along with Madeleine's little three year old boy, "Bennie".

Old Ruth or "Root", (as Papa Louie calls her), has finished her barking responsibilities and is back on the veranda by Papa Louie's rocking chair. Papa named her "Ruth" after a charming Bible character he fell in love with during his stint in Seminary years ago.

Louie Sr. offers chairs to all the men and takes his short-stemmed pipe from a beaded pukagon* pouch hanging around his neck as he settles onto his rocker.

A cool breeze is stirring the lilac bushes along the house. He taps his pipe and begins filling it with kinikinik*, then passes his little muskimoot* to Lamito, who takes one pinch of the tobacco and pokes it into his pipe. While he is tightening the string on the pouch with his teeth, Louie Sr. passes him a lit match. Lamito takes one long draw on his pipe and blows the match out with a puff of smoke.

"It's beginning now to cool down some; we will eat out here on the veranda. It will be nice once we get rid of the mosquitoes," says Louie as he takes the first squeaky drag off his pipe and points the pipe-stem at young Louie, "My boy, fix some smudges for the evening, omuh"* *Mechif comes natural in this crowd,* he thinks to himself.

"Oui, Papa." Louie says as he turns little Eulalie over to her Mama.

Madeleine gives Louie Sr. a big hug and addresses him as "Uncle Louie", which is the Metis custom among good friends.

"Oncle," she pleads, "could we have a shindig after supper? My brother Louie has been practicing the fiddle, Pierre has his guitar and Keiren plays his mouth organ. They are playing well, my Oncle, we can even dance to them now."

"I expect for you to hall* set up camp so it sounds good to me, Maddie, I tought we would have no music wit your brudder Gabe still down in St Paul wit your brudder Paul. What do you tink Julie?" Louie Sr. has resorted to English now for the sake of Keiren.

"You know that I welcome music always. Maddie, we will get these old men moving!" She gives her little quiet laugh. Julie is so happy to have them back for a visit that her French is nearly too fast to understand. Keiren is lifting his cap and scratching his red curls, "I reckon she is saying yes, tapway?"

"Oui, Tapway, my man!" Madeliene is winking at Julie, chortling away with her infectious laugh.

All of Lamito's children have the same noisy laugh that you hear throughout the Red River community. Julie's family is a bit more reserved and not quite so boisterous.

Lamito had ridden out ahead of the chuckwagons that afternoon and left the women to shop in Fort Garry. Father Taché had just happened by, also on horseback. He had chalked up their meeting as a "Devine encounter."

"Greetings to you Keiren," says Julie, shaking Keiren's hand.

"G'day ta ya, Madame Julie, et tu*, aussi* mon ami!"

Once Keiren has greeted everyone he heads for the wagon, "I reckon I best be gettin' busy with camp or Pierre will give me hell; he has the wood in his wagon."

"Dere is a lots of wood stacked in duh back, Keiren, 'elp yourself." Uncle Louie Sr. has fairly good English with a wonderful French accent; young Louie's English is much the same as his Papa's.

"Give him a hand, my boy!" he says to Louie.

"Oui, Papa. It will be great to see Pierre again!" The generally slow-moving Louie has suddenly become energized; he hitches the strap of his bib overalls up into place on his shoulders, his Mama will soon need to make him a new pair, they are getting too short. The space between the ankle of his moccasins and the bottoms of his pantlegs is getting wider as he grows taller.

Pierre pulls Joleine's team up to the house and they all scramble excitedly from their places in the wagon.

"Greetings, mes ami!" Pierre shakes the hands of Louie Sr. and Father Taché, then turns to Madame Julie and gives her a big hug; he takes her by the shoulders and kisses her cheeks. "Bonjour mon beau Tante*[3] Julie!"

Octavie and Eulalie stand and wait for their turns with their hands behind their backs; …Pierre doesn't disappoint them, he kisses their cheeks and swings them 'round and 'round, their little homemade dresses flounced out behind them and their long brown braids flying out behind!

Pierre and Joleine's twins have climbed down out of the wagon and Sara and Marie Riel run happily over to greet them with hugs. Raymone and Georgette have not seen Sara or her sister Marie, since Easter Mass and Georgette hugs them and says in her New Orleans French, "My cousins, you have grown!"

Marie L'Ambitieaux climbs down and hugs the two girls. Marie is Maddie's "sister" and is so beautiful, with her curly, auburn hair and hazel eyes; people who are not familiar with her story generally stare at her for a moment. Some people believe that Catherine had been unfaithful to Lamito.

It is so long ago now that few people ever think about all the young girls who were raped by HBC officers, Madeleine being just one of many. Marie is a fine young lady now with the discipline of Charlotte and Kokum Cardinal's upbringing.

Julie hugs Marie and comments on her beautiful curls. Marie always impresses Julie with her cosmopolitan manners as she kisses her cheeks and bends one knee.

It is now common knowledge that Marie is Madeleine's child, raised by Kokum Cardinal and Madeleine's mother, Catherine L'Ambitieaux.

She was born from a British Hudson Bay man who kidnapped her when she was eight and took her to England*. When she was near death with loneliness the captain brought her back to the Canadas.

Madeleine was just one of many lovely Aboriginal girls who were used for maids and sexual gratification in the fur trade era.*

Pierre and Joleine's twins are seven years old and both speak fluent New Orleans French and are now learning Cree and English along with their mother, who was born and raised in New Orleans.

Young Louie is in his glory, seeing all his relations. Julie gives him a nod when he asks to go to the barnyard; she is so pleased to see him enjoying the company of his buddy Pierre.

She watches him until he struts out of sight around the barn. He steps along quickly to keep up with Pierre as he follows him out to the barnyard, where the horses will be hobbled*[4] for the night.

***

Carrie Bouvette-Mason

**See Glossary:*

Footnotes:

1 *'planed'- a process using handtools to smooth lumber before the introduction of'planer mills*
2 *"My thinking tree"a solitary place to think and read.*
3 *..."ma tanté, Julie"- an old Metis custom was to address older friends as uncle or auntie out of respect, as opposed to using first names.*

Chapter Three

Riel Farm, Red River: 1857...

Keiren has unhitched the team, removed their harnesses and is busy putting their "hobbles"*[1] on their front feet. Suddenly Pierre appears around the corner of the barn with young Louie at his heels.

He leads his unharnessed team over to where Keiren is, "Dere's plenny o' grass for dese critters right here, eh Neestow*?"

"Tapway*, mon Chawam," says Keiren in his Irish flavoured Mechif, "I'll go get a few buckets o' water from duh canal and put in dis trough* to last dem to noon tomarrah... when we pulls out I reckon."

"Tapway, we will 'ave lunch before we pull out, den we will be 'ome ta Red River for h'our evening meal," Pierre says as he finishes hobbling Joleine's horses. "I will go bring h'our saddle horses over and fix dere 'obbles while you get dere water."

"Astum Louie, hep me wit duh saddle horses," he says to young Louie Jr. "It 'as bin a while since we 'ad a visit. What 'ave you been doing, mon ami?"

Louie quickly catches up with him, "I have been very busy taking my schooling from Father La Floch, and helping my Papa when I can." He speaks in mostly French.

"Well, my little brudder, never be ashamed because you wish to get your schooling. Most of h'us never seems to get past reading a bit o' newspaper, signing h'our names and h'a bit o' h'adding and subtracting. Some don't even get dat, dey couldn't sign der damn name if you 'eld a gun to dere 'ead!"

He has himself a good little laugh, at his own joke, which is his custom.

Meanwhile Louie shakes his head back and forth, enjoying a little giggle.

"Merci, mon Chawam," Keiren yells over his shoulder as he heads back to the canal. "I smells duh bannock cookin' already!"

"Dat's our women, Moonyow*[2], dey h'ar fas', just like h'our horses!" Pierre's high winnying laugh echos through the barnyard.

"Watch yer talk Chawam, my wife will thump yor head!" says Keiren with a big toothy grin.

"I know Chawam, it won't be the first time; she is a rough sister." Pierre rubs his little square fist over his curly head.

"I reckon that's what's scrambled yor brain, eh Chawam?" Keiren enjoys a few more giggles.

"Don't talk Moonyow, see 'ow yore brain is in ten years!" Pierre gives another high winnying laugh.

"Nomoya! I keeps me distance!" Keiren quickly demonstrates his side-step.

Louie is following them back to the house; he is still shaking his head back and forth. Even though Keiren and Pierre get carried away with their horsing around at times, Louie always enjoys being around them. They don't seem to have a serious bone in them and it always gives Louie a lift.

They have filled the trough with water, hobbled all the horses and turned them out to eat. Then Pierre and Keiren head back to the big two story frame house of the Riel's.

They pass the potato patch then the vegetable garden; it is framed by a rail fence, lined with raspberry bushes and rhubarb.

"H'uncle Louie is a very 'ard worker, would you say Chawam?" Pierre says as he looks around at Louie's domain … more than a decade of dreams.

"Tapway, dat he is, me frien', he has no hep so I reckon he likes it when we drops by once in a while. I remembers when we hepped 'im ta build dis fence here, hey Chawam?" says Keiren.

"You betcha! you were draggin yore hass trying to keep hup to 'im!" Pierre's laugh rings out again.

"Wuh-wah*[3]! How about you? Yore old tongue was draggin' in duh dirt, heavin' up dose shovels 'o dirt down in dat canal! Ho, ho, ho!" Keiren is slapping his knee with his cap as they pass the covered wagons, where they will be sleeping tonight.

"Get a whiff o' dat bannock Pierre! I'se a-gettin' weaker by duh minute!" Keiren begins to stagger, his knees are buckling; he grabs hold of Pierre's arm. Just as he gets close to Madeleine's fire he trips himself, grabbing on tighter to Pierre's arm; the chickens are running and squawking and Keiren is going down with loud groans. "Oh, Maddie! Maddie!"

"Wuh-wah! You lunatic! You nearly fell in the fire! K'moochiwin!"*[4]

Joleine is hooting with laughter, so Madeleine lets go the laughter she is smothering with her hand. "Good thing Kokom is not here, she would have had a heart attack!" Madeleine sings out in half Mechif and half English. "She would've gave him a crack with her ol' chicken stick."

"Go h'easy h'on my h'arm or you can pack duh wood!" says Pierre, although he is weak from laughing.

The girls have a basket of bannock fried; it is ready to take over to the heavy table under the kitchen window. Julie has just covered it with a big cloth and she sets her old cutting board at the back for the soup pot to set on.

Uncle Louie leans out the French windows and sets a big pot of stew on the cutting board at the back of the table and Julie hangs a big ladle over the rim.

Julie calls out "Joleine! If you please, bring that bannock!"

Joleine lifts the basket up onto her head, carrying it like the Creole women in New Orleans. She has both arms in the air holding the handles on both sides.

She believes it was Devine providence that brought Pierre to their home in the Bayous. He was horribly skinny, so sick, and very close to death after being held for several months as a slave on a pirate boat out on the Mississippi River.[*5]

After nursing Pierre back to health Joleine developed a strong friendship with this handsome Frenchman from the Canadas. Within a few weeks they were deeply in love and before long a big Louisianna wedding was planned by Joleine's people, the Parmentier clan.

Pierre longed to go home to the Red River but he also could not leave Joleine behind.

He could have stowed away or handled freight for his own fare but he could not expect Joleine to be dragged through an ordeal of that nature.

Finally he had saved enough to pay their expenses home. By this time they had the twins, a boy and a girl; Pierre could hardly wait to get home to show off his family!

"Don't you dare Pierre!" Madeleine hollers. He is sneaking along behind Joleine threatening to tickle her armpits.

"Now what is your crazy brother doing, Maddie?" Joleine is smiling, looking straight ahead, totally unaware of near disaster. She sets down her basket and swings around and looks right into Pierre's face, his eyes twinkling with mischief and a big wide grin showing his white teeth with one crooked tooth on the side!

Joleine chases him back to the camp, her little fist pounding on his big thick shoulder! Pierre is yelling "Owiah, Owiah!"

Soon the whole noisy lot is over at Julie's table, Uncle Louie says "Now if you all could sober up a minute we will ask Father Taché to bless the food. S'il vous plait, Monsignor?"

"Merci, mon ami! Gather the children into the circle, s'il vous plait." He proceeds to bless their gathering and gives thanks for the food.

"Merci, mon ami. Bon appétit!" says Louie Sr.

Madeleine spreads a blanket on the ground and Keiren brings two bowls of stew for Maddie… and Bennie, who is wearing his biggest smile. He looks like Keiren even though his hair is dark and curly, not red like Keiren's, and his eyes are a greenish blue, like his Daddy's.

Madeleine settles him onto the blanket and begins to blow his food to cool it down. Keiren sits down beside her, cross-legged, his stew and three pieces of bannock in front of him. The bannock is fried to a golden brown.

"You are right Keiren, dese girls can really cook!" Pierre dunks his bannock in his stew; Ramone dunks just like his father but Georgette breaks pieces into her stew like Joleine.

Metis men have spent over two hundred years depending on the beautiful women of the land to provide them with support of every description and it is common for them to brag on their women.

"Tapway Chawam! Auntie Julie's stew is always the best in the valley!" says Keiren.

"Merci, my boy, you are too kind", says Julie with a big smile. Keiren still struggles with pure French but it is his opportunity to pick up a few more words. Julie understands Mechif very well; however, she is still hesitant to speak the Cree language.

"Auntie Julie, may I tell a little bit of your Mother's story as we clean up after our meal?" Madeleine asks in French. She loves this story; Julie told it to her when they were picking berries; she is shy to tell it to everyone. For one thing she speaks all French and speaks too fast when she gets excited.

After they have eaten, Madeleine sits with all the girls on a blanket out on the veranda near the smudges; mosquitoes can be a heartless distraction at story time.

"Now listen my girls, this is a little story of Marie, Sara, Octavie and Eulalie's beautiful Grand'mére, Anne Marie Gaboury.

She fell in love with their handsome Grand-pére, Jean Baptiste Lagimodiere, kayas*, a long time ago, when our people still ruled our western homeland." She turned to Joleine and said, "It was in April of 1806, my girl, when they were wed."

Julie has washed the dishes and Joleine is quietly drying them and setting them on a clean towel in the roast pan. Madeleine accepts the cup of tea Joleine has handed her, "Merci, my girl"

"Now believe it or not, there had never been a white woman yet who had travelled the rivers out west… Tapway! The other famous woman who travelled the rivers was my Kokom's sister, Charlotte Thompson. But she was only half white." Madeleine places her right hand directly in the middle of her open left palm.

"Charlotte was beautiful also, just like our Auntie Julie's Mama, the famous Anne Marie."

Little four-year-old Eulalie looks over at eight year-old Georgette and they both hump their shoulders and cover their giggles.

"Do you know what?" Maddie stops and points to little Marie. "This little girl, omuh*, is named after Anne Marie, that is her Kokom!"

All the little girls giggle with glee!

"Sometime I will tell you of some of her adventures. She lived a hard life raising her children. She would travel on the rivers with her children even!

Her children were tough and hard workers, just like Anne Marie. All her children spoke Mechif like their Papa, most of their friends spoke Cree, but Anne Marie had them to speak to her in French. C'est ça? Auntie Julie." Julie nods.

A couple of cute episodes keep the children spellbound for a few more moments then it is time to say good-night.

Madeleine makes the sign of the Cross. "That is our story for tonight but I must remind you, Anne Marie never forgot her prayers. She taught her children to pray faithfully even though there were no Missions yet. Sometimes at night she would weep. (Maddie lays her cheek on her folded hands for a pillow.)

When all the children were asleep and Jean Baptiste was far away trading for furs, she would weep for loneliness for her people and her faith. The Cree people treated her well and she loved them but ... it was so, so lonely.

Then finally, twelve years later news came from Fort Douglas that there were Catholic missionaries on their way! Anne Marie stood on the shore of the old Red River watching with her children and everyone else, for the canoes to arrive. Then suddenly, around the bend came two Canoes bearing the Hudson Bay's flag*[6] ... was the missionaries! Everyone began to cheer!

Marie had not heard the scriptures or had the Holy Sacrements*[7] for twelve years! She was so overjoyed that she cried."

Madeleine looks around and not only are the children weeping…even the adults are teary eyed. The children are all clapping their hands to thank Auntie Maddie for the story.

"That was a wonderful story Madeleine but I have to get back to the mission and I want to see some dancing and hear some music before I go!" says Father Taché.

The men are all standing around; they had joined Madeleine's audience. "Hey my brothers, play some dance music, aspin*! She is twirling her finger for them to gather and play."

All the chairs are pulled to the edge of the veranda to make room for the dancers. In no time Louie Sr. has pulled Julie out and they dance quickly and lightly into the middle where they step to the sounds of "Soldier's Joy"! Everyone claps in time to Louie L'Ambitieaux's fiddle, Kieren's harmonica and Pierre's rhythm guitar.

"Hey, those guys are good!" yells Madeleine. "I need to steal their Harmonica player for Red River Jig, Omah*!"

She is known as the Champion Jigger*[8] in the Valley and her feet are itching to dance. Joleine is becoming a great jigger also, when Gabe is there to play guitar for young Louie instead of Pierre. The greatest sight is to have both Pierre and Keiren jigging with their wives!

Louie Riel Jr. is enjoying the music but will rarely dance unless Julie or Maddie pulls him up to help with a Square Dance, Duck Dance or Reel of Eight. He seems to be satisfied reading his book and happily tapping his beaded moccasin. All the children are jigging off to the side. The little girls are sweet as they jig in their ankle length dresses and little moccasin slippers.

Soon Julie and Louie Sr. are dancing back to their chairs and Louie L'Ambitieaux gives the famous intro for Red River Jig! Pierre gives a loud "Aye-eee" and hits an "A" chord on his guitar, and off they go! Keiren shoves his harmonica into his shirt pocket and begins jigging as soon as his feet hit the floor, he has tied his red sash around his waist especially for the occasion, as have the other men.

Madeleine jigs out to meet him and everyone claps as Pierre yells "Neemito* meewasin* Moonyow*[7]!" They dance three changes before they jig back to their seats to the sound of everyone's clapping.

Now Pierre is turning his guitar over to Keiren who also plays good rhythm, the fiddle keeps on as Pierre jigs out to meet Joleine! Keiren yells out "New Orleans Louisiana … Ay-eee!*" Joleine has become an excellent jigger and they also do three changes before jigging back to their seats.

Everyone is yelling and clapping and the Monsignor begins to make his rounds bidding "Bon soir" to all. Once again he has enjoyed the Metis culture at its finest.

Young Louie has played Soldiers Joy and six changes of the Red River Jig and he is sweating as hard as the dancers. There is no one to spell him off so he finishes up with a beautiful waltz danced by Louie Sr. and Madame Julie. Meanwhile Madeleine brings a dipper of cool water to the musicians.

Once the Monsignor has left and the dancing is done, everyone gathers over at Lamito's fire. The women lay out buffalo robes to sit on and Keiren puts some wood on the fire while Madeleine hangs a tea pail over the coals.

"Uncle Louie, could you tell us what the old buffalo hunts were like long time ago, Kayas?" Pierre asks. He remembers the last big hunt before the buffalo began to thin out. He just knows that Louie tells it well and even Pierre wants to hear his version again.

"Well my boy, I feel sad when I tell this story. I loved those days and I doubt if we will ever see them again." Louie Sr. says, as he launches into French. "I will tell it like a rock skipping across the river, a bit here a bit there. Pardon me if I leave the action to a special story teller … my friend, Pierre." He waves his hand toward Pierre, which brings applause from the seated audience, including Monsieur Riel.

Young Louie breaks more grass onto the smudge; then, he sits cross-legged beside Pierre, who will not be standing until the excitement begins.

*Glossary**

**Footnotes:*

1 *hobbles: horses needed to have their front legs set in comfortable loops.*
2 *Moonyow, Keiren's nick-name meaning 'white-man' in Cree, commonly used as an endearment among relations..*
3 *k'moochiwin-meaning, "You are crazy!" in Cree.*
4 *Mississippi River- The main highway in North America for North/South traffic...a mecca for pirates.*
5 *Hudson Bay-could be seen for miles indicating approaching Government visitors.*
6 *Holy Sacrements- The Bread and Wine representing the body of Christ used for the Holy Communion. At that time only used by Priests or Ministers.*
7 *Champion Jigger- a very special Title, given to whoever could out-jig all the dancers.*

Chapter Four

Metis Community, Red River: 1857...

Monsieur Louie Riel Sr. looks around the campfire, his eyes taking in each member of his audience ... as if to cast a mystic spell. All eyes are on him as he fixes a gaze on the fire, his eyes squinting into the flames as though he is beginning to see something.

"You must all realize ... these hunts were honored by the government of the day, which was the Hudson Bay Company. They were not small family hunts; they were becoming mammoth in size and they were not planned in one day. They had been the lifeblood of the fur industry for over two hundred years. Our people were expected to trade hides and pemmican with the Hudson Bay posts, besides feed our families. Our women worked very hard tanning hides and preparing pemmican.

The first planning meeting was generally held in October or November the year before."

He looks at Julie and tips his hand to his mouth; she brings him a cup of water.

"You also must realize that these hunts were run by our military in later years, all the more reason for spies and people of discord to be injected into our population.

Like I say, the last big planning meeting took place in November of 1839 at our secret military training camp. Some families were represented by ten or more men. Every family in our Métis Nation*[1] had representation there, it was mandatory. It is still mandatory but now you are not sure who you can trust. Many Scottish and Irish half-breeds have joined onto our nation and some of their friends are questionable."

Young Louie Riel Jr. is sitting up straight; he has listened to this story many times and never was it told with such passion! *It sounds like times are changing, this used to be a fun story; each year it becomes more serious; the hunt used to be a fun time!* Young Louie is thinking to himself, as he hears a note of regret in his Papa's voice.

Louie Sr. breaks the gaze and looks around at his audience, they are all staring seriously.

"We must cherish the memory of 'the hunt' regardless; it is the pleasure of these stories that brings joy to our hearts. We must not lose that; regardless of what the future might bring."

Tea is being passed around by Maddie and Joleine, Louie takes a sip of his tea and continues, mostly in French.

"The annual Military Training camp is vital to the success of the hunt. It is there that order is brought to this large gathering. Ever since our clash with the surveyors and white settlers; many of our people have begun to move west to the Saskatchewan River in Rupert's Land, many old faces have disappeared from the annual Training camp and new faces have been appearing every year.

The sad part is … with the diminishing buffalo herds we may never see another hunt like that one again. In 1840 the last big hunt, there were 1650 people to organize, including 400 children. Because of the necessity of having a manifest being drawn up the day before departure, we have a record of all participants and their belongings.

There are several versions of the hunt as each story teller tells it from their perspective; the only thing that never changes much is the record of participants because of the manifest kept by the scribe of the President with the hunt.

***

The Training camp itself was a large undertaking but, for the most part, it was a lot of fun. Once the Priest said the blessing and the flag was raised a shout went up, "Long live the Red River Colony!" Papa Riel takes drink of water then continues.

"Arrival time was to be an hour or two before sunset so as to give everyone time to get camp set up in a very large circle close to the river. The men cast lots the first night for ten men to a unit, each with a Captain to head up each detail."

He stopped for a moment and looked around,

"Very rarely did anyone ever oppose any assigned duties or commands given by their Captains; that is how it was."

Uncle Louie continued "…the daily chores like cooking, camp clean-up, feeding and watering of the horses, oxen and dogs, was assigned to the hunters. Some of them were also responsible for weapons maintenance.

The wood cutters were also the keepers of the fires. Supplies were all taken to one tent and five men were in charge of distribution for the next ten days.

Four men were appointed to guard the four directions and to find their own replacement each evening. They would walk the perimeter all night, from sundown to sunrise. Since the early days they had to be vigilant, always aware of attacks after dark by Sioux from the South. There was also the danger of raids by renegade outcasts, who had been sentenced into exile for criminal activity." He pauses to light his pipe.

"After supper we had small gatherings at different tents where there was maintenance being done on harnesses or rifles, games being played, stories being told, or music being played. The Captains and the Executive met together to prepare for the first day.

Each day was busy with a variety of military strategies, both distance and close combat. Most men were at there best to maintain their reputations as sharp-shooters, knife throwers, hand to hand combat and horse-handling.

There is a general gathering on a hillside to plan the next hunt. Hunting stories are a big thing and by the last day everyone has heard the latest stories and knows their responsibilities for the next hunt.

The last day of Training camp is mostly competition and the wives and Kokoms have sent wonderful prizes: sashes, belts, cuffs, leggings, hats, touques, vests and even a jacket or two, everything beaded, mind you. The same thing began to happen every year at the hunts.

Give a Metis a chance at a competition and he will do his best but ... all in all, both the Military camps and the hunts were great fun. We still enjoy them regardless if our buffalo herds are shrinking and things are changing.

Monsieur Isadore-Gabriel Dumont had been re-elected to serve as President by acclamation the year before and had appointed his secretary or scribe to keep records."

"I have sketched out the order Pierre; now could you take us to the hunt, while I drink some tea?"

"Oui, H'uncle, I love to tell about that Hunt, give our story teller a big hand!" Everyone claps and cheers for Papa Riel.

Pierre has attended military camp every year since he turned fourteen. The only time he missed was when he and Keiren were captured by some renegade Fenians*[2] and taken down the Mississippi to New Orleans.

Each of the boys has his own version of that experience as they became separated upon their escape. He missed five years of training camp right after the "Big Hunt[3]" ; he is surprised now at the shrinking buffalo herds and the changing hunts.

"'ow many wants to 'ear how big was dis 'unt? Tapway, everyone wants to hear; it is d'at exciting!" Pierre carries on in Mechif.

"We know that each family was expected to bring food and all their own supplies; same as going on a private family hunt.*[4]

According to the manifest of 1840 there were...

'*...403 horses, 536 oxen, 1240 carts and horses. There were1600 men, women and children. They had 740 guns and over ten thousand rounds of ammunitions. Over 1300 buffalo were killed in one day, a total of 2800 were butchered before the expedition returned home. 800 carts were loaded with pemmican, choice meat cuts, tongues, fat and buffalo hides on that hunt.'* – Edmonton, 1980.

... The hunt is a beautiful experience. As carts and horses begin to arrive at the traditional rendezvous; everyone is amazed at the size of the gathering. No longer can they gather in one large circle bordering the river's edge as they did in years gone by. Now each clan has their own circle and besides the little fires by each tent there is now a common fire in the middle.

With one sharp blow of the whistle, the Captain of the Hunt can summon all the officers to the fire for a quick meeting where news is told, meetings are announced or plans or orders for the next day are given. All the Captains of the clans must wear the red bandana around the neck to signify their authority. The men of the camp must wear the sash of their clan around their waist to signify membership."

Pierre takes a short break to roll a smoke and have a few sips of the tea Jolein has handed him. He looks around; the men are enjoying their tea, waiting quietly for Pierre to resume his story.

The women have pulled blankets over the little ones who have nodded off; Ramone is very wide awake enjoying the old tale he has heard his father tell several times; it makes him very proud.

The two "young" Louies are soaking it all in, as they have many times before. Louie L'Ambitieux lays some wood gently on the fire and young Louie Riel fixes the smudges and they quickly begin swirling out big puffs of smoke.

Knats and mosquitoes seem to disperse immediately. The women rub smoke on their sleeping babies' faces. Pierre continues.

"As the sleeping camp awakens, mothers can be seen making fires and feeding their families. The smell of fresh bannock fills the air. The day proceeds much like training camp with one exception, there are women and children greeting one another and even the dogs are excited.

After breakfast the clan Captain rides into the middle of the circled Red River carts and blows his whistle, men begin to come forward from their tents. They are to meet down by the river; there they will set plans in place for an early morning hunt. After the meeting they will net some fish for their camps.

While the men are off getting ready for the morning hunt, the rest of the camp is buzzing with activity.

There are so many things to do and to learn from one another as they have been joined along the way with many relations from many different regions. Each region has their various dialects of Mechif, with either Cree or Ojibwe.

The women and children are busy connecting with relatives they have not seen for at least one year. There are also Scottish and Irish half-breeds who set up close so they can visit in their own style of Mechif.

Each region boasts their own special patterns of beading and sewing and there is a great deal of pride in their own traditional lifestyle; women work as they visit.

Each day of the hunt the children are kept busy with games and chores. The little ones spend hours with their dogs picking piles of sticks and buffalo chips* that they haul behind their dogs on travois* to bring to all the Aunties for their fires.

The young girls are busy fixing the braids of their little sisters. Some of the older girls teach beading or birch bark biting, moose hair tufting and many other lessons to the children. It is said that these things teach patience to our young people.

The older people entertain the young ones with story-telling, whittling flutes and whistles and some of the older folks, who are still fine to travel on the hunt, sit around playing cards, hand-games, drumming and singing or playing fiddle music.

There is always something to do when you are camped by the river… picking saskatoons and other berries along the riverbanks, fishing and swimming, picking clams with your toes, skipping rocks or whatever suited your age group.

After the hunt and the meat is all dried and packed up there is horse-racing, dog-racing, children's racing and canoe racing on the last day before they pack up camp.

They also have prizes for the women who have the best or the most dried meat or pemmican. Prizes for the men were for who-ever killed and butchered the finest meat. Prizes for competitions were generally beaded belts, wraps, moccasins, vests and pouches, all beautifully beaded by the women."

Pierre summons Joleine for a drink of water; soon the story will be so exciting that Pierre knows his mouth will get very dry…he continues…

his French is fast, he is using the words of his uncle Louie and Papa L'Ambiteaux.

"The morning of the hunt everyone is up very early. They move quickly and quietly in the dark making every move count. Everyone is well prepared and well rehearsed for the fast-paced series of events ahead." Quote:*4

'The men set out on horseback in the dark; a traditional hunting prayer has been offered up by the Elders.

Scouts have located the herds and have reported on the size of the herds and their whereabouts.

As they reach the section of the ridge that has been marked by the scouts, they begin the climb to the top of the ridge. They have all been assigned to quadrants by Captain Dumont during their military training in the previous fall.

The first two quadrants leave the party and head in opposite directions; they will circle the herd and get into position on the other side. The other two quadrants do the same until they have connected with the lead quadrants and a complete circle encompasses the herd.'

Pierre is becoming so agitated that he stops for another cool drink of water for his dry mouth. His audience is beginning to sit up straight, as Pierre grins and runs his fingers through his hair. He is squinting off into the distance and moving his hand across slowly from left to right.

'... Once they have connected they begin to close in slowly. They are using a military strategy that is rehearsed annually during their training under Captain Dumont.

As they begin their descent down the long slope from the top of the ridge, dawn is just beginning to break. They are now speaking in whispers and no-one is allowed to smoke.

In the morning dawn, they resemble a slow moving circle of shrubs. It all begins very innocently ... Dumont signals the lead Captains who ride in first; their shots ring out almost simultaneously. It is as though an invisible floodgate has been lifted and suddenly the noise is deafening.

For the safety of their comrades they are only allowed to shoot ahead of themselves and they are only allowed to kill their assigned quota. The breaching of hunting policies can be very serious and can result in a variety of fines or punishments.

At this moment two crucial things begin to happen.

First, the lead quadrants split creating an opening in the circle; then they ride off to the side making way for the stampede.

Second, all riders move to the nearest edge of the herd; their quota has been met by the time they have reached the edge, and they park. They watch and listen.

Soon … the floodgates have closed and all is silent.

Hearts are pounding, mouths are dry; buffalo carcasses lay scattered for a square mile. Most of the men make the sign of the cross and grab their canteens for a cool drink of water.

The hunt is over and the work begins; the sun is peaking over the eastern brow.

By the time the men have skinned all the buffalo, the carts begin to arrive. The women have sharpened all their knives and are ready to go!

Before they begin cutting the meat an offering is made to thank the buffalo for their sustenance. Those who have tobacco will bury a small quantity on a hole; then they replace the grass. Others raise their cross or rosary and give thanks to the Creator for His provision.

Much like the methods of the skinners, the women will descend in pairs upon one buffalo; the men lifting and carrying as the women deftly locate the joints and present them with each quarter.

Locating their families who are waving and yelling in the gray dawn may take longer than dressing out an animal.

It looks like mass confusion; a square mile of butchering teams, shouting, singing and laughing.

However, it is in fact, a mass demonstration of meticulous organization and skill.

In a matter of moments an animal has been gutted, quartered and deboned. It is then laid in a cart on a hide that is then wrapped tightly around it to keep the dust from coming in on the way back to camp.

Upon arriving back at camp they can see the drying racks that have been put up for the meat. Poplar frames have been built ready for doing the hides. Every camp has three or four frames; you can see them for a good mile strung all along the river bank.

That evening the Elders offer up a prayer of thanks to the Creator for the wonderful buffalo who have given their lives to provide food and sustenance for the people – Calgary, 2008.

Everyone begins to clap and Ramone, who had not fallen asleep like the other little ones, jumped up and went and hugged his Papa.

**Glossary:* Metis Nation- One of the three Aboriginal groups recognized in the Canadian Constitution: First Nations, Metis Nation and Inuit Nation.

Footnotes:

1. Fenians- A group of renegade Irish militant Mariners who travelled throughout the Northern States.
2. 'unt, 'ow-Popular French accent, where the 'h' is dropped as in 'hunt' and 'how', etc. Likewise, the letter 'h' is often h'added. (added).
3. A quote taken from the writings of writer, Terrance Lusty, who co-authored "The Lagimodiere's" with Hector Coutu.
4. A quote from "My Girl" by Carrie Mason-2008, Calgary.

Chapter Five

Riel Farm, Red River: 1858...

Keiren pours water over the fire as everyone says their good nights. "I reckon no one will be a-needin' this fire. Merci, Chawam, good story, Mewasin!"

"Tapway, my friend; my wagon looks mighty inviting to me also; it has been a long day."

"Bon soir, y'all!" Keiren calls out. He climbs up and disappears into the covered wagon pulling the canvas tightly around the door to keep out the mosquitoes.

***

Meanwhile, the children have all gone to bed in the Riel house; Julie is fixing tea for her husband. He rubs his bare feet before going to bed, a habit left over from his voyageur days.

"You never told your hunting story very long, my man," Julie comments quietly.

Louie swishes the basin out the door barely missing Ruth, his old dog "Look out Root, you nearly got a bath!" Ruth is a typical Métis dog, she understands Cree as well as she does French, and yet if you call her in English she immediately obeys.

He continues to talk to Julie in his quiet, night-time tone while he scoops a dipper of water from the water pail and pours it into a blue granite basin that sits on the washstand in the entrance. "You know me very well, my love."

The smell of Julie's home-made hand soap floods the room; she adds a few drops of her mother's favourite lilac fragrance to her soap just to disguise the slight smell of lye, Louie thinks back to when he was a boy, "*…I recall the odor of Gramere Boucher's spruce-scented soap, it was a man's soap!*"

Louie washes the day's sweat from his face and neck; he scoops up a handful of water and runs it through his hair, squeezing it into his curls, then he dries his face before finishing, "… I have a lot on my mind; Julie, we are now at another crossroad and we must pray for a right decision to be made at this time."

Louie walks over to the armoire and takes down his candle, Bible and prayer beads.

Julie continues to clean up for the night; she notices the serious tone in Louie's voice. He is speaking quietly and pulling at his beard, a few hairs at a time. "Come my dear, we must talk."

He has lit his candle and is saying his rosary when Julie joins him.

Julie takes the long braids out of her hair and is shaking them loose. She is still a beautiful woman and her hair falls in ripples of shining waves; her dark eyes are searching Louie's handsome face, looking for clues.

He has just come back from Montreal; she knows his business deal for parts to build a mill was not successful. He has already informed her that they will not issue him a permit as he refuses to give up his ties with St. Paul, Minnesota.

What else could possibly go wrong? She even allows her mind to wander down an evil path of jealousy for a moment … is there a beautiful French woman waiting for him back in Montreal? *"God forbid! Forgive my thoughts, dear Mother of God and help me to be faithful, if you please."*

"My darling Julie, please have patience with me, I am searching for answers." He takes Julie's hand in his … she begins to quietly pray, *"Help me dear Saints of God, here it is. I must be strong."*Julie's throat is so tight … her eyes are beginning to burn.

"Look at me Julie; this is about our son Louie." He says in a whisper. His brown eyes are soft as he attempts a weak smile. Julie goes limp.

"You know the dedication that he shows toward our Holy Catholic faith. We have talked about how we may someday have money to send him off to seminary."

"Yes Louie, we have been praying for finances to send him to school, here at the mission they will teach only the rudiments which he already has." Julie has begun to breathe easier and now she is jabbering; at the same time, she can only wonder … *"What is Louie's dilemma?"*

"Father Taché has offered to see to it that Louie can attend seminary." Louie has finally said it.

"Oh my man, that is an answer to our prayers! Louie will be so happy that finally, he will not have to wait more than a few years."

"It is better than that Julie, He may leave next year. A wealthy patron of the church, and friend of the Father's, has offered to sponsor Louie and three other boys to the priesthood; he may be going as early as next summer."

Julie begins to quietly cry; before long she is heaving great sobs. "We have talked about age seventeen or eighteen, my man, he is too young; in October he will turn only thirteen; Louie, he is still a baby!"

She begins a mournful moan that drags up and turns into a loud sob. Louie has handed her a hankie from a drawer in the armoire. "Blow your nose now Julie; think about our son; think about what *he* may want."

"So ask him Louie, see what he wants. He is very wise; he is also very tuned to God." She has settled down a bit and the tears and sobs have subsided.

"You go and get him now Julie. He will wake up quickly." Louie is feeling somewhat relieved. He picks up his garden gloves and hangs them up high on a beam so he can find them tomorrow, "*...I am not anxious about Louie; He would leave tonight if it was up to him; Julie should know that,*" he thinks to himself.

Soon Julie comes out of the bedroom with Louie following close behind. "Come and sit, my boy, your Mama and I have something to discuss with you."

Louie is rubbing his eyes and looking puzzled. "What is wrong, my Papa?"

"Nothing is wrong my son. Your mother and I need to hear your opinion on something that Father Taché has proposed to us today." Louie Sr. is quite certain his son will be pleased.

"What is it Papa?" He looks at his Mama who has been crying, then back to his Papa who looks like he is ready to explode. Louie is worried; has he done something wrong?

"My boy, you must be totally honest with us, take your time and think about your reply." This could be very difficult for Louie; he is very devoted to his Mama.

"We have had a proposal from Father Taché; he has a benevolent parishioner in Montreal who is willing to sponsor your education with the Junior Seminary at St. Sulspice."

"Oh Papa, that is wonderful! Thanks be to God, I have been praying for this. Will I need to work for him for a few years?"

"No my son, you may travel to Montreal as early as next summer," says Papa.

Young Louie is seated right next to Julie who is looking painfully into Louie's eyes. He reaches out and takes his mother's hands and buries his face in them.

For a few moments he sits with his face in Julie's lap; she reaches one hand out and rubs the back of Louie's head, her fingers pulling at the curls. Louie looks up at Julie, his eyes filled with tears, "Mama, it is my heart's desire to go."

***

One year has passed since the intimate gathering at Monsieur Louie's. The sudden shift in destiny has given young Louie a whole new perspective. He is busy pitching hay to the oxen as his Papa fills the water trough. His mind wanders back to that day… the day he first began to realize his destiny.

Before this it seemed as though one day he would be struggling with deep feelings of inadequacy and a total lack of interest in any work-related activities. Much of the time, he was haunted with the guilt of being the eldest son of one of the most influential role models in the community. The burden of someday filling those shoes was a daunting vision that would excite him at times; then suddenly, the vision would dissipate and he would return to a hopeless reality.

He knows that his Papa has a lot of influence and is highly respected in the community; however, he does not seem to be able to accumulate money. Everyone works on a bartering system and no-one seems to worry much about money; that is a dream… out of his reach. Now that dream seems to actually be within reach!

The next day, it seemed like the world had taken on new meaning; he had a new outlook on life and suddenly he was not afraid anymore. Why he could grab a rifle and go for a hunt, perhaps he could surprise his Mama with a young deer.

He recalls the following day standing in front of Julie holding Papa's rifle with a big smile "Fresh meat in the pot Mama!" … he quotes one of the favourite expressions of the old-timers, using old French.

"My boy! What are you doing? Please put away that gun and go out and ask your Papa, he may take you hunting." Julie turns her back on Louie; she is not sure why she feels like laughing out loud. Louie looks so natural standing there with his old work jacket on … a rifle under his arm.

At that moment Louie Sr. comes through the door. "What are you talking about? Louie, where are you going with that rifle?" He hangs his tattered cowboy hat on a large spike reserved for that hat alone; his fancy summer hat hangs on a separate wooden peg.

Louie sets the rifle down, the barrel sticking into a crack in the cellar door. "Papa, I was about to go and ask for you to take me hunting."

Louie walks over and lays his arm on young Louie's shoulder. "My boy, my boy, it is a joy to my heart to see you taking an interest in real life! Excuse me if I laugh, it is only because I have prayed for you to do something besides read! First of all, my man, you do not set your rifle with the barrel down, it will become a habit; you will set it in the dirt outside and plug the barrel."

Papa Louie has a good laugh, grabs Louie's little round flat-brimmed hat and swats his shoulder," … and, you know better than to wear your hat in the house!"

Louie ducks as though he is being hit, "Sorry Papa, I am anxious to hunt!" He shrugs his shoulders like the older men when they laugh, then he giggles all the way to the veranda where he puts back on his hat.

Papa Louie follows him out to the veranda and sits down in his rocking chair. Louie sits down beside him, "Papa, since you told me that I am going away I feel like I must not waste time. There are a lot of things that I should have done with you and Mama!" His face crumples into a cry and he begins to sob.

"I am so sorry; I have not been a good son. I promise you Papa … I will make it up to you. You will be very proud of me someday!"

Julie has picked up baby Eulalie and is rocking her back and forth; tears are filling her eyes as she listens quietly to Louie Jr. … pouring his heart out to his Papa.

"Some day Mama, your prayers will be answered; I will be a spiritual leader to our people like you have always dreamed."

Louie walks around behind Julie's chair and wraps his arms around her neck from behind; he kisses her on the cheek. "If they will allow it, I will be home for Christmas every year."

Tears are rolling down his cheeks, "When I become a Priest Mama, I will serve at Red River Colony. That is my home. I belong with my Métis people," he pulls out a homemade hankie from his hip pocket and wipes his tears, then blows his nose.

***

The oxen have been fed and Louie has worked up a good appetite. "So Papa, what do you think Mama will be preparing for the evening meal? I am going to guess that she will have mashed potatoes and gravy, fried chicken and spinach and let's see, maybe rhubarb pie."

"Nich*! Could that be because you came in and cut her some spinach and rhubarb this morning?" Papa Louie grabs him by the scuff of the neck and begins to gently kick his behind while laughing heartily, they both have reverted to speaking Mechif. Louie Jr. is yelping like a dog, "Owyah, owyah!*"

They are nearing the house and old Ruth comes bounding down the stairs, barking her head off and wagging her tail.

Julie has stepped out the door and is standing out on the veranda watching the antics "You crazy guys, stop scaring me half to death; also old Ruth is having a fit!" Julie is so thrilled with Louie's new-found relationship with his Papa; it thrills her to hear their laughter.

She has to put aside the fact that Father Taché will be coming for supper and taking Louie to the Mission where they will rendezvous for the long journey to Montreal. Julie is hoping they will not leave until morning, already she feels an ache in her heart.

In the morning they will meet with the other boys who are also attending St. Sulspice and they will prepare for their long trip to Montreal. Julie has been busy baking a good supply of her French pastries for their grub box.

Upon entering the house, the savory odor of Julie's baking drifts out from the kitchen. The men begin to wash up. Near the entrance a washstand with two basins and a pitcher of water awaits them.

The hard working men begin to wash up. "We worked hard today Papa."

Louie Sr. finishes drying his hands and face then hands the towel over to Louie. Papa is using the ceramic basin so that young Louie can use his old blue granite work basin; it seems almost like a coming of age ritual.

"Oui, Oui, my boy, too bad I am losing you, just when you are getting to be a strong, hard worker." Louie is thrilled with the good feeling of being useful and appreciated.

The Riel home is designed in the usual French manner, with a large kitchen adjoining a long parlor, with bedrooms off to the side. Julie has made long blue curtains from flour sacks; they hang over the bedroom doors. A large table sits halfway down the east wall, in what they refer to as "the dining area". Closer to the kitchen area there is another smaller table that serves as a utility table for rolling out pies, buns, loaves and bannock etc. This table has many uses and if there is a crowd, the children eat at this little table, seated on wooden benches brought in from the veranda.

By the time the men are washed up Julie has supper on the table. Louie takes a face towel to the faces of his little sisters "You know, my beautiful sisters, your big brother will be going away in the morning to the Mission. There he will meet up with his friends and travel to go live at a far-away school."

"Who is my big brother, Youie?" says Sara.

"Sorry little sister. That is me. I am leaving for a far-away city. When I come home I will be a Priest." Louie gently washes their little cute faces.

"When I say good-by tonight ... I can kiss clean faces." Louie bends down and gives Sara a peck on the cheek. *I will miss my little sister. Next time I see her, the nuns will have taught her English...she will be reading and writing. Everything will be different when I return... please, dear Jesus, Mary and Joseph, help my little brother Charles not to have seizures, I am so sorry...*

"You look like you cry, Youie." Eulalie spots a tear in his eye. Louie has no idea when he will see these little girls again; it is all beginning to look very real.

After a few minutes there is the sound of horses coming up the lane.

"Well, my boy, I guess it will not be long now; Father Taché is coming. It sounds like he has someone with him." Papa Louie is beginning to look anxious.

"You will need to set some more places, my dear. I can see that Father Taché has Pierre and someone else with him.

"Tapway,* That is Daniel McDougall, Papa. We both received instruction under Father La Floch for the last four years," says Louie excitedly.

"Chasqwa,* I know that boy, he is very quiet but he is regular with Mass. I assume he is one of the boys going to Montreal" says Papa pulling at his beard as he looks out the window.

"Tapway,* Papa, we will be travelling with Louis Schmidt and a couple of the Sisters." Louie is getting excited, he has forgotten that Papa was listening when Father Taché named off the three boys who had been selected to go.

"Go help with the horses my boy; you should know by now that the animals are tended first before we eat."

"Yes Papa, I forgot; I am so excited!" Louie skips out the door shouting greetings to his hero, Pierre L'Ambitieaux.

Julie and Papa Louie are greeting everyone on the veranda, "Supper is on the table and your places are waiting for you; we are hoping that you stay the night." says Julie. Camping overnight is a tradition with Metis people, they always make time to socialize.

"Greetings to you also, mes ami!" says Pierre, as he plants a gentle kiss on each of Julie's cheeks, he begins using his best French.

"Oui, mon Tante*, Merci! We will leave in the morning to get a fresh start. I have rounded up one of your travelling buddies Louie, his parents send greetings and they will pray for you all. Daniel has bid his farewells so tomorrow when we pick up Louie Schmidt we will begin our journey.

We will be travelling with a load of furs headed for St. Paul, Minnesota, two of the sisters will accompany us; sounds like they will have a wagon load. They are carrying all the food, some of the feed, two crates of chickens, their personal luggage and that homely old parish dog named Jonah."

Julie throws her head back and has a good laugh, "Bless you, Pierre, I needed a laugh. While my heart swells with pride… it is also breaking as I am preparing Louie for his new life."

Pierre has unhitched the horses from the wagon and is taking them to pasture, "Astam* Daniel, I will 'obble dese horses while you fill duh water trough. Tomorrow we will pick up h'our freight, some will be h'in duh wagon but duh mos' will be loaded on duh ox cart. Duh trail gets damn rough in some spots before we reach St. Paul."

"How long will it be before we reach St. Paul, Pierre?" says Louie, as he steps along trying to keep up to Pierre.

His heart is pounding from sheer excitement and he nervously pulls on a handful of his hair once in a while as Pierre fills him in on some of the pitfalls of travelling overland to St Paul.

It is quicker to take the water routes but it is not for the faint of heart. Traveling the rivers with seasoned Voyageurs is something Louie would rather hear about in stories.

Louie raises his eyes to scroll the horizon and everything in between … soon he will be leaving these familiar grassy slopes. How long would it be before he again feasts his eyes on that lush green brush surrounded by bluebells and buttercups?

A lump begins to form in his throat as he sweeps his eyes along the banks of the old Seine River, he will not be grudgingly picking raspberries and saskatoons this year. *"If only I could be given one more Christmas with my Mama and Papa. I would work so hard …'if you please gentle Mother Mary, let my Mama and Papa know that I am so sorry for being a poor son', I must not let Pierre see my tears."* He is thinking in Mama Julie's beautiful dialect. *"Oh how I am going to miss her … and my Papa also …and my sweet sisters."* He rubs his eyes and straightens up, walking quickly behind Pierre.

"It will likely be three or four weeks, depending on the weather and the roads, Louie. It will be tough going sometimes but we will make it fun like we always do." Pierre has been around Louie often enough …he knows he has a lot of growing up to do.

Louie rolls over and opens one eye to peek at the morning dawn coming through his little attic window. Immediately he remembers what lies ahead …*dose little homemade flour-sack curtains on dat little window never looked so good,* he thinks to himself.

"S' éveiller*, mon garçon*, "Julie sets a short lit candle on a bookstand by Louie's bed; she sits down beside him and gently lays her arm on his shoulder, she continues speaking quietly in French, "Louie, your Papa is out at the barn with Pierre and Daniel. You must get up now and get ready for your departure to Montreal. I will not rest if we do not have a private word and a prayer before you go."

"Oui, ma Mere, we will pray then I shall get ready. I am sure I have everything packed." He sits up and takes his Rosary from the book stand.

"Mérci, I am wide awake, Mama, I have been waiting for the break of day. Such strange feelings and thoughts have been coming through my head all night. I am so excited and yet my stomach strangely hurts with a strong feeling of sadness."

Julie has seated herself at the foot of the bed holding her prayer beads.

Louie rubs his eyes and gets down on his knees; he is wearing his summer drawers but takes the time to pull on his shirt.

Together they do their Rosaries, then Julie asks for a prayer from her son. He says a short prayer in his mother's French:

"Our gracious heavenly Father, Sacred Mother Mary and precious Saints of God, hear our prayers, if you please. We thank you for our assignments and ask that you would keep us all safe while we perform the tasks You have given us. I pray a strong blessing upon my family while I am away. In the name of the Father, Son and the Holy Ghost. Amen."

"Where ever you go my boy, always take this little prayer book. The prayers are very powerful; they are from the Holy Bible taken from the Psalms of David. They will deliver you from fear of the unknown and give you strength though all your trials, always remember."

Louie takes the little green book and opens it to the back, "Oh Mama, it also has King Solomen's Book of Proverbs! I am so thrilled, Mama. Please do not worry about me. I will be in good hands."

"I must finish setting out your breakfasts …fresh pancakes my boy!" Julie steps carefully back down the narrow steps from the attic.

"I can smell your salt pork and pancakes Mama, it is making me hungry." says Louie as he pulls on his brown britches and blue flour sack* shirt; his travel clothes will do just fine, seeing they are beginning a long journey today.

Although he is dressed in his old travel clothes he takes the time to shine his boots. He washes up, hair and all, then gives his hair a good rubdown. As he combs his unruly curls he places his fingers into the curls and leaves them lying in small waves, they will remain tight and manageable until he gets excited or upset. *"Today I will be calm and contented, 'I am finally beginning to see my Devine purpose in life fulfilled, Almighty Father, keep me safe and obedient, sil vous plait".*

***

Breakfast is over and Louie Sr. rises from the table first, "It is a sad day for us to see our son leave for a distant land and yet it is also a great day to thank God for His Devine provision. We also thank you Father Taché, for arranging our son's education, and you Pierre, for taking the boys on your route to St. Paul; I hope they will not be an inconvenience on your journey."

Pierre rises and accepts Louie's firm handshake. "I must confess, sir, dese boys will be h'earning dere fare, you know how many tough spots we need to navigate between 'ere and St. Paul, dey will t'ink dey are in Paradise when dey finally board dat fancy train to Montreal."

"How soon will they be in St. Paul, Pierre?" Julie asks. Pierre musters up his best French to respond to Madame Julie.

"My guess is that we will arrive in St. Paul, Minnesota, about three to four weeks from now. There are two long trips overland, the first is to Fort Pembina and the next is when we get off the Red River Barge and head overland to catch the Mississippi barge to St. Paul."

He draws an invisible map on the table for Daniel and young Louie so they can see the distance they will need to travel by water.

"Tapway, my boy. That is the nice part of the trip. They might just as well know that there are some keespi* old trails on the way to St. Paul. You know, my boy, we have been blessed a few times and travelled by barge nearly all the way to Montreal. Mind you, it has to be the right time of the year. Things have been changing every year as the railroad tracks come further west."

Louie Sr. is standing with his one foot up on his chair, lighting his pipe, a very common stance among Metis men in Red River.

"You know I have heard that, h'uncle; I pray that we will be so lucky. We could be there in less than six weeks."

"Wuh wah*, Louie!" says Daniel. "What do you think about that?" he is chuckling and looking at young Louie who is sipping at his tea, shaking his head back and forth.

"Sounds very exciting to me, I can hardly wait to get going." He looks at Julie, "Sorry Mama. I have dreamt about this day for a long time. Now I know how much I am going to miss you all."

"It is good, my son. What more could I possibly ask. I will need to be hearing from you regularly, my boy; it will give me peace of mind."

Louie is chewing on his pipe, he takes another squeaky suck and lets out a small puff of smoke; "For me also, my son, I will be thinking about you every day. Come on then, let's get this trip started. I have a gift for you, my boy."

He goes to the armoire and opens a drawer. "I have been saving this knife for you, Louie; it will come in handy for many things; but, it also could save your life someday."

Louie reaches out and takes it, then hugs his Papa. "Merci, Papa."

"Some evening when you have settled down for the night, ask Pierre; he can teach you how to throw it at a target, and how to sharpen it properly, my boy." Papa Louie rumples his hair. Louie is swallowing hard.

*Glossary

Footnotes:

1 Mechif- An exclusively Canadian language developed during the first centuries of colonization, consisting of both the French and Cree languages.

Chapter Six

Part One: Destination Fargo, North Dakota: 1858...

The trip to the Mission is relatively uneventful except for intermittent bursts of excited conversation between Louie and Daniel who ride their saddle horses alongside the covered wagon that will be hauling them to St. Paul. Pierre's furs and pemmican will be hauled by ox cart; the wood, hay and belongings will be in the wagon.

The trail is snaky and rather lumpy at times but Pierre drives his team at a steady pace unless it is too bumpy, he doesn't want to bounce his only passenger off the wagon seat.

Father Taché is riding shotgun beside Pierre and he makes for a comical spectacle as they bounce through the ruts. He is hanging on for dear life, one hand on the edge of the seat, the other on top of his round brimmed hat; his black cassock is flying in the wind. He tells Pierre in his high-classed French, "Slow down, my boy, take it easy. You will knock my joints out of place!"

Daniel is laughing so hard that he is bouncing up and down in the saddle holding his hand over his mouth. Louie has his lips pursed in a grin but is gazing away down the road. He avoids looking at Daniel; he doesn't dare; he will burst out laughing. Finally they giggle quietly in time with the trot of their horses.

They arrive at the Mission shortly before noon and the boys tie their horses to the hitching rail, then they proceed to give Pierre a hand watering and feeding the four horses.

Father Taché has entered the Mission and is filling Sister L'Ambitieaux in on their trip. "So you had a successful trip; now you must all get washed up for lunch," says Sister Marguerite.

There are four sisters at the Mission; three are from Montreal and Sister Marguerite L'Ambitieaux who was born in Saint Boniface; she is a sister to Pierre's Papa.

Even though she is from Red River she has the accent of the highly educated. Her years with the grey nuns in Montreal, studying at the Seminary, have changed her 'dis' and 'dat', to 'zis' and 'zat'*[1], if she is not careful...a point of humor for the uneducated.

Pierre steps in the door and removes his hat, "Greetings ma Tanté, you h'are a welcome sight! I have brought you two more hungry boys, Daniel McDougall and Louis Riel."

The two boys have stepped in and take turns shaking the sister's hand, "My pleasure, Sister Marguerite," says Louie, bowing slightly.

Daniel has not developed the charm of young Louie Jr. and is blushing shyly as he limply shakes her hand. "Come now boys, lunch is waiting."

She leads them into the dining room, her starched habit rustling as she moves briskly around to her place at the table; the other sisters welcome the boys to the Mission with smiles and handshakes.

They have fed these boys many times in the past few years so the fragrance of the pea soup with salt pork is a familiar but welcome smell. Louie Schmidt is already seated at the table. He has been studying with Louie for the past few years and is accustomed to the nick-name, 'Smitty', so as to differentiate between the two Louis'.

Over the past four years the boys have spent a lot of time at the Mission studying under Father Lafloche who travels a circuit teaching the rudiments of education at various Parishes.

His students are mostly children of people who are in the freight business. They get to study on Saturday and receive their assignments for the next couple of weeks.

Later that day their parents will arrive back from Fort Garry, Pembina or St. Boniface, wherever they have gone to trade. When they arrive back they generally stay in camp for a few days where they have tents set up close to the river by the Mission. They attend Mass in the morning before going home; they may join together first for a feast, depending on the weather.

***

Seated at the table they exchange a bit of light chatter using a lot of English for the sake of Daniel McDougall.

"By the time we reach Montreal, Daniel, you will be chattering in Mechif, if not in French. Hee hee hee!" Pierre is bent over sideways slapping his knee.

"Don't laugh Pierre, he knows more zan* you s'ink*2," says Father Taché, with a quick little grin towards Sister L'Ambitieaux.

Pierre leads the way with light chit-chat. The boys are in a state of excitement and have questions for Father Taché regarding the seminary throughout the meal; then, Father Taché clears his throat.

This is a well-known signal that he is clearing the air for one of his profound exposés. "Now boys," he begins. "It is time for us to clear up any questions that you may have regarding the travelling rules. It is my understanding that the Captain of the brigade will be Pierre L'Ambitieaux, you are aware of this?"

"Oui, Father," is echoed around the table. The Bishop continues in French with the exception of a few English words here and there.

"Some of you may be aware also, that Keiren O'Brien is second in command and will relieve Pierre if necessary. We have not received word as yet if Keiren will be available. Perhaps Pierre can enlighten us on his situation." Father Taché gives Pierre a curious look.

"I can only say dat Sister L'Ambitieaux here," Pierre nods at the sister, "… she is willing to h'act as second in command if Keiren cannot make it. He may be staying behind upon Madeleine's request. She is very busy with Bennie, duh garden and Kokom Cardinal, who 'as been very ill.

Marie is doing a good job helping but Madeleine is very stressed wit' Keiren leaving on a long trip. We will be away a couple of months." Pierre ceases to pull at his young black moustache and leans back from the table.

"Merci, Pierre. We can only pray for Kokom Cardinal, z'at she will be fine. Z'at would be a relief to Madeleine."

Father Taché continues, "Sister Thérèse Valade here, is in charge of zee expenses and will do any purchasing z'at is necessary."

There will be no need for Pierre to go further than St. Paul; that is his place of business. Sister L'Ambitieaux will supervise the train travel through to Montreal quite easily with the help of Sister Valade.

"Thank you Sisters for the fine meal; we will allow instructions for the journey continue here at the table as soon as the dishes are cleared away. Good food boys?"

"Oui, merci, merci" Pierre says and the boys all clap and cheer for the sisters, including Daniel, who has picked up half of what the Father has been saying in French.

The boys listen intently as Pierre gives them the highlights on the journey for the day and where they will likely be setting up camp tonight.

He explains that, so far, there will be other freight carts joining them hauling furs to St. Paul, "We hep each udder out if der h'is a problem. Someone will be sent on horseback to take duh message down duh line."

He is mentioning that they each have their own camps, when suddenly the horses whinny and the dogs begin to bark, "Hey, sounds like we 'ave company!" says Pierre.

The boys quickly excuse themselves from the table and head outside to see if it is their companions. Coming into sight down by the river-bend, a team of horses can be seen with the driver wearing a strange little cap covering a mop of red hair held back in a string.

The horses are all moving at an easy trot and it is not long before Pierre recognizes his brother-in-law, Keiren O'Brien, driving the team…he flings his old cowboy hat in the air and gives a loud yell "Ayeeee! My Nestow*[3]!"

Kieren's old friendly black dog runs ahead to greet Pierre, "Pascatz*, we are set to go now! Here comes ol' 'Bob', Kieren's ol' buddy!" Pierre lets out a long hoot of laughter.

He quickly settles down or Keiren will be having a runaway. Soon they pull the covered wagon up to the hitching rail in front of the Mission.

"Tell us, my boy, how is Kokom Cardinal?" Father Taché is shaking hands with Keiren.

"Well I reckon you know Kokom, Father… we all got up yesterday mornin' and Madeleine went to her cabin, fixin' to check on her. Lo an' behold she was missing! We all commenced to searchin' for her and when we begun callin' her, out by the barn, here she comes,… carryin' a little pan o' strawberries, she's fixin' to make jam, fer criminy sakes!" Keiren takes off his cap and slaps his knee with it… hooting with laughter!

"That's our Kokom! By the tarnation, you can't keep her down. She's tough as nails!" says Pierre, chuckling as he picks up his old cowboy hat, whipping it across the side of his knee, keeping in time with his chuckle…; little wisps of dust are flying into the air.

"So, I reckon we load up and head out, aye Chawam*?" says Keiren with a big grin.

"You bet Nestow*[4], Tapway!" says Pierre, cramming his hat on his head.

"Astam,* you fellers, grab your luggage and set it behind duh seat close to duh hedge o' duh wagon box. I made space for it dere and dat's where it will be loaded back each night 'til we reach St. Paul. Nuttin' gets lost dat way, bedroll on top of luggage. Like I tol'[5] you at lunch, d'ere[6] are times when we need seats inside, Tapway?" Pierre is fired up and raring to go.

"Oui, merci, Pierre," says Louie.

"Tapway, Monsieur Pierre. That makes good sense, no wastin' time hunting for stuff." says Smitty, as he hands his bedroll up to Daniel, who is standing crouched in the doorway of the covered wagon.

He looks around and sees the benches where the sisters bedding has been spread out over some fur bales and covered with buffalo robes. *Looks mighty comfy, too bad I gotta ride shotgun with Pierre in the freight cart.* he thinks Daniel is a napper, if he can find a place to lay his head.

"Z'is crate of chickens can go in zee uzzer[7] wagon; Sister Thérèse and I would not appreciate listening to zem cackling h'all zuh way to St. Paul. Kieren can set zem in zuh back of his wagon where zey will not be 'eard."

Louie holds his precious picnic basket of homemade baking up to Daniel, "Sil vous plait, mon ami, we must 'andle dis baking wit' care, we would not want to crush h'it."

"Hey, hand it to me, my friend, I'll watch that for you!" says Smitty, peeking at Louie with a grin.

"Never you mind," says Daniel, "…Madame Julie baked for three days packing this basket…, don't you worry Louie, we'll put a watch on it for you."

"Not to worry, you bannock brains, Tanté Julie's pastry will be h'under duh care of Sister Thérèse!" The two sisters are standing close by and Sister Valade accepts Pierre's assignment with a quick curtsey. The sisters are both smiling and seemingly enjoying the banter of the overly-excited boys.

"Before we say our farewells, we will join hands over by the hitching rail*. As soon as the boys have tightened down the water barrels*… we will say a prayer for journey blessings," says Father Taché, quickly bringing the conversation back into order, with his educated French.

Once the prayer has been said, there are hugs, handshakes and a few tears, then the teams are untied from the hitching rail and the oxen take the lead. The horses are raring to go and Keiren has to settle down his team.

Sister Marguerite, speaking to her team in French, using a firm and assertive tone, has no problem getting her covered wagon off to a smooth start.

The Bishop and remaining sisters stand in front of the Mission doors and wave farewells until the last wagon disappears around the bend.

Louie and Smitty are trailing in the rear on horseback and they both give their final wave as they reach the bend, where they turn and disappear behind a row of aspen.

Louie takes his last long look at the old Red River flowing by the Mission grounds … a huge lump has formed in his throat, his eyes are burning. He glances over at Smitty as he roughly rubs one eye. Smitty grins at Louie and says "Could be a long time 'til we see that again."

"You could be right, my friend, but remember h'our assignment, we have been chosen and blessed." Smitty is finding Louie's strong French accent hard to decipher so he says nothing.

The sun is beginning to disappear in the west as they grind over the rough well-beaten trail. Traffic does not seem to improve the old trading trail as they wind their way along… the old Red River making a faithful appearance from time to time like a treasured friend.

Louie's constant search for a glimpse of the river is making his eyes so tired… *I would hate to be a freighter, but… perhaps now I will not need to hear remarks about my lack of courage…*

"Louie! What happened?" Smitty is yelling and jumping off his horse; Louie is lying on the ground.

"Hey, Keiren! Whoa! Hold up! Yell at Pierre!" Smitty is taking the reins of Louie's saddlehorse and the sisters are both running towards the body on the ground.

The three noisy vehicles begin squeaking to a stop as Keiren yells, "Nestow! Nestow! Astam, qwayahoh!*"

When Keiren gets excited his Mechif starts to come out. "Man down!" He yells, as though they are on a portage.

"What duh hell is goin' on!" Pierre has forgotten that there are ladies present. "What 'appened Smitty?" Pierre is looking around at the shrubs lining the banks of the river. *There were no gunshots; there must be an arrow under him.*"I see no blood!"

"No sir…he just went down like a ton o' bricks…I think he fainted," says Smitty.

Pierre is lifting Louie up to set his head on his lap, "Someone bring some water, his tongue is dry like a foxtail."

Sister Marguerite is running back to the wagon for water. "Sister Thérèse, sil vous plait, take zem a pillow!"

Louie is awake but hates to open his eyes, *Dey h'all will be looking h'at me; what a fuss!* Slowly he opens one eye... "He's coming to...give him a drink." Pierre whispers, as he helps Louie to sit up.

"What 'appened Louie? Are you 'urt?" Pierre takes the flat-brimmed hat Smitty is handing him and plunks it on Louie's head.

Sister Marguerite hands him a tin cup of water and Sister Thérèse hands him a pillow.

"Sil vous plait*, Sister, I will be fine," he takes a good swallow of water but the very thought of taking the pillow is like adding insult to injury.

"Hey everyone settle down, he is fine. Get back to your posts and prepare for camp set-up, if you please." Pierre pulls Louie to his feet.

"Smitty you stay back. You h'aught to keep in mind a couple of t'ings; first, always fill your canteens and tie dem to your saddles, needer of you boys are carrying canteens. De udder t'ing h'is... watch out fer each udder, dat goes fer you also, Louie." Louie touches the brim of his little flat-brimmed hat, "Merci, Ogemow*, tapway."

Pierre lifts his hat and scatches his head, gives Louie a nod, then heads over towards the oxcart. "You boys stick togedder now while you water your 'orses and be careful at duh river. Den you can 'obble* dem fer duh night close Keiren's wagon."

"How far are we from Pembina Pierre?" Smitty asks, as Pierre is still within earshot.

"I reckon we still need a couple o' days to get to duh Pembina area. We did alright today, for duh first day. I wanted to stop at sundown but maybe tomorrow. Duh longer we travel duh sooner we get dere."

By the time Keiren has the campfire lit Sister Marguerite is ready to start frying the bannock dough she has mixed up. Sister Thérèse has dumped two jars of beans into a heavy black pot to warm over the fire. They canned the beans last fall with salt-pork, they also have jars of canned berries for a treat once in a while.

The wagons have both been angled to look down on the river with the oxcart in the middle so as to form a half circle. All ten of the horses have been hobbled out on the south side of Keiren's wagon where the grass is the thickest.

Daniel hands Sister Marguerite the pail of water she had sent him down to the river to get. "Hey, those horses were so thirsty; Pierre was right when he made us stop and water them a couple of hours ago. I expect that's hard work pulling those wagons loaded down like that."

"Zat is correct Daniel but remember, you will not address zuh sisters as 'Hey' when you are h'at school in Montreal. Yes, we must take good care of zee h'animals and zey will take good care of us," says Sister Marguerite. "Did you see Smitty and Louie h'at zuh river?"

"Yes Sister, once the animals were all taken care of, Louie and Smitty had a good wash in the river so I figured it looked like a good idea and I washed up too," Daniel is fixing a tri-pod to hook the tea-pail on, "Looks like that water will be boiled in no time, Sister, then we can have a good cup of tea, oui?"

Daniel has a pretty little Metis mother and an Irish Catholic father. They have spoken very little Cree to Daniel and his younger sisters; his Cree is limited, much like his French.

"Tapway, my boy, merci." says Sister Marguerite. Daniel grins at the sister with crooked teeth.

Pierre has tethered his team of oxen out behind his wagon, "Mewasin, ma Tanté, dose bannocks smell good enough to h'eat!"

Sister Thérèse looks up from her frying pan with a big smile, "Merci, Pierre, vous étes trés gentil*. Soon we will eat."

Smitty and Louie suddenly appear over the riverbank, "Louie and I decided we will go back down to the river after supper and catch some fish for breakfast, aye Louie?" says Smitty.

"Tapway, mon ami, we could see dem jumping, aye?" Louie says, as he rakes his fingers through his wet curls. He is beginning to enjoy his new adventures.

"You bet, it won't take us long to fill a fryin' pan, right my friend?" says Smitty.

"Sounds good boys, meewasin*!" says Pierre as he sits cross-legged on the ground, not too far from the bean-pot.

"You are looking much better, Louie," says Sister Marguerite, "Would you be well enough to bless h'our meal?"

"Je suis navré,* Sister, "I could not stay awake, when my eyes close, I feel duh ground; I am ashame to hold up duh journey. Oui, I am honor to pray, merci." Louie reverts back to French to ask a blessing on their meal; they all make the sign of the cross and begin dishing up their fresh bannock and hot beans.

"Merci, Louie. Bon appétit,* mes ami!" says Pierre as he takes a scoop of steaming beans and a piece of Sister Thérèse's golden brown bannock, "... awe dis is duh life, aye Keiren?"

"You bet! Remember, we had bannock and beans dat time you got trapped by dat wounded moose, remember Chawam?"

"Tapway, I remember!" Pierre looks at Sister L'Ambitieaux, she is grinning and shaking her head, "...'ere we go again!"

"Quoi?"* Sister Thérèse has never heard the "wounded moose" story. "You will enjoy this story, my sister."

"Oui, oui, sil vous plait, Pierre!" Louie is more excited than usual; he has heard this story several times and still loves to hear it again.

Keiren has finished his supper; he gets up, puts his dish in the dishpan and raises his hand. "Who wants to hear Pierre's story?" Everyone raises their hands yelling, "Yes, yes! Oui, oui!"

They are making such a racket that the Pelletiers, from the wagon that is camped a couple hundred yards behind them, comes to join them at their fire.

Keiren had jumped on Smitty's horse and took the news to the LaRocque and Pelletier wagons that they were stopping to make supper. They would be setting up camp for the night. They all agree to stop for supper also and get a fresh start in the morning.

"Okay, okay… we will get comfortable after the dishes are done and the beds are made. Okay mes ami?" Pierre never tires from telling stories; he knows that it is a gift…a gift that he must share.

"Tapway Pierre, we will be ready before you can skin a wapoose*!" Daniel says, and they all run to their respective chores.

Louie reminds Smitty that they need to catch some fish for breakfast. Once the chores are done Keiren digs out a net and takes the boys down to the river to set it for the night.

The sun is just starting to get red as it sinks down behind the horizon. A few patches of willows, shrubs and the odd poplar line the crooked banks of the old Red River …it seems to follow them as faithful as the moon.

Keiren gives the boys a hand anchoring the net to a tree; they check the buoy and fasten a large rock to the bottom end of the net then Keiren heaves the rock out about thirty feet into the river.

"Dat should do it fellas, dat ol' net will be just-a-wigglin' in duh mornin'." Keiren gives one of his little 'hee-hees', and they are off up the riverbank to settle in at the fire.

Once the sisters clear the dishes away they bring their blankets and pillows for story time by the fire.

Soon everyone is settled around the fire, smudges have been lit to keep off the mosquitos and the sisters have brought out some of Julie's pastries.

Just the act of helping themselves to one piece of pastry is an act of discipline, something the sisters have been introducing into the lives of all three boys. They know that self control and discipline is going to be a shock to the system of both Daniel and Smitty. Louie has demonstrated self discipline since he was ten; it seems to be second nature.

Little does he know of what is coming ahead, and what he must indure.

*Glossary

Footnotes:

1 'zis' and 'zat'- The distinct French accent of the highly educated.
2 's'ink'-ibid
3 'zee'- as opposed to 'duh', (Red River patois), the words 'the', 'this', 'that', 'those', etc. all commonly begin with 'z'.
4 Nestow- 'My friend' or ' brother-in-law' etc. (a popular endearment among Metis men.)
5 tol'- Red River patois for 'told'.
6 ibid. –'no'd' for 'knew'.
7 'vous etes tres gentil' - French for, 'you are very kind (or nice).'
8 'Je suis navré.' French for, 'I am very sorry.'

Chapter Seven

Part Two: Destination, St. Paul, Minnesota: 1858...

"Well, it 'appened up on duh Nort' Saskatchewan on our way up to Cumberlan' House, we had portaged for mosta duh evenin'.

Jus' as we h'arrive h'at one of our traditional camp spots, I looks up and dere, about a hun"ert yard away, stands a big dry cow moose!" Pierre is using mostly English and he can see by their eyes that he is being understood.

"Well, I grabs my rifle and lines up on 'er. One shot and down she goes!" He slaps the back of his right hand firmly down onto the palm of his left hand.

"Not tinkin', I leans my gun against a tree, pulls my knife outta duh scabber and takes off runnin' towards her. Keiren grabs his knife outta his scabber too and runs to help me bleed her and dress her out. We h'allways gets a kick outta how fas' we can skin a moose!"

Everyone laughs as he exaggerates their speed and goes through the motions, as though it only takes a few seconds.

"Well, we gets up about two feet from 'er and she kicks Keiren in duh knee; ... den she jumps up!

Keiren jumps behind her to a poplar tree and I jumps behind a skinny old spruce tree right in front of 'er, I 'ave no choice!

By duh look in her eyes you can tell dat she's mortally wounded, aye Chahwam?" Keiren nods his head.

"Well, how many of you have seen a wounded moose? It's not a pretty sight to see."

The crowd around the fire seems to be complete with four others who have joined them from the other two freight-camps. Hands are going up... several have seen a wounded moose.*[1]

"She is so furious, her eyes are shootin' fire! She takes a step back, den lunges straight for me! I jumps behind a tree and she stands right in front of dat tree snortin' blood outta her nose." Pierre is so excited; he drags his fingers down over his mustache slowly, the imaginary blood is running into his mouth.

"I got no gun; ...I don't dare run! If you ever seen a wounded moose, she's mad! Dey run fast and do a lotta damage when dere mad. I am stuck behin' dis tree and I don't dare run fer it.

She is lookin' at me wit' 'er ears laid back; she's blowin' blood outta 'er nostrils and rollin' her eyes, she's only two feet away! I swear she's waitin' fer me to run. Keiren is two feet from her rump behind anudder little tree."

"Keiren catches my eye and whispers, 'Chasqwah* Pierre...be still...I's a-makin' a spear'. He takes duh pukagon string from his tied back hair and wraps it around his knife onto a stiff green poplar limb. Den he sneaks out from behin' duh tree and drives duh knife into her ribs! She staggers...den straightens up, now she is really mad!"

Everyone is glancing at Keiren who is fascinated with Pierre's rendition; … he has broken into a sweat.

"…Duh knife was not tied tight enough and h'it is collapsed! Mon Pere is standing back at duh campsite, 'Run' he yells, as he makes duh sign 'o duh cross.

'We canna' run Sir, she will be a-chasin' us!' says Keiren in a whispered yell, pointin' his lips desperately at duh ol' cow; she is a-pawin' and a-snortin!

…Finally Keiren gets his green pole sharpened into a strong sharp spear. He sneaks backwards quietly into duh bush about six yards, den …holdin' duh pole real tight in bote 'ands …he runs and jumps! He drives duh spear into duh same damn 'ole duh knife 'ad made in her ribs before! It goes deep into 'er lungs h'and she staggers once, den crumples into a big heap!"

Everyone sitting around breathes a big sigh and both Keiren and Pierre hold their stomachs and laugh their heads off.

"Wuh wah! That calls for some tea!" says Smitty, as he hangs the tea pail over the fire, doubling over in laughter.

As the laughter dies down the neighbors rise up and bid everyone a cheerful, "Bon soir!" and head for their respective camps.

Pierre stands up and stretches, "I will take duh first watch …den Louie …den Smitty; …remember what to do if we 'ave company?"

"Oui, Pierre, we wake you, right?"

"Tapway, Smitty!"

"Duh horses are your job, Daniel."

"Yes Sir!" says Daniel with a smart salute.

***

The crack of dawn is peeking out over endless prairie as the sound of the camp coming to life begins to fill the air.

"Rise and shine!" yells Keiren, "Get yer horses down to duh river, you wranglers …daylight's a-breakin'!"

Pierre is taking his two quiet old oxen down to the river and Louie decides to run alongside him with his saddle horse.

Daniel has taken Smitty with him to help water the other horses.

"Bon jour*, mon ami. Comment allez-vous*?" Louie puffs as he catches up with Pierre.

"Tres bien* Louie! Did you sleep well?

"Oui, I promise I will not fall asleep in duh saddle today. My sleep was very brief duh night before."

"Oui, mon ami, it is a very exciting time for you, Tapway?"

"Tapway, it is tres dificile* to be bote 'appy an' sad; … my 'eart is very sore to leave mon famille.*"

Pierre replied with a simple, "Tapway …tapway"

That is enough; they are both comfortably silent as they listen to the sound of the animals drawing in the river water through tight lips; the sound of the rippling waters seems to soothe Louie's aching heart.

Even the clumping of the hooves is strangely comforting … *merci mon benir Marie*. It seems so appropriate to give praise with a series of 'Hail Marys up the riverbank, in time with the hoof beats.

Finally Louie broke the silence, "Mon ami, mon Papa was going to teach me to shoot a deer."

"Tapway mon ami, we will watch for a deer along the river … when we water our horses … early in the morning." Pierre is whispering; a great sob escapes from Louie's throat.

Back at camp everyone is busy. The tea water is boiling and the sisters are frying bannock. Keiren and the boys have taken a string of fish off the back of Smitty's horse, there are seven fish on one side and eight on the other.

Sister Thérèse helps Daniel and Smitty lower the fish, six at a time into a large pot of boiling water. As soon as the water is boiling again, they begin removing the fish from the pot to lay them on a piece of canvas to cool. Once the pot is empty they lower another string of fish into the water.

Keiren takes his sharp hunting knife out of the scabbard and begins to slit the stomachs and remove the centre from the fish. Both the innards and the skins are piled onto another piece of canvas to be dumped in the bush for the birds.

Once Keiren has shown the boys how to neatly remove the two strips of cooked fish from the skins they begin helping him.

Louie is handling the knife given to him by his Papa; just the feel of the handle gives Louie a strange feeling of comfort.

As usual, once the boys catch on, it becomes a contest to see who can do the most fish. "Merci, merci, you are fine fishermen. We will use the leftover fish for our noon meal!" Sister Marguerite says, speaking only in French.

"Did you catch dat Smitty & Daniel?" asks Keiren.

"I caught that we were great fisherman!" says Smitty.

"Well, duh udder part is, we only eat one fish each, duh rest is for lunch, Tapway?"

"Oui, oui, one fish is lots!" says Daniel.

The freight brigade makes one quick stop at Fort Douglas; then, they carry on to Pembina.

There is a wet stopover halfway to Fort Pembina; they learn some of the hardships of travelling in the rain and making camp in a downpour.

"Get used to dis, boys, we will be facing a few storms before we get you to St. Paul." Pierre uses French to explain the usual stopovers, throwing in a bit of English here and there.

"Merci, Pierre. We appreciate your instructions," says Sister Marguerite, "but …when we reach Pembina, Sister Thérèse and I will take liberty to exchange for clean habits* at the Mission. You boys may clean up in the river and let your clothes dry, the Sister and I …we must take our baths in the wagon and save our dirty frocks*. They would take too long to dry if we washed them and hung them out."

Sister Marguerite is beginning to get anxious to reach Pembina. When she drops all efforts to speak English or Cree everyone knows her patience is getting thin and they do their chores quickly and stay out of her way.

Smitty and Daniel are almost cruel sometimes with their constant teasing; Louie is keeping himself contented with the books he gets from Sister Thérèse and the bantering of the boys rarely bothers him. The sisters are more annoyed with them than is Louie, unless they hide his book or jump him from behind. They get a great kick out of scaring him and when he nearly jumps out of his skin, they roll on the ground laughing.

He spends most of his time with Pierre who cuts green willows and whittles out flutes like Pierre's old Mooshom Cardinal.

"Well mes ami, next stop is duh ol' Pembina camp! Duh trails h'are smooder wit' American Cavalry troops h'up an' down; dat ol' place never changes…dere's wood an' water fer camping, dat's about it anymore. Den h'it will not be far and we will be h'at a place you will h'all enjoy. It is snuggled into duh sand hills among hundreds o' pine trees. H'as purty h'as a picture is dat Fargo, Nort Dakota."

***

Before too long they reach Grand Forks and everyone is delighted! They pull up to the Livery Stable and Pierre jumps off the ox-cart and begins pumping the hand of the old Livery man* and jabbering away in Mechif like they are old friends.

He informs the old fellow in Mechif, "We will leave everything but Keiren's team and wagon over there," he says pointing with his lips "... which we will water now and tie on d'ier feed bags over at duh Mission.

You can go ahead and feed and water these, my friend, we will be back in two or three hours ...keep those kids out of our wagons, sil vous plait." he says, pointing his lips at the spectators and their dogs gathering around.

"Awoos, keeway! Ne pas toucher! Awoos!*" the old man, in his comical Mechif accent, makes it plain to the children that they must leave ...they all scatter.

The Sisters pull out and head for the Mission while the boys stand around the trough and chatter while their saddle horses drink.

Pierre takes off his neckerchief, dips it in the trough, gives it a squeeze, then proceeds to "handsome up" his hair and face, "Meewasin! I feels like a new man! You boys take dat dollar dat Sister Thérèse gave you dis morning and go 'ave bannock and tea at Auntie Suzanne's Café omah*." He points up the street with his lips.

"Keiren and I will be dere shortly; h'after duh saddle 'orses eat...we will ride h'over."

Keiren and the boys follow suit and do a quick clean-up.

Pierre continues in Mechif..."Sil vous plait, mon ami, take good care of our t'ings and we will pay you well when we get back."

"Merci, Merci!" The old man is happy with Pierre's request.

***

Soon they are back on the road. After a few overnight stops, they arrive at Fargo North Dakota.

Most of the boys have never seen a place like this. There are fine wooden sidewalks running in front of every kind of business you can imagine... and there are people of every description walking up and down each way!

The boys stand around the trough at the Livery Stable combing their hair after they tie their wet neckerchiefs back around their necks.

The Sisters have taken Keiren's team and wagon over to the Mission; they will meet the boys back at the stables in three hours.

"Wah wah!" says Smitty. "Louie, how would you like to live in a place like this, tres beau?"*

"Tapway, my friend...it would be fine, mais*...Je préférer Riviére la Rouge!"* says Louie, with a smile, as he tucks his little green book back into his pocket.

My dear Mama would be so sad if I dropped this in the trough! Louie thinks in his Mama's French... the little book is like keeping his family close.

"Now stick close togedder you boys. We would need to call on duh Town Crier* if we lost one of yous!" says Pierre.

They head down the first street to look for the nearest Restaurant, "You can bet yor butt they won't be a-servin' no Bannock and Tea!" Keiren says as he gives one of his crazy laughs.

"Well, you might get tea but I wouldn't count on the bannock!" says Smitty, as he raises one shoulder and covers his mouth… the typical Metis laugh.

***

About the time the boys have got their fill of meandering around town and start the short hike over the dirt street to the stables, the Sisters come around the bend; they are back from the Mission, all fresh and clean. Their black frocks and white habits are sparkling.

Smitty says to Sister Marguerite, "Sister, how did you dry your dress so fast?"

Sister Marguerite says, "Now that is a miracle, yes?" as she opens a basket of fried chicken and fresh buns. Keiren is rubbing his belly and acting faint.

Sister Thérèse says, "Smitty, non*, non, she teases you. We leave them our soiled laundry and take clean ones, vous plaisantez,* oui, Marguerite?"

Sister Marguerite is making the motion to circle for prayer, "My dear Sister, you always insist on spoiling my jokes."

"Wuh wah! How easy…and you look very nice !" Smitty says sincerely.

"Merci, merci, Smitty. Vous étes trés gentil!"* says Sister Thérèse, showing a slight blush, while doing one twirl, holding out her clean vestage.*

By now it has become a habit for young Louie to give the blessing on the food, seeing how his parents have given him years of practice.

"Do not forget to give thanks to our good companions, St. Christopher, St. Francis and St Joseph," says Sister Thérèse in her usual command of both the French language and the issue at hand.

"Oui, Sister, you are so right," says Louie," …our travel has indeed been blessed."

Pierre and Keiren gently tap out there cigars and put them in their pockets.

After a wonderful lunch and a few interesting tales of the sights around Fargo, North Dakota it is time to prepare the animals for the last stretch of the day.

"Well gang, h'are you ready to 'it duh trail again?" says Pierre, he and Keiren are both lighting their cigars.

"Oui, oui Pierre, we are now excited for duh train ride in St. Paul," says Louie as he checks the cinch on his saddle.

"Tapway, my boy, but you will first be 'avin' duh pleasure of a ride down de ol' Mississippi River in a few days. Firs' we 'ave to make it over a stretch of rough trail on land, but you fellas can handle 'er now, eh mes garçon?"

"Tapway, Monsieur Pierre. You and Keiren have been good teachers," says Daniel.

"Merci, Daniel. We 'ave already made it out of a few good mud-holes, fixed a broken axle, repaired a stretch of rotten corderouy* …we will be fine."

The Freight Brigade has now grown into six separate camps and they make their way over the last stretch of trail that winds around seemingly endless sand hills. Dotted over the hills are beautiful little pine trees that seem to grow in clumps …as if in families.

As the sun begins to set over the hills …the landscape begins to transform into a splendor of reds …like a woman cloaking herself in a panorama of fine silks, getting ready for bed; night is falling like a dark blanket spreading out over the land.

Louie reins his saddle horse up to a stop and fixes his eyes on the beauty of God's magnificent creation. Through the distance he can see glimpses of what must be the great Mississippi River. He must move on; he knees his horse back onto the trail.

He hears Pierre call out his signal to rein the teams into a circle. As they begin to circle for the night, Louie listens to the sound of the other captains reining in their freight wagons.

A strange sense of excitement fills the air as everyone anticipates the riverboat experience, some for their first time.

As he catches up with their company he can see that the Mississippi River is now in plain view …as he squints he can see what can only be the dock that Pierre has been talking about.

Pierre spots the ancient fire pit they have used for generations, he lines up his Red River cart so as to be in the centre as the wagons pull up on either side; they form a half circle facing the river, not too close to the fire-pit.

He unhitches his oxen first and heads down to the water-hole close to the river. Hand-made channels have been dug to provide an inlet and an outlet giving campers easy access to fresh water.

"Keiren, could you send one of duh boys down wit' two bucket, sil vous plait? We need to get our cookin' water omuh*, before the animal stir up duh water." Pierre is taking his time with the oxen, there is a fairly good slope down to the water holes.

Soon Louie comes bouncing down the hill with two water buckets, "I am 'appy to get duh water, mon ami."

Louie knows that he will be saying farewell to Pierre when they reach St. Paul. Once he is finished his business at the tannery he will be ready to head back to St. Bonifice.

Louie is not looking forward to parting with Pierre or even Keiren, for that matter.

"We 'ave 'ad no luck shooting our deer, my friend, time is running out, tapway?"

"Tapway, mon ami, I regret to say we may have to leave that for now. But I promise you we will shoot one as soon as you come back from Montreal. It will be a great time, we will have 'meat in the pot', as the Old-timers say!"

"Oui, merci, mon ami. You 'ave been a pleasure to journey with, I will miss you terribly,"

Louie turns his head to push the tears away with his fist.

"Well Partner, you can bet we will not forget you. Guaranteed dere will be candles lit every Sunday at Mass, especially for you boys. Some of us will be t'inking of you often, Louie. Time will pass quickly, jus' you watch and see."

Everyone has finished watering their animals and soon they are busy hobbling them for the night.

After an hour or so of chores the boys gather around the fire to watch the sisters as they drop dumplings into a large black kettle. Sister Thérèse has a long peeled pole that she is using to give the soup a good stir once in a while, the fragrance is overpowering.

A generous gob of egg noodles pop up occasionally to the top, making their mouthwatering appearance; the boys are mesmerized by the tantalizing sight.

They are boiling two cut up chickens that they have been feeding since they left the Mission at Fargo. They are quite plump, as the Mother Superior made sure they had enough chopped oats to feed them through the crates until they are all gone. Daniel left four behind, still cackling in the crate, when he lifted out the two squawking sacrifices from their noisy purgatory.

***

Darkness is falling over the old Mississippi River, several barges and crafts have drifted by during supper, now they resemble little black toys bobbing along in the dark, lost out in the middle of the great old river.

Keiren is whittling his stick, he says he is making each of the boys new flutes. He will put the date on them and his name. They will need to put their own names on as Keiren is not a speller.

"Cousin Pierre, sil vous plait, mon Papa instructed me to ask you to teach me how to use dis knife and how to care for it." Louie has taken his Papa's knife out of its scabbard.

Pierre speaks back to him in English, he is happy to hear Louie using all his languages, on several occasions.

"You know Louie, it will only take about 'alf hour to show you 'ow to sharpen it an''ow to hit a target hif you trow it proper; first give me a minute, omah, to h'explain to h'everyone duh morning chores."

"Astam, gadder over 'ere, omah. I mus' h'explain h'our boarding rules, so pay attention! It will be different, we h'ar not climbin' h'on a hayrack, we will be boarding a large steamship. You will recognize it as it will be duh only steamboat dat comes into sight blowing its whistle h'an' ringing h'it's bells … h'it will pull right up to dat huge dock over dere."

He points both with his lips and an outstretched arm as if to emphasize its grandeur.

"First, duh sisters, Keiren and I, will speak to duh Captain and receive our instructions and tickets. Den duh sisters will pay our fare and we should be ready to board.

Animals to duh lef' down duh ramp to duh belly o' duh ship, after duh freight wagons are parked and numbered. Black porters will load our suitcases onto a luggage wagon and follow us to our quarters. Be polite to dese fellows, dey are our brudders, you will address dem as Sir, duh same as we address our Captains in duh Militia or on a Hunt."

All three boys are gaping at Pierre; their mouths hanging open.

"Are dere any questions?" Remember, you are going to a seminary … not to duh gallows!*"

Louie gives the other boys a quick grin. "No fear, jus' h'act honorable. You will soon get used to h'all dis."

"Wuh wah! We should all stay togedder, tapway?"

Smitty is staring bug-eyed at Pierre.

"Aye-huh*, if you pay attention and behave yerseves you should 'ave no trouble. Tapway, Keiren?"

"Tapway! Daniel wants to know, where do we eat?"

"Good question. Just follow your nose," all the boys laugh. "Chawah, no, stay close to duh Sisters, dey got duh money!" They all laugh again, mostly out of nervousness, only Pierre and Keiren have been on the River and their stories were not too encouraging.

The boys have all heard both Keiren and Pierre's versions of their lives on the Mississippi river.[2]

During their days in captivity on one of the infamous pirate ships that sail the Mississippi river, they served as slaves to these heartless pirates; their reign of terror moved inland as they robbed and looted gambling boats.

Also, runaway slaves, both Black and Irish, who refused to serve in a renegade Irish Militia, were sold as slaves to pirate ships. They travelled the river from Montreal to New Orleans and along the Eastern seaboard.

Louie questioned Pierre about his famous escape[2] as they tramped through the muskeg to a secluded spot a half mile from their camp, "Astam, mon ami, dere is not much to t'rowing a knife once you take an' learn a couple o' tricks, h'it is h'all in duh balance and duh motion o' duh wrist*. Start at eight feet, den keep stepping back. You will soon become an excellent marksman at twenty or t'irty, my boy, keep practicing but always be careful dat no-one is in your line 'o fire. You could take someone's ear off...or worse."

"When we get back to camp I will instruct you in duh sharpening. Duh firs' ting you mus' remember h'is to h'always clean your blade before putting h'it in duh scabber*. You could h'easy forget, h'if you are busy working wit' meat. Duh blood will h'eat spots from your metal blade ... I will teach you 'ow to sharpen h'it on an h'axe 'ead and also to give h'it a fine h'edge wit' your belt or duh rein from your bridle ... anyting dat h'is ledder. When sharpened proper, it will slice one hair in two...wit' one stroke, tapway?" He finishes up in French.

"Oui, Tapway, mon ami," says Louie.

Louie finds himself lifting his round brimmed hat and running his fingers through his curly hair as he places it back on his head and gives it a little shove back, just like Pierre does with his cowboy hat.

After a few bad throws Louie finds himself placing the knife right in the middle of the target that Pierre has carved on the tree. Pierre is very proud of Louie; he shakes his hand and they both sit cross-legged under the tree for a few moments.

"Merci, merci mon ami, I will remember dis forever, mon Papa will be so proud to see me hit dat target!"

"We will carve our initials and the date here omuh, mon ami," says Pierre as he lifts his hat and scratches his head again. Both of them carve their initials; then Louie carves the date, June 21st, 1858; then he resets his hat.

"Merci, mon ami, I will never forget dis day!" They head back to camp, both feeling very satisfied with their accomplishments.

***

Sister Marguerite hangs the big pot back in the corner of the wagon, then claps her hands, getting the boy's attention, "Make sure your belongings are all packed tightly in your bags or trunks; this will be the last we will be needing the wagons."

Her French is very clear ... with neither a word of Cree nor English. She looks the perfect nun; her tall black and white form silhouettes against the slits of red western sky peeking through the darkened trees.

"It will be just breaking daylight when we get lined up on the dock ... so offer your prayers and try to get right to sleep, Good night." Her French is very trite, but understood by all.

A resounding, "Bon Soir" is heard from the boys as they make their way to bed.

Louie is settled into his bed roll; he pulls out his little green prayer book and his rosary ... before he has finished his prayers he is sound asleep.

As the crack of dawn begins to widen in the east, Pierre moves around camp stopping by each wagon, "Wunskah!*...water your horses you fellas, the Steamboat will be pulling up soon."

Keiren jumps out of the wagon and pulls his little cap over his unruly red curls. He grabs his riding boots from the wagon and pulls them on, "Criminy! It seems like I just got to sleep."

Louie has stepped down and is pulling his flat brimmed hat over a mass of dark brown curls, "Wuh wah! I woke up when Pierre took duh las' watch. Hit is so exciting, 'ow can a guy sleep?"

"Me too!" says Smitty, "Wuh wah, it's my turn to light the fire, astum* Daniel, you need to water the horses!"

Just about the same time as the breakfast was done and everyone was packing up, a very loud and low whistle sounded as the big steamboat came into sight. It was barely visible on the dark waters of the massive Mississippi river.

"Holy crap!" says Keiren, "She's a big one! Look at the stacks on 'er!"

"Tapway! Dat ol' girl will hol' a lot 'o cargo," says Pierre. "Well we bes' git our teams hooked up. These guys don' like to wait fer no-one."

*Glossary

Footnote:

1 Moose experience- This author is a moose hunter; the experience of standing face to face with a wounded moose was 'yours truly'.

2 Famous escape- story taken from 'My Girl', by Carrie Mason.(Pierre's escape from captivity by Mississippi Pirates.)

Chapter Eight

Mississippi River, Minnesota, U.S.A. : 1858...

As the steamer lets down her big ramp, the Sisters are the first aboard, "Greetings to you sir!" says Sister Marguerite. "Sister Thérèse here will be paying fare for all three teams, including the oxen, sil vous plait. I am Sister Marguerite" she extends her hand to a smiling black Porter who has given Sister Thérèse a warm handshake and is greeting them in his finest New Orleans French.

"Bon jour, Sisters, welcome aboard the 'Bon Julie'! Jacob here," he says, pointing to a younger black fellow,"... will assist you down the ramp, Madam; one wagon at a time, of course."

The women insist on following Jacob down to instruct him in loading the luggage cart that will be stored in their room for the three-day journey, down river to St. Paul.

By the time the boys walk back up onto the deck, the deck hands are pulling up the ramp and hooking the huge chains on each side of the gate. The anchor is hoisted and the big boat gives another loud blast; clouds of black smoke swirl into the air and all five of the boys tramp along the edge of the boat holding onto a big metal hand-rail. The familiar smell of the river almost makes Louie feel at home.

However, there is a strange feeling of excitement as his heart pounds to the rhythm of the old paddle wheel. The strong rippling of the water carries him off to exciting places he has only read about in books at the mission.

"Holy smoke!" yells Keiren. "You can say dat agin sir!" Jacob has caught up to them and is having no problem keeping his balance as he gets in step with Keiren.

"How long do ya reckon before we gits to St. Paul, sir?" Keiren asks Jacob, they have made friends down in the galley and both have a great love for the old Mississippi, which Keiren is also very familiar with from his childhood.

"Well, you know it all depends on the stops, Mistah, it could be by tomorrow night sometime, iffen we don't have too many stops, ya see." Jacob pulls a cheap pocket watch from his over-alls, "I reckon we'll be at St. Cloud about lunch-time tomorrah, sir. Then it's not far to Minneapolis, 'course ya knows duh St Paul Settlement is only a couple 'o miles overland."

"Sounds good Jacob. Is dat duh dining room trew dem windows?" Pierre asks.

"Yes sir, you fellahs go in and find yor party, dat's where dey'll be."

"Merci, mon ami", Pierre says as he shakes Jacob's hand, then motions for the rest to follow him.

All of the boys are finding it difficult to quell the excitement of their first ride on a steamboat. Even Pierre and Keiren, as much time as they had spent on the Mississippi, could not believe the size if this boat, "Nestow* what do you tink 'o dis little craft?"

"I'll tell you what, brudder, it is mighty fine, I could drift along on dis ol' ship forever. You can see all duh sights along duh shore ...Criminy*[1], it's purty!"

Keiren is trying to stay at a loud whisper, the dining room is elaborately furnished and he removes his funny little cap when he realizes the boys have all removed their hats, "Paskutz*! dese people look high-toned! I'd best be a-usin' me manners."

Louie glances over at the two Sisters who are in conversation with the Captain. He bids them a fair journey to St. Paul, using a very dramatic New Orleans French. The nuns are delighted!

They seem to be enjoying his lively animated story; *I would say that years of dedication to God have not robbed them of their sense of humor,* Louie thinks to himself, with a smile.

After wrestling with the animals and their harnesses, the boys have worked up an appetite. Pierre waves a waiter over and informs the boys at the same time "...you need't worry about duh lunch. Duh Sisters paid fer h'ar meals wit duh tickets."

All the boys are glancing at each other, trying to contain themselves, the menu items have them rubbing their bellies and rolling their eyes until Keiren, who doesn't read well says quietly, "Wah wah! What in duh hell is all dis?"

The boys expel a variety of strange noises resembling muffled laughter, "Tapway, Moonyow!" says Pierre. "It's all written in bote French h'and English; Master Louie, could you please read out duh menu to h'us? H'it looks like we 'ave two choices, tapway?"

"Tapway Sir!" says Louie, and he proceeds to read out the menu.

When the food arrives, Louie is also nominated to ask the blessing.

As night begins to fall over the old Mississippi, the landscape seems to take on a haunting mystique. It is as though the shadows of the changing tree-line against a back-drop of darkening blues from the sky are rudely interrupted by an occasional little lamp-lit window.

As Louie stares at the beauty of the moon-light reflecting off the rippling waters, it takes him back to a miniature version of the same beauty he has experienced from a scow* along the old Red River.

His thoughts are of Papa and Mama and the quiet of the evenings; when all the babies are sleeping… and he can read. *Now I regret not using more time for Sara, he muses. I did read to her though!*

He and the boys have opted out of cabins and are sleeping under the stars on the top deck so they can watch the shore-line for little villages where happy sounds and barking dogs can be heard.

Over the constant putting of the engine there seems to be haunting suggestions of ancient tales from the old Mississippi coming from the changing shadows of the endless shore-line.

"Pierre, if'n we try to be quiet, do you reckon you could give us one of your stories before we go to sleep?" Kieren is standing over Pierre's 'nest', or so he calls it, when his bedroll is just the way he likes it.

"Well mon Chawaum*, by duh looks o' dat starry sky, duh night is ripe for story -telling. What do you say guys?" he says in a loud whisper as he looks around at the other three boys rolled up in their beds.

"Oui, oui, Pierre!" squeaky whispers are rising from the bedrolls that are perched on the brow of the deck. They had chosen the highest point to roll out their beds; this way they could watch the shoreline for the points of interest that seemed to sparingly dot the riverbanks and break the monotony, from time to time.

"Oui, mon ami, we will be quiet as mice!" says Louie as he moves his roll a little closer to Pierre's.

"So, do you want to hear about duh Band o' renegade Sioux dat raids camps on duh Red River or about duh Pirates dat robs steam boats on duh Mississippi?"

Daniel wants to hear about the Pirates of the Mississippi, Smitty wants to hear about the Sioux raids and when it comes to Louie's turn, he wants to hear about the great Metis uprising in 1849.

Suddenly they all are awakened by a series of blasts from the old fog horn of the steamer.

"Wuh waaaah!" says Keiren, as he rears up, scratches his head and places his little red cap square on top of his head.

Each one does their yawning and stretching rituals as Pierre stands up with his bedroll under his arm, "Bon jour mes ami! I see duh Sisters are back from duh chapel after dere Mass. You can grab your bedrolls and we will go and knock on Sister Marguerite's door, she will be fine wit keeping our bedrolls in 'er and Sister Tèrése's suite wit duh res' of our tings. Den we will 'ead down below and see 'ow Daniel is making out wit duh h'animals."

"Oui, mon ami, but where shall we be going to the toilet and where do we go to wash up?" says Smitty.

"Good point, mon ami, dere his a little cabin downstairs 'specially fer jus' dat."

Down below, Pierre pulls out a bag of hay from his Red River cart to feed the oxen. He unties the burlap bag tied with twine and pulls out a couple of armloads for old "Bob and Ben", his faithful old oxen.

The bag of hay is Pierre's seat and it is getting low, "Before we heads 'ome Nestow, we need to fill dis bag again. Dere's lots 'o good hay at duh train station. I only needs it when duh grass is scarce."

"You fellers are in fer a treat on duh way home; we'll be unloading about seven hun'red pounds over at duh train station."

"Where are duh pelts going Pierre?" quizzes Louie.

"Oh my pelts are well-known by dis old guy at duh train depot. He pays me on duh spot and dey are loaded fer Minneapolis where duh 'ledder'* factory pays top price fer all pelts shipped by Monsieur LaMontane, 'old Joe' we calls him. H'ar Canadian pelts h'are top quality 'cause 'o duh long, cold winters 'o course."

"You see dat shovel Louie? H'open dat trap door halfway up duh ramp and pitch out duh poop. You'll see an old wheelbarrow over by duh horse stalls. We got two saddle horses, two teams and a team 'o h'oxen, dey'll lay a few nice piles fer ya."

"Daniel h'an Smitty are 'elping Keiren wit duh feedin' an waterin'. Den we'll go h'up to dat fancy Dining room an' h'order h'up a petit' déjeuner*.

The sisters are seated and waiting for their boys to arrive for breakfast. They spot their wards coming across the deck and begin jabbering excitedly in French:

"Here they come! What a variety of personalities we have here!" says Sister Marguerite, as she squirms her skirts into place on the red velvet bench near the window.

"They are a delightful lot, are they not?" says Sister Thérèse, she seats herself across from Sister Marguerite so that she can enjoy the beauty of the shore-line.

"Bon jour mes ami, what a grande voyage, too bad it will end this evening" says Keiren as he extends a handshake to both women.

Pierre is next in line, as he comments on the beautiful weather, "Bon jour, bon jour, mes ami!" Each of the boys shakes hands and greets the ladies. Just as they all get seated the same pleasant waiter comes over to their table.

"Bon jour mes ami, comment allez-vous?" says the friendly little black waiter, as he smears a smile over the table, "Trés bien" echos around the table and the orders are quickly taken.

After a delightful breakfast, there seems to be not much choice for the boys; but, to enjoy themselves for the rest of the day.

Louie does a lot of reading while the rest find a variety of places on deck to explore, the Sisters lounge in the sunshine reading their prayer books.

Smitty comes up to Louie hiding something behind his back, "I got a gift for you, my brudder, lay an eyeball on dis!"

He presents a piece of fruit he has taken from the fruitbowl. "Smitty, did you steal dat?"

"No, no, Louie, duh Sister said to take one, it's what you call a 'orange'. I et one and it smarts duh lips but it tastes good after you eat a bit." She says der will be wooden bowl 'o apples and oranges nailed to duh tables on duh Train."

"Wuh Wah!" says Louie, "You better get used to strange things, I read dat Montreal is duh biggest most modern city in duh Canadas. Dey say Quebec City is grander, but not as big. Take duh St. Lawrence river, dey say it is a splendid sight, tings are shipped in dere from all over duh world." Louie is peeling his orange so slowly, Smitty is watching every move.

"You know Louie, you are so smart, I wish I could read dose books." Smitty shakes his head back and forth.

"My Chuwuam, I hate to scare you, but you will be learning to read dose books. You 'ave to know 'ow to read good, my brudder, so learn fast."

"Paskutz, Louie, I can read!"

"No, mon Chuwaum, I mean, well... you said I was smart...I do not know anyting if you read dose books. You will see. I 'ave a real tough time to h'unnerstan' dose books!"

"Tapway, Louie! You don't need to get mad!"

"You can sure rile a guy! Louie h'is not mad, look h'at me...h'ime smiling."

"Yah, yah, dat's when you might be duh maddes'!"

"Merci, mon ami, dat was a very good h'orange."

Keiren and Pierre even find a Poker table upstairs to spend a little time at, though their pockets are so empty they soon find other interests. "You know Moonyow* I t'inks we deserves to allow ourselves about ten dollars on duh way back, Tapway?"

"Tapway, mon Nestow*I think so aussi*, but no more dan fifteen at duh mos', right Chawaum*?"

"No more dan fifteen, Moonyow, Tapway!" It has been a long time since they have seen their wives and children so the trip home will be lighter and faster. The heaviest freight will be orders of flour, sugar, and bullets. The salt, tea, tobacco, tallow and seed for next spring is not heavy, and they will be five passengers and one wagon lighter. The Hudson Bay Company rarely ever bothers them any more since the last showdown. They travel in freight brigades that regroup at the train depot.

They begin to see small villages along the shore with a few very impressive Ports and docks. The dock-hands seem to be almost exclusively Black men who move around rolling cargo to various stations with an air of efficiency; all the while exchanging the odd comment in a rich New Orleans accent.

The big steamer stops only for the larger settlements and there is an air of peace and quiet for long stretches of water.

Pierre and Keiren are both laying back on lounging chairs on one of the south-ward decks when suddenly the stacks belch out a black cloud and with it the bloodcurdling blast of the fog-horn.

"Holy Crimination!" Keiren jumps off his chair taking it to the floor with him!

"Wuh wah! What a commotion! I don't blame ya Brudder, what a racket, I more'n likely dropped a little puddy in duh pants meself!" Pierre doubles over holding his stomach enjoying his most painful laugh that is a cross between a horse whinnying and a wolf howling! Whatever it sounds like it generally initiates squeals of laughter from those close by.

Just at that moment, around the corner comes Louie, Smitty and Daniel."What in the Sam Hill blazes is goin' on!" Smitty is laughing his head off as he sees Keiren lying on his back on the floor.

"Well," says Keiren as he picks up his chair and screws his little tweed cap back on his head, "Dat ol' horn sounds so purty comin' off duh river, you'd never expec' it to soun' like dat up close, … mercy!"

"Tapway, it don' 'elp too dat we are right by duh stacks," Pierre lets out another one of his high whinnying laughs as Keiren continues to shake his head back and forth.

"Well, it was a little loud down stairs but not all dat bad." Louie says as he grins, covers his mouth and laughs silently at Pierre and Keiren's antics … his one shoulder raises up like his Papa's.

The sun is sinking slowly in the west and a shimmer of evening fog lays over the old Mississippi; the outline of large buildings can be faintly seen in the distance.

"Duh sisters 'ave asked for a gaddering in duh Dining Room at eight o'clock dis evenin' to prepare for departure in duh morning," says Pierre. "I reckon we will kind of be saying our last good-byes, for …it could be a long spell."

Pierre is sounding kind of choked; Smitty is looking at him with big full eyes. Louie is also pushing away tears and hiding his face.

"Wuh wah, Pierre! It may be years before we see you again," says Smitty, glancing at the stunned look on Louie's face.

"Well, we still have to go 'an listen to what duh sisters 'ave to say; den I will take a couple of you to hep me unload dese bales of pelts. You can yank dem by duh twine and manhandle dem but it's hard on duh back. Bes' for two to work togedder"

"Don't you worry, Pierre, for as much as you done fer us it won't hurt us to go give a hand, tapway Daniel?"

"Oui, Pierre has been good to us."

"Well, merci, mes ami. It will be appreciated. Only ting duh train pulls out at eight so we all have to roll out of duh sack hearly."

Pierre sticks his old cowboy hat on his head and rises from his chair, "We best be showin' hup at duh Dining Room about now, hit's sundown and we'll be unloading at duh docks in duh next hour, we're slowed right down now."

The Sisters are already seated when they arrive at the dining table."Bon soir mes ami," Sister Marguerite greets the boys and points them to their chairs.

"We shall celebrate tonight before we go our separate ways in the morning," she continues in her regular French.

"We shall order up some fine food, since Father Taché's school budget is paying for it." She gives a cheeky little smile.

"I am sure we all appreciate Pierre and Keiren's kindness in allowing us to join their freight brigade. Give them a hand and then we shall order our food."

After they have all eaten, the Captain appears at their table. He introduces what turns out to be a short speech with three loud claps, he speaks first in French, followed by English:

"Ladies and Gentlemen, many of you will be disembarking at our next stop. Before we part company tonight I would like to extend a sincere thank you to all of you who have chosen to cruise down our fine American

Jewel, the 'Mighty Mississippi'…" he pinches at his little black mustache as he surveys a roomful of smiling faces "… aboard one of New Orleans' most comfortable cruise vessels, the luxurious 'Bon Julie'! Give her a big 'and, she's a fine little liner!"

He checks the crowd again, extending a hand to the nearly all black crew lined up at the back. With that, everyone gives a loud cheer and a round of applause for the, 'Bon Julie' and her crew.

"Now, Ladies and Gentlemen, I would like to introduce you to some of our outstanding passengers that we have aboard this passage. They are five people who will be departing from St. Paul's lovely Train Depot tomorrow morning enroute to Montreal, Canada.

There, three of these fine young men will be attending Canada's famous St. Sulspice Seminary in preparation for the Priesthood, please rise, you boys. Give them a hand!" There is a loud round of applause.

The Captain continues…"It has been our pleasure to accommodate the two Sisters here, on their journey. Please bid them farewell… it is not often you will find on our Rivers, vessels that offer both a small Gambling facility and a fine Chapel for those who choose. Give also, if you please, a warm farewell to the men in charge of their freight Brigade. Pierre and Keiren, please rise!"

Two slightly red faced young men rise from their chairs, then sit down quickly…both grinning profusely.

"Thank you all for travelling 'Bon Julie', we will be docking soon, enjoy the rest of your evening."

The boys have not stopped blushing for five minutes; however, they are all smiles! "Wow! 'ow did dey know all dat?" Pierre is grinning at his Auntie Marguerite.

"Well, tapway, Pierre! We have been sitting with them every day, we had to talk about something!" Sister Marguerite gives a hearty laugh; she is so happy she is even using a bit of Mechif.

She is not only pleased with the big send-off for the boys; she is more than pleased to get one up on her nephew, Pierre!

Daniel and Smitty are quietly getting short interpretations from Pierre, until the Captain resumes his broken English after each comment.

Soon the time has come to leave the "Bon Julie' and get ready for a whole new experience…the train ride Sister Marguerite has been telling them about!

Once they have disembarked, Pierre is given the money needed for a Hotel room by Sister Thérèse. The boys head over to the stables and the sisters give them instructions to be at the train Station by 7:00 in the morning.

"If you ask at the front desk they will knock on your door as early as you like," says Sister Thérèse.

"Merci, Sister, we promise to go to bed h'early, Tapway, mes ami?" Pierre checks over his shoulder for their response.

"Tapway, Pierre, I reckon we will need to get our rest. But man, oh man! It'll be hard to get to sleep…dis has to be duh mos' exciting night o' my life. To think we will be riding on a train, omuh*." Smitty is rubbing his hands together.

Louie is shaking his head back and forth in awe, not saying a word.

*Glossary

Footnotes:

1 "Criminy!"- A common expression used by the Irish.
2 "Criminiation!"- Ibid.

Chapter Nine

St. Paul, Minnesota : 1858. . .

The sun is beginning to set by the time the sisters arrive at St. Joseph Mission; they are greeted by Father Saville who shakes their hands and help them down from the covered wagon.

"You sisters go right in, the other sisters inside will be delighted to see you!"

"We are just finishing supper but there is plenty left. Come, we will set some places at the table."

"Just a basin of water and some soap will do me, we must look like a couple of hedgehogs!"

They are all laughing as Sister Marguerite helps herself to the pitcher of water down the hall, the girls are excitedly exchanging comments in the foirier as Sister Therese awaits her turn at the basin. Sister Marie heads for the kitchen, "I will heat the food right away."

Suddenly a familiar figure appears in the doorway, "Monsieur Riel! Where did you come from?" They are all jabbering in French at the sight of Louie Riel Sr.

"I arrived here on the last little steam Freighter yesterday. I have been trying to catch you up to travel with you to St. Paul. I must have got ahead of you as you camped at Pembina."

"What is your mission here at St. Paul?" says Sister Thérèse, "Sister Marguerite! Come see who is here!"

She offers her hand as Louie bows to deliver his traditional kiss; by the time he has greeted all the three of the nuns and shook Father Saville's hand, Marguerite appears wearing a curious smile, "My dear brother in Christ! What are you doing here?"

Louie laughs as he hugs Sister Marguerite crumpling her starched habit, "My Sister, you look like you seen a ghost!" The rest of the nuns join in on the laughter.

"I received a telegram to come and pick up a grist mill. It has been a sore spot with the Hudson Bay Company and my order was finally approved." His French is now very strong, clear and fast.

"When I arrived at the train station there was nothing. I sent a telegram asking when it would arrive. They telegraphed me saying there would be no grist mill, it had been opposed by the Governor. I was very upset for a while but now I am excited to see my boy."

"Come, Louie! Join us at the dining table where we can visit while you eat," says Sister Marie as she shoos everyone through the large swinging doors, where a long covered table is set for one person.

A long chandelle possesseur* in the centre of the table floods the room with the light from twelve candles. Louie muses as he notes one chair pulled out at the head

of the table with a plate of steaming food set and waiting. *I do not feel worthy of a candelabra**2 *of fresh candles...*"My dear ladies, I am so flattered, a bowl in the kitchen would have been sufficient!"

"We are all too nosy to wait to hear why you are here; you are more than welcome of course!" Sister Marie is laughing as she uses some familiar French idioms to get a laugh from the sisters.

"Father, you have been listening to the latest news on our boys travelling to Montreal to attend St. Sulspice Seminary, right?"

"Yes, we are so very proud of these young Indian boys going into the priesthood!" Father Saville says with a smile.

"I am so very proud also, Father, my boy Louie is one of them, you know."

"Yes, I have had the pleasure of meeting young Louie at St. Boniface Mission one time. He is an obvious candidate, being so devoted to our Holy Catholic Church."

"Thank you Father, I came as quickly as possible to try to catch my son before he boarded the train to go east. I had urgent business in St. Paul so I travelled alone on horseback to try and meet with him, it may be years before I see him again…"

His voice trailed off as his eyes filled with tears. "I am so sorry, I know that it is a seven year baccalaureate and most demanding. I doubt if they will pay his way for a visit. I did not last my third year in seminary. It can be very lonesome."

He pulled a large red handkerchief from his vest pocket, wiped his eyes and nose then with two quick folds, he put it back neatly into his pocket.

"There is no reason to apologize, my friend. You are very brave and also very dedicated to your faith, think no more of it. You did amazingly well, being fresh off the rivers. You have obviously prepared young Louie with strong discipline and spiritual conviction, he has a great advantage over you, my friend."

"Louie we are thrilled to have you here; you are welcome to go and bring your son back here to spend his last night with you in a comfortable dorm," says Sister Superior, as Sister Marie removes his plate, "Would you like a piece of apple pie, Monsieur?"

"I would love a piece, my dear, but I am too anxious to see my son. We will enjoy a piece of apple pie together before retiring tonight, thank you Sister. The chicken was delicious!"

"Monsieur Riel, you are welcome to hitch your saddle horse to my little black carriage out in the garage if he is harness broke," says the Father.

"Oui, Father, I will accept your offer. Do not worry about my 'Blackie'. He has pulled everything from logs to dead moose, he will do fine with a harness."

Louie excuses himself and reaches for his hat, "Pardon me, I don't like to be rude but time is precious and I am anxious to see my son."

"Go ahead my friend," says Father Saville, "…we will see you when you return."

***

The night air is cool and refreshing; Pierre and Keiren have brought the three boys over to the little sidewalk café known as 'Aunt Peggy's' and they have all been enjoying a cool Sasperilla seated around a little table with a striped umbrella over it. They are watching the traffic go by, a small group of men on horseback saunter along the cobblestone street behind a team and wagon, loaded down with lumber.

The rich hollow sound of hoof-beats echoing off the cobblestones gives Louie a strange feeling of excitement. He is awestruck by the high buildings, beautiful windows, pillared steps going up the Courthouse stairway, as though leading to a higher intelligence... he has never seen this type of a building before except in books!

Suddenly a lone figure appears in a little black buggy. He squints as he stares at the black horse pulling the carriage… he begins to pull at his curls…it can't be!

He jumps to his feet, "Papa, Papa!... is dat you Papa?"

Louie Sr. reigns in his horse and parks right in front of the little Café, the street lamp has lit up his face, the secret is out!

"My boy, you were so easy to find! I thought I would be searching for you! How wonderful it is to see you again!"

"Oh, my Papa!" I cannot believe my eyes! What brought you to St. Paul?" He reaches for his hand but Louie grabs him around the shoulders and gives him a big bear-hug. The other boys are all over Louie's papa, shaking hands and hugging, they are a noisy bunch and 'Aunt Peggy' is soon out the door looking to see what is the commotion.

"Is everything okay?" she says.

"Everything is fine, Mademoiselle, we are having a reunion!" says Papa Louie.

The well-endowed, middle-aged lady pulls her long skirts off to the side and swings the door open wide, "Well, come on in, the coffee is on me!"

Papa Louie, one of her regulars, takes her right hand and kisses it, "Merci, Mademoiselle, I will have a visit wit duh boys, dey have come a long way."

"Will you all be eating?" asks Peggy, as she sets out their coffees.

"Coffee will be fine for me, have you eaten, my boy?" he turns to young Louie.

"We just finished having a great meal," says Pierre, as they all rub their bellies.

"Well, my boy, I would like to steal you away to come back to the Mission with me. The sisters have invited us to spend the night in their Dorm. We will sit up and visit a bit before we retire," he tells Louie quickly in French.

"What do you tink brudder? He asks Pierre.

"Now, Louie, I tink dat sounds great. You go and spend a farewell evening wit' your Papa! We will meet you at duh Train Depot at 8:30 wit' our wagon. My ol' oxen are teddered*[1] at duh Livery Stable where we lef' dem h'after we h'unloaded at duh Trading Post."

After travel stories have been exchanged the boys pull on their hats and bid the Riels, 'Bon Soir'.

***

Darkness has settled over the Mission and Louie can hear sounds coming from the mission as he and his Papa put away the buggy, water Blackie and turn him into a small corral made of peeled rails. *I remember me and Papa peeling rails for his corral. I cut myself and he sent me to the house to get bandaged.*

He glances over at his Papa, he can see the silouette of his cowboy hat and mustache in the moon-light, "Papa, remember the time I cut my thumb helping you peel rails for our old corral?"

"Oui, my boy, I do remember that day. It had begun to rain and the rails were getting slippery. I am so sorry that we never stopped sooner, you would not have that big scar on your thumb if we had stopped." For some reason Papa Louie is choking up.

"Papa before we go in I would like to tell you ...that I love you very much and I am so sorry for not being a good son." Suddenly his voice cracks and he begins to sob.

Louie scans the rolling hills through tear-filled eyes. He rubs the blur from his eyes with clenched fists.

It must be the protection of the darkness... or the splendor of an endless sea of stars, tenderly lighting a rich, majestic blue landscape that whispers freedom, and with it, the permission to express his deepest and most intimate thoughts ...*a scene never to be offered again*, Papa Louie thinks to himself.

He seems to sense that this is an opportunity he must seize now… he grabs Louie by the arm and pulls him to his chest, "My son, please… do not think those things. I have always loved you…and you have been a good boy…in your own way…" he rocks him back and forth. *Papa's heart is pounding, just like mine*, Louie muses.

When Louie stops sobbing…his Papa takes out his big handkerchief and wipes his son's eyes and nose. Then he wipes his own, "Thanks be to God for this time together, my boy, it could be a long time…" his voice is very husky and he clears his throat "…morning comes early, my son, we had better get in there and eat our apple pie!"

Young Louie rubs his hands up and down on his pants as they enter the porch, "Tapway, Papa!"

Papa Louie raises the knocker on the door, just as Father Saville opens it, "Welcome back Louie and greetings to you, my boy, you look much like your father." Louie thanks him and shakes his hand.

Sister Thérèse appears in the doorway, "I heard your horse trotting to the stable when you arrived so I dished up your pie. You have permission to take your pie and some tea to your room as long as you bring the tray back when you come up for breakfast."

"Merci, it will be a treat to enjoy dessert with my son tonight," says Papa Louie as he sets his hat up on the shelf and hangs his jacket on the coat tree. Young Louie does the same.

Sister Thérèse continues with her instructions…"You may take your usual dorm Louie. Young Louie can help himself to a lit candle from the hallway so you can see to set your tray on the table, have a pleasant evening. The bell will be ringing at 6:00 in the morning." She gives them her little smile and makes her exit to the other hallway leading to the Residence.

Papa Louie wastes no time once they have finished their pie. During the drive out from St. Paul they had at least a half hour for a brief update on the latest happenings since they said their good-byes in St. Vitale, "Which side of the bed do you want, my boy?"

"I would like to be against the wall Papa, merci."

It has been a long day and when Papa Louie says, "Promise me you will not worry about my problems with the supplies for the mill being refused Louie. God will take care of us, tapway, my boy?" There is no answer… and Papa Louie smiles as he hears the gentle snoring of his precious son.

Louie is suddenly awakened by the familiar ringing of an old mission bell, he rolls over and there is Papa at the washstand pouring water into the basin, "Wunskah*, my boy, we need to get down to breakfast. The Sisters will be waiting."

So I guess it was not a dream, thinks Louie, as he pulls on his britches, "I am so happy it was not a dream, Papa, you are really here!"

'Oui, my boy, we must enjoy our last few hours together before the train leaves for Montreal. It will make stop at Chicago tonight but you will likely have a bunk or berth, they call it, on the train. They feed you very well on these trains, you will enjoy your journey. It is very long but also very pleasant, the countryside is beautiful in the summer."

"Tapway Papa, it will sure beat that old trail we had to travel in the mud. We rode inside the covered wagons all the way to Grand Forks in a big rainstorm!"

He can't help but giggle as he buckles his belt. He feels excited to get on that train… yet a deep feeling of sadness keeps pulling on his shoulder blades and he feels tension tightening his chest. He brushes it off and says, "Papa, you must have been travelling right behind us, too bad they did not bring your telegram one day sooner!" *Papa is so quiet…he must be thinking.*

After eating a hearty breakfast, when everyone has bid their adieus, Louie and his Papa go out to the barnyard and harness the team. They have been fed and watered earlier and are snorting and happy by the time Papa Louie pulls them up to the door for loading.

The sisters have everything sitting outside, ready to load up, Louie rides up on Papa's black stallion beaming with pride and excitement; he dismounts and ties the saddle horse to the back of the covered wagon for the trip into town.

"Father Saville has blessed our journeys and gone to the chapel to prepare the Mass for today," says Sister Marguerite, "The train will be leaving at eight thirty so we are doing well for time."

Soon they are loaded and on their way, they reach the Train Depot just as Pierre and the boys are saying their good-byes, Louie's heart is pounding, *it will be so hard to say good-bye to both Papa and Pierre,* Louie's heart is in his throat, *Sweet Jesus and Mary, give me strength to say good-bye, I do not want to cry again in front of my Papa.* He smiles bravely as he climbs down from the wagon.

Pierre comes up to Louie, speaking quietly in Mechif as he gives him a hand lifting down his two bags, "Bon jour, mon ami, I have to say, my heart is heavy as we say good-bye. I wish you well in your studies and hope to see you before too long," their handshake turns into a big bear-hug.

Tears are flowing shamelessly down Louie's cheeks as his Papa hugs him to his chest once more, "Good-bye for now, my boy, take good care of yourself and write often," Louie rubs his wet cheeks with the back of his hand, "Good-bye Papa, I love you," Papa is saying something that is drowned out by the loud whistle of the train.

Porters are busy tagging and loading their luggage, "You' all ready to board, young man?" says a handsome old black Porter with a white beard; he is wearing the dark blue cap and uniform of the Northern Pacific Railroad line.

He takes Louie by surprise, "Yes sir!" he says ... as he steps up into a strange new world.

*Glossary

Footnotes:

1 ‘teddered’- patois for ‘tethered’, meaning : tied up with a bit of slack in the rope to enable the horse to eat.
2 Candelabra- an honorable table centre, a 12 candle holder may indicate very special guests.

Chapter Ten

Part Three: On to Montreal: 1858...

Louie cannot believe the size of this monstrous machine, or the sound of that engine, it screams like a thousand demons. He trips as he steps into the passenger car to follow his four travel companions, "Watch your step there, young fella," the Porter says behind him.

"Yes sir," says Louie as he catches up with Smitty, who turns around and says, "Wuh wah!" with a big grin on his face.

"I guess this is really it, mon ami," says Louie with a slight roll of his dark eyes, a half a smile, and a shrug of one shoulder.

"Pierre says to pay attention for game. He says they don't stop for animals, they just run over them and leave them," Smitty says, shaking his head in disgust.

"Wuh wah!, says Daniel, who is eavesdropping on Louie and Smitty's conversation. "I guess we best be ready for some surprises."

They come to a stop as the two Sisters look back at the boys, Sister Marguerite explains the seating arrangements in her slowest French which she spices with the odd English word for the sake of Daniel and Smitty, "This is a comfortable car, it is close to the Dining car and the toilets, the next car after the Dining car is an Executive Coach. After the Executive Coach there are sleeping coaches for Men or Women. You boys will be under the care and discipline of a Railroad Conductor; you must be quiet and pay attention to their directions."

All three of the boys nod their heads and say, "Oui, Madame."

Louie snuggles up as close to the window as he can get. He removes his little grey, flat- brimmed hat and lays it on his lap. He has to see if he can see Papa or Pierre. The train begins to move slowly along the platform and sure enough…there are Papa and Pierre tipping their hats to the Sisters who are seated in the next seat to the three boys. Suddenly Louie catches the eyes of his Papa, he is smiling and waving…Pierre is standing right beside him; he is waving both arms in the air and smiling…it is a sight that Louie will hold in his heart for many years to come.

As they move along to the edge of town Louie keeps his eyes on the sights of St. Paul until the only thing he can see is prairie, sagebrush and scattered Aspen trees.

He can hear the voices of Smitty and Daniel but they are fading…

Louie is awakened by the sound of the train whistle, as he looks out the window he sees huge buffalo, their large curly horns smashing up against the sides of the train. He looks back and as far back as he can see…there are buffalo, many are lying wounded along the track, *I guess this is what Pierre was warning us about, it is an awful sight…* ; he watches until the animals are out of sight, then he drifts back to sleep.

The next time the whistle blows it was lunchtime and the Sisters were shaking the boys to wake up. Sister Marguerite is straightening out her habit and rubbing the sleep from her eyes as she instructs them in her best English, "We will h'all follow Sister Térèse to zee dining car where she will be buying all h'our meals. Please remove your 'ats has you pass trough zee Executive Coach, den h'again when we h'enter zee dining coach. We will first proceed to zee toilets to wash up, sil vous plait?"

"Oui, merci, merci," they are all saying, as they straighten out their clothes after a long morning sleep.

The train ride is very long for three young fellows. By the time they have had several nights in their bunks and seen many unusual sights, they are beginning to get bored.

The only one who is not asking permission to go for walks down through the various cars of the train, is Louie. He has brought a very thick book that he borrowed from Sister Thérèse; she was happy to accommodate him.

All three of the boys straighten up and pay attention as they go through the process of changing trains in the massive train depot of Chicago, Illinois. Louie is petrified at the sight of all the buildings and masses of people, *who would have ever thought that there were things like this happening as we went about our business at Red River. I heard Papa talk about it but you have to see it to believe it.*

There is a two hour stopover until the next eastbound train; everyone agrees…they are all starving!

"Smitty, we need a box of sandwiches, come with me, sil vous plait; we will see what they have," says Sister Thérèse.

Louie looks up at the high ceilings; voices and footsteps are reflecting tones new to his ears, "Daniel, do you hear dose echos?" They both stare up at the ceiling, "Tapway, my friend. I think we died and went to heaven! Look at all the strange looking people!" Daniel lets out one of his noisy laughs, then quickly shuts up, the echo of his laugh rings out all over the station. People are turning to look at them.

"Wah waaah!" whispers Louie, "We best be quiet." But he can't help but snicker at the look on Daniel's face.

He notices people taking brochures from a rack on the wall, "Sister Marguerite, h'ar we hallowed to take one?" Louie asks. It would make for great reading, "Oui, mon garçon, you may indeed. D'ere are odders d'ere you may like h'also," says Sister Marguerite. Louie looks around; no-one is paying attention; he takes one for Cleveland and Detroit also. *Bon, tres bon les carte!* Louie is thrilled with his new information; he has maps, train schedules, hotels, restaurants…for three major cities. *Someday I will travel…for sure!* As he walks along glancing at the brochures he suddenly realizes he has lost his way back to the benches where his companions are seated…he scans the crowds…people are looking at him strangely…*sil vous plait, dear Jesus, which way do I go?*

Suddenly he hears the sound of a child crying, *My God, it is baby Charles! He has followed me to haunt me! 'Please sweet Mary, take away the memories of that day…I cannot stand the sound of his cries!'* The scene of that dreadful day plays over in his mind once more.

A moment later he hears the sound of his sister Sara's voice. *It is very strange…hit sounds like duh voice of Sara…mais; Sara ne parlais pas anglais*[*1]*!* A young girl is saying, "Look for an Exit sign!" Louie quickly glances around, there in the distance he sees an exit sign…and not far away is Sister Marguerite, sitting on that bench. *"Merci, merci, dear Jesus!"* he says under his breath, he gathers his composure and smiles as he approaches the bench, "I was went duh wrong way!" Daniel lets out a loud hoot of laughter. Louie giggles to himself as he sits down straightening out the curls he had been pulling at. "You looked like a raving maniac for a minute!" says Daniel. Then they all enjoy a quiet little giggle, including Sister Marguerite.

He continues to watch the floods of people as they move in waves, back and forth, to and fro. Louie is beginning to get dizzy trying to look at all the fancy dressed people… *some day I will buy a suit like dat; I will buy oxfords like dat also, just like Father Taché wears on Sundays. The women! Some have yellow hair and some have hair like Marie L'Ambitieaux, back at Red River. Some are just as pretty! Papa warned me dat dere are many beautiful women out here.' Sweet Mother Mary, send your holy angels to protect me from evil.'* He is thinking in English again, it has become a habit on this trip.

Smitty is handing out sandwiches, "Pull in your eyeballs there Louie, they will drop on the floor."

Louie takes a chicken sandwich, "Merci, mon ami, you also, I see you bump into dat man, gawking h'around." Louie raises his shoulders and has a little laugh to himself.

The sun is setting as the small entourage from St. Boniface, Red River begins boarding the train for Detroit.

Louie is getting settled onto a larger seat. The boys have learned that you can sit alone if there are not too many passengers; then you can stretch out and have a sleep. They also learned that stopping at a high water tank usually means that there is a town coming right up. Louie has been paying attention, for instance, if you are the first one to excuse yourself from the table, you likely will not find a line-up at the toilet.

He hears Sister Térèse talking; she has slowed down her French to allow for Smitty and Daniel to translate. Louie sits up to listen, "We will now stay on this train until we reach another big city called Detroit, Michigan. There we will begin taking several Stage Coaches to Toronto… then on to Montreal. Settle down now and enjoy this last train ride," she looks at Sister Marguerite and grins.

"Oui, mes ami. Z'is train ride will be like heaven compared to some of z'ose rough wagon trails we will travel to reach Montreal." She looks at Sister Térèse and gives a little laugh as she looks at the boys…they are not laughing.

Sister Térèse waves her hand, "Oh, it is not so bad. In some ways h'it is more h'interesting zan zuh train."

"Oui, my Sister, you are correct, stopping at all those relay stations is quite fun. Especially when we change Coaches and have a meal; the food and the people are always different. The drivers speak English until we reach Quebec." Sister Marguerite has been using her broken English during much of the trip to Chicago.

Louie has pulled his book out from the Muskemoot* Pierre gave him … a gift from Kokum Cardinal, Pierre's Gramere*. He loves this little bag because Kokum always spoke to him in Cree at Mass, *she always told me that I was a good boy, that made me feel good. I will always think of Pierre whenever I use this bag,* Louie thinks to himself. It has beautiful flowers beaded on one side and is made of pugakin*. It has nearly lost the smell of smoke as it is only slightly tanned. The puckering string smells the strongest, it is darker in color like the seams.

By the time they reach Detroit they have eaten two good breakfasts and had two fairly peaceful sleeps except for the occasional train whistle which is no longer startling. They have just finished breakfast and are having a short rest as the boys take their turns at the toilet; the sun is just coming up. The train is slowing down as Smitty says, "Louie, do you get kinda sick looking at the blurry trees?"

Louie is shaking his head, "Mon ami, I never would 'ave believed it if I did not see h'it for myself, no horse could gallop dat fast! Tapway?" "Tapway, mon chawaum*." says Smitty.

The train has slowed down to a nice speed that allows the boys to have a short look at the edge of the city. They all look at one another in relief as they see the station coming into view. The train Depot at Detroit is not quite as overwhelming as the one in Chicago, yet the boys are showing signs of excitement again.

"Here we are in the big city of Detroit," says Sister Marguerite as she straightens her habit and the boys begin to get their hats and coats from the shelves overhead.

"Wah wah! I guess we need to stay close together again, eh Sister?" says Smitty as he sets himself back down to let Sister Marguerite take the lead.

"Oui, my boy, we will go in and 'ave a Porter to gazzer h'our luggage. Dere will be plenty of buggies and Coaches parked by z'uh platform."

"Perhaps we can have a Porter move our luggage straight to an East-bound Coach for Toronto," says Sister Térèse, in her usual slow French, she uses when giving directions.

"That would be excellent; we would not have to handle it until Toronto where we will be spending the night," says Sister Marguerite.

The boys are all excited as they make their way through the Station and out onto the huge platform, where people of all kinds are moving in all directions.

Sister Marguerite is taking the lead as they scan the platform for east bound traffic.

Soon a voice calls out, "Sister, Sisters! H'ar you looking for h'an H'eastbound?"

Everyone stops and looks back, "Oui, mon ami! Dere h'ar five in h'our party, sil vous plait!" Sister Marguerite is pointing around in a circle at their entourage, as Sister Térèse begins taking her bag from off her neck.

"Combien est-ce que je vous dois*[2]?" she asks the driver, who is seated up in the driver's seat, reins in hand, and crooked-stemmed pipe clenched in his teeth. He's a rough looking character with the legendary shotgun in a scabbard standing by the high, wide wagon seat that sits solidly over the front end of the stage coach.

He pushes his crooked old cowboy hat back on his head revealing a crop of coarse gray hair; pointing his pipe around he says, "Dese boys will ride half-price, ...altogedder I reckon it will be fifty dollars, dat includes duh ferry toll."

"Merci, monsieur, trés bien*!" says Sister Térèse as she is counting out the money.

The agile little driver jumps down off the stage coach, stuffs the money into his pocket with a quick, "Merci" and begins to help the three boys as they hand the luggage up to the young fellow who is riding 'shot-gun'*.

He has moved from the right side of the driver's seat, up on top of the coach into the luggage rack, "Toss 'em up boys!"

He grabs each piece of luggage with skill and precision, placing them carefully into position. When the last bag has been hoisted up he snubs everything down tightly, "That should do 'er boys!"

He jumps down and shakes hands with all his passengers, "Howdy Ma'am, they calls me Smiley, we 'll be a-visitin' at all duh stops, nice ta meet ya! Old Pete here is always in a rush ta get-a-goin'."

"Well son, we got a dead-line to connect wit' duh Tronto stage by noon tomorrow. You folks will be staying tonight at duh Morton Inn. It will cost you two dollars a bed; it is clean and comfortable, and dey serve a nice breakfast for two more dollars."

Smiley is holding the door open for the Sisters to climb aboard. There is no room to spare as the three boys get settled across from the Sisters. Smitty pushes Daniel in first, then Louie, "You might just as well sit in the middle Louie, you always read your book anyways. Me and Daniel, we need to look out the windows."

Sister Marguerite was right about enjoying duh train, dis is got to be duh roughest road I ever was on! Louie is finding it hard to read his book with all the bouncing around.

After a couple of hours trying to focus his eyes Louie is tired of reading and falls asleep with his head on Smitty's shoulder.

Smitty and Daniel are getting restless; suddenly, Daniel spots a small black piece of cloth sticking out from the side of his seat. He begins to pull on it. It begins to stretch until it is getting longer and longer. "Hey, mon chawum, look at this!"

Smitty reaches out with a puzzled look on his face, he grabs the end of it and pulls. It keeps getting longer and longer, "What is z'at?" says Sister Marguerite as she leans back, careful not to wake Sister Térèse.

"Wuh wah! It is nothing but a stocking!" says Smitty.

"Oh, my heavens!" says the Sister "…H'it looks like zuh stocking of a dance-hall girl, like you see in zuh newspapers!"…Her broken English making it even funnier.

"Holy smoke!" Smitty is trying to be quiet but he is getting the giggles. He puts his finger to his lips, "Scusé, sil vous plait…he whispers to Sister Marguerite …this will be so funny!"

He quickly twirls it into a circle around the mass of curls on top of Louie's head; then he slowly lets it dangle over his ear. Louie rubs his nose and continues to sleep. Sister Marguerite is trying not to laugh when suddenly Daniel lets out a smothered whoop. Sister Térèse wakes up, "Smitty! What did you do?"

"Just havin' a little fun Sister. Sorry." Louie has awakened, "What duh Sam?" He sees the end of the stocking and grabs it. He gives it a jerk, looks at it, and drops it like it burnt his fingers.

"K'moochiwin*[3] you, Smitty!" says Louie, his eyes flashing in anger, he begins rubbing his eyes and soon he is shaking his head and grinning. Both boys have lost it and they are laying back holding their stomachs, laughing their heads off!

"Hey, hey now, boys. You will frighten zuh horses and we'll have a run-a-way. Zen you will not be laughing!" Sister Marguerite sounds so serious with her French accent; the boys simmer down to a snicker, their hands over their mouths.

The sun has gone down and it is beginning to get dusk when there is a squeak over-head and the trap door opens to the Driver's seat, "Ten minutes and we'll be pullin' into Morton's Inn!" says Smiley, "Thank you, sir," says Sister Marguerite.

"Boy, oh boy!" says Daniel, "Those sandwiches are a long ways down!"

"You are not kidding, mon ami, mine are down in my boots!" says Smitty.

Louie stretches out his legs, careful not to kick Sister Térèse. He peers out toward the north window and although it is nearly dark he can see the huge body of water on his left…*it seems like we are still in duh same place.*

Smitty is looking out the south window, "Hey look at this! We must be at that Inn old Pete told us about!" A cozy two-story log Inn sits back from the road; a small livery stable can be seen in the rear. A veranda with a swing, a bench and a couple of chairs out front overlooks a glassy endless lake that disappears into the darkness. A lone loon can be heard as they climb from the coach.

"What a relief! I cannot wait to stretch my legs!" Sister Marguerite is arranging her habit and skirts for the step out to the ground.

Old Pete is hollering "Whoah, Whoah now!" to a tired and hungry team of four horses. Smiley opens the doors for the ladies to step out of the coach.

"Merci, merci, mon garçon!" Sister Térèse is teetering around like a drunk.

"So sorry, Madame! I reckon ya needs ta gets yer land legs!" Smiley gives her a hand but is having a hard time to not laugh.

Once the luggage is inside Pete and Smiley go out to take care of the horses and the sisters deal with the Innkeeper.

A cheerful well-groomed old gentleman takes care of them and gives them two keys, so the boys can take the luggage and lock it in their rooms while they have supper.

When the boys get back, the Sisters are seated at a table. "You boys can sit wherever you like; we will be having stew and dumplings. We will need to retire before long as the stagecoach leaves at eight o'clock. Enjoy your supper." Sister Marguerite offers a part of her Newspaper to the boys; Louie is the only one interested and he accepts it with a smile. "Remember prayers in our room, after supper," Sister Térèse usually reminds the boys each night.

The next morning they are all ready and rejuvenated after a good sleep and a hearty breakfast of pancakes and boiled eggs. Old Pete pulls the stagecoach up to the door and the boys begin handing up the luggage to Smiley as Pete helps the ladies up into the coach.

The journey to Montreal consisted of many uneventful days much like the first leg which had brought them to Toronto.

The most striking features of this stop-over were the majestic Cathedrals, the many sophisticated buildings, including the Nuns Residence where they are welcomed for one night.

Now as they enter the city of Montreal, Louie is suddenly overwhelmed by the feeling he has for the ancient architecture and the enormous Cathedrals. *Dis h'is jus' like I have seen in books, it all seems like a dream.*

The buggy that has picked them up at the Staging Depot is made of very elaborate woods, fine leather seats and ornate black metal trims. The sound of hoof-beats on the cobblestone streets echo like a grand scene from one of his favourite books; Louie is gaping shamelessly as they move from one amazing sight to the next.

The carriage pulls up to the back step and Louie is suddenly back to reality. The Driver is helping the sisters down and giving them all a fine scripted welcome to Montreal, French now being the order of the day.

Life as it had been, would never be the same again, for three young boys from the old Red River Valley.

*Glossary

Footnotes:

1 *'Sara ne parlais pas d'anglais'*- Louie is thinking he hears his sister Sara's voice, as someone says, ' Look for an exit sign!'

2 'Combien est-ce que je vous dois?'- Sister Thérèse is overjoyed to speak French, she asks how much she owes.

3 Louie is upset with the tricks that Smitty keeps playing on him, 'K'moochiwin', he says, 'You are crazy!' (in Cree)

Chapter Eleven

St. Sulspice Seminary, Montreal, Quebec: 1858...

Despite subtle tips and short anecdotes about Montreal and Seminary life from the sisters, on rare occasions ... no one has prepared the boys for what is ahead of them.

They will be spending their first three days at the Grey Nuns Convent for assessment and orientation; then, they will be taken to a school of their entrance level.

Sadly enough, the three boys are never given much opportunity to continue their close relationship as they adjust to life in Montreal, Madame Masson, their kind-hearted patron, makes an effort to have them gather at her Estate for a few days during Christmas and Easter and two short summer visits.

Daniel becomes so homesick within the first two years he has to be taken home; he is unable to apply himself to his studies and becomes very pale and thin.

Smitty also begins to have serious health problems, and he also has to be taken home to Red River in his third year. Louie's life has been so busy with keeping up with the demands of his baccalaureate he barely has time to miss them.

In the summers of '59 and '60, the three boys are able to spend time together at the Nun's Residence or Madame Sophie's; however, by 1861... Louie is the only Red River student left in Montreal.

Louie's strong devotion to his Catholic faith, his steady progress and amazing achievements carried him along for six years.

Though life at St. Sulspice is drab, and the curriculum very demanding, Louis finds a great deal of support from his patron, Madame Masson, and his Uncle John Lee who was married to Louie Sr.'s sister, his Aunt Lucie.

Louie's thirst for knowledge and his passion for religious studies is copiously quenched through the many challenging disciplines. He feels very honoured to receive instruction in such respected classical studies as Greek, French and Roman Philosophy, History, Literature and mathematics.

He receives his first reprimand on his first day of classes. He begins to read the Fall Outline given to him by Sister Josette, as he sets out to follow Sister Matilde to his room; her French is clipped and fast.

"Do not read as we walk, there will be plenty of time for that. Pay attention to where you are going, if you expect to find your way around." She points to her left.

"Pass three doors down this hall and you will be at the Dining Hall." Louie swallows hard and looks around, the halls are dimly lit and he can smell the odour of coal oil* fumes mixed with Lye*. He can feel his shoulders tighten as their footsteps echo over the brick floors, his eyes begin to burn.

Once he settles into his dorm room, Louie is left to himself to await the six o'clock bell, his call to supper.

He sits on the edge of the narrow, stuffed mattress, *It seems soft, I wonder what it is stuffed with... I think not goose down*... it would be softer?*

He stretches his long lank body out to see if he can reach the footboard, he has to slide down off the little stuffed pillow to tap his toe on the footboard. He wiggles back up onto the pillow and lies there looking around.

"Wah Wah!" *These walls are so high! Paskutz!* The ceiling is as high as duh one in Chicago Train Station!" What would my Mama say? Oh, my Mama, she is likely crying for me right now, at this very moment! I should be at her supper table.* His thoughts are pulled back and forth between French and Mechif; his feelings are pulled back and forth also; he is excited; he is sad…

Oh my dear Jesus, Mary and Joseph, please be here with me. Send your holy angels to minister to me in my loneliness. I am so sorry…but…I miss my Papa so! My Mama also, and the kids … especially Sara, please, keep them safe. Thank you for bringing me to the place my Papa tried so hard to endure, please give me the strength to do Your will… amen. His prayer is in French, as usual … he begins to feel steady as he makes the sign of the cross.

Louie rolls over to face the wall; he can feel bitter tears welling up, his throat is so tight…

***

Loud bells are pealing out over the campus, Louie wakens with a jump… *my God, it was not a dream. I am here.* He feels the dried tears on one side of his face, his pillow is soaking wet. *Come on Riel, smarten up,* he gives his face a couple of slaps. *It works for Pierre, it should work for me!*

He jumps to the wash stand and quickly dumps a small portion of water into the basin. He splashes his face and rubs water through his hair. After he rakes his little comb through his tangled hair, he pushes his waves into place. *Now that looks better!*

He heads out the door and down the narrow corridor to the hall that Sister Matilde pointed out to him.

Wuh wah! I am so hungry; I can smell salt pork already! I hope it is beans like my Mama makes. He begins the trek in a rush, then, he remembers… *I will not know a soul here, 'Jesus, Mary and Joseph, help me, I feel so alone.'* His throat hurts and his hands are clenched as he nears the door.

Upon entering the dining room he senses the need for an attitude of acceptance; nothing is ever going to be the same again. A strange feeling sweeps over him, a feeling of calmness, *It is the prayers of my Mama and Papa, I can feel peace coming into my heart. It must be the Holy Spirit.* The drained feeling is leaving his body and that strong feeling of anxiety has turned to excitement.

A smiling nun comes towards him and he finds it easy to smile back. "Welcome to the Convent of the Grey Sisters, I am sure you will enjoy your stay."

Louie reaches out and takes her hand, he bows and kisses it gently as he was taught by his Papa.

"Come with me Louie, I am Sister Marie-Genevieve; I will introduce you before dinner."

She leads him through the tables covered in white linen, up to the front of the long narrow room. Splintered rays of sunshine spray over the tables through tiny panes crowded into a row of high windows, the only visible scenery are endless roof tops and two steeples.

The rustle of starched habits grows louder as nuns stream through a giant doorway at the front of the room. More than a couple of dozen young boys, looking very much like chickens being herded to the chopping block, begin to file in through the door Louie had entered moments before.

Sister Marie-Genevieve stands with hands folded waiting for all to be seated. Louie stands with hands clasped behind his back, a favourite stance of his father's when surrounded by a crowd.

As the noise subsides Sister Marie-Genevieve gains the attention of the room with three loud claps..."Good evening gentlemen, on behalf of the sisters I would like to introduce you all to... (she presents Louie with a wave of her hand)… Louie Riel. He is sent to us by Father Taché from the St. Boniface Mission at Red River Settlement." She looks back at the boys who are all gawking at Louie, making him feel very uncomfortable.

She continues, "Because tomorrow is the Sabbath, we will gather after Breakfast in the Chapel. After Mass you will be free to roam the grounds until the twelve o'clock bell. We will then meet back here, of course. This evening you may visit on campus until the eight o'clock bell; then, you must go to your room to prepare for bed."

Louie's French is not crisp and confident like Sister Marie's; however, he responds to the nun's introduction with a quiet, "Thank you Sister Marie, I am pleased to be here." He gives a nod to both sides of the room and follows Sister Marie to his place at the table.

He is seated between two contrasting characters; he shakes hands with each one in turn as they say their names, Joseph, a skinny kid with a limp hand, Louie quickly concludes *…he looks like he needs a good feed of bannock* and Romaine whose hands are stiff and heavy, like horse hooves *…I think I will stay out of his way*; they both smile weakly.

There is no conversation as Louie looks around to see if he can spot Daniel or Smitty…*no sign of those two, they must be here somewhere, I feel so sorry for my buddies, they will not understand half what the Sister just told us.*

After dinner Louie goes out to the grounds and finds a bench to sit down, he watches the boys as they spread themselves around the grounds *…they look like pigeons looking for a place to land, or drop their blessings…or like they are lost souls in a strange land…just like me…*

"Wuh waaah!" Louie nearly falls on the ground, someone has jumped on his back! *That is an old Red River trick!* He turns around, sure enough! "Smitty! You son of h'a gun! Where you guys were?"

"We could see you; we didn't want to butt in."

"Oh well, I wonder where we will h'all be sent!" Louie says as he searches the puzzled faces of his buddies.

"You know Chawaum, I got a feeling we will not see much of each udder. I reckon we are bein' put in grades, Daniel and I don't fit in your grade, for sure, we can't hardly read good!" Smitty sits on a bench and shakes his head back and forth.

Daniel pats him on the back, "Don't be sad Smitty, you will make us sad. You always cheer us up! But you are right. I heard what the sisters were saying too. We will be split up. If I knew where to start … I would find a ride back home tonight!" Daniel buries his face in his hands.

"Oh Daniel, buck up! I reckon we are close to bein' men. We can do it, tapway Louie?"

"Tapway, mon Chawaum! We will be just fine! We will put our faith in God, the saints will be with us!"

Louie has talked himself into accepting their fate for now, Daniel and Smitty have also cheered up.

Louie puts down his head to form a huddle, for a minute they stay quiet while Louie gives them the instructions Sister Matilde gave them in French. "Wuh waaah; merci, mon ami! We would have been so confused, merci, Louie!"

"Tapway, mon ami, make sure and tell dem you do not understand French!" Just say "Je ne pas parlais de Français*[1]. Tapway? Aussi*, ask dem for a French dictionary."

"Oui, oui, mon ami!" says Daniel.

"Merci, merci, mon ami! We needs dat good talk, I reckon we can write each udder, hey Chawaum?" says Smitty, his eyes beginning to fill up.

"You bet, mon ami, now do not forget!" The bell begins to ring, Daniel sticks out his hand, Smitty brings his elbow down. Louie remembers the old "Red River elbow" and sticks out his hand, both boys take a turn at smacking their elbows down on Louie's hand. The bell stops ringing and they all head in different directions.

The silent hallways that Louie navigated, leading up to the dining room at supper time, are now alive with the sound of undisciplined voices echoing off stone hallways. He takes a wrong turn and ends up on the wing of the Sister's dormitory. *Dear Jesus, send me a guide, sil vous plait.* The first nun he sees will be his guide.

"You are going where, my boy?" A kind voice comes up behind him, *she sounds like an angel!* He swings around, a smiling face greets him. Louie is so grateful he bows to the sister and says, "You have the voice of an angel, my sister."

He has just won the heart of the Sister Superior who will also become very good friends with Louie's favourite sister Sara, in years to come.

The results of the testing in the next few days will bring Louie Schmidt, no longer 'Smitty', to St. Hyacynthe College and Daniel McDougall to the Collège de Nicolet.

Louie is assigned to the second level of an eight year program at the Collège de Montréal under the St. Sulspice program.

Only one month after he starts his first term he ranks twenty fourth out of thirty seven students in his class. Three weeks later he has jumped to thirteenth place.

In the following years Louie becomes very well respected in all aspects of the Catholic community which would include: the Academic circles of Montreal, local Politicians in later years, and even the legal community, due to his studies in Law.

Madame Masson, his wealthy sponsor, soon begins to receive good reports regarding the success of her young patron and he becomes a welcome guest at her Estate on Terrebonne and the Mansions of several other members of the local Aristocracy.

Louie has received a strict upbringing by his Papa and is well versed in the vocabulary and social etiquette of the French Aristocrats who flaunt their 'old money' and wear benevolence like a coat of arms.

Women think he is charming and men enjoy taking him around just to surprise the upper class with this "...articulate young man from the wilderness of the West."

He becomes somewhat of an entertainer as they introduce him to a local speaking circuit. Being from St. Sulspice, his speaking engagements will generally be expected to contain a spiritual flavour. Audiences are often made up of Catholic socialites looking for a positive exposé on the joys of being kind and generous, as taken from the Holy Scriptures.* 2 Corinthians 9: 6,7&8. KJV

His crowds rarely contain many English-speaking people; therefore, one of his most appreciated topics by his male followers is that of the history of the French in both Old France and the New World.

The Director at St. Sulspice is pleased to allow Louie the liberty to attend these engagements, seeing as how great contributions are being received by the College.

On occasion Louie is well rewarded for his work and he finds it a blessing to be able to dress appropriately. He loves to patronize the exquisite Taylor Shops in Montreal. His allowance allows for the finest in leather boots, jackets of a fashionable cut and his wavy hair and dark moustache trimmed in the latest style.

By the age of nineteen, after four years of coaching and grooming by Madame Masson, he has become very well-known as a debonair and very articulate young man.

He is also very handsome and women shake their heads and say, "C'est un chic*2 type." …as if to say… "What a waste; to think that he will be a priest!"

In 1864, Louie is riding high and his Uncle John and Aunt Lucie are proud to attend his engagements and to enjoy sharing in his accolades.

While finishing his evening meal at his posh residence on the grounds of Madame Masson's Estate one evening, he was visited by Father La Fontane, one of the junior instructors.

He suddenly appears in the doorway of the dining room with his large black hat in his hands, "…sil vous plait, entre," Louie is smiling. Father La Fontane does not smile. "May I be seated? There has been a telegram from St. Boniface, my child."

Louie is beginning to feel uncomfortable, *a few gray 'airs does not give 'im zat* right, he only uses zat term when he needs to get personal, when he is disappointed or worse…*

"I do not know how to tell you this, Louie, but your Father has passed away."

"Do not say that… there has been a mistake!" The Priest, who is usually very calm, is taking Louie by the shoulders, "Sit down, my child."

Louie again jumps to his feet, "I will not sit down! And I am not your child!"

"Where is this telegram?" Father La Fontane hands him a small piece of paper.

"Who sent this? Louie reads it and spits out the word…Taché!" He grabs the arm of his big stuffed chair "…Dear Jesus, Mary and Joseph…oh my God… it is true!"

He shrivels into a fetal ball, his head resting on the arm of his chair. Father La Fontane seats himself on a chair by the dining table…it is beginning to get dark. At last, fearing to disturb the crumpled ball that is sobbing and heaving; he quietly sees himself out.

When Louie finally rises, he staggers to the street and flags a carriage going by, "Mile Bend, sil vous plait!" The driver closes the door behind him, he squints at his face, "Is this Monsieur Riel?" There is no response.

He takes the short route to Mile Bend, opens the door of the carriage, "Bon soir, Monsieur Riel," Louie raises his head … the driver jumps back in horror at the distorted look on the face of …the once handsome, Louie Riel.

Safely up the stairs of Aunt Lucie's front veranda, Louie staggers to a wooden swing. This is where his Uncle John finds him, staring blankly, his hair dishevelled and his bow-tie dangling.

"Louie… my boy, my boy! What are you doing? Are you intoxicated?" John Lee, Louie's closest uncle in Montreal, is shocked at Louie's appearance; he has always been well groomed when he arrives home.

"Oui, oui, mon oncle, I am intoxicated with grief!" Louie looks up at John, a strange and twisted look of anguish written all over his face.

"What has happened, my boy?"

"He is dead Oncle, he is dead." Louie rolls his head back and forth.

"Who, my boy!... Who is dead?" John is frightened at the demeanor of his nephew.

"Mon Papa! Louie cries out in anguish … mon Papa, mon ami, mon héros!"

"Oh my God Louie, I am so sorry!" John gently takes his arm and stands him on his feet, "Come inside, my boy. Your Auntie must be told…I will fix you both a nice hot brandy!"

As they enter the foyer, Lucie appears from the parlour, "What is happening?"

John sets Louie on a chair, then takes Lucie and sets her down, "Your brother Louie has passed away," he kisses her forehead and says, "Take it easy Lucie…I am fixing you both a hot brandy." Lucie grasps her nephew's limp hand and holds it to her wet cheek.

That evening Madame Masson arrives in all her splendour…her chauffeur escorts her in and seats her in the parlour where Lucie and Louie are wiping at their faces'… they both greet Madame Masson.

"I cannot tell you how sorry I am. It breaks my heart to see Louie receive this news so very far from home. I would be pleased to hire a carriage to get you to the train. I will be responsible for all of your expenses."

She looks as though she is desperate to help.

"Non, non, Madame. I cannot even imagine arriving there in one month … for what? To view a grave covered in bird droppings?" Louie is gripping the curls above his ears with both fists; he shakes his head back and forth and heaves out a ragged sob… "Oh, my God! How cruel, six lonely, useless years, how very cruel!"

"Please excuse me, Madame, I am sorry for being so uncouth, but I do not even care, I am angry!"

Madame Masson is mopping back tears; her most precious patron is suffering and there is nothing she can do; even money is of no consequence.

Louie continues…"No one knows the strong vows that I made to my father …only Louie Riel can deal with that… it is not for anyone else to be burdened."

Time is given to Louie from St. Sulspice, to deal with his grief.

Upon his return to classes, Louie is no longer carrying himself with dignity and grace; he is withdrawn, quiet and anxious to return to his room.

After a month of absences and late arrivals the Director calls Louie to his office. After a lengthy discussion among the Director, two residing Priests and limited words from Louie, it was finally decided that Louie should spend his remaining residence at the Grey Nuns Convent to finish the few months left before graduation.

Louie is slowly dropping in attendance, ratings, popularity and interest in general. He cannot seem to find comfort in attending Mass, which had always brought him out of a slump in the past.

After several meetings with sisters at the Convent he decides to drop out of St. Sulspice, he tells Sister Superior, "You have been a faithful friend, my Sister, can you understand that my heart has dried up?"

He sits with his head down, his fingers gripping his thick curls, "I have lost the desire to learn; I have not been able to read one book since the death of my...Papa."

He ends his sentence with a deep sob.

"Louie, I cannot say that I understand exactly how you feel, I gave up my family for the Lord many years ago; I rarely see any of them. I can see that you are deeply grieved, but, no one but God can help you. You must be willing to try to help yourself, however. It may help for you to write your mother. I have a letter from her that you may take and read, she also is very grieved, but ...she needs to hear from you Louie."

"Sister, I was fulfilling my Papa's dream; I was nearly there. I would have gone back to Red River next year. We could have worked together to help our people to build a strong community." He pounds three times on her desk then... laying his face in the crook of his arm, resting on her desk, he takes two deep breaths and whispers in a raspy voice, "Now… h'everything h'is gone."

Suddenly he rises from his chair, "Merci, mon ami, I will remove my belongings from here and move them to my Uncle John's home at Mile End. Bid the sisters farewell for me."

A strange feeling runs down his spine…as though he is about to journey into a strange land…perhaps forbidden territory…*I will write my dear mother as soon as I am settled in at aunt Lucie's.*

"Louie, I will not try to stop you. You have made up your mind, may God direct your paths and do not forget that you will always be welcome here, we have grown to love you." Louie takes her hand and kisses it; then he kisses her forehead, "You have treated me well, my Sister, merci." Then he is gone.

*Glossary

Footnotes:

1 'Je ne pas parlais de Francais.' Louie tells Daniel, '…just tell them that you do not speak French.'
2 "C'est un chic type' – equivalent to: 'That is one cool guy!' – so much as to say, '…and he is totally unavailable!'

Chapter Twelve

Mile End, Montreal, Quebec: 1864...

Life at Mile End is very quiet and Louie is having much trouble dealing with silence. Auntie Lucie is very pleasant and her cooking is wonderful; however, Louie has no appetite. His wonderful wardrobe is beginning to sag on his skinny frame.

"Sil vous plait, my boy. Tell me what I can fix for you to eat. Have a shave and comb your hair. You are too handsome to waste away to nothing, my boy."

Aunt Lucie is at her wit's end, "Get cleaned up Louie and go to your Coffee House and go listen to those braggers." Lucie is not particularly educated except for the rudiments; therefore, her French and English are simple and unadorned; Louie loves her untainted character which is genuine and rather course and comical at times. She reminds Louie of his father, for a woman of the times she is not bashful and can be rather bossy. *...my, my...Auntie, she is so like my Papa...good looking and bossy. It is no wonder that I battle with an ego problem.*

Louie has several old haunts in downtown Montreal, places where he can meet up with friends. The 'Chez de Café' is one place where he can meet with other University students and enjoy lofty intellectual conversations.

He has not been there for two months, even now, he has no desire to go there. He has purchased his favourite international blend of coffee and is content to drink gallons of it. Black and syrupy, spiked with three teaspoons of sugar… he stirs and stirs…and stirs.

He stares blankly out his little attic window. He tries to read some of his Greek, Latin or philosophy text books. Nothing interests him. Even the Bible that he has always loved to read… is laid down gently, as though he does not want to offend Jesus, Mary or Joseph, who even without looking up, he can envision all three… standing before him, hands on hips.

The time has come for me to write my Mama, he takes pen in hand, then, with eyes blurring with tears, he begins his dreaded letter: 'Louis Riel', Maggie Siggins.

Dearest Mother, dear little sisters, dear little brothers:

> *After I received the news that plunged me, as you can imagine, into the depths of pain, I was advised not to write immediately so as to be better in control of myself, and not to sadden you over much. But I cannot contain myself any longer…*

Louie spends a great deal of time in his room; his mood is beginning to improve…ever since he mailed his letter to his Mama. His heart aches to see his Mama and his siblings; they are so far away.

His interests in writing are beginning to awaken since he accomplished a letter to his Mama. *I shall write a letter to my Law professor Laflamme first, if he has no room for me as a legal assistant, I shall try Georges Cartier. He may need me to write his speeches again, I still consider him a friend; he was excellent at promoting me when I was doing speaking tours. Even if he could get me into the bureaucracy, as he once suggested, a toe in the door, so to speak. I am not too proud to start off as a 'paper goon', as he calls it. Heh, heh.*[*1] (Louie's connections with a large influential following while doing the speaking tours at theatres in Montreal and Quebec City had resulted in a season of popularity. Louie goes downstairs, has a bite to eat, then goes back upstairs. When he returns he is looking very handsome in one of his favourite outfits.

"I will walk by the Post Office and mail these letters, ma tanté; then, I shall go over to the Masson Estate, Madame is still happy to see me. She is willing to continue an allowance for me you know, as long as I do some writing and prepare for some speaking engagements. I have been spending time in her guest house by the gardens. She sends paper down with Moses when he brings my meals and 'Le Soleil'*[1] ...but I am only writing bits of poetry, nothing fit for publication."

He is wearing Madame Masson's favourite jacket. Whenever she accompanies him to a theatre she requests that he wear it, the fabric is a fine fashionable import and the cut is a smart three quarter length, with a collar that is very chic, even more so when Madame slightly raises it for him, after she straightens his cravat*.

Madame always exhorts me when I am feeling down. She believes in having the very finest of everything...it is no wonder she makes me feel special.

He takes down his top-hat, brings down the small hat brush hanging in the closet and gives his hat a few brisk brushes. *Madame notices everything, I must not have dust on my hat or my shoulders, she will think I 'look like a tramp'.* He used to get a kick out of his thoughts and have a private little giggle over these humorous little remarks from back home. These days he rarely manages a weak smile.

He sits in the foyer checking the shine on his high boots. Auntie Lucie is watching from the parlour door, "Don't forget your walking stick, my boy."

"Oui, merci, ma Tanté. Do not save dinner, I will be eating with Madame, sil vous plait."

"Greetings, mon ami! Do you care for a lift?" Louie is startled, he swings around to see who is driving the one-horse buggy he has been hearing, as it clips along on the bricks, behind him. *Now what? He will be asking too many questions! I cannot bear to be interrogated at this time!* "Merci, mon ami, I am getting exercise with a brisk walk to Madame's."

"Bon jour, mon ami, enjoy your stroll!" Jacques McGill is a law student Louie has spent time with for two years each Tuesday at Chez de Café. He breathes a sigh of relief as the one-horse buggy clips on down the street.

I bet today is Tuesday, I have no idea anymore. Time is passing and I have not written mon mere, except for a small note. What can I say...I am no longer pursuing the priesthood? My God! What have I done? Mama will die of shock; Papa's lifetime dream will never be fulfilled. Six years! I would have now been moving into my final year...Papa's only hope for me has now been shattered!

He is approaching the huge iron gates of the Masson Estate. He opens the small gate on the side and enters...nothing has changed.

He stands on the door-step and surveys the massive manicured gardens that surround the ancient stone Manor...he has spent hundreds of hours for the past six years sitting under a tree in the farthest park, reading, praying or simply thinking and meditating.

A narrow brick walk circles the park and two straight paths cut across, with benches along the way for those who need to a place to sit and rest. The long garden path is entirely lined with a thick, well-manicured hedge. Lush bordered flower beds appear from time to time, claiming their stations amidst the greenery.

I must visit that garden again...things could almost feel normal sitting listening to the birds and smelling all those wonderful flowers. I could even visit my thinking tree, way up at the other end...away from everyone. I cannot spend the rest of my life cooped up in that Guest house or sitting at the dormer of Aunt Lucie's. I must shake off this darkness and gloom.*

Louie is sitting on a white swing up on the brick patio; one of his favourite ways to take a break from study has been to spend time at Madame Sophie's, studying the architecture, the ornate stoneworks. Even here on the patio, polished patio bricks gleam in the sunlight between a stately semi-circle of tall white columns. He is staring out over the stone wall at the splendour of the city... when a carriage pulls up to the front gate.

An old black gentleman bows to the driver as he holds the gate open. Louie has developed a great friendship with the old black fellow; he serves as gardener, gate-keeper, and even as butler if he happens to be indoors, his name is Moses.

"Louie! I had no idea you were out here; you must meet our guests!" Madame Sophie has just appeared in the doorway. Louie ponders their status, here at the manor...*they must be business associates, I have never seen them here on week-ends...*

A tall dark haired man is coming up the front steps; a beautiful young girl behind him, lifting her skirts as she steps onto the patio.

"Louie, please meet Monsieur Joseph Guernon and his lovely daughter Julie-Marie."

Louie is very embarrassed as he has seen this lovely lady a few times recently... walking in the garden. "Louie Riel, sir...I am pleased to make your acquaintance ..."

He has risen from the swing to give Joseph Guernon one of his firm handshakes. "...and you Mademoiselle, you are lovely indeed. He bows and takes her hand to kiss it lightly. "We have never met though I have seen you from time to time."

"I am pleased to make your acquaintance also, sir." Julie is blushing profusely.

Madame Masson holds out her hand toward the wide door being held open by Moses. "Come, come, mes ami, Millie will fix us some refreshments." She is herding them into the parlour.

"Monsieur Joseph and I have a quick business meeting; then we will visit," a cheery black maid, wearing a starched white apron, takes her leave for the kitchen, as she hears the indirect request from her mistress.

"My apologies, Madame, I have only one hour, then we must leave. A pleasure meeting you, my man," he tips his hat in as much as to say, "Be off, un-hand me!"

Louie takes his hat and excuses himself, "I will be back later Madame Sophie, I must finish my walk."

He trots down the steps and heads for the garden. *A guy has to know when he is not welcome. I need to read my mama's little green book, zat* will make me feel better.*

Louie thinks and speaks in English more often in recent years. It comes with the territory when international students and faculty are using both English and French. His accent has improved in the sense that he no longer uses the Red River patois such as, 'dis and dat', but has been elevated to the use of words like 'zis and zat'*, much like the language of the French nuns.

He walks all the way out to his old 'thinking tree' and past the guest house that he has been accustomed to occupying on many of his week-ends.

He settles down with his back against the old rough trunk…*perhaps one day I will again occupy zuh guest house, it feels so good, zis old tree… I may take me a nap when I have read awhile.*

He cannot see the house from his tree and it feels very safe and secluded. He pulls his little green prayer book from his jacket pocket. His mind is racing back to the last time he seen that lovely Guernon girl. The words on the page are a blur…

What is wrong with courting Marie-Julie? Am I not released from those impending vows of celibacy?... the singing of the birds seem to provide a melodic interlude to his romantic thoughts that bring a tingle to his belly, the music is fading… *Dear Jesus, Mary & Joseph, can you still hear my prayers or have I moved too far from your Holy presence? I am blinded to your Word…*

…am I dreaming or is that Marie-Julie standing on the path staring at me?

"Bon jour, Louie, you look so sweet when you are asleep," Marie-Julie begins to move in his direction, "May I?"

Louie is mesmerized, their eyes are locked. Marie is stunned at his eyes, they are so sensual with the remnants of sleep almost hidden by his long squinted lashes.

"Pardon me, Mademoiselle, your presence began as a dream but it is real… you are here." He reaches into his vest pocket to retrieve his handkerchief. As he wipes his eyes, she reaches out to touch his arm, "Please Louie, call me Julie. I must apologize for the rude behaviour of my father. He is a rather shrewd business man, with very little compassion, as you can see. He always addresses me as his 'dear Marie."

"I have been waiting to meet you, Julie…I suppose it is the price I must pay to finally make your acquaintance. I peeked at you often, afraid I may meet your eyes. I have been betrothed to the Priesthood and have recently left the Seminary. Just the sight of you made me a candidate for confession, you are so beautiful…my heart races and I cannot bear to look at you."

"Louie, look at me. I have waited so long to meet you also. I know you are studying to be a priest; I could not bear to look at you either. I feel like a Jezebel.[*2]" She gazes into Louie's eyes; her pale skin and dark ringlets cause her hazel eyes to stand out. They have an almost hypnotic effect on Louie.

"Never feel that way; you are no Jezebel! I am as available as any young man. It is just that it is very difficult to realize…" His voice trails off.

"Julie, would it be inappropriate for me to invite you to the Guest house for refreshments?"

"Well, Louie, of course it would not! You will need to learn a bit about women. At least we can sit at a table to drink our lemonade!" her laughter is infectious and he also giggles. *It has been so long since I have laughed; the sound of it startles me.*

"Your wish is my command, Mademoiselle!" He takes Julie's hand and pulls her up, *she is so close...*he lets go of her hand quickly, as though it is hot...*I cannot let her know that I am trembling.* "I will call on my friend Moses to bring us some cookies and lemonade."

"Race you to the Guesthouse!" Julie lifts her skirts and leaps quickly over the cobbles*; Louie feels like he is back at Red River; he runs and leaps like a deer!

"Ha, you will not get in without this...!" He holds a large key up, dangling it on a string. He unlocks the door and slips the key back into his vest pocket.

"Carry me over the threshold, sil vous plait?" She looks up into Louie's eyes. His eyes are laughing.

"No, my dear, it is much too soon for that." They both throw their heads back and laugh.

"Watch this Julie!" He takes the poker and shovel from along the fireplace and strikes the shovel three times as it dangles from his fingers, then he comes back in, closes the door, and returns the tools to their places.

"Now, sit here like a lady and wait a few moments." He sets her down gently, then, takes his place at the other side of the small round table.

He takes his watch out of his vest pocket holding it by the fob*, he taps his fingers on the linen tablecloth..."Now watch, the door should open any moment."

Two quick knocks and the door comes open. "You called, sir?" Moses eyes are as big as fried eggs when he sees Julie.

"Miss Julie, I reckon I figured you wuz gone. Yor Daddy lef' an' said you wuz to walk home if you wuz gonna dilly-dally, he says."

“That is fine with me Moses. I can take my time and visit with Master Louie.” Julie is beginning to realize Louie’s status here at Madame Masson’s.

“Moses, mon ami, thank the good Lord you came. I could have looked really stupid, you are my friend indeed! I began to think you were inside helping Madame Sophie, and had not heard my signal.” They all have a good laugh.

“What is it you need Massah, Louie?” He looks at Miss Julie, “You bes’ be lockin’ yo’ door, Massah, I don’ wanna be disturbin’ yore visit.”

“What would you like for refreshments, Miss Julie?” Louie turns to Julie with a smile.

“I shall have whatever Miss Millie has ready for Madame Sophie, Moses.”

“You are always so gracious, Miss Julie, and you, Massah?”

“I will have the same, my friend.”

“Madame’ll be tickled to hear yer back in the guest house today, sir.”

He gave a nod and disappeared out the door. Moses will always be grateful to Madame Masson for her hand in bringing him to Montreal and from spending years in slavery in the Carolina’s.

Julie walks over to the fireplace and begins to stand on her tip-toes to see the plaques standing in a row on the mantle, “What is all this Louie?” Julie is straining to see.

Louie begins to run his fingers through his dark curly hair. He is embarrassed as he brings down the first two Awards, “Julie, these are gifts I received from speaking engagements the past few years.” He hands them to Marie-Julie.

“Oh Louie, I am so proud of you, I have heard my parents speak of you after attending an evening of speakers at the Theatre. May I see them all?”

Louie brings down a stack and sets them on the big four poster bed that dominates the room, sitting grandly in the far corner. Louie lights three candles and sets the bronze candelabra on the nightstand.

Sweeping aside the heavy drapes from a large oak corner-post, he makes a place for Julie to sit and look at his trophies. Louie's embarrassment slowly turns to a warm feeling of appreciation…*I suppose it has never occurred to me how significant these Awards are to a boy from the Red River valley. Praise be to God.*

Louie has nearly finished showing Julie his framed awards and plaques when a knock comes to the door, "One moment Moses, I will let you in."

He opens the door to find Moses standing with a wagonful of treats from Miss Millie. "Sir, Miss Millie is so happy to send you her extra treats again!"

Moses begins to unload the cart. He begins by taking a large bouquet of fresh flowers and placing them in the middle of the table.

Julie is still sitting on the bed looking at news articles, "Did you know Moses that we have a celebrity with us?"

"Yes Ma'am. I knowed that for some time now. Madame Sophie is very proud of Massah Louie."

"Moses, you must know that I have left the Seminary." Louie searches Moses' eyes, "Yes sir."

"Do you think Madame thinks less of me now?" Louie knows the honesty of Moses and is desperately searching his face.

"Massah, I mus' tell you the truth…she was very saddened…she would not accept company for one whole month." Moses looks very hurt to tell Louie this sad news.

Louie says "…and what else?"

"Well sir, I hear her telling some folks off good for sayin' you lef' the church; she says, 'You have no right to judge that boy. That is the job of God alone!' They shut up, sir ...besides...they offered apologies."

"Moses, your few words have meant the world to me; I feel like I can go on living now."

"Think nothing of it, sir. I am only tellin' the truth." Moses understands every word of French being spoken by Louie; however, Moses speaks very poor French and will only speak it if the occasion demands it.

"Merci mon ami, you know you are special. Madame says for you to call for a ride when Miss Julie is ready to go. If you don't mind, sir, she would like for you and Miss Julie to go in for a minute."

"Well of course, Moses. Tell her we will be there in one hour." He glances at Julie and she nods."Merci, Moses, we will see you soon." Moses bows and leaves with a big smile.

Louie steps over to the door and locks it, "I suppose Moses is right, if this is not locked from the inside we could have servants coming and going."

"Do you think there is a cloth I can dampen? These things are covered with smoke and dust." She brings the remaining trophies to the table.

"Yes, Julie, I will bring two cloths; then I can help you. I will begin by wiping off the mantle."

When they have finished, Julie flops over the width of the bed and lies there staring up at the canopy. "Louie, each time I saw you...I knew we would someday meet."

Louie is so nervous that he takes his time wiping down the fireplace ...*what have I got myself into now...Oh, Jesus, Mary and Joseph, do you hear me? Sil vous plait, help me out of here...or give me the grace to be a regular man.*

"Louie, could you bring that tray of fruit for us to eat while we talk?" Julie is not sounding nervous at all, yet she appears to be very young and innocent...*is she experienced...or simply naïve?* Louie takes the tray from the table, his hands are trembling.

He sets the fruit between them, leans back on his elbow, and takes a twig of grapes. "I am beginning again to feel like I am dreaming." He closes his eyes for a moment.

"Louie, you have such long eyelashes, may I touch your eyes?"

He feels her fingers caressing his eyes, he opens them and she is right there. Before he knows it, their lips have met and nothing else matters in the world... *her lips are so soft, I know this is a blessed union.*

Their kisses are sweet and slow, Louie wants more but is not about to frighten her.

When they finally stop and look at each other, Louie speaks first. "Julie, I could go on and on, you are so delicious and beautiful. I must savour this time together and take you home before it is too late."

"I know you are right Louie, but...just one more before we go." He kisses her lips, her eyes, her nose, then they have a long kiss good-bye. They both know that this can not be public...*this is all so bitter-sweet, the scripture says 'forbidden fruit is sweet'. I must not torture myself with these thoughts.* Louie is struggling with an overactive conscience.

As they rise from the bed they see the grape juice on the front of their clothing, "My goodness, Louie! What shall we do?"

They both bend over in laughter, "Oh my Julie, we will be in trouble!" They scramble to find cloths to wipe off their clothing; it can barely be noticed, except for the dampness. "Oh well, we must be going," says Julie.

After a short visit with Madame Sophie, she calls for a carriage to come to the gate. "My boy, I still am very proud of you, we need to take in a Theatre soon; we will also take Julie with us, right Julie?"

This may be an exercise in defiance but Louie is familiar with Madam Sophie and her strategies, the community does not frighten her.

"Oui, Madame. I would be delighted!"

"Give Moses our apologies, sil vous plait; we did some cleaning but the table is messy, I would like Moses to take care of it. Leave the fruit; we will be back tomorrow. The carriage is here so if you ladies are finished we will wish you a loving, bon soir!"

Louie and Julie make a run for the door, waving as they slow down for the stone stairway.

"I know your Papa does not like me; it is too light out so I will lie down on the seat as you leave the carriage." Louie is serious … *I must do something to get Monsieur Joseph's approval.*

"Oh Louie! I am so sorry that my Papa is so rude!"

The driver, an old black fellow named Ezra, chirps out a giggle "I remembers dose days, you chillun be careful now. We don' want no shootin's." He enjoys one more giggle before he stops the carriage and helps Miss Julie down from the seat where Louie is lying as flat as he can get.

"Bon soir, my darling, walk to my uncle's tomorrow like we planned. Ezra will pick us up there and we will circle over to Ms. Sophie's" His whisper, coming from the floor of the back seat is raspy and Julie is getting a kick out of it as she steps down from the carriage.

"Bon soir, mon ami, Ezra!" She waves good-bye as she runs on tip-toes through the front gate of the Guernon residence. Louie gives her one quick wave; his heart is racing.

*Glossary

Footnotes:

1 Le Soleil- 'The Sun', Louie's favourite newspaper where his speaking engagements are generally announced. This public exposure now results in an aversion to being seen out walking. Many of these admirerers would remain loyal to Louie's cause throughout the years.
2 'Jezebel'- When Marie Julie expresses her guilt feelings to Louie, she says she feels like 'Jezebel', the infamous female infidel of the Old Testament.

Chapter Thirteen

Mile End, Montreal: 1865...

As Louie enters the house, Aunt Lucie is waiting in the parlour, crouched in a chair watching for Louie's mood ...*please, dear God, let him begin to heal from this dark place he is in.*

Suddenly the door flies open and Louie enters, like the charming man he has always been; he lifts his little Auntie in the air and swings her around, a typical merry greeting from a Metis man, "There is hope for me still, mon Tanté!"

"Louie, Louie! Put me down! You will break my back. What has gotten into you?"

Lucie is frightened ...*has he finally lost his mind?* Lucie is searching his face, *he looks normal; he looks happier than I have ever seen him.*

"My sweet Tanté, I am so happy. I am in love!" Louie has set her down gently and is brushing her hair from her face, "Oh my little Auntie Lucie, I am so happy. God has given me grace to be a regular man, a man who can love a woman."

"Louie, do not speak so boldly of such a thing...have you gone mad? Did you actually break with your celibacy? Oh, my God, Louie!"

"Non, non, mon Tanté, but I have at least known the lips of a woman. Be happy for me Tanté, I will still need your prayers. I am in love with Julie-Marie Geurnon, Sir Joseph will be very unhappy with me, if he doesn't kill me!"

Louie buries his face in his hands, "Oh my little auntie, what can I do? You must give me your blessing!"

"I am sorry, my boy. Give me a chance to get over the shock…I must tell your Uncle John."

"I am very tired, tell uncle John I love him. I will come down and join him for breakfast before he goes off to work. Pray for me that I do the right thing, sil vous plait, mon Tanté?"

He hangs his coat and hat, puts away his walking stick and goes up to bed.

Louie is in the habit of trying to read until late, then, he sleeps to noon. Today he is wide awake and down stairs to meet with his uncle John as soon as he is clean and dressed. *Well, he will not shoot me. I must face him and hope for the best.*

"Congratulations, my boy. You have found a woman! And a pretty classy one, I might say." Louie has swallowed the lump in his throat and is all smiles.

"Merci, my uncle! Merci! I am so happy you are not angry with me." Louie shakes his hand.

"Well, my boy. Your Papa made three years in the Seminary, you made six. Perhaps your first son will make the seven." He throws his head back and laughs.

"John, do not be so crude, it is no laughing matter." Lucie is wagging her head.

"I have suffered from so much guilt Auntie. Uncle John's laughter is like a healing balm." Louie joins his uncle in a hearty laugh, "I think I will have a daughter who will be a nun instead. Those women stick together and are much stronger than us men."

"I believe that, my boy!" and he has one more, good laugh before breakfast.

A small horn sounds outside the gate, Louie swallows down his coffee. It has no sugar yet, but for Louie, there are more important things to think about. "Bon Jour, mon oncle. I must go. See you tonght, mon Tanté!"

Louie can see Julie, tapping her umbrella as she rounds the corner, just up the hill from the Lee's, on Mile End.

"Good day Ezra, how are you today?" Louie tucks his walking stick under his arm as he unlocks the front gate, "It is a good day, Massah Louie, and don't you look fine!"

"Merci, Ezra, you stay seated, I will help Miss Julie up to her seat."

As Louie greets Julie he can see Auntie Lucie peeking out the window.

"Good morning, ma chêre, you look very lovely!" He sets her up on the right side of the rear seat; then, he goes around and climbs up to his place beside her.

...I am already trembling, it must be love "I slept like a baby last night, Julie. It was my first good sleep in two months."

"I too slept like a baby but I was too excited to eat breakfast, we are like two little kids going to the circus and we don't even know where we are going, do we?" Julie tosses her head in musical laughter.

"I am sure Madame Sophie will be expecting us for breakfast, right Ezra?"

"Dat's right, sir. She says to bring you aroun' to duh back door."

"Well that suits me fine. Sometime I would like to ride in a canoe again, I have not even seen one since I was a little girl." Julie is as fidgety as a little girl.

"You just watch, Julie, we will be doing lots of things. I know Madame will not mind us taking a buggy. You should see the vehicles in her coach house. We will need to be discreet until your Papa gets to know me, we will take the back roads for a while."

"You are right Louie, I hate lying but he asked me where I was so late, it was only quarter of nine...anyway I had to tell him I was helping Madame. He is fine with that because he likes her business."

Soon they are at Madame's back door. "Do you want dis buggy later, Massah Louie? Dis ol' mare is easy to handle. Ain't you Sarah?" Sarah snorts a bit and Julie gets a big kick out of it.

"She knows her name, Miss Julie." Ezra chuckles.

"Why not? Merci, Ezra. Just tie her up with a feed-bag on*. I will water her before we go."

Madame is delighted to see Julie and Louie again, "Come on in and sit at the table. Millie will have your breakfast before you can blink an eye."

"So what does your father think, my girl?" Sophie sits in her place at the head of the table, looking grand as usual, her wavy white hair pulled back in a loose bun.

"We are feeling so guilty, Madame. He does not even know. I almost had to lie last night. I told him I was helping you, then he was alright."

"My dear, you are helping me. I am suffering the same sense of failure as my boy here. We need to accept his change in careers and go on, regardless of what Bishop Taché is saying."

"What can I do to help, Madame?" Julie asks.

Madame Sophie goes to the armoire and opens a drawer, "My dear, I have been crocheting on this white tablecloth forever it seems, do you crochet?"

"Why yes, Ms. Sophie. I am actually quite good at it." Julie is all smiles.

"Then take this bag with you and do as many of those large white roses as you can do; the thread and hooks are in the bag."

Julie takes the bag and peeks inside, "Oh Madame, you are so kind. I will be happy to help you with your beautiful tablecloth."

"Thank you Millie. That breakfast looks wonderful!" The table is already set; all they need to do is dish up. "Louie, will you be asking the blessing as usual?"

"Of course, it will be a pleasure. I have not abandoned God, Madame," he says bravely.

After breakfast and a short visit, the happy pair leave out the back door, "Madame, could you tell Moses we will be back in a couple of hours and we will take our lunch at the guest house, sil vous plait?"

Madame Sophie is looking as fashionable and well-groomed at eight o'clock in the morning as she does at eight in the evening; she smiles and gives a little wave, still sitting at the breakfast table in her lounging gown.

"Yes, my boy. We will be watching for your return."

"Which way should we go?" Louie asks Julie, as he brings Sarah back from the water trough.

""I can tell you that my father never goes along the river, he may run into one of his poor relatives." Julie has a good laugh over that and gets Louie to giggling…*when was the last time I was laughing at eight thirty in the morning?*

Louie takes a left turn and taps Sarah on the rump with his little buggy whip. They trot merrily down toward the old St. Lawrence River, when they reach the river road it is a sight to behold, "Oh Louie, look at the way the trees hang over this road!"

The sun is lighting small ripples on the water. They flash every few seconds between the tall aspen trees that line the river banks, "I wonder how far this road will take us."

Julie has opened her umbrella and is enjoying the light breeze that is blowing through her hair.

"I suppose we will see; we will watch the time and turn around in one hour. I don't like to be late for Moses' lunch." Louie is stealing a look at Julie, pretending to gaze around at the scenery.

"Julie your hair is beautiful when you let it hang loose. It looks great when it is up in ringlets, don't get me wrong."

"I will remember that Louie, I prefer it loose above ringlets anyway." Their conversation becomes intimate once in a while then swings back to the scenery.

"We need to turn around now Julie," Louie says, as he checks the time on his pocket watch.

"Oh Louie, please park over there by the river," she is pointing down to a shady area nestled in the trees and shrubs.

Louie helps Julie down to the ground, then, takes a folded blanket from the seat, "Where should we sit, Julie?"

"This will be fine, right here." She points to the ground under a big tree overlooking the river. "Right here by these shrubs, Louie."

Louie spreads out the blanket and immediately stretches out on it, his hands under his head. Julie sits down and arranges her skirts to cover her ankles.

"Louie, may I lay my head on your chest? I have no pillow."

"Of course, ma chēri, I shall never bring a pillow." Julie giggles as she snuggles up to Louie.

The sound of the water slapping at the shore is soothing and they lay in silence. Soon they can hear rapids up near a bend in the river, Julie rests her cheek against Louie's, she can hear his heart beating in his chest "Your heart is pounding Louie."

"I know, ma chēri, I cannot help it." He feels rather embarassed at how his body is reacting to the nearness of Julie. He rolls over and wraps his arms under her head and buries his face in her hair. "Oh that I could die right now and never have to watch our lives be torn and tormented."

"Please, Louie, we cannot be wasting precious time worrying." She plays with his lips for a moment, then, kisses them sweetly. She can hear him breathing, his heart is pounding in his throat.

Finally they are kissing frantically and Louie sits up straight. "We must be going Julie. You are driving me crazy."

"Oh Louie, it is not that bad, just a few more kisses then we will go."

Louie takes her in his arms, he kisses her gently, over and over, rocking her back and forth, back and forth.

Then, he rises from the blanket and pulls Julie up onto her feet. Shaking out the blanket Louie goes to speak and he croaks, his voice will not come out...*I will shake this damn blanket until I stop trembling...Oh Lord, what am I saying?*

Julie is laughing, "You sound like an old bullfrog! Ha, ha, ha, sorry Louie, but you sound so comical!"

Louie takes out his comb and combs his hair viciously, then calms down and pushes his waves back in, "Here, my sweet Julie, you too have some wild hair." He gives a little giggle and heads over to the buggy with the blanket.

Moses has brought a lovely lunch down to the guest house and Ezra has taken care of the horse and buggy while Julie and Louie go for a walk in the garden after lunch.

"Louie, could I ask you to do something?" There is a mystical look in Julie's hazel eyes, Louie's heart is melting from her sheer beauty and the 'innocent little girl' tone in her voice.

"Well of course, my dear, what is it?" Judging by the look in her eyes, Louie is guessing that she is not asking for a soda pop; he suddenly feels a bit uneasy.

"Now please don'tlaugh at me. Louie, your penmanship is so grand; I wish that you would write my parents a letter." She turns and looks Louie right in the eyes.

"Oh my god! Julie, do you know what you are asking?" Louie is visibly shaken.

"The way I see it, my darling Louie; they will either agree or give us reason to run away together. I cannot bear going back to that endless sneaking!" She is almost in tears. "Give them your credentials, Louie, you have more education than a professor! Please, you have a lot to offer; you have nothing to be ashamed about!"

"I hate to say this, my love, but his greatest dread has nothing to do with my potential; it has everything to do with my pedigree."

After a few days like these, Ezra shows up at the Lee's residence and honks for Louie. He is climbing up into the buggy with a big smile when Ezra says, "Massah Louie, I got bad news. Monsieur Guernon has taken Miss Julie to Quebec, I knows cause he came and got a bank note from Madame Sophie... when he lef' he said he was takin' a trip to visit their relations."

"I cannot believe that man... he is cruel!" Louie is enraged. "How long will they be gone?"

"I wish I could tell you, Massah Louie. Can I do anything for you? Do you needs a ride?"

"No, Ezra. I must go in and tell my aunt Lucie, she will be worried."

Louie turns and begins the short walk, to the gate and up the sidewalk to the door. *How can I tell Aunt Lucie that my dreams have been shattered again? If she is not in the parlour I will get up the stairs...I am feeling so tired...*

"Louie, Louie come down for dinner. We are having your favourite cream noodles." *Now I remember...I walked right past her and came up to bed.*

He looks at his watch; it is five o'clock and he has slept for hours with all his clothes on!

Louie is silent throughout the meal. Aunt Lucie is feeling rather uncomfortable...*something is wrong. He has not combed his hair...I wonder if he even washed his hands?*

"Do you care for more, my boy?" she ventures to break the silence.

"Merci, mon Tanté, I am not well. Monsieur Geurnon has taken Marie-Julie out of the country. I need to try to read my prayer-book ; then, I shall try to write Mama a letter."

He lays his napkin down and rises slowly from his chair, "Bon soir, mon Tanté. I shall see you in the morning."

Back up in his little room, Louie is very weak after climbing the stairs. He takes out the little green prayer book his mother gave him the night before he left St. Vitale.

With a deep groan he falls across the bed ...*what have I done? Is this my punishment for abandoning you Lord? Where do I go from here; shall I get money from Madame Sophie and catch a train to New York? I could look up Father Barnabe at Keeseville, I am sure he would welcome me.*

Opening up his little book he looks down to see what the Lord has for a message...*do You have a word for me; or am I too unworthy?*

The words are a blur before his eyes...Psalm 61:

> 'Hear my cry, O God; Give heed to my prayer.
>
> From the end of the earth I call to thee, when my heart is faint;
>
> Lead me to the rock that is higher than I, for thou hast been a refuge to me;
>
> A tower of strength against the enemy, Let me dwell in thy tent forever;
>
> Let me take refuge in the shelter of Thy wings.' KJV.

Louie's voice is a whisper as he reads the last line...*oh, my sweet Mama, how I miss you...why did I ever leave you...how will you ever live without Papa?* Louie pulls the pillow in tight to his face and lets the hot tears flow. Finally he is asleep.

He awakens to the sound of the midnight train whistle...*I must write my Mama.* He sits up to the little table in the corner.

After the candle is lit he takes out the special box of paper and envelopes given to him by Madame Sophie at Christmas...using his best French and his usual neat penmanship he begins:

Dearest Mother,

I regret to send you such a letter at this time. I am still in much pain at the loss of my dear Papa as I am sure you will be for a long time. I pray for your comfort as you read what I must say. There is no easy way. I have left the Priesthood, a few short months from graduating. It grieves my heart for several reasons.

First, of course, it would never be my intention to hurt you, particularly at a time like this in your life; I should be there to comfort you. I could not bear to tell you in my first letter upon hearing word of dear Papa. My life was in such a turmoil; I thought it wise to keep it brief.

Secondly, it is most regrettable that I have let down so many people, my parents, my people at home, all who have received splendid reports on my progress. My Catholic church and all my spiritual and financial supporters; most of all, I cannot face Father Taché.

I feel that I have wasted six years of gruelling study and Madame Masson has wasted hundreds of dollars on my education.

I cannot bear to face anyone at this time, I love you dearly, Mama… please give my most sincere love and regrets to my dear siblings,

Your loving son always, Louie. ('Lagimodiere' by Hector Coutu, et al.)

His wonderful penmanship has graduated to a flat and wobbly scrawl; nevertheless, he folds it and slips it into the envelope.

He sits motionless for twenty minutes; then, he undresses for bed, blows out the candle and crawls in. After seemingly hours of restless review of the past six years, he sinks into oblivion.

Upon rising, Louie begins a daily regimen of washing and combing his hair and satisfying his auntie by joining her in a light breakfast. He is barely responsive to her attempts at conversation.

Back in his room, he sits up to his little writer's desk. *I feel no desire to write to anyone, there is nothing to say.* He takes his little green book out, that his Mama gave him, and after a few attempts at reading his prayer book he resumes his work on his most recent poem.

He pours out his disappointment in himself, lashes out at the cruelty of Marie-Julie's father or speaks of his love and passion for his beloved 'Julie'.

Once a week he walks to Madame Masson's to replenish his writing paper and see if Madame Sophie has heard anything from Joseph Geurnon.

After a walk in the garden and a nap in the guest house, he walks back up to the Manor to visit with the staff or to have lunch with Madame Sophie. It has been one month since Marie-Julie has left and Madame is becoming tired of Louie moping around.

"You must try to get back to your senses, my boy. I realize your suffering takes time to heal but you must begin to try to write or take a light job or something. Anything that will motivate you...I know some good friends who would be honoured to have you tutoring their children. Think about it, there is an elderly instructor by the name of Father Francois Champagne. He is very fond of you and has enjoyed many of your lectures. He is retiring and would be delighted to take you into his classroom to learn the basic principles of tutoring. With your education he may get you a teaching licence quite easily. I believe you would make an excellent teacher!"

"Thank you Madame Sophie, you are too kind. I feel I have let you down to the extent that one more favour would be taking advantage of you. I cannot bear to abuse your kindness any longer." Louie's head is bowed and the lines of worry can be seen on his brow.

"I will tell you again, my boy...God has given me this assignment. I am not in the least disappointed in you. You are a fine young man...given time you will find your niche in life. Now, remember that my shock of your leaving the Priesthood is past, I have forgiven you. Now you must forgive yourself."

"It is the least I can do, Madame. I will contact Father Champagne immediately and keep you informed on my progress, merci, merci boucoupe*."

Madame Sophie is seated in her favourite chair near the fireplace, she takes a sheet of paper from a small note pad on the lamp-table,

"...here you are, my boy, this is his address, it is not far from Mile End; it is within walking distance from your Uncle John's."

"I will accept your kind offer and have Ezra take me over there as soon as possible." Louie gathers up his top hat and walking stick; he bids Madame Sophie adieu*, thanks Miss Millie for lunch and leaves by the back door. *I am beginning to feel better already, I would love to teach. My dream of helping my people could still be possible! I could share the gospel with my people and give them a practical education at the same time!*

Ezra is bent over working on the hoof of one of his black mares; Louie switches his thinking over to English as he waves to Ezra, who greets him with a big smile.

My, my massah Louie, you looks real good today!" Ezra is a runaway slave from North Carolina who Madame Masson has had on staff since he arrived by the underground railway several years ago, his wife, Polly, arrived later and has been a treasured housekeeper for Madame Sophie ever since.

"Good day to you Ezra, I am feeling much better since I have a job to attend. If you are not busy I have an address here for you." He takes the small paper from his vest pocket.

"Well now that is good news massah Louie. We will leave as soon as I gets Sarah harnessed up; she will be happy to have a run."

Louie is beginning to feel like there may be something to live for after all.

Chapter Fourteen

Montreal: 1866...

The home of Father Champagne is quaint and comfortable; it is much the same as Madame Sophie's main guest house that Louie has used for years. The only difference is that he has a bed that is curtained off from a small kitchen where his care-giver, Sister Hȇlene, may fix a snack for him and there are numerous portraits of Christ, Biblical characters, and events.

He greets Louie with a firm handshake and a gentle, "Bonsoir, vous allez bien?"* in the typical French of an elderly gentleman.

Louie gives him his best smile, removes his hat and shakes his hand, "Ḉa va, et toi?"*

"Tres bien, tres bien!*" *He seems like a friendly old gent,* Louie thinks to himself.

The old man asks Louie if he knows English and Louie answers him in English, "Why yes father, my people in Red River are all trilingual."

"How wonderful! Now zat would be le français, d'anglais h'and...?" Father Champagne is pleased to speak some English; he looks questioningly at Louie.

"H'our sird*[1] language h'is Cree; zere is also Ojibwe; however, h'it is not used h'as much." He switches back to French. "I have been sent here by Madame Masson, Father, she believes I should take up teaching."

The father responds in French, "I must admit, my son, news of your change in careers came to me immediately. That kind of news travels fast you know."

Louie can feel his heart racing and the blood coming to his face, "I am so sorry, father, I am suffering much grief for my decision, but I must carry on." His head is hanging down.

"Raise your head, my son, God will still guide you, if you ask." The old man has pulled a chair out from his little table.

"It is very hard to face my Catholic peers, I still love my church dearly." Louie has sat down and set his hat on his knee, dusting it gently with his fingers.

"It is not for us to judge, remember: 'Judge not, that ye be not judged,'...as taken from the Gospel of Saint Mathew in the Holy Scriptures."

"Has Madame Sophie spoken with you in this regard?" The father has taken his place at the table. He reaches for a string that will ring a bell and summon the nun who has been serving him faithfully for several years.

"Yes we have discussed your exceptional gifts and your potential to move into the teaching field, I am happy for you. Teaching can be very rewarding; you will enjoy it; I am sure."

"Thank you father, your words are very encouraging." Louie's heart is settling down and his face has ceased burning.

"If you are serious we will begin making preparations." He gives the rope two quick jerks. "First we must order tea and snacks." He looks at Louie and grins. Louie is feeling more comfortable all the time...*I like z'is fellow, I s'ink we will get h' along fine.*

"Z'at sounds like a wonderful place to begin!" Louie says with a big grin.

In a few moments there is a tap at the door, Father Champagne opens it, and Sister Hễlene enters; she is bearing a tray of tea and pastries, "Now you understand why I wear a large belt on my tunic?"

The father laughs and Louie laughs with him, even though he has spent the past five years learning to fast*[2] and discipline his eating habits.

The men of Red River love to eat; there has always been an unspoken contest among Metis men with regards to who has the best cook. They work very hard from spring to fall, staying trim and hard, then, like an old autumn bear, they put on the winter fat, unless they are trapping and running dogs *[3].

Louie has found that, coming from a culture that is steeped in feasting and celebrating, one of his most persistent sins is gluttony. It is a demon he deals with from time to time and the practice of prayer and repentance has helped him to keep from over-eating. *Back home there was a lot of jigging to dance off a meal; rarely have I seen jigging in Montreal. I suppose I am not in jigging company any more, just the time my uncles came to visit with their fiddle and a jug of wine...I woke up to hearing them being chased out for fighting. Oh my people...I get very lonesome for them, nevertheless.*

Today he feels honoured, however, to break bread with an elder.

Life may be good after all, Louie thinks to himself as he smiles up at Sister Hélene.

"Thank you Sister, your pastries are very tempting but I generally only have one or two at the most." He takes a croissant and stirs a spoon of sugar into his tea, he consciously resists stirring too much...auntie Lucie has scolded him for incessantly stirring his coffee.

The old man takes a freshly baked biscuit from the tray and reaches for the honey.

"If we stay on track you will learn the fundamentals of teaching very quickly. Then there is an exam that will give you your certificate after we do your practicum with a few children. I have an ideal class for you this week; they are rough little Irish boys, many of them are orphans, recent refugees from Ireland. You may use a bit of French but it is not your job; you teach them reading, writing and arithmetic, what do you say?"

"That would suit me fine father. My goal now is to go back home and teach the children of my community. The only other thing is, I would like to incorporate a bit of gospel and have prayer in the morning and at close of day; I am sure that would be a part of your curriculum, right?" He is pulling at his moustache.

"Why of course, my boy! The gospel is our prime purpose; you have learned well. We will get along just fine. Next month we will take the train to Keeseville where we will stay at Father Barnabe's mission. He has a group of Mohawk boys. They are fast learners and I have a feeling they will adore you. Strangely enough our reading books that are issued from the Hudson Bay Company, are all from Britain as is our other classroom materials"

I guess if I am forbidden to see Marie-Julie I had better be making a career at something. Funny how God moves; I believe He is still caring for me, what does He have in store for me now?

Once they have finished tea, the father takes Louie into his study to show him all the teaching aids and explain a bit of the basic principles; Louie picks up on things very quickly.

"Well, my boy, you can meet me at the little classroom behind the Cathedral at 7:00 a.m. on Monday morning, we will prepare the classroom before they bring our little Irish students over."

Louie is grinning ear to ear, *I am so nervous but I am also very excited. I can hardly wait to tell aunt Lucie and Sophie!*

Louie is now in his third day of teaching eleven young boys from ages 6 to 12; they are all taking the first grade of Reading, Writing and Arithmetic.

He is seated at his desk looking up at the big clock on the wall, it is three o'clock in the afternoon and they have just heard a story from Louie about the 'Hare and the Tortoise.'*

"So, boys, what do you say is zuh morale of zis story? Please raise your hand."

A little boy with a ruffy red head raises his hand. "Yes?" says Louie.

"Sir, could ya be tellin' me what is a morale?" The boys all hoot with laughter.

"Excellent question, my man. I told you on Monday, it is zee lesson to be learned…but it has been a long time since Monday, right my man?"

"Yes sir!" the little fellow is beaming; the Schoolmaster did not laugh at him.

"Does anyone else have any idea what zuh morale of zuh story h'is?"

One little boy in the back raises his hand…"Sir, I reckons dat we needs ta pay attention." The boys all laugh again.

Louie rubs his hands together in a rolling motion, like is his habit during his lectures, "Now zat is zuh answer I have been waiting for... very good!"

"You will never be a winner if you do not pay attention! How many believe zat?" Every one raises their hands. "Very well! You have all done very well today and I believe you have paid attention. Now, who would like to come forward and lead us in the Lord's prayer?"

Just as Father Champagne steps in the door a small, skinny boy comes forward, "I reckon I would like to pray, sir."

Just at that moment, Father Champagne enters the room; he joins Louie at the front of the class, "Wonderful Danny! Now all rise."

Louie does not know that little Danny is an Irish refugee who lost both his parents in a military skirmish before the children were herded on board a ship headed for the Canadas. It is the first time he has spoken, and Father Champagne is in tears. On their way to the father's quarters he explains the story to Louie.

"I knew there was something strange about that little boy...how miraculous!" says Louie shaking his head back and forth in amazement.

"Yes, that boy has finally come out of a state of dumb shock, he has definitely felt safe under your care; I believe you are in the right business, my boy!" The old fellow is laughing with joy as he pulls the cord to summon Sister Hēlene for tea and a snack.

Every day holds new experiences for Louie; his new career has brought him out of a major depression...however his darling Julie does not stray too far from his mind. When his nights get long and lonely and his Mama's prayer book does not put him to sleep, he writes poetry...romantic poetry.

***

Three weeks have passed since Louie's first day of teaching, he is enjoying his days, keeping busy with lessons for the boys...but evenings are long.

After supper he sometimes helps Auntie Lucie clean up the dishes before they retire to the parlor with Uncle John who is resting in front of the fireplace with his crooked stemmed pipe. The smell of his pipe drifts over to the kitchen...it smells good. It reminds him of his Papa; the aroma is different but it still gives Louie a good feeling.

He asks Uncle John what is in his pipe and he says, "Same tobacco your Papa smokes, only difference is, he mixes his with kinikinik, a wild tobacco they traded for in the west, it is apparently the bark of red willow bushes."

Louie hangs a towel over a heavy cord string that auntie Lucie has strung from the stove to a spike, over buy the kitchen window; Lucie dries her dish towels and strainers* on this little line every day. Both he and auntie Lucie join Uncle John in the parlor.

"How was school today, my boy?" he takes a drag from his pipe.

"It has been going very well Uncle; next week I will be taken to New York state to teach some Mohawk boys." Louie folds his hands and leans back in a comfortable old chair that is covered with a colourful crocheted chair throw.

"Well you know my boy, I think that job would suit you perfectly. You always loved to read, you are a good speaker, you can be fun, but you can be serious. You will take those boys in hand."

They are using a dialect of French used by men who work on construction; Louie has no problem with this casual dialect as it is very close to what was spoken by Louie Sr. and his Mama Julie.

"Thank you uncle, I feel like I will enjoy this career; it is still a way of helping my people. Your pipe smells wonderful! May I have a taste?"

"Well now, my boy, you certainly may! Now that you are doing a regular job you can afford tobacco. As a matter of fact I have a pipe for you; your Papa left it here years ago. Here, have a pull, if you like it you can have your Papa's pipe."

Louie takes the pipe and draws in a good puff; he begins to cough, his face is red, mostly from embarrassment.

"Oh, oh-h …how come you do not choke, my uncle?" Louie is gasping for breath.

"Well, you don't smoke like that. You take small puffs and let some of it fill the air around you. Relax and take it easy, small puffs, small puffs." He demonstrates. "See? Slow and easy…the way you love a woman, my boy"

"John, watch your tongue, you can be so embarrassing!"

"Relax Lucie, he is no longer a Priest." John is having such a good laugh that Louie cannot help but join in...*it feels good to laugh*, he thinks to himself.

"There now, I have cleaned your Papa's pipe and loaded it for you, take a little drag."

Louie takes a couple of small drags, this time it is smooth, he only tastes a little bit, *so this what my Papa enjoyed every night before bed!*

"I must tell you, my boy, the pipe is a pacer for men to time themselves on a trip or a job, or even a break from work. Your Papa would have told you how the voyageurs used their pipes to name parts of the rivers. They would always have a pipe after any rapids, he may have told you that. One pipeful is about a mile, upstream."

"It has been such a pleasure to visit downstairs with you and Auntie. But I must be off to bed. I will leave the pipe down here, I may try it again this week, sometime. Good night."

"Good night my boy," says auntie Lucie.

Louie fills the basin on the vanity half-full of water from the large pitcher nearby. Refilling the pitcher is his job, so he makes it last for three sponge baths. He has a nice refreshing sponge bath; then, sleep comes as soon as his head hits the pillow.

The next morning, he is just finishing his grooming ritual when he hears his auntie call him for breakfast. "Louie!" There is a happy note in her voice these days; the days of calling up to him with a note of uneasiness in her voice seem to have passed. *I am so sorry for my little aunt; I know that she is afraid of me sometimes when I am depressed. Hopefully those days are past.* He skips down the stairs; he has dressed down a bit for the job, however, his old black oxfords* are polished to a shine.

***

Sitting on the train next to the window on the Grand Trunk Railway, Louie watches the landscape as it changes from the rocky slopes of Upper Canada to the rolling prairie in New York State. Louie has brought his mother's little green prayer book and he has tucked it back into his vest pocket as he rests his head for a nap.

A total review of the previous week rolls through his mind as he pulls his top-hat down so he can peer around and take note of the passengers without being noticed.

He recognizes the signs of the executive car that he once scampered through like a scared mouse. The drapery and fine upholstery are made of heavy expensive fabric and brandy is being passed out to the well-dressed passengers. *If Smitty could only see me now, he would have something to say about these high-classed people.* Louie chuckles to himself and hides it by pulling on his moustache. *I remember thinking about him when I dressed up to go deliver a lecture, he would have had something to say about that. But...I could not very well show up looking like a tramp!*

Their arrival is without much ado; there is a horse and buggy parked beside the small train station; the driver is looking straight at them. He must be sent by the mission.

"Father Champagne?" queries the friendly looking driver, wearing what was likely a smart looking outfit at one time.

The father says, "That would be me, thank you sir." The little man nods his head and says, "Climb aboard." They scarcely get sat down and he taps the horse with his little buggy whip. The horse is a trotter and they arrive at Keeseville mission in no time. There is very little conversation so Louie enjoys taking in the sights of the Keeseville he has heard so much about.

Arriving at the mission, they are greeted by Father Barnabe who walks out to the buggy to help with the luggage and to pay the driver he had ordered up.

Shaking his hand, Father Champagne introduces him to young Louie, "This is the teacher in training I told you about. He is looking forward to teaching your little Mohawk boys."

"Why yes," he shakes Louie's hand, "… you will enjoy those little rascals, I am sure. They are full of fun and they love to play tricks."

"I am anxious to meet them, sir." Louie gives a tip of his flat-brimmed hat and a slight bow, then, they unload the luggage. Father Barnabe insists on paying for the ride, "I had a Mass to conduct for the locals at the same time as your arrival, my apologies for not meeting the train."

"No need to apologize. We have had a very enjoyable trip; nothing much has changed; the farmers are as busy as ever."

"Yes, they are busy year round, an ambitious lot they are."

They are greeted very cordially by two sisters and a tall good-looking woman who is introduced as Father Barnabe's younger sister, Evelina. The nuns excuse themselves and return to the kichen, while Evelina ushers them into the parlor.

"How was your trip?" she asks Louie as she settles into one of the tightly upholstered Victorian chairs. The room is quiet and carpeted and Louie walks over to seat himself in the chair next to Evelina. "Please, make yourself comfortable. How was your trip?"

"Zuh trip was quiet and uneventful, merci, no run-ins wit buffalo, train robbers, or Indians." Evelina laughs, a hearty, musical laugh, "But you know, sir, all are entirely possible."

She has not a trace of an accent, which is unusual for Louie, considering the multitude of European and Canadian accents encountered in the average day, living in Montreal. He is guessing; … *She has at least a grade ten education, if not more. She is definitely not without letters,* he thinks, as he gives her his best smile. Most of his acquaintances either speak French or have a strong accent of some sort.

After supper Father Barnabe excuses himself to attend to evening prayer, "You are both welcome to join us for prayer; however, my sister will show you to your quarters so you can get set in for the night, whenever you like." He takes his leave for the chapel.

"Well, my dear, it looks like you are in charge of our hospitality." Father Champagne has known Evelina since she was a little girl. Her father is a military man, stationed in Virginia and her mother passed away many years ago, leaving her older brother to care for her.

Once again she responds with her infectious laughter. "Well, you know that I am good at that, Father!"... she continues to chortle as she leads them with their luggage over to a bunkhouse. Louie can feel a strong attachment growing towards this girl and he feels a strange excitement mixed with a familiar uneasiness.

Father Champagne follows Evelina along the wooden sidewalk with Louie following close behind, "Louie, I will be spending the night tonight, but as you know, tomorrow I go back to Montreal. You will be spending the next three weeks here in training; Barnabe will introduce you to the children Monday morning. They are housed at a boarding school, which is financed by the Government and the Catholic Church…"

Evelina unlocks the door of his room. "…then in three weeks you will catch the train back to Montreal," he continues. He sets his little carpet bag down on a chair inside the door.

"I am sure every'sing will be fine Fozzer; I am looking forward to working wis' z'ose little fellows. You go on to zuh prayer meeting; I will look around for awhile"

Evelina says, "If you need anything just pull that string and one of us will answer your bell." She looks at Louie and laughs, "Sorry, you do not get the same services as the Father. You have to walk over and knock on the door." Louie joins her in a good laugh. *If she only knew, I was in his category only a couple of months ago,* he continues to laugh.

Somehow it feels good to be classified as 'regular', Louie muses to himself.

*Glossary

Footnotes:

1 'h'our s'ird'- '...our third', (Louie's Montreal accent).
2 Fast- An habitual refraining from earthly pleasures, (generally food), for a period of time in order to practice self-discipline.
3 'running dogs'- or 'using sled dogs' for winter travel. (This would provide excellent winter excersise in order to stay trim.)

Chapter Fifteen

Keeseville, New York State: 1866...

Louie sets his larger sized bag in on a chair as Evelina stands in the doorway, "Would you like for me to show you around, Mr. Riel?"

"Why of course! Zere are many buildings around here; you can tell me where everysing is; you may even tell me who I should not hang around wis'. I see a lot of tough looking hombres around." Evelina laughs.

"Now Mr. Riel, you should know better than to travel with that crowd, especially unarmed!" They both laugh. Then Louie pulls his coat-tail back, revealing a knife scabbard hanging from his belt.

"So what do you call zis?" He pulls out the fancy handle revealing a six-inch blade.

"I would call that the hunting knife of a voyageur; I'm not entirely ignorant you know!" Then she points at him and laughs.

"You've got me H'evelina. Zee only s'ing zis has ever been used for is to cut or clean my fingernails!" They both have a good laugh as he slips it back into the scabbard. Evelina is laughing even harder at his heavy emphasis on 'nails'. She doesn't hear such a strong French accent very often.

They begin their tour with the Cathedral and all of it's splendour, then they go on to the grounds of the Residential School which look as though they are gasping for some greenery.

After that they visit the coach-house. There are several types of buggies, wagons and coaches and across the fence there are several nice mares chewing on the grass eenerywhile fighting a losing battle with the flies and mosquitoes. In the distance Louie squints as he sees a few heavily treed areas that punctuate the edges of flat fields against a clear blue sky.

Next to a long pasture are two large barns with rail corrals around them; the lofts are filled with hay for the cows and horses.

Not far from the corral is an old chicken house with a large pen out in front. A big white rooster stands on the edge of a water trough; as Louie and Evelina approach he stands up tall and crows loudly out over all his kingdom.

Louie is mesmerized; he has not felt so close to home in years; a large lump is forming in his throat.

"Do you ever see chicken pens in Montreal?" Evelina asks, as Louie leans on the fence looking longingly at the crowing rooster.

"Oui, I have seen a few animal pens in zuh city...but not h'up close..."

"Well, you may as well get used to it; he will be waking you every morning about six o'clock." She punctuates the news with a ripple of laughter while Louie looks on with a smile, pulling on his moustache.

"The older Indian boys do all the farm chores; the bigger Indian girls help with the cooking and cleaning. I teach them to sew. We make all those blue uniforms you see them wearing."

After breakfast the following morning, Louie bids Father Champagne farewell with a handshake while thanking him profusely for the opportunity to get his teaching credentials.

After seeing Father Champagne off with a wave as he rides away in the buggy with Father Barnabe, Louie flings his book bag over his shoulder by a wide strap and sets off for the school.

Before long he has reached the wide steps leading up to the double doors of the Residential School. He lifts the heavy knocker and drops it three times; the door opens and he is welcomed by a small nun with small blue eyes. "You are sent by Father Barnabe?" Louie removes his flat-brimmed hat and shakes her small, limp hand.

"Oui, Sister. I am finishing my practicum here wis' you, zen when I return to Montreal, if the good Lord is willing, I shall become a certified teacher." The smile fades from his face as she answers him in a very cool manner.

"Very well, Mr. Riel; you must remember, we do not speak French here, and by the way, I am Sister Pauline Carriere."

"Excuse me; I will attempt to refrain from speaking French, Sister."

"Very well, Mr. Riel, come with me now and I will introduce you to the class. Their ages vary from eight to twelve but they are all at the first level."

She opens the door and ushers Louie into the room. A hush falls over the room. Like a row of blackbirds on a fence, their eyes are all fixed on Louie, then Sister Carriere speaks, "Good morning boys, this is your teacher, Mr. Riel. He will be teaching you until your teacher returns from New Hampshire. Now repeat after me:

"Good morning Mr. Riel."

Like a roomful of little parrots, they all stumble over her words in a chorus of varying Mohawk accents.

Louie removes his round-brimmed hat and bows. Then he raises his right hand and with a sweeping motion across the room he addresses them, "Good morning, my friends. I am very pleased to meet you." The little boys all break into a broad smile, Louie gives them a friendly smile as he sets his hat on a book shelf by the chalkboard. *The poor little fellows, they must be happy to have an Indian teacher.*

"I am sorry, I do not speak Mohawk. My native language is C'wree," he says with a strong French accent.

"Excuse me Mr. Riel, we do not allow any native languages in our classrooms. As you know, we are partially funded by the Government and we are governed by a policy which forbids native languages; they believe we would be defeating our purpose of assimilation." Her feet are planted as firmly as her statement and she has taken Louie by surprise.

"Well, excuse me Sister, I will tw'ry to remember z'at." *Wuh wah! She must have slept on a lumpy mattw'ress!* Louie is so dumbfounded and disgusted that his Mechif suddenly returns!

For three weeks Louie drifts in and out of a sea of emotions. He is missing his Papa, still having bouts of regret; and his Mama is never far from his mind. He wonders how she will manage without her hardworking husband. Louie has already considered sending her a bit more of his pay, but until he is a full-fledged teacher, he will likely be receiving the same meagre pay.

Louie prepares for bed; tomorrow will be his final day of teaching. It has been good...his mind has been occupied daily; nights are still his hard time, when he is reminded of all his failings.

He often thinks of Father Taché, how he trusted him and looked forward to his return as an ordained Priest. *I remember Mama saying in one of her last letters before Papa died, that I would be returning home by train with Father Tachē after he attended my Ordination...my God, can you ever forgive me? I have broken the hearts of my Mama, Madame Sophie, but most of all... Father Tachē. How can I ever face him? I suppose I shall stay away until he has gotten over the shock of it.*

Then, slipping in and out of these thoughts is the haunting memory of Marie-Julie. *Shall I ever get over the smell of her hair...or the feel of her tiny fingertips on my face? How can I forget the feel of my heart pounding in my throat as she stroked my moustache... my eyebrows... my eyes? Oh, my precious Mother Mary...what have I done?*

He takes his prayer book and opens it to Psalm 149: "*Oh to feel the forgiveness of God once more like David...I need to be free from the guilt of abandoning the priesthood! Oh well, I must be thankful for my health, my job and for good friends. Evelina has been a good friend; Father Barnabe has also been very kind...I can't say as much for Sister Carriere...I am so sleepy; thank God...*"

The crowing of the rooster is pleasant to Louie's ears; he rises and pulls the curtain back to look out at the sun shining out over the barnyard as it comes to life; the horses are switching away the flies as they sip their first drink of water for the day.

I suppose I should be excited about getting back to Montreal but the only thing to look forward to is my Teaching certificate if I am approved. I dread not seeing Marie-Julie but she will not be returning to Red River with me after all. So... I will get a job and send money to my Mama, she will like that. It has been nearly six years and Sara will be almost sixteen. Mama is hoping for her to be a nun...that would help her to get over my failures. Oh well, I must face the day and be thankful; those little boys know I am leaving; they are sad. I pray that nun treats them well; she is obviously the 'bad apple in the barrel', like the saying goes. I am happy she cannot stop me from thinking in French.

He finishes trimming his moustache, throws his water out the door and puts his hat on just as the breakfast bell rings.

***

"Good morning, my friends!" Louie says as he sets his hat up on the shelf.

"Good morning, Mr. Riel," the boys echo back.

The day passes fast as the little Mohawk boys hang around Louie every chance they get. They have hid his chalk, then his brush. They are happy to clean the board and sweep the floor for 'punishment'; Louie can see the look of regret in their eyes as the day comes to an end. *Poor little guys...I hope their teacher treats them well.*

"Will you come to teach again, Mr. Riel?" One brave little fellow ventures to ask.

"You know, my boy, I certainly hope to; I am going to miss you all."

There are tears in their eyes as they bid farewell to their beloved teacher of three weeks. Father Barnabe looks on as Louie shakes the hand of every little boy. There is a look of pride in their eyes as they shake his hand; they blink back their tears with a brave smile. Louie places his hat on his head, slings his book bag over his shoulder and pulls the door shut behind him.

"Now z'at was a hard s'ing to do," he tells Father Barnabe as they stroll up the path to the mission.

"I suppose that is a part of the job, mind you, they are generally there again in the fall. Their parents have them for one month, then if they fail to send them back on the train, the government is no longer responsible for their health or rations. They soon send them back when the food runs out; there is nothing much for food on those reserves, you know."

"Actually, no, I did not know zat. I have been so busy wi's ancient studies, I have lost tw'rack of zuh conditions of my people z'ese days."

"It has been a pleasure having you here Louie. I have been meeting with Father Champagne today; he has a complete report from sister Carriere and myself to finish up his application for your certification."

"I shall be very thankful to have a career. My efforts in the pursuit of a political career or at least a position in government have been unfruitful. Obviously my old friend from my Laval speaking engagements, George

Cartier, is too far advanced to answer my letters. He is too busy 'ob-nobbing wis' John A. Macdonald to care h'about my career."

"I have enjoyed zuh opportunity to work wi's z'ese boys zuh past sw'ree weeks. I am beginning to get anxious about having a career in teaching; it is a commitment if you are taking it sew'riously. I get zuh feeling sometime z'at my fo'zzer would be pleased w'is my change in ca'wreers."

After supper they bid farewell to Father Barnabe and the sisters, as they load their bit of luggage into the buggy, "I guess I will take you men for a wicked, fast ride, seeing it's my pleasure to see you off on the train." Evelina enjoys a good laugh, but they need not worry; she is a good driver, she does a lot of driving for her brother when he is busy with Mass.

Louie is a bit sad with leaving and saying good-bye to Evelina, as they have become good friends, "Now you take care H'evelina, I will miss you. We have had some good talks."

Evelina finishes his sentence with "…and some good laughs, too, Louie. Send a telegram if you come for a visit, otherwise write to us once in a while."

Louie waves out the window as the chugging of the train picks up speed. Evelina is waving good-bye and wiping tears from her eyes. *She must like me more z'an I realized,* Louie thinks to himself, as the train speeds up and Evelina disappears out of sight.

There is something about riding on a train that gives Louie a strangely pleasant and unexplainable feeling. Perhaps it goes back to the day that he, his pal Smitty and Daniel McDougall all boarded the train to begin their first train ride. Or possibly it is because that was the last time he would lay eyes on his Papa.

Still, there is something even more strange and elusive…it has something to do with the smell of the coal smoke from the steam engine, the odour of the leather seats, or perhaps it is to do with the air of excitement created by so many people anticipating new adventures.

Yes, it could be the people getting off to meet with loved ones and the sheer happiness of a homecoming, mixed with the sound of "All aboard!" as people rush to climb up those three metal steps onto a modern monster of a machine that will propel them to places unknown.

Then there is the din of all the tidbits of excited conversation, spiced with accents from various exotic places. *I seem to always get a funny feeling in the pit of my stomach when I settle back on a train,* he thinks to himself. *I believe I shall spend a while writing poetry. I will pretend that I am going to meet Julie...the love of my life. I shall take her away on a speeding train, bound for a secret place of safety.*

He stands up and retrieves his book bag from the overhead; he is beginning to feel quite comfortable on the train. *Something I enjoy most about riding the train is ...I am among strangers. No one is going to judge me...I am simply your average, well-groomed and well-mannered gentleman.*

Louie is beginning to feel sleepy, the sound of the endless 'clickety-clack' broken only by the whistle as they take a fifteen minute stop or slow down for a crossing in one of the small communities along the way. He has only begun to write when he feels his eyes getting heavier...he is feeling hypnotized... *the sound of this train is so repetitious, but strangely enough, it is not annoying...I will work on this when I get to Auntie Lucie's...*

Suddenly Louie is awakened by the loud scream of the whistle as the train begins to enter the outskirts of Montreal. He stretches his legs and glances across the isle at Father Champagne who is combing his hair and is obviously also wakening from a sleep.

Many of the streets are already lit up by a fellow who stops a small buggy at each street lamp; he reaches up with a small torch to touch the gas wick* that lights up the street for a city block.

"We will catch ourselves a carriage to my place; then you can take it from there to your uncle's house," says the father, as Louie hands him his bag.

"Oui, I expect they will be up; it is only ten-thirty," says Louie, pleased to be using his French once more.

The carriage pulls up at the gate of John Lee, Louie's uncle; the light is still on. Aunt Lucie has the door open before Louie can get up the stairs, "You are looking well, my boy. Let me see your hat and cloak while you put away your bags. I will fix a quick lunch; Uncle John is still up reading in the parlour."

Louie hands Lucie his hat and cloak, "Merci, ma Tante." He takes his bags upstairs to his room then comes down and settles into his favourite chair, "Good evening Uncle, how are you?"

"I have been working very hard in this good weather; stonework goes well in the heat but my old body does not do so well," says Uncle John as he takes a drag from his pipe.

"Yes, I am even a bit stiff from that train ride." Aunt Lucie hands Louie a tall glass of lemon aid.

Louie is pleased to be speaking French again. "Merci, mon tanté."

"How was the teaching, Louie?" inquires Uncle John.

"I believe it went well, I suppose the truth will be known after I write my exam on Monday. If I do well I shall receive a Teaching certificate in the mail this month sometime."

"That is so exciting Louie!" says Auntie Lucie clenching her hands as though she were watching him open the envelope. *It is so good to hear Auntie Lucie's French; it is like listening to my Papa.*

Louie is getting ready to go upstairs when Aunt Lucie says, "Louie, Ezra, the nice old driver from the Masson Estate was here yesterday, he wishes to speak to you when you get back he says."

Suddenly John jerks the pipe from his mouth, “Oh my God! I hope we’re not hearing from that Geurnon girl, I have had enough of that! I don’t want this place turning into a damn zoo again!”

“Oh settle down now John, perhaps the Lady Masson has a speaking engagement for Louie.” Lucie is not anxious for anything to upset Louie’s life either; he is doing so well.

“I am truly sorry, Uncle, for disturbing your lives so. Nothing has been the same since Papa passed away. It still seems strange to even say it. I hardly believe he is really gone, yet. We will see what becomes of Ezra’s visit tomorrow. If it is Julie, I must insist on a marriage or I will leave within the month…certificate in hand.” *If only I could feel as certain; if it is God’s will, all will be well.*

***

Morning brings a dark and wet day, “Good morning, my boy! It is so good to have you home. Pay no attention to Uncle John. He has no time for Joseph Guernon, he was like that before you ever met Julie. They had a violent quarrel years ago; there has been bad blood between them ever since.”

“I never knew that Auntie, no wonder Joseph Guernon has no use for me.” Louie sits down to join Aunt Lucie in a breakfast of crèpes and sausages.

“I missed your wonderful breakfasts Auntie; you are almost as good as my Mama.” *Since I left the priesthood she rarely asks me to say the blessing; we seem to bow in silence, then make the sign of the Cross, and that is it.*

As they are finishing their breakfast there is a knock at the door, Aunt Lucie goes out to answer it. After a moment, she returns. Louie is somewhat alarmed at the look on her face, “It is for you, my boy,” she says in a whisper.

“Merci, mon tantē,” Louie says, as he rises from the table wiping his mouth, “Who is here?”

As he steps out to the foyer, he sees Ezra, hat in hand, wearing a nervous smile, "Massah, Louie, I has good news for you. At leas' I hopes it's good. Miss Julie is over at Madame Sophie's and she's a-hopin' fer me to bring you over."

Louie's heart is suddenly stuck in his throat, "Ezra!" he croaks, his voice is not coming out right, "What are you saying? I s'ought we were finished!"

He sits down on the chair next to the cloak closet,* his face is in his hands, "Oh, Ezra, I have dreamed of zis moment. Now I am not sure what I should do!"

"Well, I just follows orders, Massah Louie."

"I realize zat Ezra, I h'am so sorry to get you involved." Louie is shaking his head back and forth.

"Don' worry about Ezra sir. I bin through so much suffrin' comin' up here from duh Carolinas, nothin' much scares ol' Ezra anymo'. Duh good Lord knows; you jus' do what you gotta do."

"Well, you go ahead and visit wi's my aunt Lucie, I will finish getting dressed." Louie heads for the stairway.

Lucie says, "Yes, you are very welcome, Ezra."

"Thank you Ma'am, but I'll be a-goin' to tend to my carriage. My ol' girl, Sarah, is good, but someone could spook her an' way'd go yor gate." He gives a little giggle and he's gone.

He hardly gets out the door and Louie is down the stairs, looking handsome and dashing in his good clothes, "See you later, Auntie. Wish me luck," he says as he kisses her on the cheek.

"Bon chance*, mon garçon*," Lucie says, as she turns to hide the look of disappointment on her face. She raises her palms and gives a shrug, *here we go again, just when he was getting interested in a good future, 'Please save* *our boy from harm, precious Mary, Joseph and Jesus'.* She makes the sign of the cross as she scrapes out Louie's plate.

*Glossary

No footnotes in this chapter.

Chapter Sixteen

Terrebonne - Montreal, Quebec: 1865...

Louie is silent. He counts the brick houses while they clop along the cobblestone streets; finally they reach the alley that will lead them to the rear of the Masson Estate. As they pull up to the carriage house in the rear of the mansion, Ezra breaks the silence.

"Massah Louie, you otta be smilin', Miss Julie will be hurt." Ezra says in a tone that is next to an order.

"You are right Ezra; I had better be counting my blessings. I have had it pretty good lately. Merci, Ezra; you are truly a friend." Ezra begins unhitching Sarah as Louie points his shiny oxfords in the direction of the Masson rear entrance.

As he is skipping up the steps, Julie appears in the doorway, "Louie, Louie! Oh, how I have missed you!" Louie grabs her waist in both hands, then lifts her in the air and looks at her, *she is so beautiful, oh, how I have missed that long soft hair!*

He lets her down gently as she takes his face in her hands and finds his lips...they are caught up in a long awaited kiss as Madame Sophie appears in the doorway.

"Oh! My children! Come in; Millie will fix us some tea and biscuits." Sophie is in her usual fine lounging attire and Polly has already made her beautiful; she is ready for the day. Her graying hair has been swept up into a French roll, the style of the day; a gold clip holds it in place.

"It is so good to see you, Miss Sophie, I 'ave been so busy for zuh past mont'...I would have been here zis week to see you regardless. I just h'arrived back from Keeseville, New York, where I 'ave been finishing my practical training for a teaching certificate."

"Oh, Louie! I am so proud of you!" Julie sits herself on Louie's lap with her arm around his neck, and Sophie seats herself in her padded chair at the head of the table; she calls out to Millie for a pot of tea. Louie taps his fingers on the table as Julie runs her fingers through his curls.

"You know Julie, h'it amazes me 'ow God still blesses me after my unholy behaviour. I suppose He 'as heard my cries of repentance but I still feel I have distanced myself from Him."

"Now don't be worrying about those things. I want to hear about your new career. Do you like to teach?" Julie is totally taken up with the news of Louie's new venture.

"Teaching zose little boys gave me more of a sense of satisfaction zan delivering any of zose lectures I gave over zuh past few years. Zuh looks on z'eir little faces each morning h'as zey would say,'Good morning Master Riel' was so rewarding; I was set for a good day before we h'even got started." Louie's face lit up when he spoke of his little students.

"Do you think that will be what you will be doing the rest of your life?" Julie inquired.

"It could get tiresome if h'it was only considered h'employment, but Julie, I h'am still feeling zuh call to serve my people and teaching z'ose little Indian boys gave me a sense of satisfaction, like I h'am still answering zee call of God. Remember I 'ave not received my teaching certificate yet, wish me luck. If zuh good Lord h'is willing, I should 'ave it in zuh next week or so."

Sophie holds her hand over her heart, “Louie, it makes me so happy to hear you say that. If there is anything that I can ever do to help, never be afraid to ask me.”

Millie has set the teapot down on the table. Madame Sophie proceeds to fill their teacups, “Help yourselves to the biscuits; you know Millie, Louie; they are fresh out of the oven, just don’t burn your fingers.”

“You are too kind, Madame, we appreciate everys’ing you have done for us.” Louie lightly butters his biscuit, “…and Millie, you make zee best biscuits in Montreal, you always ‘ave.” *Good thing my breakfast was interrupted; I wouldn’t have the heart to turn down Millie’s biscuits.*

Before long they have enjoyed a good conversation and have finished their tea.

“Do you think we can go to the guesthouse to visit for a while, Sophie?” Julie asks.

“Of course, I don’t expect you lovebirds to catch up sitting at my table!” Sophie is delighted to see them enjoying each other’s company again.

Louie reaches for the key in his vest pocket; he has never returned the guesthouse key and Sophie has never asked it from him for over five years. The door opens easily with one turn of the key, “Do you think it smells a bit musty, Louie?”

“You are absolutely right, mon cheri; we’ll leave zee door open for a while and let in some fresh h’air.”

Louie finds some fresh mint candles in the cupboard, “Here Julie, you can set zem in zuh sticks* while I wrap zee old ones and put zem h’away. I don’t s’ink Madame would use zem; I believe Moses gazzers zem up for zuh servants.”

Louie walks over to the fireplace and removes the shovel and poker, “Don’t you s’ink we need some refreshments, ma chére?[*1]”

"Why yes, Louie. That's just what we need, some grapes to squeeze all over my breasts!" Julie has already made herself comfortable on the edge of the bed. She has unlaced her ankle high shoes and kicked them into the corner. Her light, cotton, sky-blue dress spreads out over the white lace bedspread.

"Oh my Julie, you 'aven't changed; I used to chuckle to myself h'at times, remembering your crazy sense of humor. Zen zee h'aweful truth would set in; I s'ought I would never see you h'again." He steps out the door and taps the edge of the swinging shovel; the familiar ring sounds out over the orchard; he turns, looks back at Julie, and grins.

"Oh Louie, you are so good-looking when you are happy." Julie is brushing out her long wavy brown hair. She stuffs her brush back in her bag and hangs it on the bed-post*[2].

Louie steps inside and closes the door behind him. "We 'ad better keep zuh door locked like Moses instructed h'us; he should be 'ere in about ten minutes."

"I will bet you a good foot-rub he is not back in ten, I will say fifteen minutes."

"Okay, Miss Guernon, you h'ar on!" They both have a good laugh while Louie hangs the tools back on their hooks.

"Those mint candles are giving off a beautiful aroma, Louie."

"Oui, h'only zey smell even better when you h'ar 'ere, my Julie." Louie sits down beside her on the bed.

Julie reaches up and takes a fistful of Louie's dark curls, she falls back on the bed bringing Louie down with her. Louie takes her in his arms and they begin with a long tender kiss; soon they are making up for lost time; they both lay back to catch their breath when suddenly there is a knock at the door.

"Fifteen minutes Louie, you owe me a good foot-rub." Louie gives her a wink, then goes to the door and lets Moses in with a tray of drinks, fruit and pastries.

"Come on in Moses; zat looks like a genuine feast, my man!"

"Miss Millie sends greetings to you both. 'Bon apetit'!"

"S'ank you Moses, we will try to leave zuh place decent." Louie is so anxious for Moses to leave he nearly shuts the door on his coat-tail.

"Let's eat first; then you can rub my feet." Julie takes the tray and sets it on the bed; Louie lays leaning on one elbow, "Just like back in zee Roman days, Julie. Zey used to stretch out h'at zee table on couches and eat lying down." Julie breaks into laughter, "That is so funny Louie!"

"Apparently h'it is true; no wonder zee men all had large stomachs." Louie never meant it as a joke but Julie bursts out laughing again.

"Sorry Louie, I just imagined you with a big stomach!"

Louie reaches for the kiss she is offering, "You do 'ave an imagination, my love." He feeds her a grape, "You know Julie, I am not hungry at all, not for food, at any rate. I 'ave dreamed of being wi's you again h'and we were not eating grapes."

"You are so right Louie, set this tray on that night stand. I want to hear more of your plans. I have been missing you too, Louie. What are we going to do?"

"I will tell you what we are going to do; we h'ar going for a canoe ride tomorrow!" Louie is wearing his biggest grin.

"Oh Louie! That sounds like fun…I will wear my riding clothes." Louie lies back down and takes her in his arms. After a few more kisses, Louie sits up again; he takes his hair in his hands, "Julie, I need you so… zat my every fibre aches to 'ave you as my wife…to make love to you like any uzzer husband. I cannot bear z'is sneaking h'around and zuh closeness of you h'and knowing h'all zee time zat h'our love is forbidden. It h'is driving me crazy…I want you h'as my wife, Julie."

Julie pulls him back down,"Louie, I feel the same way. I could make love right now but that is not your way…we have no other choice but to run away and get married!"

Louie's fingers are tangled in his hair, "No Julie, I know a better way, a way zat will make us married before man h'and God."

"How, Louie? What are you talking about?" Julie is sitting up straight on the edge of the bed.

"Julie, I have disappointed a lot of people but zere is one person who still trusts me and h'is not disappointed h'in me."

"What do you mean, Louie? Who are you talking about?"

"Now don't s'ink me foolish Julie, I h'am going to suggest a solution to h'our dilemma zat I believe will be acceptable in zuh sight of God. What appears foolish to man may not be foolish to God, it is written by St. Paul in his letter to zuh Corinthians."*

"Oh Louie, you are so wise, yet sometimes when you speak in riddles you leave me puzzled…who are you talking about?'

"I am talking about God, h'our Fazzer. He knows me, He understands my weaknesses. Each time I meditate on zose s'ings zat I regret…He seems to say quietly, to my heart, 'You will someday understand why you have had to h'endure zis…take heart, my boy, remember zuh faitfulness h'of David'*."

Louie glances up at Julie; he is desperately trying to make his hair lie down. Julie hands him a comb and he begins to smooth out the curls he has unravelled with his fingers and settle them back into place before he continues.

"I believe zat living six years h'in obedience to God gives me zee aus'ority to perform a ceremony zat will unite us h'as man h'and wife, in zee sight of God."

Louie arises and pours a bit of water from the large ceramic pitcher into the matching floral designed basin. He dips his fingers in the water and wets his curls rubbing it through evenly; he combs his curls back into place.

Then, he retrieves a small black book from a drawer in the nightstand, "Zis, my dear, is zee Bible. I 'ave read it s'rough to zuh best of my ability. It is full of mystery at first…zen God lifts a veil from h'it and allows you to h'understand many s'ings… in part…whatever you h'are seeking. We will take it h'along tomorrow h'and we will have a marriage picnic."

"But Louie, we will need to partake of the sacraments first and say our Mass." Julie is beginning to feel comfortable with the idea.

"Yes my love, tonight I will prepare a ceremony zat you will h'enjoy; it will contain h'our commitment to h'each uzzer, and to God."

"What about the legal document you made up, separating our properties and declining a dowry from my parents, do you still have it?"

Louie reaches for the nightstand, "I 'ope it h'is in z'is drawer, I had forgotten we completed z'at document; when Ezra came wis' zuh news of your leaving I fell into a deep depression."

He pulls out a flat page of paper containing several neatly written paragraphs. Three lines have been drawn alongside the names of Julie, Louie and Moses.

"Look, h'all it needs is signatures!" Louie is ecstatic, "Come my love, we will 'ave a glass of lemonade and some of Millie's goodies." Louie is trembling as he pours them each a glass of lemonade.

"Oh Louie, I am so excited! We are finally getting somewhere with our heartbreaking dilemma." She sits down at the table and takes her glass to clink for a toast, as she raises her glass, Louie stops her, "Take h'it easy, my love. We will 'ave a snack, z'en I must leave, if zuh good Lord is willing we will be clinking glasses by tomorrow evening. Ezra is expecting to take h'us 'ome before too late. I will h'arrange for 'im to load a canoe into zee back of a carriage. Madame Sophie will be pleased to loan us a carriage so z'at we may drive h'out to our little lake tomorrow."

"I can hardly wait Louie, we must say our prayers tonight; This so exciting I believe I will not sleep a wink tonight."

"I 'ope your enthusiasm remains when you bid your parents good-bye and board zee train to begin h'our journey to Red River settlement. My muzzer will love you Julie; not only do you 'ave zuh same names but you 'ave zuh same soft 'earts."

There is a light knock on the door and Louie opens it to a smiling Moses, "How is you'all doin' Massah Louie?"

"We are doing so well Moses z'at you can be zuh first to know zat we will be wed tomorrow."

"Oh, Miss Julie, you will be havin' yo'sef a fine fella fo' a husband. He is hones' as duh day is long, Ma'am!"

Louie takes the document over and lays it on the table. "Not to change zuh subject Moses, but, can you read z'is?"

Moses takes out a pair of round-rimmed glasses and squints at the paper, "Sir, not only is it blurry but I needs to be hones' wit' you too. I reads very poorly, sir. Kin you read it to me, Massah Louie?"

"Of course Moses, we need you to witness our pre-marriage promises; z'en, if you don't mind we would like you to sign as a witness to h'our marriage h'also." Louie is imagining Monsieur Geurnon at the door any moment.

"Sir, I reckon I likes to have Madame Sophie to read dis paper; she will be mighty pleased, Massah Louie, she's been honest and kind to me an' my missus. I reckon I don' takes to doin' anythin' behin' her back."

"I totally h'agree Moses; we will go h'up and break zee news to 'er now. Is z'at agreeable wis' you, Julie?" Louie is praying for patience; *I must not look agitated.*

"Why of course! I think it is only fair that Madame Sophie knows what we are doing. After all, Louie is almost like a son to her. She would be hurt Louie, no doubt. My foot rub can wait until tomorrow night." She smiles at Louie and he gives her his best wink.

Louie slips the paper into his vest pocket while Julie helps Moses load the cart to be taken back up to the kitchen. "Miss Millie will get dese treats for her chillun', Miss Julie, you watch an' see."

"I believe you Moses. Sophie is very kind to z'ose children." Louie has witnessed Miss Sophie's kindness for years. *It is 'ard to stay agitated with a man like Moses, but h'it is not like me to state a wrong birthdate on a legal document, forgive me dear Mary, Joseph and Jesus! Do I have a choice? Please, dear Saints of God…give us strength to make it through this difficult time. My shoulders are sore from feeling so happy and yet so guilty…*

As they break the news to Madame Sophie, her eyes get big and she looks at Louie in silence, she searches his eyes, "My boy, I am so sorry, I cannot participate in your marriage plans. As much as I love you children and wish you the very best, the most I can do is give Moses my blessings as he witnesses this document. If all goes well, be sure to come by, I will have a gift here waiting for you."

"I understand Madame Sophie, my father can be very ruthless; he may even be dangerous. We will most likely need to catch the first train out and head for Red River." Julie's voice breaks and she bursts into tears.

"Take it easy Julie, my love, we are getting carried away. We will pray for zuh blessing of God and hope for zee best." Louie holds her in his arms for a moment until she settles down.

"Louie I am going to give you enough money to get to Keeseville, in case things go wrong; Julie is right, I have seen her father in a rage."

Louie has pulled his chair up closer to Julie and is brushing her hair back from her face; he takes his handkerchief from his vest pocket and gives it to her. It happens to be one with his initials embroidered on the corner; Sophie had given him a box containing a dozen for his birthday last October. "Oh no Louie, I can't clean my nose on that!"

"Why of course you can. You h'ar going to be my wife; h'ar you not?" He hands her back the handkerchief as he gives Sophie a wink.

"Yes Louie, I am going to be your wife. I need to keep telling myself that; it does sound so strange."

"Tomorrow will be a better day, my dear. If Ezra can take us 'ome now, I will prepare everys'ing for h'our ceremony, including zee holy sacraments.

Early the next morning Louie rises feeling refreshed and ready for the day...*this is the day that has been haunting me for weeks. I have prayed for God's will to be done; I am missing my parents dreadfully this morning...such an important day and yet I feel so alone. God help me to be feeling better before Ezra honks his horn for me.*

Auntie Lucie greets him as he comes down stairs "Good morning Louie, you are looking very handsome today. Is something special going on today, my boy?"

"Oh Auntie, I am so nervous; I will only have coffee and perhaps toast. Julie and I are having a secret marriage ceremony this afternoon." Louie takes his place at the table.

Uncle John steps into the dining room, just in time to catch the last sentence. "Oh my God, here we go again! God help you Louie, if you tangle with Joseph Geurnon, he can be a very unpleasant man. I can tell you one thing. If he comes shooting his mouth off at me around the brick plant, I'll have no choice but to belt him right in the mouth!"

"No, please John!" Lucie is in the middle of pouring Louie's coffee.

"Mark my words, that little loudmouth does not scare me...I'll give him what he should have got years ago! In fact it will give me great pleasure!" Uncle John bursts into one of his loud boisterous laughs.

Louie has dipped three teaspoons of sugar into his coffee and is stirring furiously. "Now Uncle, I never intended to cause you to make enemies from this...please, I hope he stays away from you." Even Louie is speaking French rapidly, which is not usually his style.

"Do not worry, my boy. If that did happen, everyone at the plant would buy me a drink!" He throws back his head and laughs even louder.

Just as Louie takes his last swallow of coffee, there is a squeaky little toot out in front. "Well, there's my ride. Wish me well and thank you Auntie... even your toast tastes magnificent!"

He kisses her on the cheek and grabs his bag, puts on his flat-brimmed hat and says good-bye as he goes out the door. *I get a kick out of my uncle, he never fails to come out with some of his favourite French idioms and I am soon feeling better...sometimes he can make me laugh in the midst of a crisis.*

True to his word, Ezra has strapped a small canoe onto the back of the carriage and after a short visit with Madame Sophie in the back entrance, Louie lifts Julie up into the carriage; she looks radiant with her hair tied back loosely, wearing her split riding skirt.

Before long they have turned onto the familiar road that once took them on their first buggy ride together; it has grown to be quite familiar to them.

It is still quiet, deserted and beautiful; the early morning sunshine is dancing on the narrow tree-lined road as Louie taps Sarah lightly on the rump with Ezra's gentle little quirt. He knows exactly where he is taking them; he cannot wait to see the shoreline of the little lake where they will paddle over to a small island.

Millie and Sophie had prepared them a small feast for after their ceremony and Louie has placed it in the back with his black bag; it contains all the necessary elements for a legitimate Catholic wedding ceremony.

As they pull off the road, Louie looks down at Julie, "Here we h'ar, ma chéri. We will load zee canoe wis' h'our picnic basket and my valise; it 'olds everys'ing we will need for h'our special day."

Julie is wiping her eyes with a small hankie, "Louie, I am feeling so frightened!"

"If you have any doubts Julie, say so now!" Louie is also beginning to feel nervous and is almost agitated with Julie.

"No Louie! That is not what I mean. I am so afraid of what my father will do to you!"

"Hush now Julie, once we get on the water they will hear us all over the lake!" Louie unties Ezra's knot and lifts the canoe down onto the ground.

Julie settles down and helps Louie carry the canoe to the water, "You get seated ma chéri, I will get us started." He lifts the canoe into the water, climbs in and sits down. The sound of the water rippling as they cross over to the island is a soothing cheerful sound, "Oh Louie, I feel like singing."

"You go ahead and sing, ma chére; z'at is what we need… some wedding music!"

Julie is just finishing her song as they slow down to line up for a landing, "Here we h'ar; I believe h'it is safe to say we h'ar all alone except for God and zee birds; z'ey are singing us a welcome song Julie!"

"No Louie, I think they are singing us a wedding song!"

"No, I believe z'at will come after zee ceremony." They both burst into laughter and their voices can be heard resonating across the water. It feels so good to laugh.

Once he ties up the canoe, Louie leads the way to a flat grassy spot under a large birch tree. There he spreads out the picnic blanket, sets the basket to the side and flattens out a square white linen cloth. Julie watches him as he unwraps each brass item needed for the taking of the sacraments, "Louie, you look so natural doing those things…it's as though you have done it a thousand times."

"Not to boast Julie, but it is likely almost z'at many times. I 'ave to h'admit…it feels wonderful to do it once more." Louie makes the sign of the cross and bows for prayer. Julie suddenly feels a sense of pride as she sees the look of genuine devotion on Louie's face; she makes the sign of the cross and bows her head.

After they have had the communion, Louie gives a handwritten set of vows to Julie, "They have been blessed with both my prayers and my tears, Julie."

Julie has no problem accepting Louie's adept handling of their wedding ceremony.

"That was wonderful Louie, I have witnessed a few weddings and they weren't much different."

"I 'ave to admit, I also 'ave witnessed a few weddings and h'our vows were as meaningful as any one of z'em. Zee only s'ing is …zuh groom always gets to kiss zee bride… z'is time it h'is my turn."

Louie grins, then takes Julie in his arms and kisses her long and sweetly; then he rocks her back and forth, back and forth, "Oh Louie, this is so beautiful; never would I have dreamed of such a wedding."

"Do you wish to 'ave some lunch now Julie? Or would you like a glass of wine first?"

"Louie, do I have to tell you what I would like?" She grabs him by the curls and brings him down to the blanket. He takes her in his arms and kisses her lips, her eyes; then her neck, "Oh Louie, I have dreamed of this. You know that I have never had a man like this, I am so happy… but so frightened."

"I will take h'it so easy wi's you, ma chéri. Just let me 'old you for a while…I too, have never had a woman h'eizzer." Julie enjoys his embrace; then…she takes the initiative. When she discovers that he is not ready… he becomes extremely embarrassed.

Just like I always dreamed! I am unable to… function! Louie sits up and takes his face in his hands.

Julie wraps her arms around him and kisses his cheek, "Please Louie, I am nervous also. Let us have some lunch and a glass of wine."

"Of course, ma chéri, we are bote 'ungry, look at me…I h'am trembling like a little boy shooting his first deer." Louie holds out his trembling hand. "Me also Louie, look at this…" She holds out her hand next to Louie's; they are both trembling. Julie begins to laugh, "Here, I will pour while you hold the glasses."

"No Julie, I am to pour while you hold zee glasses, z'is way I get to 'old your beautiful wrists." He looks at her and winks.

Julie raises the glasses, "Oh Louie, we are already arguing!" She continues to laugh as Louie holds her wrist to carefully pour the first glass.

"Just one glass, we will 'ave anuzzer wi's Madame Sophie when we return."

Julie spreads out the sandwiches and cakes. "Oh look Louie, Millie sent us some more grapes to crush!" They both have a giggle while they take their first sip of wine, "You may pray a blessing if you like Louie." They both make the sign of the cross, then carry on.

"One sandwich is enough for me…I will 'ave some grapes…" she hands Louie a grape. "…here, my man," she pokes it in his mouth, then she kisses his lips. She lays back and brings Louie down with her…her fingers are wrapped in his curls, "Oh Julie, you h'ar so delicious…" he kisses her over and over. Julie nibbles softly on his lips.

Louie makes his move, she is waiting…and he is ready. As they gently make love on the grass, the birds begin to sing, "Listen to them Louie." Julie whispers.

"Oui, zey h'ar singing to h'us… h'our wedding song."

Louie is almost delirious, he wants to say more, but his heart is pounding so hard in his throat…no words will come. *I knew it would be good…I never thought I would ever see this day.*

*Glossary

Footnotes:

1 'Ma Chéri' – 'My Dear'
2 Bed post – Luxury homes commonly had large canopy beds and fireplaces built into their bedrooms.

Chapter Seventeen

Terrebonne Mansion – Montreal: 1865...

Ezra is at the carriage house polishing tack as he hears Louie and Julie returning with the horse and carriage.

"We is all a-waitin' to hear if yous got married, Massah Louie!" Ezra has relieved Louie of the reins and begins to unhitch old Sarah as Louie takes Julie's hand to help her down from the carriage.

"We 'ad a wonderful ceremony Ezra and we h'ar now officially... Mr. h'and Mrs... Louie Riel." Louie presents Julie to Ezra, he kisses her hand.

"Congradulations, Madame Riel an'Massah Louie; I hopes dat all goes well for y'all."

"Merci, Ezra. We appreciate everys'ing you 'ave done for us, you h'ar a good man. If h'all goes well, we will be catching a train for Keeseville soon. I 'ope to 'ave my teaching certificate in zuh next few days so I can become a paid teacher. We will keep in touch wis' Madame Sophie by mail, she has an address for Father Barnabe in Keeseville and will be sure to forward my certificate. Leave Sarah hitched up, Ezra. We will need a ride to my h'uncle's."

Louie lifts his hat and scratches his head.

"I must impose upon you once more, my man. Tomorrow night at five o'clock could you bring me h'and Julie to zuh main train station? I 'ave a feeling she had better pack lightly and be prepared to leave town tomorrow."

"Yes Massah Louie, you can count on me...Good Lord willin'."

Julie has lifted the picnic basket from the rear of the carriage; Louie lifts out his bag and they walk together up to the back door; Louie lifts the metal knocker and lets it drop; Millie opens the door.

"Bon jour Monsieur Louie and Mademoiselle Julie." Louie hugs Millie with one arm and presents Julie with the other, "You now may address Julie as Madame; we have been married for three and one half hours..." He pulls his gold watch fob from his vest pocket. "... nearly four hours actually."

He grins at Miss Millie and winks; she shakes her head and wipes her eyes.

"Oh Millie, it has been so exciting. We had a wonderful ceremony!" Julie shows her the golden wedding band that Louie had surprised her with, as he lifted it from his bag. "It was wrapped in a hankie; Madame Sophie loaned it to him."

"I gave it to him child; it was the least I could do; you must remember; he is like my own son." Sophie calls out, her voice filled with emotion... from her seat at the kitchen table; she is wiping tears from her eyes.

"I wish you well... but I hope you can leave town soon. The suspense is unbearable, your father would not harm me physically but if he knew I participated in what he will perceive as deciet, he could sue me for everything I own. No, that is not it; I am afraid what he will do to... my boy" She reaches into the sideboard with a hankie in one hand and hands Louie a banknote; she pinches her nose with the tiny hankie.

"Of course I wish we could celebrate but I am a bundle of nerves. Please write me a letter when you are settled in Red River." Louie kisses her on both cheeks and wipes her tears with his handkerchief.

"Millie we will say farewell for now...please, get Sophie a glass of brandy, merci."

With that they are gone and the room is suddenly silent, except for Madame Sophie's sniffing.

Louie instructs Ezra to take him and Julie to his Aunt Lucie's, "I can't think of anozzer place zat would welcome h'us like h'uncle John and Aunt Lucie, Julie...zey are very kind people. Zey will gladly welcome you. Zen tomorrow we will need to take you to your mozzer to say good-bye. You may want to grab a few s'ings, zen get out of zere before your fazzer gets home from work."

"If you likes sir, Ezra'll be here at four in duh aftanoon, two hours before duh whistle blows at duh plant!"

"You are too kind Ezra, but h'on second s'ought, Aunt Lucie will take us to zuh train station in her little buckboard, I am sure. No need for h'us to implicate you and Miss Sophie h'any furzzer."

Ezra reaches for Louie's outstretched hand, "Merci beaucoup, Ezra. Take h'our love to Miss Sophie and zuh staff."

As they watch Ezra drive out of sight, Louie feels a stabbing fear; it is so difficult to feel safe... now that connections with Miss Sophie have been severed.

As they step up to the rear entrance of John and Lucie's home, Louie says a short prayer, *Father God, precious Mary and Joseph...hear my prayer. I am feeling so confused...forgive my weaknesses and set me on a straight path, sil vous plait!*

The door is opened by Auntie Lucie, "My boy! What is going on, where have you been...are you alright?" She is jabbering in French and Louie finally has to speak harshly in Mechif, "Muh, mon tanté!" Lucie settles down.

"Oh my boy…I have been so nervous all day!" Louie sets her on a chair by the table and pulls Julie in the door by the arm and sets her near Lucie.

"Sil vous plait mon Tanté. I need for you to sit here with my Julie…, we 'ave exciting news for you!"

"Julie, I would like you to meet my Aunt Lucie, she is as sweet as I promised you. Please excuse zee excitement Julie." Julie is smiling as though she is amused, "Forgive us Miss Lucie; we are so sorry for barging in."

"I have been worried all day about my nephew Louie; let me get you a cup of tea."

"You stay sitting Auntie, I will fix tea for you and Julie." Louie quiuckly puts the tea kettle on to boil for tea.

Auntie Lucie is holding her forehead, "Would you like a cold cloth or cold drink, Madame Lee?" Julie has squatted down beside Lucie on one knee, "You are so sweet my girl; I need a cold drink, sil vous plait."

Louie is too nervous to wait for a tea kettle to boil, "Julie, I will be back down before the kettle boils. I need to pack a bag." *Our next move should be to take the nine o'clock Southbound; Julie can write her mother for a bag and send our regrets.*

"Yes my love, I will care for your Aunt Lucie." Julie is holding out a glass of water for Lucie, "Merci, my girl. I am so afraid for you young people… you should have waited until things could be done proper."

"Yes, Madame, you are right. I pray all will be well." Julie sits down at the table and looks around Lucie's cozy little kitchen …*obviously Lucie has been taught by a fussy mother, judging by her needlework.* "Your mother must have been a wonderful embroiderer, Madame Lucie."

"Merci, my dear, she was good with any needle. She sewed most of our clothing, knitted and crocheted very well. Oddly enough; however, I was taught embroidery work by the nuns of the community." It is times like this that Julie regrets having such poor French…Lucie speaks very fast.

Just as the tea kettle begins to boil, Louie opens the stairway door with his valise in one hand and a large carpet bag in the other; he sets them near the corner of the doorway to the parlour.

"Tea coming up!" he says cheerfully. Footsteps can be heard coming up the back steps…they all look towards the door.

The door flies open and Uncle John steps in and looks around, "So what do we have here?" Louie steps forward and nods at Julie, "Uncle John, this is my wife Julie, sil vous plait, Julie, my Uncle John."

"My god you brought the bees nest into my home? You know that Monsieur Geurnon is out looking for his daughter? The whole plant is laughing about it; it may not be so funny."

Uncle John lifts the teapot from the table to sip from the spout*[1] (a bourgeois Metis tradition), "This damn thing is hot!" Julie bursts out laughing.

John spins around with the teapot in his hand, "My God, you the perpetrator, you laugh?"

Julie covers her mouth, "I am so sorry Monsieur Lee. You do not deserve this after working hard all day! I shall leave now!" She jumps up and steps toward the door.

"Sit down, my apologies! Lucie, pack a lunch for these children, sil vous plait, they need to go hide somewhere until they know what to do. He will look here first."

"There is no need for me to remove my coat; I will go and hitch the buggy up again." He grabs his old crumpled work hat and plunks it on his head,

"Hold on Uncle I will come and help you." He bends down and kisses Auntie Lucie on each cheek. "I love you Auntie; you have been very good to me." He grabs his bags and heads out the door.

"Julie you can be bidding Auntie Lucie farewell, we shall be leaving immediately."

Just as Louie is setting his bags in the buggy, a strange sound whistles through the air and a buggy whip catches him around the neck. He jerks himself loose and grabs the whip; he gives it a yank. A man comes stumbling out of the darkness and lunges toward Louie, "I will kill you, Riel! Marie-Julie, get in the buggy, this moment!" A shot rings out, there is a flash and Louie yells out, "My arm!"

Julie runs for the buggy of her father as Louie is yelling, "No Julie, come back! My God! You cannot go with him…he is a maniac!" Louie raises his boot and catches Geurnon in the stomach; he sends him flying backwards. John comes forward and lands an uppercut under Geurnon's chin that sends him flying. Guernon falls backwards into his buggy, "Now get to hell out of here, you son-of-a-----!"

Geurnon jumps into the seat of his buggy and whips his horse with the lines, he spits his foul French curses out over his shoulder, "You phony priest, you are a joke; you are nothing but a savage!" His voice echoes up and down the back alley, … Julie is hanging on, nearly falling out, as the buggy speeds away into the night.

"That bastard is a lunatic!" John comes to look at Louie's arm.

"It will be fine Uncle, do not be worried; it is a mere flesh wound." Louie has rolled up his sleeves; blood is spurting from his forearm.

"It is not bad but your aunt will fix it or it might get poisoning. Come, we will go in the house."

"No, my uncle, I must catch the ten o'clock train; I shall tie a handkerchief tightly around my arm. My bags are loaded and I have kissed Auntie farewell. I will go to Keeseville and await my Teaching Certificate. My life here in Montreal has ended; I must begin my journey home to Red River.

The sound of the cars clacking over the rails is comforting, *Thank God that is over! My mind is strangely at rest as I look out over this beautiful land preparing for winter. My ride through here last month was filled with apprehension. I wanted to see Julie; yet in a way…I dreaded it. Now I feel free to go about my business…and hopefully, it can still be ordained of God. I will look to Father Barnabe for some wisdom. I will also be counting on Evelina for some good solid advice…spiced with a bit of humour as a bonus!* Louie smiles to himself. *I am sounding rather selfish…perhaps even heartless; but life goes on. I need some maturity in my life. That is exactly one good reason why I am so attracted to travelling by train! What a perfect place to reflect…to shed my sins unto the good Lord, in privacy, and to count my blessings as I watch the world pass by. How better to reach forward to another monumental change in my life? I now have a mother and siblings to be concerned about. Sailing along over the prairies I can spend time fondly remembering my Papa, instead of feeling bouts of panic and grief and suffering the agony of feeling trapped… I can begin making plans.*

Louie reaches inside the waist-band of his trousers and feels for the leather lace that is anchored to his hidden purse, *my dear Papa used to refer to his port-monnaie* as his "wampum belt*", he always wore his little moneybag tucked inside his trousers.* Louie unpuckers his money purse and pulls out the bills Madame Sophie folded into the banknote she stuffed into his hand, *I could not believe my eyes when I counted my money; maybe I made a mistake.* He glances around the coach to insure his privacy. *It is no mistake; there is a little better than two thousand dollars here, all told.*

Suddenly there is all kinds of traffic in the isle. Two smelly cowboys walk by about the same time the doctor arrives to check his wound.

"Good evenin' Laddie! How is the arm feelin?" He sits down across from Louie and sets his bag on the seat beside him.

"You are lookin' a wee bit better now laddie. Would ye mind removin' your coat agin'? We'll have another look at that wound, it kept the bullet from entering your ribcage anyway; otherwise, ye would be passin' out daisies." He gives a little laugh and Louie surprises himself by joining in his laughter, "Doctor Graham I am so gratefulful for your services, I will pay you well. Do you serve zuh Railroad Company?" Louie rolls up his sleeve.

The doctor begins to remove the dressings from Louie's wound. "Laddie, you can thank your lucky stars, or the angel your mother sent alongside you. I just happened to be returnin' to New York from Montreal and spotted you looking pale layin' back in this seat. I asked you if you were ill and you passed out when I said I was a doctor. Of course I could see the blood soaked through your sleeve.

There you go, it has stopped bleedin' but take it easy, it may start up agin'. Thanks Laddie. Here is enough brandy to see you through for a couple of days." He takes the folded up bill, stuffs it in his pocket and goes back to his seat.

Louie is beginning to recall, *no wonder I was feeling no pain. He dropped that brandy in a cup of strong black coffee before he sewed up my arm.* Louie has a little giggle to himself, then realizes he is in dire need of a trip to the lavatory.

As he steps from the toilet he smells a strong familiar smell. "Those damned stinkin' range rats…" He feels an arm wrapped around his throat; then, a gruff voice says, "Hand over that roll you drunken dandy!" He feels an unfamiliar rage.

The nerve! First I am not drunk, second he has no idea what a Frenchman can do wit' a loose h'elbow! One quick move and Louie has given him a taste of the 'old Red River' elbow, as his old buddy Pierre refers to it. He drives his elbow into the fellow's ribs so hard you can hear the wind whistling up out of his throat. The whiskery stranger tries to grab a-hold of a sturdy iron hand-bar…he misses it; his screams fade into the night, as he flies out between the two moving cars.

Louie swings around and sees the other fellow hanging onto the railing on the other side. He swings his leg and lands his foot in Louie's stomach, before Louie can think he grabs his knife out of the scabbard and drives it into the leg that has landed in his stomach. The fellow yells out, "You son-of-a----!" as he is sucked out between the cars onto the gravel.

"Next stop Keee-isville!" The conductor yells out in typical railroad fashion. The train is beginning to slow down as Louie staggers back to his seat to retrieve his bags. He had combed his tousled curls in the toilet before the attempted robbery but as he runs his fingers through his hair he can feel a tangled mess. Quickly he combs his hair and straightens his tie. *If Madame Sophie could only see me now...*he has a bit of a snicker, then thinks of his Mama...*my God, if my Mama were to see me now she would be disgusted!* He brushes off his sleeves and pants; a sharp pain stabs through his arm and he remembers his wound.

Not a bad fight...for a cripple! He remembers the words of his Papa, "This knife could very well save your life someday." He feels a quick twinge of grief hearing his Papa's familiar French words...but he is too worked up to dwell on the past.

Wait until I tell Evelina; she will laugh her head off. Louie allows himself a quick belly laugh before entering the Executive Coach. By the time he has put on his coat and top-hat, gathered up his walking stick and bags, the train is screeching to a stop.

There seems to be no sign of the old freighter this time but Louie spots a familiar driver they have used before and gives him the signal, "Which way you headed, young feller?" He waves Louie over to the buckboard* tied to the hitching rail.

"S'ank you sir, I h'am headed for zuh Catholic Mission, a couple of miles from town, down by zee river." Louie is loading his bags and climbing up into the passenger side of the buckboard. "That will be thirty-five cents my boy."

"S'ank you sir," Louie says as he pays his fare and sets himself onto the wooden seat of the wagon that once was painted green. "It has been a wet harvest, down here in New York State, hopefully it will begin to dry out soon. You a lawyer?"

"Well, I 'ave studied law, but I find zat I enjoy teaching. I will be awaiting my teaching certificate. Could you please check for mail for Mr. Louie Riel? If zere is anysing, I will pay you fare for delivering h'it to zee Barnabe residence."

"Why certainly, sir. I will be pleased to do that for you." The old fellow takes out his watch, "You know that it is after midnight' is someone expecting you?"

Louie shakes his head, "No, but zey will not be zat surprised, zey knew I would be 'ere sooner h'or later."

"Well these dogs sound pretty vicious but I don't think they will bite you."

"No, zey will not bite; zey know me. 'ere Rags, come to Louie!" The old black and white dog comes running to Louie, wagging his tail like crazy, "Good boy, good boy, now settle down. It is wonderful to know zat someone is happy to see me! Heh, heh," Louie is getting a kick out of old 'Rags'.

"My name is Steven," He reaches for Louie's hand. Louie hands him thirty-five cents, "Well I h'am Louie, pleased to make your h'acquaintance," He notices his heavy emphasis on the last syllable, *I 'ave to get used to H'evelina's teasing h'again; she likes my accent*; he gives Steven a firm handshake even though it causes him some pain in the shoulder.

"Just h'in case I am not h'around when you deliver zuh mail. I h'at least know you 'ave been paid."

"Thank you sir, here comes your welcome committee." He climbs up on the buckboard and hands Louie his bags, "So long for now, Louie."

As Louie swings his bags to the ground he sees Evelina approaching, "Louie, Louie! It is so good to see you. Come in and have some supper and tell me some new stories!"

Louie is suddenly overwhelmed with a strange feeling, he grabs Evelina and gives her a big hug as he realizes …he feels *safe.*

"It will only take a minute to get your supper warmed up. Take your things down to your cabin while I fix supper. Everyone is asleep…at least they were until the dogs began barking!"

She breaks into that infectious laughter, Louie puts his finger up to his moustache, the way his Papa did when the babies were asleep, "We 'ad best be quiet, h'easy wis zuh jokes" He is suddenly overwhelmed with the giggles…he covers his mouth and doubles over. He is in a giddy mood; overcome with a strange feeling of directionless freedom.

He grabs his bags and begins to head down the board side-walk to the bunkhouses. "There's a candle inside the door on that light-stand. You can light this lantern for that dark path down to the bunkhouse"

"S'ank you H'evelina!"

He raises the globe of the lantern with his left thumb and strikes a match with his right hand. Soon the pathway is lit and he sees the doorway. He tries the door latch; it opens. Once he has set his bags on the floor, he sees the narrow bed with the familiar patchwork quilt and cannot resist flopping on it. *What a good feeling! Thank you, Lord Jesus, Sweet Mary and Joseph. It is so good to feel safe.*

Once he has gotten his bearings, he lights the candle, has a wash and combs his hair. *My breath is still filled with the taste of brandy… but the pain is strong again. I will need to have my dressings changed; I will give H'evelina her first story when I get up there to h' eat.*

Louie is not long getting up to the kitchen, he taps on the door. "Come on in Louie, sit down to the table, your supper is nearly ready."

Louie bows his head and makes the sign of the cross...*Almighty God, I am truly thankful for your protection and provision, merci beaucoup.* He makes the sign of the cross once again as Evelina sets a plate of beans and pork before him.

"Thank you H'evelina, it is so comforting to be in the presence of your calm and pleasant spirit once again. It seems as though I 'ave been to Hell and back...since I last seen you." He looks at Evelina and smiles; his eyes are wet with tears.

She can see the pain in his eyes. "First have something to eat Louie; we will talk later." She puts a kettle of water on to boil and gets the big salt shaker from above the cookstove.

"How will you be taking your brandy, Louie?" she says as she sets out bandages, scissors and Iodine.

"I will take h'it with hot water and honey, if you 'ave h'it, for sure I will need h'it before zuh h'iodine." He gives a little giggle. "My dear Mama h'always used h'it h'on our wounds, It hurt like blazes but h'it is h'every bit h'as effective h'as pine pitch." Louie's heavy emphasis on 'pitch' brings a smile to Evelina's face.

"Oh Louie, I sure missed our walks and talks, especially your wonderful French accent." She is about to sponge some Iodine directly into his raw wound.

"Owyah!" He responds to the Iodine like he did when he was five. "I was h'about to say, I must find work, but we will remember to visit once h'in h'awhile. Zen you h'attacked me!" Evelina gets a great kick out of Louie's pitiful remark.

"I must impose on you again, dear H'evelina. Zere h'is a Teaching certificate about to h'arrive from Fazzer Champagne h'in Montreal. Perhaps I could spend a few days 'ere waiting for h'it. Zen I shall be off to meet wis' an h'acquaintence I met h'up wis' h'on zuh train during my return to Montreal last time. He has a Law h'office h'in Chicago; he too writes poetry. We renewed an old friendship h'on zuh train and he gave me his h'address, his name is Louis Fréchette. I shall give you his h'address before I leave for Chicago."

"You are more than welcome, you may get to meet my suitor, Robert Whitelaw. He is the Indian Agent who serves our Indian Residential school."

"Merci, my dear H'evelina, you h'are very kind; my certificate should be 'ere before zee h'end of zee week. You be careful keeping company wi's an Indian H'agent; I hear some h'awful stories of 'ow some of zem steal supplies from zee Indians and sell zem to white people."

Louie speaks quietly as if someone may overhear him gossiping; he examines Evelina's dressing on his arm. "Merci, my dear; you h'ar a good nurse!"

"Thank you. It will need to have clean dressings for a few more days; that salt will dry it up fast." Evelina is looking questioningly at Louie… "I thought you were going to teach Louie."

"Oui, I plan to teach; however, in order to 'elp my people I must be well-versed in zuh British political system and z'ere law which now governs h'our country."

"You'll be busy learning Louie, how will you find time to teach?" Evelina is making Louie think too much while he is in pain. He grabs a fistful of his curls that are hanging over his forehead.

"I am trusting zat God will provide funds, students, whatever I need. I must go to bed; z'ere h'is a lot of pain now." Louie begins to get up.

"No Louie, relax, I will get you another cup of hot tea and brandy."

Louie sips on his brandy for a while watching Evelina moving around in her housecoat, as she tidies up for the night. "H'evelina, you h'ar so kind, I 'ope zat Indian h'agent treats you well."

Evelina gives a quick little laugh, "He will be kicking horseturds down the road if he shows any signs. I only went to the horse-races with him twice. It's not a place where you discuss your deepest feelings Louie."

"Yes my dear, you h'are right." He clears his throat, then says, "You know zat you h'are one of my dearest friends H'evelina, I h'only want you to be 'appy."

Evelina hands him his hot drink, "I know that Louie; don't worry, I will keep your words in mind. Now, tell me what you've been up to since I last seen you."

Evelina leans back in one of her brother's favourite chairs with a cup of tea. She can see Louie beginning to relax by the way he is sitting. "We must remember zat h'it is late and Fazzer Barnabe is asleep. If I tell you something, promise me you will not keep me h'up all night questioning me."

"Of course Louie, I promise. I have to teach sewing instruction in the morning at the Girls school so I need to get up early." But he has captured her curiosity and she is leaning ahead, waiting anxiously for his story.

"H'evelina, now keep your voice down; Julie and I were married yesterday." Louie takes a large gulp of his hot lemon brandy.

"Louie, where is she? For Heaven's sake!" Evelina's voice is now in a loud whisper.

"Quiet, quiet, mon ami, I told you! Now simmer down, zuh marriage will not be recognized by her fazzer; zere was no time to register. He hates me because I 'ave no 'h'old money'* and besides I h'am part Indian."

"Oh Louie, that makes me so sad. But I knew it was coming, just by your story last time we talked. You seem to be taking it quite well, or are you post poning your grief like last time?"

"You could be partly correct on zat, my dear. I will be so busy tomorrow; I believe I will be fine; I 'ave a lot to do. I 'ave set aside some money to send to my Mama, so I must write 'er a short letter to mail wis' it tomorrow. Zen I need to travel to Chicago while I still 'ave some money."

"I'm sure you'll be able to work for the Indian Department, teaching those little boys again. Then they will go home for the month of August."

"You are very kind, H'evelina." He begins to relate a few details of his experience with Julie; his eyes tear up as he tells her how their beautiful wedding day ended so tragically.

Evelina is listening with her head bowed down, "You have suffered a lot my friend." She looks up at Louie; there are tears in her eyes.

Louie takes his hankie from within his vest pocket and wipes his eyes. He heaves a big sigh and carries on.

"Tomorrow I must mail zat letter h'and some money to my dear muzzer, Zen I can go spend a little time in Chicago wis' Louis Frechette, my poet friend from Montreal. He claims I can learn more from him h'in one week, preparing for court, zan I could learn in a t'ree mont' Law Semester."

"Your plans sound impressive Louie. This Fréchette sounds like an interesting fellow from what you told me last month. It would likely be good for you to write poetry; it's obviously very comforting to you. We need to check your wound early in the morning before I go to the school. It may need a fresh dressing." She brushes the wave of brown hair up to her hair pin and gives it a quick tuck.

"Bless your heart, my dear H'evelina. I would love to see zose little boys h'again but I must be honest wis' you…tomorrow may be very painful when zuh brandy 'as worn off and I 'ave to face h'up to what 'as transpired in zuh last few days."

"Yes Louie, I am sure it won't be pleasant, especially to have a painful wound on top of it all."

"Well, I will bid you, bon soir, my dear. If my certificate is not in tomorrow I shall catch zee evening h'express anyway to begin my journey to Chicago. If you don't mind, you may forward my certificate when h'it h'arrives."

"Of course I will do that for you Louie; see you in the morning."

Louie is awakened at seven to a familiar sound. *That old rooster must know that I am here. Well, praise be to God.... I planned on attending Mass this morning, before Evelina works on my wound...praise be to God, for that old rooster.*

When Mass has ended and Louie is back in his cottage he sits down at the little table with pen and paper...*Dear Mother Mary, precious Jesus and Joseph,... send your holy angels to inspire this letter I am about to write. Give me the words that will comfort my dear mother. May I be cheerful for the sake of my siblings and as brief as possible. Lead me on a good path that I may begin to heal and find the ambition and wisdom to persue the destiny you have for me, in the name of the Father, Son and the Holy Ghost...Amen.*

He makes the sign of the Cross and picks up his pen and writes:

> *My Dear Mother, August 10th, 1866*
>
> *You are always in my thoughts. You all know how much I love you, my good mother, and my little brothers and sisters. I am sad that I cannot make you as happy as I would like...* Quote: Siggins.

*Glossary

Footnotes:

1 ...from the 'spout' – A common tradition among metis men. Wives would leave cold tea in the tea pot especially for the men to drink from the 'spout', she would then rince the pot with boiling water and make a fresh pot of tea.

Chapter Eighteen

Chicago, Illinois: 1866...

Like the dawning of a new day, the train whistle increases in volume with each blast. Louie squints as it comes into view.

He rises from the station bench out in front, and gathers his walking stick, top hat and two bags. Then he heads for the metal steps that will take him up to the passenger car.

This shall be my sleeping coach until I reach Watertown. Thank the good Lord for the gift of sleep. I know that today is Friday; I expect I should reach Syracruse by Saturday night, then, by Sunday night or Monday morning... I should be in Chicago.

As he settles into his window seat he leans his head on a train cushion that he has squashed up against the window...*now, every time we cross a prairie ...I shall sleep, oh, the blessing of sleep...* As he begins to doze off he notices a calendar on a wall across the isle...; *it is now June 23rd. and I am finally heading west...*

Louie's plan for a long sleep is interrupted only twice. Once by a fuel and water stop and again a slight exchange of a few passengers at another stop.

Soon he is gathering his belongings to disembark at the Illinois Central Rail Line main station. The Chicago main Train Depot is breath-takingly huge and after ten years, the city is a mass of smoke stacks and high buildings… Louie's heart begins to race.

As the train begins slowing down he squints his eyes at Taxi carriages that are lined up along the platform. He spots a West-side Taxi…*if I hurry I can take that one, Fréshette lives on the North-west side.*

Louie settles himself into a west-side Taxi and digs out the address of Louie Fréshette; he hands it to the driver. "I hope you know, this is gonna cost ya!"

Louie nods his head, "Yes, sir."

Louie is not totally surprised at the growth of Chicago; there is often some mention of Chicago and New York in the papers that Uncle John shares with Louie after supper, so he is somewhat informed on some of the changes he will encounter.

Still, the sights and sounds of such a large, busy city is fascinating to Louie. He is nursing a sore neck from scanning high buildings by the time the carriage pulls up in front of a six story tenement building.

A wide stairway leading up to a pair of tall ornate double-doors, appears to be the neighbourhood meeting place. Two little boys chase after each other up and down the stairway, while a couple of gentlemen stand at the top of the stairs smoking their pipes and chatting. A couple of ladies exchange remarks as they climb the stairs carrying brown paper bags filled with groceries.

Louie excuses himself with his two bags, one slung over his shoulder, the other on his left side as he tucks his walking stick under his arm to open the door, "'ere you h'are, Madame," he says, as he opens the door for two young women bearing grocery bags in gloved hands.

"Why thank you sir, you're very kind," says the first one through the door, "Merci, monsieur," says the second one.

Louie is so pleased to hear his language that he bows and slightly tips his top-hat.

Now, I must go to the third floor, he can hear the conversation between the ladies until they bid one another 'good day' at the second floor. They sound like a couple of young girls as they exchange comments on his good looks and debonair manners. *They must not be accustomed to manners around here.* Truthfully, he is rather pleased that no-one is around to see him blush.

Now, here is # 305, I hope he is home. He knocks twice "…Mon ami, bienvenu, bienvenu!"

Fréshette is pleased and excited to see his old Montreal commrade; English will now be a rarity, as they shake hands and begin to chat cheerily in their familiar University French.

"How was your trip? You are looking well!"

"I am doing well, thank you. I am so happy to finally be here, mon ami!" Louie sets his bags down and hangs up his coat and hat on a coat tree near the door.

"Come on in and make yourself comfortable. Sorry, but I still have no wife, I am still trying them out." He lets out a familiar loud laugh, something Louie has always remembered him by.

"The lady of the house will soon have our dinners ready. Then we will retire to my study where we can catch up. In the meantime, would you like a glass of sherry?"

Louie is looking around the apartment; the place is decorated with extremely shiny oak panelling and furnishings *…there is no shortage of books here,* "No thank you, my friend. I will have some brandy if you have it."

"Why of course! Have you been writing any poems lately?" He hands Louie a snifter of brandy.

"Yes, every chance I get. That is still my best therapy…you may not enjoy my recent work. It is either: very joyful, very depressing, or very pissed off! If you know what I mean; pardon my vulgarity, but I have been dealing with a very predjudiced, selfish father-in-law."

"You mean you were married? Louie! I never heard. What about your baccalauréat? What about the Priesthood? You have to be kidding me." He settles into his big stuffed chair and looks square at Louie.

"Oh, my friend, you have no idea. I have been to hell and back since the death of my dear father." Louie sets his drink on a small table beside the big comfortable chair Fréchette has waved him into with a large hand bearing a large gold ring.

He crosses his legs and clasps his hands over his belt buckle, as though to gird up his loins for a very painful confession.

"I am so sorry Louie; I am away behind with Montreal gossip. When did this happen…where is your wife?"

"If I may light my pipe I will fill you in briefly." Louie retrieves his Papa's pipe from his bag.

As difficult as it is, Louie brings him up to date with a very brief version, as his father would say, "Like a stone skipping over the water."

It proves to be therapeutic to Louie, giving him some relief from a heavy burden, much like his talk with Evelina.

The next week is spent catching up with the latest news, sight-seeing around the city and meeting with the Louie Fréchette mutual admiration society.

Louie endures the company of a myriad of influential French nationalistic types, who are in the Construction Industry. They are all great friends of Fréshette and are quite impressed by Louie's charm and intellect.

However, the only one he is well acquainted with is a fellow named Rodolphe Laflamme, whom Louie had served for a short time as a legal apprentice during his discreet romance with Marie-Julie in Montreal.

Laflamme is held in high esteem with Louie…he has built a respectable reputation within both the halls of Justice and the halls of Academia as a professor of Law at Laval University.

Now, along with Fréchette, they resume their passion for the classical poetry of Hugo and Lamartine.* It is common to have Laflamme drop by and report on the happenings with the French community who live in a neighbourhood of construction people.

Their loyalties are not necessarily with the Canadians and Louie sometimes finds himself getting caught up in Many of them are part Mohawk and Laflamme has insisted that Riel and Fréchette attend a couple of their parties.

Their music is lively, their food is delicious and they tell very funny stories; legends and tales that have been handed down through the Elders of the Mowhawk ironworkers.

Freshette is a wonderful host and Louie enjoys the luxury of having his clothes cleaned and pressed by Freshette's friendly Mohawk maid. Her name is Chakky and she turns out to be also a fine cook.

She takes care of the mail and leaves Louie's mail on his bed after she makes it up. Louie loves to lie back on the big patchwork quilt and read his mail.

He receives a few invitations for speaking engagements in the evenings, *Praise God for these opportunities to speak; I need to keep in practice. It is like dodging bullets preparing speeches for such an American audience; I suppose I should stick to the Ancient Arts and play it safe with these patriots. I have no problem speaking to a French audience, they always appreciate the historical parallels marking the Anglo Saxon conquests; the more money I can send my Mama the better.*

As 'water finds it's own level', it is not long before Fréshette's circle of friends has shrunk to a smaller circle consisting exclusively of poets, Laflamme also being one of them. Freshette does not announce his Indian blood; he feels some things are best untold, "...half-casts are not treated very well in the academic world, unfortunately." Louie does not announce his Indian blood either, yet he is proud of his heritage.

They meet regularly and enjoy themselves emmensly reciting their poetry, both old and new. They play a game, once a week, which can only be enjoyed by poets. The game is called "Mot de le Jour"*, depending on how many are in attendance you are generally only allowed to pull one word from the hat. Each participant writes one word on a paper and drops it into a hat. Upon retrieving a word from the hat, each poet has one minute to conjure up a title; then, at the sound of the bell, he begins to recite an impromptu poem. The time-keeper sounds a five-minute bell, at which time the poet is allowed one final moment. The winner is determined by the applause and receives a prize from the host.

Much fun arises from these single word selections. In the mean time, the men help themselves to hors'deurves, the drink of their choice, and either a cigarette or cigar. Louie eventually fills his Papa's old pipe and has one glass of wine or a brandy. His self-discipline with food and drink always remains intact.

The sky is the limit as the poet makes his selection; subjects range from critical, comical, beautiful, romantic to morbidly horrifying.

Louie enjoys the company of his friends and even grows to understand court proceedings very well while on the payroll of Louie Fréchette. His greatest pleasure comes from reading a variety of law books from the massive selection in Louie Fréchette's library. It totally fills the north wall and consists of a large open section and a smaller section that is covered by sliding glass doors.

***

Winter comes and goes and Louie is relieved and happy when the icy Chicago winds begin to slowly warm up. He is walking back from the Courthouse when he feels the spatter of warm rain; he looks around the streets and the ice and snow is all but gone; he suddenly feels a longing for Red River stirring in the pit of his stomach. There is something about the sky; it is as though a cold and clammy hand has been lifted off the city of Chicago.

The time eventually comes when he finds himself lying on his large four poster bed, staring up into the dark. He feels uneasy...like he is wasting time, as he fixes his stare on the high ornately decorated ceiling of his private suite in Fréchette's upscale apartment. *I must move on, soon. I am continuously, tormented at night by memories. I feel that there is a healing for me at St. Paul...in fact...I crave it. This will be my final week with my friends. I believe God has blessed me with their company. Now, I must proceed with my commitment to my family.*

Louie chooses to make the announcement regarding his soon departure as the weekly Poet's Circle is concluding..."My dear friends, I have enjoyed extremely, our weekly exchange. I must now bid you good-bye as tomorrow I will be catching the eight o'clock Western Pacific for St. Paul Minnesota."

There is a lengthy exchange of handshakes as Louie and Fréchette prepare to leave. Louie Freshette has been aware for some time of Louie's restlessness.

Rodolphe Laflamme has also been aware of Louie's strange behavior; being the sage of the Law-firm he wisely counsels Freshette, "There is nothing wrong with Louie except he is lonely; we get to go back to Montreal every few weeks to see our families; he sits here and pines for his people in Red River. Now that he is not doing the Lecture Circuit anymore he is bored. You will see; one day he will pack up and catch the first train heading west." Laflamme punctuates his remarks with a tapping of his pipe into a heavy metal ashtray.

"Your assumptions are generally correct, my friend. I believe also the spring air could be rousing his Indian blood and he is restless to move on." They both enjoy the humor of Freshette's remark.

True to their words Louie begins to have his clothes readied for packing the next day.

***

As Louie boards the noisy bustling train he feels an overwhelming relief flooding over him...*Finally, I will be getting home to my family.*

Louie Fréchette has given him many of the favourite books he has been reading during his stay in Chicago. *I will now begin to start my own library with such a collection of classic poetry, law and history. I cannot believe that he entrusted to me some of his collection from behind glass. He says he can replace them...I hope he is not mistaken...they are a treasure...*

He takes his little green Prayer book from the pocket of his vest and begins to read; the sights of Chicago fade into the distance. *Oh, what a pleasure it is to emerse oneself in the comfort of scripture without the prompting of anyone but the Holy Spirit. I must read once more the third chapter of the precious Proverbs: *(SeeFootnote)...ah well, does it remind me of forgiven weaknesses and the faithful love of my Holy Father...*

Louie is awakened from sleep several times as he continues his journey to the west. He sees no reason for a sleeping coach or the confinement of a berth*. A pillow against the window is fine and he can take in the lights of a few familiar places as the stops are called out...he recalls the trip out east ...so long ago...

Oh, sweet Jesus, Mary and Joseph...watch over my dear mother and brothers and sisters. When I think about going home my stomach begins to hurt...is it guilt about my poor widowed Mama? ...or is it guilt about my little brother Charles...or is it...fear of facing Father Taché and the sickening guilt... about my betrayal of his vision for my Devine destiny?

I am actually getting thinner...eating has no appeal to me. Finally, I will be able to face up to my guilt...I will seek out the appropriate Confessor to oversee my repentance. I look forward to seeing my siblings...I would reckon that Sara and Marie are beautiful young women. Eulalie and Octavie are likely still doing all the talking. Joseph should be eleven, old enough to do chores for Mama. Then, she has had Henriette and Alexandre, whom I have never seen...I have spent many sleepless nights wondering about Charles.

He turns his face to the window to hide the pain that always pulls at his face...when he thinks of Charles. *I wonder if he still... He will be thirteen when I get home to Red River. I wonder if my Mama is still beautiful...or is she getting old and grey? I dread seeing Father Taché. My stomach hurts at the thought of seeing him.*

They are beginning to see buffalo; the herds are getting larger.

Madam Sophie's money should be lasting fairly well. I have not squandered money...$500.00 to my Mama to catch up with debts and buy cattle and seeds...a few dollars on some good shirts and the cleaning of my clothes. A few meals, drinks and Taxies were paid for from my wages at the Law office...Fréchette even deducted my board, which is fine. Now, I must be more observant as I visit the lavatory to count my money. It seems there is always a creepy figure in the shadows.*

He rises from his window seat and hangs onto the balance rods behind each seat and moves through the fancy Dining car. The Executive coach is next to the lavatory; there are a dozen or so wealthy passengers seated in the elaborately decorated Executive Coach, the seats are green leather and the windows are draped in green velvet.

He enters the lavatory, locks the door, and takes his money purse from the hidden pocket in his vest...*It looks like I have done well, there is still sixteen hundred dollars here...I will be able to arrive home with some money.*

He settles back into his seat as the Conductor comes down the isle calling out, "Next stop Madison County!"

Time begins to pass quickly as he recognizes some familiar sights. The grassy mounds, mottled with stunted pine still provide a shady resting place for the buffalo.

Louie recalls his shock and disgust back in '58, as the east-bound train ploughed through giant herds of buffalo, leaving hundreds of dead and wounded amimals in its wake. Somehow he felt guilty…as though he was an accomplice to a criminal act.

He and Smitty discussed the tragedy in great length; they felt as though they should be yelling at the railroad conductors to stop. *The least they could have done was to chase the buffalo away from the tracks!*

He now is saddened by the small clumps of buffalo scattered sparcely through the hills. *I knew that this was one of the atrocities I would return to…my dear mother has been trying to prepare me for some of these changes. She says I will not recognize the settlement of Red River. I must be cheerful; she says we have a wonderful Cathedral at St. Boniface. I am still looking forward to it… even though I will not be one of the local priests.*

"Next stop St. Paul Minnisoo-ata!" The old black Conductor had sneeked by Louie and yelled right behind him; Louie rared up from a half-sleep with a squawky yell that brought stares from all the passengers at the front of the car. He could not keep from coughing and laughing. The old Conductor says, "Sorry there, young fella."

As the porters set Louie's three boxes of books on the trolley, he picks up his three bags and follows them into the Station, "Here you are sir," says a young red headed porter, looking grand in his red WPR* uniform with a red and gold striped beanie*on his head.

"Merci, my man!" says Louie as he drops a few coins into his outstretched hand. *Now that fellow reminds me of Kieren O'Brien from the L'Ambitieau clan. I surely missed those lively, musical people. Hopefully I will see them soon after I arrive home.*

He registers his boxes for storage and writes a note on them: 'Ship to Red River when notified-L Riel. *I feel I am not ready to go home until I have a retreat. I will go to a Cathedral and look for an appropriate confessor…Lord knows there are a few Churches and Cathedrals around here. What a huge place! I barely recognize anything.*

The old muddy streets have now been transformed into cobblestone or gravel; beautiful buildings, boasting the latest in French architecture line the busy streets. Lovely draped carriages have replaced many of the old hooded surreys waiting at the train station, the hollow ringing of hoofbeats, punctuated by the occasional winny of a horse, fills the air. Even the little old train station has been replaced by a magnificent Train Depot, complete with shoe-shine boy* on the platform.

Louie sets his bags down on the platform and begins his panoramic scan of St. Paul; it offers many of the same characteristics as Montreal with giant trees now surrounding all the old familiar Cathedrals. Most have had expansions and are now much larger.

Louie finds himself a room at one of the nicer hotels and is received very respectfully by an old black porter, "Jus' make yersef' comfortable, sir. Would you like yer dinner brought up?"

Louie removes his top hat and hangs it with his walking stick on the hat rack inside the door.

"No s'anks, my man… I h'am exhausted, 'ere is a dollar for your trouble. Good evening to you."

"A good evening to you too, sir." The porter flashes him a smile as he closes the door.

I should not be tired after all the sleep I have had in the past few days. I will freshen up in the morning and go look around. St. Paul is not the same little place it was last time I was here…it is a good sized city now.

Louie takes out his little green prayer book, which after almost ten years has become faded and dog-eared. It falls open to Psalm 150, *I feel such a kinship to David the psalmist, there is nothing like David's famous praises to soothe the soul in times of uncertainty.*

Louie's mind begins to wander…he wonders where he should begin in his search for a confessor to guide him back to God before he has to face up to his Mama, his siblings and worst of all…Father Taché. His eyes are getting heavy. He reaches out and turns down the stylish oil lamp by his bed, the wick rolls down and the room is swallowed up in darkness.

***

Louie's heart is pounding with excitement as he descends the long stairway down into a luxuriously carpeted lobby. Large, red leather upholstered chairs matching the drapes and carpet are here and there. He takes in a deep breath …*nothing like the smell of bacon and coffee.* He steers himself in that general direction.

Seating himself at a small round table, he sets his hat on a chair beside him, "Would you like breakfast sir, or just coffee?" A pretty dark-haired girl is asking him in French.

Louie looks up at her with a big smile, he answers her in French, "It is wonderful to hear my language again! Yes, I would like bacon and eggs, sil vous plait, madamoiselle, but coffee, most of all." She gives him a short curtsey and a big smile, "Coffee coming right up!"

After Louie has enjoyed a good breakfast he is ready for a stroll around town. As the young girl gathers his dishes and gives him his bill he asks her, "Do you know where I could find a Priest in St. Paul?"

"Sir, where are you from, there are Priests every where you turn in St. Paul?"

"I am sorry Madamoiselle. I just came in on the train from Chicago last night. If you point me in the direction of a nearby Cathedral, I shall find a Priest."

"Yes sir. When you leave the Hotel turn left and go about five blocks, it is St. Paul's Cathedral…you will see the steeple right away."

"Merci, mademoiselle, have a good day." He tips his hat and heads for the cashier.

***

Louie stands on the corner looking back at Le Grande hotel to his right, and St. Paul's Cathedral to his left. It cranes its steeple over the city like a caring mother goose. *I guess I should not get lost here like I did a few times in Chicago, three blocks and I shall be back at the hotel.*

Climbing the wide stairway to the double-doors, Louie lifts his hat to a Priest coming down the stairs. The priest smiles and asks him in English, if he is new in town.

"Why yes, sir. I just arrived from Chicago." The priest steps across and shakes hands with Louie.

"My name is Father O'Hara. Have you been sent to a post here?" Louie replaces his hat and shakes the father's hand, "I am Louie Riel, Father. I am seeking guidance at this time…I have endured some troubled times."… *there has to still be an air of spirituality about me…he thinks I am a priest.*

"Well! Allow me to welcome you to St. Paul's. We are very proud of our recently completed Cathedral. Please, come in."

Louie removes his Irish Bowler* and smoothes his unruly curls. Upon entry he takes walking stick and hat in one hand as he dips his fingers into the holy water and makes the sign if the cross as he lowers one knee to the floor, then up again.

"Follow me, please." The priest leads the way to the confession booth. If you wish we may begin with your most recent confession."

This is too fast for me. I am not prepared to stir up sleeping dogs that have been put to rest … for the time being, at least.

He begins to feel dizzy, *I must excuse myself…I am going to throw up.*

"I am so sorry, sir. I am not feeling well. I must go out and get fresh air. Perhaps I should return tomorrow if I am well."

The Priest is looking at him strangely. "Well, you do look a bit pale. Be on your way, I will be here tomorrow."

Back in his room Louie is regretting his adventure. *Now what shall I do? I feel panic overtaking me…dear Jesus, Mary and Joseph…guide me, please. What shall I do? He will be after me now…I am not ready…*

His first beautiful, fair morning in St. Paul, Minnesota, has turned into a nightmare.

He lies crossways on his fancy, fresh bed to soothe his sick stomach, it may as well be a bed of ashes…soon he is asleep. His sleep is fitful, with visions of people he has been longing to see for years…now he is dreading the burden of guilt he will need to deal with when he encounters Father Taché, Father Lafloche and L'Ambitieaux family…they were so proud of him. Even Pierre and Kieren…he longs to see them…they were always so kind… *I must find Father Lafloche, he has always been my favourite confessor…*

*Glossary: 'Irish Bowler'

Footnotes:

1 Lamartine- A well-known Poet and colleague from Montreal, during Riel's popular stint as a circuit speaker and Poet.

2 'Mot de le Jour'- A game played among people of the 'Arts'. ('Word of the day': a word is pulled from a hat which will serve as the key word in a poem which must be composed 'on the spot'.)

3 Shoe-shine boy- Most Rairoad stations in major cities provided a shoe-shine stand, set up on the platform next to the tracks. Men could sit on a chair and put their feet up on a stool to receive a quick shine on their way into the station for five or ten cents. A 'modern' convenience of the times. Traditionally, the stand was run by a cheerful young black boy.

Chapter Nineteen

St. Paul, Minnesota: 1867...

Louie is awakened by the sound of church-bells. *I shall be packed in ten minutes, then I shall take a coach; they may tell me where I can find a descent room with a reasonable rate. I must send money to Mama, she is worried about raising crops. I cannot believe that white men are taking over Red River...no wonder she is worried.* The terror he had been feeling when he fell asleep has subsided and he is no longer nauseous. *I will look for work as a Teacher when my certificate arrives.* He brushes lint from his cuffs *...another chore today will be to locate a Laundry...my dress clothes must be cleaned before I hang them in my room.*

The sound of a steamboat whistle can be heard coming into port on the mighty Mississippi, Louie pauses on the steps as he leaves the hotel with his luggage. *What a welcome sound, I was a mere boy when I last heard that whistle blow!*

He flags a carriage as he steps out onto the street. *I cannot believe the activity in this place. People are coming and going in every type of buggy and wagon imaginable. Even the smells are different now...I might as well be in Chicago...the factory smells are the same.*

A quiet little buggy pulls up and a well-dressed driver pulls the little bay mare to a stop, "Mornin' sir, set your bags in the back and climb aboard!"

On second thought I never heard that in Chicago, heh, heh. A good long nap has put Louie in a much better mood…the thought of hearing his beloved Metis language again is a thrill to his lonely heart.

"Bon Jour, Monsieur, could you take me to a 'otel where zey speak some French, sil vous plait?"

"You bet, I know exactly where you want to go. It can get a bit noisy at times but they are a friendly bunch."

"There you go sir." The driver sets Louie's bags on the sidewalk. Louie pays him and bids him good day. *I saved a few dollars there…I have grown accustomed to service to my door. I shall enjoy carrying my own bags; the exercise will do me good. My arms will look like sticks alongside Pierre L'Ambitieaux's. I shall be so happy to see Pierre! Mama has been telling me a few things about my school buddy, Smitty…I look forward to seeing him also, even if he drinks a little bit too much.*

Louie enters the hotel and squints as he looks around for the clerk's desk. The lobby is full of people. *That driver was not mistaken, it sounds like St. John Baptiste Day in Montreal!*

Louie excuses himself through the crowd and sets his bags down, "Sir, do you happen to have a room for rent?" He is very doubtful… *perhaps there is a circus in town…or a hanging.* He smiles to himself at his own joke.

"Yes sir, we actually do! This crowd is from a fur Auction down on the river hill, it just finished and they are all checking out." His French is fast and muddled with Lakota Sioux.

"Great!" says Louie. *Now, there is my first miracle in St. Paul, Minnesota. I could have been here last night.* "Is there a place to have a lunch close by?"

"Oui, there is a bar straight through that door, where you can order food and there is a Café just up the street. First we will get you registered," he is very efficient and remains pleasant as he bids adieu to his guests.

Louie is happy to be on the second floor and he is even happier that the rent will be manageable until he has completed his retreat and confession, then he will be ready to head north to Red River. *It would please me greatly if I could teach for one term and arrive at Red River with an established career.*

As Louie walks the two blocks over to the café, he notices a lot of Metis people walking up and down the street *...looks like I am in the right part of town.* He has a little giggle to himself. A husky-looking Metis man tips his cowboy hat as he walks by, "Tansi, bon jour.!"

Louie nods back... his smirk turns to a smile as he returns the greeting, "Bon jour, bon jour." He tips his little bowler hat and squints down the street into the morning sun.

"Where from, h'ar you, monsieur?" The cowboy stops and pulls his tobacco pouch from his shirt pocket.

"I just got in last night from Chicago. Where are you from?" Louie is a little uncomfortable about using his old Mechif and he sticks to French. Even Auntie Lucie used very little Mechif, it was rarely heard in Montreal. The cowboy answers him in English.

"I h'am from Red River, my name is René Bannatyne. I h'am in charge of my Papa's h'orders for duh store in Red River. Me and my two younger brudders will be hauling freight home once all duh h'orders are filled."

He finishes rolling his cigarette, then tightening the puckering string on his pouch with his strong white teeth he stuffs it back in his pocket. He strikes a match on the hitching rail that follows the sidewalk.

As René lights up, Louie smiles and offers his hand for a handshake.

"Pleased to meet you René, I h'am Louie Riel, you may have known my Papa who is now deceased."

"You h'ar duh long lost son of Monsieur Riel?" He pumps Louie's hand up and down like he has just met royalty. "What a downright pleasure to meet you. I 'ope we 'ave duh pleasure of taking you home wit h'us, we freight by steamboat until we head west, den we h'unload our wagons h'and leave duh Mississippi to 'ead nort' to duh Dakotas. It's a helluva long trip but we rest ar h'asses about h'every fifteen miles or so, if h'it's not too rough." He rares back and has himself a familiar loud Metis laugh.

"You know, René? I h'am so tempted, I would love to travel wis' you but I 'ave business to finish h'up 'ere in St. Paul before I h'am free to leave." *No use mentioning my retreat, he likely would not understand. But I truly intend to be 'free'… free from my sorrows and sins of the past few years.*

"I wish to work for a while and 'ave some money to take 'ome to my poor widowed Mama. But now, mon ami, would you join me for breakfast?"

"You bet! Don't be surprised if we're joined by my brudders, Jules and Paul, dey h'ar noisy, but dey h'ar good hones' boys. We can buy yor' breakfast, mon ami."

"No, h'it will be my pleasure." They have arrived at the doorway of 'Polly's Café' and are welcomed by a charming Metis girl. "What will you be 'aving sirs?" she asks as they get seated.

"What do you say Louie? I will 'ave two flapjacks and two broken h'eggs upside down, and coffee, sil vous plait?" His order is punctuated by a cheery smile.

"Oui, sir, et tu?" she asks Louie.

"I shall have toast, two soft boiled eggs and black coffee, sil vous plait."

"Madamoiselle, do you 'ave fresh bannock?"

"Oui, we do, sir." She says with a smile.

"I s'ought I could smell fresh bannock! I shall change zat h'order, sil vous plait, merci, merci!"

Louie sends his hat and stick with the waitress, he smiles like a little boy as he pokes his curls back into place, "I 'it zuh jackpot 'ere René!"

"Remember, mon ami, we h'ar in St. Paul…the home of the Metis. You will notice that over half the people you meet here are Metis. There are even more over in St. Anthony and St. Joseph"

"Wonderful!" says Louie, as he looks around the room, "Tapway, tapway!" says Louie as he leans back in his chair to await his bannock.

Breakfast is pleasant and the boys prove to be as noisy as René had predicted.

Louie has taken the liberty to extract some very valuable information regarding the current political climate in Red River.

Paul, the youngest of the boys is very opinionated and his remarks are rather bitter toward the 'high' people in the community. When he begins to speak of the greed of some of the new immigrants, he becomes so enraged he speaks rapidly in straight Mechif.

Louie quickly picks up on the stressful situation in Red River. It has brought the Metis people to extreme behavior with the new settlers. The 'high' people have become very aggressive. Fistfights in the saloons are common and are generally between the French and British frieghters, or anyone who has loyalties towards the Canadian Orangemen from the east "…who," Jules shakes his head as he looks sadly at Louie "… own most of the local businesses."

Louie's Mama has mentioned a man named Schultz who is taking over Red River. It has been a mystery to Louie as he is not accustomed to remarks that appear to be of a gossipy nature coming from his Mama.

He is beginning to see what has been meant by some remarks he has been hearing, *I had better be getting things straight before I step right into a hornet's nest.*

"I 'ave enjoyed h'our visit, mes ami, now I must 'ave a look h'at what zere is for h'employment in good old St. Paul; I can 'ardly believe it is zuh same place I left in '58."

"I believe you Louie; we will be at the hotel for two more days if you change your mind and want to go home." René speaks French very well; therefore, much of their conversation is in French.

Louie rises from his chair, puts on his Boston Bowler hat and takes his walking stick from the hat rack. He is still dressed very chic, for the Metis side of town.

"You may do well to check out some stores, Louie. You dress like a store-keeper."

"Merci, mon ami. I will begin zere, merci." He gives a little bow and the boys all tip their cowboy hats.

"Merci, mon ami. The breakfast was good," says René with a big smile.

Louie pays the bill and heads up the street to a dry goods store a few blocks away. He is nearly at the door when a familiar voice calls out, "Louie! Louie! You son- of- a- gun! Where did you come from?" Louie squints his eyes in the morning sun.

"Smitty? For the sake of St. Peter! Where did you come from?" They are both laughing and their hearty handshake becomes a huge bear-hug. With tears in their eyes they explain themselves and Louie invites Smitty to his room.

"It is on zuh second floor, right at zuh top of zee stairs, room #202. I was h'about to ask for a job in z'is store. I 'ave saved enough money to pay my way 'ome, 'and to give my Mama for bills. We want to buy more land, though, before the good land is h'all taken h'up. Mama says it is going fast."

"I reckon you will get a job fast in that slick outfit, wuh waaah!" Smitty sings out his 'wuh wah' in a long drawn out laugh. *I never realized how welcome those silly old expressions could sound.* Louie lets out a giggle.

"Well, you need to dress accordingly, mon ami. If I was h'applying for a job h'at zuh stables, zen I would dress differently."

"Tapway, mon ami, tapway! You darn sure haven't changed!" Smitty lets out a roar of laughter. *This guy is as crazy as ever,* Louie thinks as he flashes Smitty a big grin.

"Well, my friend, let us take a stroll h'around town. You can give me the names of h'all zeze places; I will write zem down."

"You bet, Chuwam! I can even tell you who to talk to in some of the places."

***

By 3:00 p.m. Louie and Smitty have made a circle around the Industrial area and the commercial part of St. Paul. "What a filthy smell coming from z'oze faczories! Zey are worse z'an zuh lakeside factories in Chicago!" Smitty looks at Louie and laughs, "I can't believe you actually lived in the city of Chicago, my friend."

Finally they have arrived back at Polly's Café. "Merci, my friend. I h'appreciate zuh tour. I h'am beginning to feel a bit more comfortable. Now, shall we indulge ourselves wi's a bowl of soup and some fresh bannock?"

"Hey, I reckon dat sounds mighty good, Louie. Remember all the fried bannock we ate on the journey from Red River to the Mississippi steamboat?"

"I do recall zat trip. I s'ought of it many times over zuh years; it made me very homesick; I tried not to s'ink of z'oze s'ings too h'often…h'it was too painful. I would quickly begin to study."

"Well, Louie, when I heard you left the Seminary I was shocked and disappointed, but, my welcome home was not that great either…by the Priests anyway.

My parents were so happy to see me dey never even gave me hell." He has a big chuckle.

"Yore Mama will be so happy Louie. Just try to forget what the Priests will say. It should be Madame Sophie who would be upset…she bid us farewell and gave us hugs. Daniel told me, she never scolded him a bit. Of course we both got sick. You know it was sheer loneliness, my friend."

"Tapway, my friend, I felt that way a few times; they made me pray and bath, pray and bath." Louie looks at Smitty with a grin and Smitty shrugs his shoulders and laughs.

After they have enjoyed a hearty bowl of chicken soup and bannock they stroll back over to the Hotel, Smitty refers to it as 'Montreal House', on Minnesota Road.

"It is the only real French speaking Hotel in town and all the Red River people gather there." Louie is passing a group of Metis men who all seem very familiar, most of them have moustaches or beards and they all dress alike. Their pants are either blue or tan; they wear riding boots and cowboy hats or touques, and their tanned leather vests are beaded in the beautiful style that was worn by his Papa…the last time he saw him. Most of them wear six-shooters on one hip and a knife on the other. They all have colorful sashes tied around their waists.

"I have no clothing of z'at style h'at all. I suppose I look strange, eh, my friend?"

"Have no worry, Chuwam, you look just fine to me. It's about time we had a gentleman in our midst." He slaps Louie on the back and they have a little chuckle.

"H'as I recall, most of zee men of Red River zat I knew h'as a child were gentlemen, especially my Papa. Do you not h'agree, Smitty?"

"You bet, Chuwaum, he surely was a gentleman. He spoke much like you Louie, you are his spitting image."

"Merci, merci, mon ami. I shall take zat h'as a compliment." He raises his hat and gives Smitty a solemn nod.

As the two men sit comfortably in Louie's room, they waste no time in answering all the pertinent questions regarding their most recent years… both in Montreal and Red River. Time stands still as they fill in the blank years that had nearly made strangers of two boys who were once as close as brothers.

"Would you like another quart of beer brought up, my friend? You have been nursing that same mug of beer for an hour, I'll go down and grab us a quart!"

"Non-merci, my friend, two is my limit. You go ahead and get yourself a beer; z'is is enough to wet my t'roat before I retire for zuh night." Louie raises his mug to Smitty, "Go ahead, my friend!"

The door closes and the room is as silent as a clam. *I cannot believe I am really here with Smitty. I am beginning to feel a bit better about returning to Red River to face my shame. The white settlers in Red River were good friends with the Metis when I was still home... my heart aches for the old days and I have not seen the division of our people yet.*

He pokes a pillow behind his head, then goes back to reviewing the news of Red River.

Half-breeds at the north end of town under a Protestant minister and Metis at a half dozen Catholic Parishes scattered from Pembina to St. Anne in the east. Orangemen cashing in on all the profits and the Metis getting all the menial jobs, it gives me the shivers, thank God for Smitty who can prepare me for these deplorable conditions.

The door opens and Smitty enters with a jug of beer in one hand, wearing the smile of a Chessire cat.

"Did you miss me, my friend?" He sets the beer down on the little round table beside the shaded coal oil lamp. Louie is still sitting in the big comfortable chair with his legs crossed smoking a cigar.

He is amused at Smitty as he becomes a little bolder with each glass of beer; he offers him a cigar.

"Here Chuwaum, try one of these."

"I will smoke a half a cigar, zen I must retire."

"Sorry, I tried a cigar one time and it made me deathly sick. Do I get to sleep on your chesterfield*, Louie?"

"Oui, my friend, you lay right there, you may 'ave one of my blankets. I will slock z'is cigar, it may make you sick. I generally smoke my Papa's pipe when I want to relax."

Suddenly Smitty lets out a loud hoot of laughter, "I can't believe you still say 'slock'. The Red River people still say that when they ask you to snuff out the lamp." He takes a big swig of beer and rolls back and forth laughing.

"Well of course I remember the Red River patrois, I just 'ave not 'ad zuh pleasure of using it for nearly nine years." Louie lies back and soaks up the pleasure of listening to Smitty's stories of old friends and family back home, they are spiced with everything from laughter to total digust.

"Well Smitty, tell me a couple more stories of Red River, while I smoke my pipe. You will enjoy zee fragrance...it shall remind you of my wonderful Papa."

He smiles as he pinches a half a pipeful of tobacco from a small bag; he puckers the string and returns it to the inside pocket of his vest.

The two men continue to enjoy one another's company on into the wee hours of the morning; Smitty is still talking as his long lost friend dozes off…

***

Louie awakens to the loud snores of his buddy, *I shall let him sleep and go back to that little grocery store h'after I 'ave my toast h'and coffee.*

Louie opens the window to let out the stench of beer and smoke; he writes a small note to let Smitty know to meet him at Polly's for lunch at 12:00 noon; then, he leaves it on the table and finishes his grooming before going downstairs. He listens for a moment to the faint ringing of a church bell… *probably St. Paul's Cathedral,* he muses.

By noon Louie is back at Polly's Café. As he enters the room he squints to look around; his eyes are blind from moving in from the sunny street to a darkened room.

There are not many people sitting around at the little round, gingham* covered tables. He recognizes the figure in the corner…head down sipping coffee, hat sitting back on his bushy blonde hair.

"You beat me back here, Chuwaum. Wuh wah! You look razzer tough! A good bowl of soup will fix you h'up." Louie notices a strange feeling of freedom as he begins to enjoy the old Metis expressions.

"Oh, my friend, I'm still sick and I slept until noon. Thanks for opening that window, you may have saved me from an early death." He looks back at Louie and curls his shoulders up in a chuckle.

"You h'ar a mess my friend; you should 'ave washed your face and combed your hair. Remember z'at when you travel wi's me. Is z'at too much to ask, mon ami?"

"Of course not Louie; I will go wash up; you order my toast and coffee… I'm not in shape for breakfast yet."

Soon Smitty is back at the table and coffee and toast is being served.

"Now does zat smell pretty good, mon ami? You look much better; I shall enjoy my toast…take a guess where I have been hired, zuh fellow knows you well."

"Oh for cryin' out loud, did you get a job at ol' Eddie Langevin's grocery store?" Smitty waits for Louie's reply.

"I certainly did! What is wrong w's zat?" Louie looks puzzled.

"Well, nothing really, I know him well; he spends a lot of time in Red River. He owns a grocery store there too. He's a greedy little Frenchman, always tryin' to get a dime ahead of everyone!"

"Well, he seems to me to be a nice friendly fellow; he offered me a fair wage and more if I am a good worker."

"Oh, he's alright, we are still good friends. He just kicked my ass out of his store a couple of months ago…I was trying to buy a bottle of vanilla early in the morning, ha, ha, ha…" He rubs his belly with laughter.

"He says I can begin work tonight h'unloading stock off a steamboat down at zuh docks."

Well that's real good Louie, I am so happy to see you back that I hate to leave you and go home. Your Mama will be so disappointed you never came home with me."

"You might h'as well be honest w'is her Smitty. I am not ready to go home until h'after my retreat…until then…I do not wish to see anyone. You may tell her zat for me. H'it will save me from writing a letter h'at z'is time."

"I'll be happy to do that for you, my friend. I just don't understand."

"God knows my heart, mon ami…I h'am still very h'upset from leaving zuh Priesthood, h'after six years of study…and unrequited expense."

"Okay, we'll leave it at that. I don't feel any guilt at all any more. It bothered me for a while…then I just said 'To hell with it; I can't let it ruin my life."

"You do 'ave a good point, mon ami. I will s'nk h'about your view to a certain extent…I h'am still committed to zuh Catholic Church h'and to my God, 'owever…h'it gives me peace."

"Good for you Louie, me too. To a certain extent! I must say good-bye, my friend; thank you for the breakfast." He reaches out and shakes Louie's hand.

"Merci, mon ami, I h'appreciate h'all your h'information h'on Red River. H'it will make h'it easier to go back now…h'after I do my retreat."

***

Louie catches on fast to all the workings of the retail business. He manages to get along very well with Monsieur Edward Langevin.

He has established himself at St. Joseph Mission, which is…incidently, where he spent his last night with his beloved Papa, back in 1858.

As a special confirmation from the Lord; Louie is overwhelmed when he learns who actually is serving as the Parish Priest at St. Joseph. *H'it is another miracle of Divine providence,* Louie thinks to himself as he pumps the hand of his old instructor, Father Lafloche, from St. Boniface.

After a long visit answering questions and reminiscing the days of his Greek and Latin instruction, in preparation for the Seminary, Louie feels very content with Father Lafloche. He vows to himself that he will attend Mass every Friday night and Sunday morning. *He could have been very upset with me; I suppose he got over it in time. '…oh blessed Mother and almighty God, grant that Father Taché may also get over it.' Mama says he is still bitter.*

Another great thing that has happened to him since he arrived is his little black saddle horse. He purchased it at the local stables and he quickly decides to name him Blackie… after his Papa's old saddle horse.

The fellow that runs the Livery stable has become a good friend of Louie's and he has also given him a nice little black Collie dog, her name is Madame. Louie is overjoyed with his 'petit famille'.

"Merci, Marcien! I can barely wait until I get back to Red River now! I want to give this little 'Madame' to my brother Charles. I may give 'Blackie' to my little brother Alexandre...he is a nice, quiet, well behaved horse, yet he has lots of spirit. He gets me to Mass ten miles away in fifteen or twenty minutes...tapway, merci!"

"Oui, mon ami, they make a good pair!" says Marcien. Blackie snorts and Madame wags her tail happily; Louie has won himself two faithful friends.

*Glossary

There are no Footnotes in this chapter.

Chapter Twenty

Antoine Gingras', St. Joseph, Minnesota: 1868...

Fall has turned into winter and Louie is still enjoying his job at Monsieur Longevin's; however, he is becoming restless. His Teaching certificate has arrived months ago and he still is enjoying his new career in retail. *I will know when it is time for me to teach; now is not the time.*

He has been putting Antoine Gingras off for three months, to go to work for him in his dry goods store at St. Joseph and the temptation is strong to go to work in a clothing store.

Monsieur Gingras has become good friends with Louie through meeting him at Mass every Sunday at St, Joseph Mission.

Antoine was immediately struck with the poise and charisma of young Louie...he had been very good friends with Riel Sr. and Louie appears to have all the same attributes as Louie Sr., and more.

Monsieur Gingras carries a line of men's clothing that caters to a clientele that is much more refined than he. His own wardrobe is of a better quality of shirts, hats and trousers; however, he is short and dumpy and no matter what he wears, he looks short and dumpy. He also caters to a large Metis clientele who appreciate his beaded vests, his sashes and riding boots. He is obviously covetous of Louie's handsome build and refined mannerisms, which is good for Louie's badly damaged self-image.

In some ways Antoine reminds him of his Papa. He loves to sing Metis River songs and tap his feet in time to his mouth organ. Some of his family dance the Jigs and Reels that Louie has missed so badly. He also sings 'scat' with his River songs that reminds him of his buddy Pierre L'Ambitieaux, "Tum-dee-dee-dum-dee-dee-dum-diddle-dum"...his feet tapping out the beat of an old traditional French song.

"I know that there are other grocers that Eddie could train, even though he may miss you. But, my friend, I need a man of your calibre to pitch the old line to my upper class clientele...you have it, I can see it!" He gives Louie familiar Metis wink; again...he is reminded of his Papa. "Think about it Louie, I could even put you in a store at Red River... in time." He chatters away in French which suits Louie just fine!

"You nearly have me convinced Antoine. If you find me a place to board at St. Joseph I will take you up on it." His French is a bit faster than usual... he is obviously excited.

"Well, I have been after you since you arrived at St. Joseph, I would even be willing to give you a room free of charge."

***

The change in jobs has been good for Louie and he loves outfitting Antoine's clients with the latest in fashions from Chicago and New York.

Winter has gone by very quickly with all the responsibilities that Antoine has given him. He has so much confidence in him he leaves him to run his dry goods business without a worry.

Louie takes his job very seriously; however, by the time the May birds are singing and the pastures have become yellow with crocuses, his heart is yearning to head north...home to see his family. *I must speak to Father Lafloche and make arrangements for my retreat very soon.*

Louie has left Mass and the sun is shining as he throws the saddle back on Blackie, tightens his cinch and climbs on for the familiar little ride out to the 'hill'. As he reaches the top of the little hill he wraps the reins around the saddle horn, unties the bedroll from the back of the saddle and spreads it out under his 'thinking tree'. He has brought his Bible and prayer book to read awhile, until his eyes get tired.

Sometimes he has a good nap under that old tree…it has a somewhat archaic appearance…Louie feels the comfort of the huge canopy as he nestles his back up against the bark.

He opens the lid on his canteen and has a long drink of water and pours Madame a drink into his hand before he takes a bite from the piece of bannock that Madame Gingras prepared for him this morning.

He gives Madame a bite; then, as he raises his eyes to give thanks, he scans the familiar beauty of his precious and most private, panoramic view. Then…he sees something that he has never seen out here before...

Three eagles are moving down from the rise, far off in the distance. They glide down closer and continue to circle within view…deep within his spirit he hears the words… "My son, remove the shoes from off your feet… for the ground on which you stand is Holy ground." He removes his riding boots and rises up from his blanket.

The little Collie dog is lying on the ground looking up at Louie; she wags her curly black tail, as though to express her approval. Louie squints his eyes to the skies, the eagles are still circling, "My Holy Father…what must I do?"

"The time has come for your cleansing and communion." Louie listens for more instruction, but there is a long silence. The sound of a crow in the distance breaks the silence…Louie has to smile at his rudeness.

Suddenly, a great feeling of peace floods over Louie and he watches as the eagles finish their last round and fly swiftly to the ridge and disappear up over the horizon.

Louie looks down at his dog, "Madame, did you see that?" he asks in French.

His dog lies down beside him as he pulls back on his shoes. She licks his hand as he straightens his pant cuffs, "No one would ever believe this, my friend. But, we shall gather our things and head for St. Joseph as soon as possible. My time has come."

Louie holds Blackie to a trot as they head back to St. Joseph, tears are streaming down his face and a large painful lump has formed in his throat. *I have looked forward to a retreat for two years but now, for some reason...I am dreading it. I guess facing up to the truth is never easy.*

He waters his horse; then, ties the reins into a loose slip-knot around the hitching rail. Then he goes back to the trough and gives his face and hair a good sopping. He pulls the neckerchief from his neck and dries off. Then he combs his hair and pushes the waves back into place.

I shall wait for an opportune time to get Father Lafloch alone...then I shall ask him if he will be my Confessor. I feel he will work with me and not be judgemental towards me. He already knew about my sin of abandoning the Priesthood and has never judged me for it. Tomorrow is Saturday...I shall ask permission to meet him in his office after my day is done at the store.

As Louie steps up onto the front veranda of the mission, he can see Father Lafloch through the screen door.

He greets him quietly as he comes through the door. "Bon soir, Father. May I 'ave a word wis' you for a moment?"

"Most certainly, my boy, what's on your mind?" They both seat themselves; Father Lafloch has chosen the rocking chair and begins to rock gently, back and forth.

"My Father, there is something I must tell you." He reverts back to his Montreal French; the old priest is comfortable with the familiar dialect of the Seminaries.

"The sisters are about ready to serve our evening meal; we have a few moments if you prefer to talk privately, or we can talk at the table, if you care to join us."

"Thank you, sir, but I would prefer to talk privately. I shall be brief, but I must decline your invitation to dinner. I am fasting until after I have had confession and communion, sir... due to what I am about to tell you."

"Go ahead, my boy, I am anxious to hear what you have to say." He takes off his spectacles and slips them into his tunic pocket.

Louie's dark eyes are beginning to fill with tears, "I have finally heard from God, Father." He squeezes at his moist curls; the old priest nods his head, "Go on, my boy."

"It happened this afternoon, out on the rise, as I sat in meditation under my thinking tree." He looks deeply into Father Lafloche's eyes, "Father, it was a very brief encounter...I wish it had been longer."

"Yes, yes...go on." Lafloch is rubbing his long white beard and smiling. He has heard Louie speak of his tree and he is enchanted with Louie's stories of the beauty of nature, the sounds of the birds and the freedom of the animals out on the prairie.

Louie relates to him the glory of the atmosphere as he is compelled to be silent and to remove his shoes. Father Lafloche is staring at him intently, he says not a word until Louie is silent, staring out at the sunset, "My time has come Father; we may begin my retreat."

"It shall be my pleasure to work with you on your journey through, what may be, a painful experience."

The old priest shakes his hand and Louie agrees to meet with him on Sunday afternoon.

He unties his horse and reins him back out to the road; Madame follows along faithfully, wagging her tail as she trots close behind.

Louie reflects on his meeting with Father Lafloche all the way back to his comfortable residence at Monsieur Gingras' Trading Post.

Sunday afternoon Louie saddles up Blackie and heads back to the mission. He has had a lot of time for looking back over the changes in his life that have unfolded since the death of his father in '64.

Sometimes it all seems like a dream and during times of sleepless nights and fitful dreams…it seems much more like a nightmare. Louie remembers a verse from his Bible: "Come unto me all ye who are weary and heavy laden…and I will give you rest."* KJV.

I am beginning to feel more comfortable about this retreat, even after spending time with my Mama's prayer book; I tossed and turned all night. Strangely enough, I am not the least bit tired. My mind, body and spirit are all set for another encounter with my Lord…I can hardly wait.

He reins Blackie over to the hitching rail, if Father Lafloch is ready he will take his horse over to the pasture, "You stay and keep Blackie company, Madame dog."

"You curse your dog?" Sister Saville is holding the screen door open for Louie.

"No, no, my Sister…it is a joke. Is the Father in?" Louie is still standing by his horse.

"Oui, he is waiting to see you." Sister Saville is as abrupt as her brother, Father Saville, who was serving here at St. Joseph, back in '58, when Louie was leaving for Montreal.

"I will be back in 10 minutes; I must tether my horse in the grass; he had water before we left, I just wanted to make sure the Father was in."

"I will tell the Father that you are here." Sister Saville pulls her skirts through the doorway, goes back in and shuts the door quickly; the mosquitoes are best left outside. He unbridles his horse and walks him swiftly to the pasture closeby.

Before long Louie is greeting Father Lafloch; the feeling of excitement he has had in the pit of his stomach is slowly turning to nausea.

"Good afternoon, my boy, you are right on time. Come into my office and get comfortable" He glances at Louie's palid face, "Would you like a glass of water, my boy?"

"Oui, merci, Father, I am feeling a bit faint."

After a few moments, Louie is settled in a padded chair across from Father Lafloch, who is leaning back in an easy chair waiting… Louie takes another long drink of water.

"You are welcome to put your feet upon this footstool; there is room for both of us. If Sister Saville brings refreshments we will have to sit back; she may want to set her tray on it."

"I am feeling much better, Father; I may get sleepy if I get too comfortable. I will not be eating until after my confession and communion." Louie sets his hat on the floor and sits up straight.

"Well, my son, where would you like to begin?"

"That is where it all began; please forgive me Father; I love to hear you call me 'my boy', you were close to my Papa and you are close to me. But when that young Priest at St. Sulspice brought me the news of my Papa, he called me 'my child'. I got very angry with him, almost violent. He was ripping my world apart and treating me like I was a snot-nosed child. I have never seen him since but if I could…I would tell him how sorry I am for treating him like he was guilty of my father's death. That was where my sinful path began… I would think."

Father Lafloch excuses himself for interrupting, "Before we go any further Louie, would you like to ask remission for your actions at that time? It is not unlikely that a person recieving such news would be in a shocked state of mind; however, it is not up to me to judge; you may ask and receive absolution as we pray." Louie begins by making the personal sign of the Cross.

"Father God, I do so pray. Absolve me of those haunting memories of my father's death, and the guilt of my behavior that follows also, amen."

Father Lafloch makes the sign of the Cross on Louie's forehead using his blessed Holy water, "In the name of the Father, Son and the Holy Ghost. Praise be to God."

There are many things that have haunted Louie over the years; he is careful to confess everything that he has been remembering...the tears are flowing and Louie can feel the burden of guilt lifting from off his shoulders.

While he is being honest, it occurs to him that he needs Father Lafloch's opinion on Bishop Bourget's ultramontane Theology.

"Father, I must ask you if some of the conversations I have had with Bishop Bourget are out of line."

Father Lafloch leans forward, "I am ready to listen...I remember how you spoke of Father Bourget and how you held him in such high esteem, go ahead, my boy."

"Being so ill with depression at the time, it may sound a bit strange, but... our discussions, at times by correspondence, were always very open. It was not unusual to speak of a new 'Catholic System' in the 'New World'. We spoke openly about new policies whereby... Priests would eventually marry, but only to nuns who were also dedicated to God." Father Lafloch interjects, "Is this because of your marriage you say was annulled?"

"No, although I felt qualified to speak to the subject. But, consequently, I learned some very disturbing history regarding the sins of the 'old world', the corruption that resulted in excommunication from the Church...the sin of sexual deviancy, it became rampant, apparently."

"Those things are rarely spoken of, except for in the confession box." The Father sits back and drums his fingers on the arms of his large overstuffed chair.

"Now that is what I am concerned about. At this point it may seem irrelevant to my life today but, no, it is very relevant. Am I to confess my concession to an unorthodox ultramontane theology that even led me to believe..." Louie hesitates to continue, "I am sorry Father..." Father Lafloch smiles at Louie, "Continue, my boy." ...that Father Bourget could be in standing as the new Pope for the 'new world'?" *Surely he is not going to laugh...*

"Now, just a minute, my boy... one thing at a time; I will deal with your first question...yes, I believe you would certainly find some relief in repenting to God... an infatuation that may or may not have merit, but is definitely out of your league or at the least...none of your business. Excuse me Louie for being so blunt...but thank you for being so honest. Now, let us pray."

Once Louie has poured out his heart to both God and man, he begins to sit up straighter and he feels the tightness leaving from around his face.

He lets out a big sigh and smiles at the Father, "Merci, merci...I finally feel free, thank you Jesus, precious Mary and Joseph; I have waited for this a long time, merci."

"Now, my boy, go and sin no more. That is to be our goal, we are human; we will make mistakes. But we must learn from them and if we do fall into sin we must be quick to repent before it grows into a wall. That wall will separate us from God, every time, until we humble ourselves before Him, once more."

"Thank you Father, I am ever so grateful for your gracious prayers and unconditional love, praise be to God."

"Oui, my boy, praise be to God. You are more than welcome to break your fast with us at supper tonight or you can also take your communion right here in my study."

"I guess I would prefer to continue our time together here in your study. If you don't mind we can finish up with a private communion."

Louie is still in his chair basking in the glow of forgiveness.

"Of course we can have a private communion, my boy." He lifts a little brass bell from his desk. It has barely tinkled when Sister Saville knocks on the door.

"Come in, Sister. We will need a tray of Communion elements, sil vous plait." She smiles and leaves.

"She will be back in a few minutes, Louie. It has been a good day, has it not?"

"Oui, it has been a good day, Father."

"I expect you will be seeing Father Taché before long after you arrive back in Red River. If you find him aloof don't let it bother you too much. He has changed over the years; maybe he is just showing his age.

He showed me a letter he received from the Director at Sulspice. I remember one thing it said was …better that you would be a good Christian than a bad Priest."* Louie looks at him and smiles,

"I would have likely taken offence to that yesterday…today I am inclined to agree. What did Taché have to say about that?"

"Well, my boy, you have to realize there is a lot of truth in that statement. Some of the Priests we accepted from the old country are expulsions from their duties in France. Unfortunately, one of the most common confessions are regarding sexual deviancy, that is why Paul said in the new Testament, "It is better to marry than to burn."

"Oui, Fazzer, h'it is so true." Father Lafloch studies Louie's face, "The light is back in your eyes, my boy."

"The last time I visited him, he had lost the light from his eyes; they would light up his countenance when we would speak of you. You must realize, my boy, he had also lost sight of his goal in life…we must pray for him also. He will need to forgive you."

He scratches at his beard. "I do not wish to judge him, but you asked. There is nothing wrong with having a goal; that is good. I believe it becomes wrong when you begin to take credit for your success. Then if things change you do not have the flexibility to allow God to reveal a different path. It may not be the same path exactly, but it is still His will. You see what I am saying? It can become a personal vendetta instead of a divine destiny, or even worse…it can become an obsession. That is not healthy… you stop looking to God for guidance." He takes his spectacles from his pocket, hooks them behind his ears and looks straight at Louie.

"Your countenance is aglow with the glory of God. Sit for a while and enjoy it; you have been given a fresh start, my boy; now take it easy and continue to seek God's guidance."

When Louie arrives back at the Gingras' Trading Post, he sees a Pinto horse tied outside the front veranda, *I guess I will retire to my room, I don't even feel hungry…it looks like they have company…that horse is not familiar for this time of day.*

He enters the foyer, hangs his old black felt hat on the hat tree and puts his riding boots in the boot shelf.

Suddenly he is grabbed by the hand and spun around, "Louie, you son-of-a-gun!"

Louie looks up and there is Pierre wearing a big old Red River smile. Louie grabs him in a big bear hug, "Pierre! Where 'ave you been? Mama usually brings me greetings from you."

"I just rode in from St. Paul; I 'ave been h'in Montreal, you big goof! You h'are now a man, and a damn good-looking one at dat! Hee, hee, hee, hee!" A high winnying laugh fills the room.

"Much 'as changed in zuh last ten years but s'ank God you h'ar not... you still look zuh same, sound zuh same, (he sniffs his shoulder) and still smells zuh same!" Louie is so excited; his old Red River patois is suddenly showing.

"Louie, you can't imagine 'ow I 'ave looked forward to dis day." Pierre's eyes are glistening with tears.

"Me also, mon ami." Louie takes out his handkerchief and blows his nose. *I will be careful to refrain from the Montreal accent now that I am back with my people of the Red River patois.*

"Well, my friend, are you ready to go home?" Pierre is looking at him with a big smile.

"You bet I h'am ready, Chawam*! First I must speak to my boss."

Madame Gingras appears in the doorway, "Antoine is out back unloading supplies for the store. If you hurry you can give him a hand." Louie has grown fond of Madame Gringas and her 'no nonsense' French. She speaks her mind and eliminates the fancy talk.

"You lead duh way, Chawam. You should know yore way around 'ere by now."

"I can guess what Antoine is doing; we got a shipment of flour, sugar, oatmeal and beans in from St. Louis yesterday."

Pierre makes a big job of rolling up his sleeves; then he flexes his muscles as they enter the shed,

"Do you need two good men, my friend?"

"Yes, you won't be so frisky when we get that wagon unpacked." Antoine gently tosses a fifty pound sack of flour up onto a pile; then, he stands back, raises his dusty old cowboy hat and wipes the sweat off his brow with his handkerchief.

Pierre is tickled with Antoine's remark, he giggles as he begins to count his trips balancing a fifty pound bag on his shoulders, hanging onto the corners; then, swinging the bags around, he lets the momentum carry it up onto the pile.

Louie has decided to take care of the twenty pound bags of suger; he knows he's not in the shape that Pierre is, "Your years in the freighting business is showing on you my friend; I will not be competing with you, I'm afraid." Louie gives a little giggle.

"Merci, mes ami, you shortened my day, merci." Antoine is ready for a cup of tea and a pipeful.

As they take turns at the basin Madame Gingras meets them at the door. "You are finished Antoine?"

"Oui, my friends made a quick job of it." They all stand back and brush the flour off their clothes and tap their hats on the railing of the veranda. Then they step up to the outside washstand to freshen up before supper.

"It is very nice to see you Pierre. Louie has been speaking of you every day." She ushers them into the huge dining area between the kitchen and parlor. Antoine loves to have parties and like most Metis homes, the only rooms closed off are the bedrooms; they need a lot of room for feasting and dancing.

"Make yourselves at home boys; we will smoke and rest until supper, come sit down." He pulls two chairs out before he sits down to fill his pipe.

Louie generally has a half a pipe after supper, but he has refrained from smoking during his fast. Pierre loads his pipe while Louie fills Antoine in on his plans to return to Red River soon, "I would love to go with Pierre but I don't wish to leave you before harvest."

Louie is so enjoying the old Red River French; but, he is also eager to hear the old Metis slang when he returns to Red River.

"Louie, I knew that you would want to go home with Pierre, the boys are bringing in one of their friends to pitch hay. You go and don't worry about anything; we will be fine. It has been a pleasure to have the son of my old friend here with me."

"I could say the same, sir. I sometimes can almost feel the presence of my Papa as you speak." Louie rakes his comb through his hair and pushes it into place.

"You have a fine sounding French now, my boy. Your Papa sounded a bit like you." Antoine takes a drag from his crooked stemmed pipe and lets a set of smoke rings drift into the air. "I suppose he would have sounded just like you if he had stayed around the Priests as long as you did." He is enjoying a steady gaze at Louie Junior's features; it has only been two years since he lost his old life-long friend, Louie Sr. He has an identically thick moustache but has generally been clean shaven otherwise.

Strange how I do not feel any judgement coming from Antoine; I believe he is a genuine friend. "Pierre told me the same thing; he says I grew up to look like my Papa."

"Well, mon ami, when you get dressed up in your fancy duds you look like a professor or a politician!" Antoine has a little chuckle as he holds his pipe firmly between his teeth.

"Don't laugh Antoine, I saw the boxes of books we have to ship out to Red River!" Pierre begins to chuckle as he says,"Besides, the bugger has a Teacher's certificate!" Then he bursts into a loud laugh. Louie sits with his legs crossed taking it all in with a grin; he knows that Pierre is brimming with pride.

"You could have been over here at the mission teaching instead of scraping horseshit out of my barns!" Antoine throws his head back and howls with laughter. He is nearly as loud as Pierre.

"Non Monsieur, I needed to do that work; I have been feeling very healthy lately."

Madame Gingras enters with her large round cuttingboard bearing a large oven-baked bannock and a wide-bladed butcher-knife, "Antoine, bring the pot of stew, sil vous plait."

The conversation ends as the boys pull up to the long gingham covered dining table. Before Antoine can return with the large pot, Madame has cut large pieces of bannock and set them on the edges of the cutting board, "Pierre, I know how you like to tear off your bannock when h'it's hot, but I made dis bannock last night, it's still nice and fresh."

"Oh, Madame Cecile, you are duh bes' bannock maker h'in St. Joseph, tapway Louie?" Pierre looks at Louie who is deep in thought, "Oui, mon ami, she h'is a superb cook, no doubt." *It will be the last time we break bread together for a long time, if we are leaving for St. Cloud tonight.*

Antoine sets the big pot of stew on the cutting board and begins dishing everyone up, "Do you mind saying a blessing, my boy?" He looks over at Louie; he gives a nod.

Once they all receive their bowls, they bow their heads, "In the Name of the Father, Son and Holy Spirit we give thanks for this food. We ask a blessing upon these wonderful hosts, upon their home and upon their family. We ask a blessing upon this food and upon the journey, mon ami, Pierre and I will begin tomorrow, back home to our loved ones. We thank you for your blessings upon us, merci, merci…amen."

*Glossary

There are no Footnotes in this chapter.

Chapter Twenty One

St. Vital, Red River: 1869...

Antoine steers his team carefully as they pull his wagon up onto one of the big plank docks at the St. Cloud landing*, on the Mississippi River.

Although it is just getting dusk, two black dock hands are busy lighting the lamps along both edges of the docks. A steam Freighter is chugging away patiently, while two rough-looking river rats unload cargo from a wagon. They pile it onto a large dolly, then they wheel it down a ramp into the waiting boat.

As soon as they pull out of the way, Antoine drives his team of bays up closer to the ramp. Pierre holds onto his and Louie's horses as Antoine helps Louie load his three boxes of books onto a dolly and take them on board.

Once the two saddle horses are tied and given feed, the two men go back up to say their good-byes to Antoine. By now the moon is shimmering on the river as if to welcome Louie home from his long absence.

"Man, don't dat ol' Mississippi look good tonight, Chawam?" Pierre and Louie make their way back out to where Antoine has turned his team around. "Tapway, mon ami, I h'am so h'excited I can scarcely breathe." Louie says, as he rubs his eyes.

"You boys 'ave a good trip 'ome, now. Bon voyage!" He reaches down and shakes each of their hands, then gives them a salute, touching the brim of his old cowboy hat; then, he clucks his tongue and the team continue their treck up the river hill.

Pierre asks a dock hand standing by, "How long now before the steamer pulls out?"

The husky black fellow smiles at Pierre, "Well, you knows, sir, it always seems to take at leas' fifteen minutes, den we gits a blas' o' dat ol' fog horn an' its time ta raise duh landin'."

Pierre pulls a couple of coins out of his pocket and hands it to him. "Would you mind not raisin' duh landin' until Louie an' I gets back on board; we got somethin' urgent to do?"

"You go right ahead sir. Be back in fifteen minutes d'ough or dey'll have my hide!"

Pierre turns to Louie and says, "Astom, mon ami, head for dat talles' tree over d'ere!"

They run and jump through the shoulder high willows until they reach the tall oak timbers, then Pierre sneaks along over to a tall tree, squatting and squinting, "Here it is Chawam! Look, bote h'our initials, 'P.L. & L.R. 1958.' Can you believe it?" Pierre grabs Louie and swings him around twice. The third time Louie trips and lands on the ground! Like two little boys, they jump and holler...then, they run as fast as they can back to the boat; Madame is happily keeping up with them.

Just as they hit the draw bridge the fog horn belches out its long drawn out sounds that echo up around the river bend. "What a sight, my friend, look at dat ol' moon shinin' on duh water!"

"Pierre, I will never forget dis night, what a sight!" Louie gets a whiff of the animals on the lower deck, "Should we check on duh horses Chawam?" Louie is a few steps behind Pierre,

"No, don't worry, dose boys downstairs takes better care of our horses dan dere own kids. Heh, heh, heh!"

"I shall keep Madame up 'ere wit' me; she h'is very well-behaved.

***

It seems like no time at all before they have disembarked from the steamer at Cross Lake Landing and loaded their luggage up onto a stagecoach. Louie and Pierre tie their saddle horses to each side of the rear of the coach then they climb aboard. They are greeted by an old grey-haired couple, "We're Molly and Sam, pleased to meet you both."

The elderly lady is pleasantly plump and has obviously brought a bit of Ireland to the new frontier. Louie gives them his most handsome smile, invoked mainly by her shawl, which is crocheted in one of his Mama's favourite patterns.

"Nice to make your acquaintance, Ma'am. We h'ar Louie h'and Pierre, he motions to his buddy. Where h'are you headed?" Louie tips his hat and slips into the patois of the west.

He is not fooling anyone, "Nice to meet you too, son. That's a great French accent you have…different from folks around here. We'll be getting off at Pine River; how about you?"

"We will be changing coaches h'at Fargo, Nort' Dakota, zen we shall head nort' to Red River."

"We call it Winnipeg nowadays but it's in duh Red River area. I reckon we will travel by steamer a fair spell. Louie will be surprised at how duh river traffic has grown since he left home and lived h'over in Montreal for six years." Pierre is the talker so Louie takes out his Mama's prayer book and reads until he dozes off.

He awakens in time to bid the old couple farewell as they board a coach and go on their way.

Then Louie and Pierre settle in for the night at Pine River so they can rise early for a fresh start the next day.

After making a few stops at little roadside Inns where they water and feed the horses, have a bite to eat and freshen up, they finally arrive at Detroit Lakes where they spend one day looking around.

They check in at the Stage Depot to tag their baggage for Fargo, North Dakota then they take their saddle horses for a good trot and find a big tree to take a nap.

Louie can hear their hobbled horses chewing grass; there are familiar birds singing in the trees. He listens to a sound that triggers a memory…a memory that brings a twinge of sadness and yet a strange feeling of joy… it is the sound of water slapping at the edge of the lakeshore. The smell of the closeness of the grass…then the fragrance of Marie-Julie's hair…

Louie is suddenly awakened by the sound of Pierre's angry shouts, "Get to hell outta here!" Two fellows, one white and the other Indian, are sneaking to their bareback ponies, packing away their saddles. "Drop dose saddles, right dere!"

They quickly drop the saddles and take a running leap up onto the backs of their ponies; one turns and fires a shot at Pierre. As quick as lightening, Pierre draws his six-shooter and fires, the pistol flies from the hand of the white fellow and he digs his bootheels into the flanks of his frightened pony. In moments they are out of sight.

"Now you see, Chawam, why I insisted h'on wearing my gun; we h'are not h'in Montreal now." Pierre blows the smoke from his gun barrel and slides a bullet into the empty chamber.

"You h'ar so right, mon ami; I reckon I felt we were inviting trouble. You are a heck of a shot, my friend. Do you suppose we can get a deer when we h'ar on land?"

"You never forgot, Chawam! We will start 'unting h'as soon h'as we get close to 'ome. It gets so hot h'in July, h'our meat would not last. We would need to spend h'anudder day to dry duh meat. I don't blame you for being in a 'urry to get 'ome, but I could 'ardly talk you h'into taking dis break today."

Once they had walked, stretched and rode, they were hungry and tired, "Well, mon Chawam, we will be back on duh road at seven in duh morning. H'as soon h'as we feed and water h'our 'orses we will 'ave supper h'and hit duh hay."

"Sounds good to me, my friend." Louie gives him a firm quick response in French; they have used very little French for several days.

***

Arriving in Fargo is like seeing a strange new city; so much has changed, Louie is mesmerized by the industry that has gone up on the edge of the city, "I will not be letting you h'out of my sight, Chawam; dis place 'as grown so drastically; I don't see one t'ing dat I recognize."

"Don't worry, mon ami; tomorrow morning we will be boarding a steam freighter on duh ol' Red River. For sure you won't recognize old Fort Garry; it is very quiet dese days."

The docks are buzzing with activity as the two men arrive in a shuttle wagon to load their luggage onto the last steamer on their journey.

Louie hangs back with Madame and the horses; he needs to savour the sights sounds and smells of the old Red River, it seems to be not so green any more. It must be caused by the steamers that have taken over the freighting industry. *For some reason it just doesn't smell quite the same.*

Still, nothing can take away the thrill of being back on the banks of the old Red River. Louie takes their horses below while Pierre helps tag the crates of books and the trunk Louie bought in Chicago for his mama. He has been buying little gifts and surprises for his siblings for over a year now and there is still room for Louie's good clothes in the top bin of the chest. It is a fine piece of furniture and generally fits snuggly up against the wooden crates of books. Their tags will take them to Pembina, then on ahead to Winnipeg by stagecoach.

The men will arrive the next day by horseback, after a short visit with friends at St. Agathe.

***

Louie is not certain, even after a few hints, who it is that lives in St. Agathe. He just knows that it is a relative and that it is someone who always says, "Instant deer, guaranteed!"

It sounds so familiar that it keeps Louie puzzled for over an hour, "Hey, Chawam, for duh love 'o Bessie, who h'are we meeting up wit'?"

"Can't you h'allow me duh pleasure of giving you a surprise?" Pierre shakes his head back and forth, "For cryin' h'out loud; h'it's someone who knows how to yodel!"

"Now dat's not fair ei'der, half h'our relatives know how to yodel, for criminiation!" Now he is definitely back in the patois. His mind quickly flashes to Madame Sophie, back in Montreal, her hand to her forehead in shock: '*Oh, what a waste of six long years... of classical academia at dat! I remember a saying of St. Paul, 'When in Rome, you do as duh Romans do.'Now I know damn well my Sophie would not behave like dat. She is a humorist...she would laugh...* Louie suddenly bursts into the loudest, longest laugh Pierre has ever heard; and he has heard some winners.

With every 'ha ha!', Louie slams down his fist on the saddlehorn until Blackie can't take any more. He rares in the air and Louie goes for the bucking of his life. He hangs onto the horn with one hand while reaching for his reins with the other.

"Hang on, my friend, 'ere is your udder line. Now snub 'eem down evenly wit' bote reins, Settle down, now Blackie!" He commands, and Blackie stops in his tracks.

Louie slides down Blackie's shoulder and is piled up on the ground, still laughing, "You crazy ass! K'moochiwin!" (You are crazy)He t'ought he 'ad a stranger on ee's back. Now, tell me what was so damned funny?"

Pierre hands Louie his reins, "No, not 'til you tell me where we're going." Louie looks up at him from the ground, smoothing his moustache and lowering one eyebrow like his Papa.

He takes the reins, both in one hand, and grabs the saddle horn with the other and swings into the saddle. He begins to rub Blackie's shoulder, "Sorry dere boy, take it h'easy."

"I told you it's a surprise, now we only 'ave about five miles to go; dat ole sun is a-tellin' me it's close to supper-time. What do you say, mon ami?"

"Sounds good to me, I needed dat laugh more dan you'll ever know, my friend."

"I believe you Chawam, dere h'is nuttin' more healin' dan a damn good laugh. You can only take so much pain, den you gotta laugh, see your Priest, or howl at duh moon like a coyote."

"You know, Chawam, coming home, getting dis close…I feel all giddy. I really don't care if Bishop Taché is standing by duh door, I will grab him and hug him; I don't care if he uppercuts* me when I walk t'rough dat door." Louie begins to laugh all over again.

Upon reaching the top of a rise, they let the horses get their wind.

Louie sits back in the saddle and surveys the splendor of the old Red River, winding its way through the valley, everything is green and fluffy clouds are drifting along the horizon, "Man, dat is a nice little spread, my friend. I have dreamt of having a nice little spread like dat some day."

"Louie, you know what is really sad? Most of us boys do have a spread like dat; we just don't know how long we can keep dem."

"What are you saying, Pierre?" Louie looks at him puzzled.

"I have been hinting at it for days, to get you prepared. But I hated to be blunt wit you. You said you didn't like to come home to a bees nest; well dat's exactly what you h'are coming home to. Duh Canadian Government does not recognize h'our homeland, Chawam. Dey are chopping it into square farms, 160 acres a-piece and only duh rich farmers can afford duh lots next to duh river. It is as bad as your Mama says...she is not hysterical. She knows you are educated enough to help us keep our land...you know duh law, my friend."

Louie is squinting his eyes at two children and two dogs leaping and bounding towards them.

"Oncle, Oncle! Where wuz you?" Pierre pulls up his horse and dismounts, "Well, well, you h'ar a fast runner, my boy! Louie, remember Madeleine h'an Keiren's son, Bennie?" He hugs them both before climbing back up into the saddle.

"Pierre, you doggone trickster you! I am pleased to meet you, Sir Benjamin." He shakes Bennie's hand and asks, "Now who might dis charming young lady be? She is duh spit and h'image of Madeleine, except for duh red hair."

"Dis is Amy, onclé, what is your Mama cooking, my girl?" Pierre asks, as he pulls little Amy up onto the front of the saddle.

"Wah wah, onclé, I don't know!" She shrugs down low, giggling, with both hands over her mouth. Madame is barking and wagging her tail like crazy.

"Well, what kind of a cook's 'elper h'ar you, my girl? Bennie, grab aholt of Onclé Louie's hand." Louie pulls Bennie up high enough to reach the stirrup that is dangling empty; Bennie gives a heave and Louie has him seated behind him.

"You have grown tall since duh last time I saw you, my boy. How old h'are you now?" Bennie sits up straight and gives him a short answer, "I reckon I'll soon be twelve, sir."

"You know, I swear I 'ave seen your 'at somewhere before, Sir Benjamin. It looks familiar." Louie is grinning as he takes another peek at Bennie's hat.

"Sir, it is not a hat; it is a cap." Bennie lifts his little green cap up off an unruly mass of red hair.

"Did Keiren not wear a cap just like dat, Chawam?"

"Oui, you are right, mon ami. He could not find one for Bennie so he got his sister-in-law to make one."

"I bet it was your Tanté Angelique who made your cap; it is trés chic*, my boy." Louie tells him. "Merci, merci, mon onclé."

In the distance, there are two figures outside on the veranda, waving their welcome. In a few moments you can hear Madeleine yelling, "Hurry up, you guys, duh supper is ready, you slow-pokes!" The sound of Madeleine's mild accent, as she sings out her words, is music to Louie's ears.

As they pull their horses up to a stop, Louie is choked with emotion, *I really do not want to frighten these children by crying like a baby…*"Maddie, you h'ar a sight for sore eyes, I must 'ave a hug!"

While Pierre swings his sister around, Louie and Kieren have a big bear hug, "Man it's good to see you Louie; it's been a long, long time." Tears are glistening in their eyes; Bennie and Amy are looking on; they look anything but frightened; they are all smiles, making friends with Madame, who is licking their hands and wagging her tail.

"Come on inside; I will stir up a bannock that I can 'fry on the go', while we eat our stew. I learned how to can buffalo meat, Louie. My stew is nearly as good as your Mama's now, but not quite. Now that Keiren has learned how to cut blocks of ice and put them away in the root cellar in sawdust, we hardly make pemmican for ourselves, and I do a lot of canning. Help yourselves to the basin in the foyier. Throw out the children's water and take some clean out of the pail, we haul our water up from the river on the stoneboat.*" Madeleine has not changed; she rattles on whether you are listening or not.

The men gather around the table, Pierre rubs his hands together.

"What can I do to help, my sister?" Pierre is trying to tie on an apron and getting it all twisted. "Just stay out of my way; you might get scalded!"

"I think we have time for a half a pipe, my friend." Keiren pulls out two chairs at the table, "Astom, api*, mon ami."

"I reckon I'll join yous in a minute…soon as I get down Madeleine's big bread bowl."

"Bennie, you set places for your uncles, sil vous plait. My grease is nearly hot so I need to quickly stir up my dough." She scoops out one heaping dipper of flour into her bowl, puts the dipper back into the fifty pound flour sack and quickly ties it. From a shelf above her utility table she takes down three ten pound lard pails, one contains salt, one contains sugar, the other is filled with tallow* mixed with bacon drippings. After she shakes out a handful of baking powder, she throws in a pinch of salt and a small handful of sugar, and lifts it a couple of times to sift it and mix it, then she scoops back the middle and makes a 'well' for her water. She rubs a small amount of tallow into it before adding a half a dipper of water.

In a matter of two or three minutes she has her first four pieces of bannock sizzling in the skillet and turning a golden brown.

Amy is standing by watching her Mama, she removes her thumb from her mouth long enough to say, "Your bannock smells good, ma Mama."

"Merci, mon fils, you stay back now, this grease is 'tres chaud'*, my girl."

"Do you want me to set duh pot on duh table yet, Maddie?" Keiren has poked a few puffs of tobacco into his pipe and is listening to Pierre telling little stories.

"You know we 'ad a lot of fun on duh trail, tapway, my friend?"

"Oui, oui, mon ami, we 'ad a lot of laughs. Tapway, Tapway." Louie leans back and takes a long drag off his pipe.

"I bet you never dreamt a couple years h'ago dat your black robe was gonna turn into a pair of buffalo chaps*, eh Chawam? Heh, heh, heh."

"Well, you know, mon ami, I have begun to learn a lesson from St. Paul's writings, and dat is: …no matter what state I am in I should 'therewith be content.' It is a good thing to remember. You never know where your destiny may lead you."

"You know it's darn hard fer me to get over Louie being a grown man, let alone a philosopher and next ting to bein' a Priest. I have to say Louie…I am damn proud of you." Pierre gives Louie three good ones on the back.

"Well, if that's true, I am proud of you too, Louie. Now, would you mind saying a prayer before we eat?"

"Madeleine, I am so t'ankful h'and 'appy to be 'ome, I would be honored to pray for us."…Louie offers up a short, sincere prayer of thanks for all the blessings they have enjoyed throughout their journey…and now a sweet prayer of thanksgiving for the pleasure of this little family…blessings upon their home and upon their meal. He finishes the powerful French prayer with a "Hye, hye", a blessed Amen… in his beautiful Cree language.

"Thank you, Louie, you have beautiful prayers. Now Keiren could you fill our bowls, sil vos plait?"

"It is sad that Kookom and Mooshom passed away in your absence, Louie, but it could be worse. Everyone else is still here and still healthy even though there has been some violent clashes between our people and the greedy Orangemen. They keep sending more white settlers in, now there's a big Anglican Church in the Northwest surrounded by a whole settlement of them." Madeleine has always been known to speak the truth, no matter the cost. She is still full of grit if circumstances require it.

"Well, I know dat Madeleine is right, Chawam, but you gotta know dese are innocent people, dese settlers. Dey are sent out here promised all kinds 'o tings. 'Duh Promised Land' dey are callin' it in dose Eastern newspapers." Even though Keiren is tough as nails if need be, he generally opts to chose the peaceful route if possible.

"Tapway, my man, don't forget I was one of the first to take supplies to them when they were set to starve that winter. We all had to pitch in for them." Madeleine is speaking Mechif and Louie is spellbound by their conversation. Not only are they confirming his suspicions about what he is about to encounter when he arrives back at St. Boniface, but he is amazed at how well Keiren, the 'little red-headed Irishman' can speak Mechif.

"Do you fellows want your pie now or wait until the dishes are done?"

"Let's wait guys, it will taste better after we have some music." Keiren begins to move the chairs to the edge of the room. He rolls up the round braided rug and parks it in front of the fireplace.

"It looks like we are going to do a little steppin'," says Pierre.

Madeleine has filled the dishpan with warm water taken from the reservoir* at the right side of the cookstove. She sets it out on the cutting board and hands the children each a dishtowel. "We will join you in a minute boys, it will not take us long to do up these dishes, tapway, my children?"

"Oui, Mama, I want to jig!" Amy is all excited, "Settle down dere little sister; you will be breaking duh dishes." Bennie has rolled up his sleeves and is ready with his dishtowel.

Kieren gets out his harmonica and Pierre takes a guitar down from the wall, "What do you want to hear, my friend?" Louie is honored to be given the first request, "You know, one of the few familiar songs I used to hear in ballrooms when I was on a speaking tours in Montreal was 'Sailor's Hornpipe', I would be so 'appy to 'ear it done by my own people."

"Sounds good to me," says Keiren as he begins tapping his feet and playing a good, peppy version of 'Sailor's Hornpipe'. Pierre is smiling like a 'cat in the creamcrock'as he keeps up a nice spunky rhythm.

They play a couple more tunes then Pierre says, "Kieren, my brudder, 'ow would you like to go get a deer in duh morning?"

"Dat sounds like a great idea, one deer, guaranteed! I always know when he has work for me, he calls me, my brudder. Heh, heh, heh."

"Well Maddie, I guess it is up to you to take dese two young 'uns fer a couple 'o changes!" Keiren strikes up the familiar intro on his 'A' harmonica, then Pierre yells, "Red River Jig, omuh!"

"Astom, my boy. Come jig for your uncles!"

Louie sits and weeps bitter tears all the way through the song… clapping in time and wiping his eyes with his sleeves.

*Glossary

There are no footnotes in this chapter.

Chapter Twenty Two

Riel Farm, St. Vital: 1869...

After a two-day visit, some apple pie for the road, and a crock of canned deer meat, Louie and Pierre set out on the last leg of their journey, home to Red River.

Madeleine had insisted that she make hotcakes with chokecherry syrup for their breakfast.

"Oh come on my sister, you know dat h'it is only one hour to Madame Riel's house. You just need to steal some more visiting..." Pierre is back in the house from getting the horses fed and watered, ready for the road.

"Well of course, you crazy fool. We have not seen you for two months. We want him to stay one more night, eh, my children?"

"Oui, oui, mon onclé, stay, stay, sil vous plait?" Amy is jumping up and down. "Oui, mon onclé, we missed you, tapway!" Bennie is also pulling on him.

"You h'ar making h'it real tough on me, my favourite little people. You 'ave to t'ink of Onclé Louie, he is anxious to see 'is brudders h'and sisters... h'and especially 'is Mama... t'ink of h'it...he has not seen dem for ten years!" Pierre has seated himself at the table with both children hugging on him.

"Go ahead and make hotcakes, my sister. We will 'ave breakfast…tapway, mon Chawam?"

"Of course! We need to visit some more, tapway, mes ami?" Louie is grinning at the children, more than happy to accommodate them.

"Oh goody, goody!" Amy is off his lap leaping up and down again.

"We need to get washed up now…come h'on, mes ami!"

***

Louie gazes off in the distance at the beautiful old trail he left behind so many years ago, he smiles as he recalls the excitement of the morning, "Boy, doze crépes were delicious, mon ami."

"Tapway, dey were just what we needed to finish h'off h'our visit, meewasin!" Pierre is rubbing his belly.

"Now we shall be a bit more calm as we h'arrive h'at mon Mama's, instead of descending on her like a pair of hungry wolves…not dat h'it would bodder her. I cannot wait to see her face!"

Before they know it, the steeples of the St. Boniface Cathedral are coming into view, "Pardon moi, mon ami…I need to go in h'and pay my respects to my Lord wit'in duh walls of duh new cathedral. H'it broke my 'eart when Mama wrote me of duh fire*."

"Tapway, mon ami. H'it broke h'all our 'earts. Some even said dat it was arson…by duh Orangemen 'o course."

"Well, if dere is no proof, one should not be bitter about somet'ing dat is mere speculation." Louie ties his horse out front and walks, for the first time, up the solid new steps of St. Boniface Cathedral. He pulls open one of the big doors and makes his entrance…with a mixture of great reverence and a shadow of trepidation.

He bows his knee and dabs his fingers with Holy water, makes the sign of the cross and begins a five minute prayer of repentance and thanksgiving.

The Cathedral is empty, but he can feel the warm glow of a long-awaited blessing.

Pierre is waiting outside with the horses and Louie's dog; he knows how precious this time is for Louie.

They ride out onto the street again and suddenly a large black stallion is galloping toward them, "Now who in the hell are you draggin' into town, you trouble-makin' Lamito bastard!"

Louie is so startled he pulls his horse to a sudden stop. "Who is dis Pierre?"

"Oh, I would not waste my time worrying about dis useless mout' piece; he's nuttin' but a six-foot pile 'o bullshit!"

Louie leans on his saddle horn and stares down this stranger with his famous penetrating stare. The stranger rides past Pierre and suddenly hacks and spits; it misses Pierre and lands on Louie's dog. "The nerve, I will have to clean that!" Louie says in French with a look of disgust.

"You're in Canada now Frenchman, speak in English!"

"You get to hell outta 'ere, Scott. You h'are blocking h'our path!"

"Well, well, try and make me, you Lamito bastard!"

Pierre suddenly rides up to the black stallion and gives him two strikes with his reins across the flank, like a bullwhip. The stallion rares in the air and his rider lands on the ground like a ton of bricks.

"Who is dat, Chawam?" Louie asks as they ride away.

"Oh, you will likely see a lot more of him. Dat is Thomas Scott, and he likes to torment Metis people...he 'ates us and lets us know every chance he gets."

***

Louie cannot help himself; the last half mile is a trot that turns into a gallop as he sees his Mama out on the veranda shaking out a rug.

"Mama, ma Mama!" He jumps from the saddle to the ground and runs up onto the veranda, "My boy, my boy! Pierre! Where did you boys come from? Precious Jesus, Mary and Joseph! My boy has come home!" They rock back and forth in a tight hug, "Oh, ma Mama, I am so 'appy to see you! Praise be to God!"

Louie is shamelessly weeping, as tears flow freely. Julie is sobbing uncontrollably...Louie sets her onto the swing and sits down beside her, as he holds her hand to his wet face.

"Where are my siblings, Mama?" He has taken a clean white handkerchief from inside his vest and hands it to Julie.

"They are all gone off to work for the day and the younger ones are at school." Julie still prefers to speak French to her children. "They will all be home for supper except for Sara and Marie; they are at their missions. I am sorry Pierre, help yourself to the feed and water for the horses; I will go in and fix a lunch for you boys."

"Mama, let me look at you for a moment; you look so young for all you have been through. Even your hair, there is scarcely any white!"

Julie begins to slice some bread, "You know, my boy, it seems like you have been gone forever and it is so hard to believe my skinny little son has grown so big and strong!"

She puts bread and butter on the table and dishes up some chicken soup from off the stove into three bowls. "This soup is fresh from this morning;

there is plenty for our lunch. I was going to hang it down in the well to stay cool for supper. You can do that, my boy, when we are finished eating."

Pierre comes in from tending the horses, "Your garden looks good, ma Tanté."

"Yes, we will have some vegetables after all. Without any rain everyone is in a panic; but, our boys are not lazy. They have been hauling water up from the river on the stoneboat every evening. That way it has all night to soak into the ground."

"Tapway, Tanté. It is looking nice h'and green; Keiren 'ad to do duh same for his garden. Louie will be helping mon Joleine to keep h'our garden alive also. Sorry to be rude, ma tanté; I will need to head on over to my family h'as soon h'as we h'eat lunch."

"Well, do not worry, my boy, I understand. You have been gone a long time; your twins will have a fit when they see you coming!"

"Tapway, dey will tear my h'arms off! It is hard to be away."

"Ma Mama h'and I will be visiting h'all h'afteroon; I 'ave so much to tell you Mama; some will be happy news…and some will be sad." He scratches his head, just like his Papa.

"Me also, my boy; I will need to fill you in; I mostly told you of our family. There has been a lot happening here in the old valley; you will be surprised."

"I have tried to prepare him for the population explosion, Tanté and the changes in our churches and schools. He knows there is a lot of trouble with the Canadians, especially the Orangemen." Pierre explains to Julie in French.

"Meewasin, dat soup is delicious, Tanté Julie, merci."

"Give my love to Joleine, Marie and the rest of the clan."

"Oui, oui, ma tanté, I will tell dem. Take care now, Louie. I know you are going to Coutu's Meat Market tomorrow so h'if you run into Scott, just ignore him…he is h'all mout' h'and no action!"

***

Louie is curious about this new place Julie has moved into, "Do you mind, Mama, if I take a look around outside?" He peers out the back window at the barnyard.

"You just make yourself at home, my boy. Why don't we try and have you moved upstairs before they get home?"

"Oh, Mama, I would just as soon have them to help me move my things upstairs. It will take a little time, even with the boys helping; we can get to know each other that way." *When I unpack I want to see their faces as they receive their gifts.*

"Alexandre just fell asleep for his nap; he generally awakens just before the children arrive from school." Louie stands and looks down at Alexandre, "He will be rested and happy; he is a cute little guy. I shall have him polish my shoes."

"You are still a good planner my boy; that is good."

"I must admit, my boy, I am a bit nervous. Do you prefer that we speak in English?"

"Not at all Mama; it is wonderful to hear your French again." Julie grabs her old chore shawl and swings it over her shoulders; her hair is hanging in soft brown waves around her face, then folds into a gentle fat braid. "I shall come and show you around Louie; your Papa would have loved this place. There are all kinds of berries around here and I brought my own rhubarb root."

They walk around the full circumference of the garden and barnyard; Louie is delighted with Julie's little herd of healthy looking cattle and horses; she even has a nice pen of chickens and a couple of pairs of ducks and geese wandering around, "Have you gathered the eggs yet, Mama?"

"No, my boy, you go ahead, see if they are frightened of you." Louie bumps his head on the top of the doorway going into the henhouse. *Every once in a while I feel like a little boy…I suppose I need to remember to duck my head.*

Moments later he returns with his neckerchief filled with eggs, "They acted as though they knew me Mama."

"They see your mannerisms; you move like me and speak softly, like me"

"How long before the children get home from school?"

"They will ride right straight to the barnyard and tend their horses before they come in."

Louie gets a strange little impish look on his face, "Cést bon!* I will wait in the barn and when it is safe and the horses are eating…I will jump out and surprise them!"

Julie's eyes fill with tears, "Of course, they will never forget such a greeting as that, my boy!" She is laughing, but inside her heart is breaking, *my poor boy, he was robbed of ever playing with his brothers and sisters."* She dries her eyes with her apron.

"I am so sorry to be crying on such a special occasion; I am just so happy to see you home at last. The children will be home soon; I will go in and mix up some dumplings to go with our chicken. You can bring the chicken up from the well and set it on the stove to warm, then come back to the barn for your monkey business."

"I can hardly wait to see their faces, especially Charlie." Louie is beside himself with excitement.

“Remember, they may not know who you are!” Louie is washing up and getting his hair combed, “I will tell them right away; I don’t want to scare them to death.”

Louie has found a big comfortable Maple tree to lean his back up against as he sits under its wonderful shade. He takes out his Mama’s prayer book and reads Psalm 150*; he is feeling so blessed to be home at last. *Thank you my Lord and Savior for healing my broken heart and for…*

***

The sound of hoofbeats suddenly coming down the lane wakens Louie and drives him to his feet; the riders are barely coming into sight as he snuggles in behind the barn door, peeking through the crack. He grins as he sees them slow down for the corner of the garden fence, then their trot becomes a walk as they step up close to the water trough. *What a cute little boy, that must be Joseph, he looks to be about ten. Wah wah, dat must be Charlie; oh, for the love o’ Bessie, that must be Eulalie, what a lovely girl! Now I am embarrassed; should I jump out and yell? Oh well, God hates a coward!*

“Surprise!” he jumps around to the doorway of the barn…and everyone stops and stares. No one says a word. “Eulalie, you must remember your big brother Louie, from Montreal?”

“Oh Louie, Louie, Louie!” Eulalie has wrapped her skinny arms around Louie’s big frame and is jumping up and down…Julie runs down from the house and is laughing so hard she is holding her stomach.

“This is our Louie! We have waited for ten years to see him…he has grown into a man!” Each child takes a turn shaking Louie’s hand or hugging him…Louie begins to tremble, then collapses into a pile of hay with his face in his hands…he sits and sobs for two or three minutes. Then he pulls his big handkerchief from his vest pocket, wipes his eyes, then takes out his comb and combs his hair.

“Is all the straw out of my hair?” The girls jump over and quickly begin pulling the straws out, one at a time.

"Merci, merci, my beautiful sisters; I feel much better now!" Eulalie is pawing at Louie's hair, wishing there were more straws, "I cannot believe how handsome you are, my brother!"

"Oh, so you thought I was pitifully ugly!" Louie throws his head back and laughs; you can tell he has been hanging around Pierre. "No, no, no! Mama has a poster of you on stage at a theatre in Montreal, its hard to see your face," Eulalie rolls her eyes as she finishes, "...all we could see is your high-classed clothes you are wearing...oo-la-la!" She lifts the collar of her dress and pats her hair. They are all laughing as they stand back and watch their brother comb his hair.

When Louie finishes combing out the mess the girls have made of his hair, Charlie offers a hand to help Louie up and he accepts. Louie lays his arm around Charlies shoulder and gives him a squeeze, "You know little brother, a day never went by that I didn't pray for you. Sometime when its quiet I will tell you why. Maybe we can go and sit under my old thinking tree and I shall tell you all about it."

Charlie is grinning ear from ear, "You look and act just like Mama told us you would; she said you were a lot of fun, rather serious, and mighty handsome."

"Now Charlie, you are making me blush; you are a mighty good looking fellah yourself with your little patch of hair under your nose. Heh, heh, heh."

"Come on girls, we need to get back to the house and fix supper." Julie raises her skirts up to her ankles and trots up to the house, her long thick braid slapping against her back. All Julie's girls seem to have opted for the one braid down the back; Louie's photo of Sara has her long braid wrapped around her head; he would study it when he went to missing his Mama a lot.

Louie is already unsaddling the girls' horses and taking them to water, "I can't believe you are really here, my brudder; we have waited for so long." Charlie is a slow speaker but seems as smart as any. *I think Mama exaggerated when she told me Charlie showed some brain damage from being under the water too long. He looks mighty fine to me, thank the good Lord.*

"Tell me again where our three older sisters are, Charlie. I am getting confused once in a while; I am not used to all this excitement."

Charlie and Joseph anchor their horses close to the water trough with a quick half-hitch* of the halter rope around a corral rail behind the trough. They both sit up on the corral railing while Louie sits on the rim of the trough.

"Tapway, it can get crazy around here sometimes. Sara is the only one who doesn't come home every Sunday for mass. She is stationed at St. Charles mission serving as a nun."

"That doesn't surprise me at all. All the time I was gone I could count on her letters; she always gave me a report on her religious studies. She seemed to me to be almost or more dedicated than I. Don't get me wrong, I was always very dedicated, and still am, for that matter. The death of our father sent me spinning into a dark depression; I was like King David, you know, how he would lose direction once in a while. But he always remained dedicated to the Lord, as did I. Now, where is Marie?"

"She comes home every Sunday and sometimes during the week. She bought herself a little old Surrey* and travels around with a quiet little mare pulling her buggy. She has been paying back Bishop Taché for all Mama's seeds. She is a school Teacher…"

"Don't forget, Charles, she painted that buggy black and it looks very nice…" Joseph has butted in.

"Yes, and she sewed up every tare in that old buggy; she looks high-classed, brother Louie, just like you on that Poster!" It is not hard to see how proud Charlie is of his big sister.

"Well, and where is our sister, Octavie?"

Joseph jumps in quickly so as not to miss his turn, "She is a cook at the St. Boniface mission school, at least she is a helper. She also helps the teacher with all those little Indian children, they like her because she speaks Cree and Ojibwe. She has her own pony; she will be here soon."

"Well let us go and see how Mama is doing; I love to just sit and look at her working; it still seems like a dream; I have to speak to her and get an answer…just so I know that she is real. Heh, heh, heh."

They finish up and head back to the house; just as they are washing up in the foyer, Louie hears a whimper from the couch *…at last, Alexandre is awake, I better take it easy and try not to scare him…*

"Good day, little man, would you like me to wash you up for supper?" Louie is standing there smiling like the friendly witch… with a facecloth in his hand.

Alexandre is shocked, "Mama, Mama, there is a devil wants to wash my face!"

"No, no, my boy, that is your big brother, Louie. He waited all afternoon to see you." Julie takes him by the hand and leads him over to his brother.

"You is Louie?" Alexandre asks in English.

Louie is peeking from behind the facecloth. "Oui, my brother, may I wash you?"

"Mama, it is Louie! He is washing my face."

Once the victory is complete, they all sit up to the table. Julie asks Louie to set the pot on the cutting board.

"Now if we can have your big brother to say grace for us we will have chicken and dumplings. I promise you Louie; tomorrow we will have fresh bannock for supper."

"Sounds like a good deal to me, Mama. Tapway, I would love to say a blessing."

Louie commences to say a most beautiful blessing in his mother's French. He gives thanks for their reunion, for the tender care of his mother and siblings now that Papa is gone on to Paradise and for the reassurance that their dear Papa is in glory having as much joy as are they.

He offers a special thanksgiving for the priviledge of breaking bread with his loved ones and he pronounces a blessing upon the food and the Riel home, all agree with a "...praise be to God, " and Charlie begins to dish up the bowls of chicken stew. Eulalie follows close behind with a bowl of dumplings; she carefully sets one big fluffy dumpling on the edge of each bowl, she has wrapped her apron around the bottom of the hot bowl.

"Tapway, meewasin, my boy. What a joy to hear your prayers once more!"

"I am 'oping duh boys will help me move my belongings upstairs h'after supper."

"Of course we will help, Louie. Just tell us where you want it." Charlie is more than happy to help his big brother.

"That will be good, my boy...the girls can help clean up then we will gather in the parlor."

There is no partition between the parlor and the kitchen, the large open area provides a large room for family gatherings and parties.

Suddenly the door flies open, "Did we miss supper?" Octavie has entered the room with a young gentleman, "Look who I found up at Coutu's helping in the slaughter house!" Louie's mouth drops open in surprise, his sister is beautiful, and who should be holding the door open for her but Louie Schmidt!

Louie jumps up from the table, takes his sister in his arms and gives her a squeeze, then kisses her on both cheeks. He grabs Smitty's hand and pumps it twice, "Pew, my friend…you smell like a back-house!"*

"I know, I had no time to clean up, even Monsieur Coutu scolded me!"

"Excuse me Mama, I am finished and Smitty can have my place at the table.

"I am doing great, my friend, I shall grab you a set of clean clothes."

"Who is this fine young man, Mama?" Octavie gives her Mama a quick wink.

"Louie, you know this is your sister Octavie, she is a Teacher's apprentice, and doing very well."

"It is so good to see you Louie! Go ahead and help Louis get cleaned up. Lord knows, he smells to the high heavens!" Smitty's nick-name is not used by Louie's sisters or Mama.

"We shall be back momentarily!" Louie says as they close the door behind them.

"What the Sam Hell took you so long to get home, Riel?"

"Oh, I had a lot of t'ings to do before I was ready to come 'ome. Do not worry, I 'ave kept up my responsibilities wit' Mama. Where do you t'ink she got money to buy more land and stock?"

"I figured it was all comin' from Bishop Taché. He said when your Papa died he would look after the family."

They are at the river and Smitty jumps in clothes and all. It is like old times …back on their journey to Montreal in '58!

"'ere, rub d'is lye soap all h'over your wet clothes, den scrub dem wit' dis brush." Louie tosses a hand brush out onto the water and it floats towards Smitty. "That looks like your Ma's floor brush; you got your old accent back."

"H'it is duh scrub brush, use it. Don't be counting too much h'on Bishop Taché; I t'ink he has washed his 'ands of me. Duh Montreal accent does not ring in my head anymore. I can hear nothing but Red River patois… thank the good Lord!

"Whenever I fall off the wagon, he washes his hands 'o me too, that is 'til he needs some dirty little chore done. Then he treats me kinda white fer awhile."

Louie bends over laughing, "Well, we shall see; I have nothing against him and seeing how I am forgiven by Madame Sophie and the good Lord Himself; I shall not be sneaking h'around scared of 'im, my conscience is clear. I still am trying to relieve him of responsibilities to our family.

Our family acts like they h'ar so indebted to him. Later h'on I will set dem straight on dat. Heh, heh, heh." He hands Smitty a towel.

While Smitty is drying off and pulling on Louie's clean clothes, he makes an observation, "I sure do like your change in attitude, Louie…keep it up, it looks good on ya."

In a matter of minutes they are back up at the house, Eulalie dishes up Smitty while the rest of the family have canned blueberries from last fall, and a big piece of cake.

"Bring that biggest trunk over here you boys, sil vous plait." Louie turns his chair around so as to pass out gifts to his family…he has waited a long time for this.

There is much joy around the Riel farm as they revel in their first family evening together in ten years.

The little circle has grown since the last time they set the chairs in a circle for evening prayers. They have just wrapped up the scripture reading for the night and have blown out the candles at the little family alter by the window, when… crash!!!

A big rock smashes through the window! A note is tied to it with a string.

Kids are screaming and Smitty is swearing, "I know exactly who that was! It is that bigshot Scott with his gang of Orangemen. He swears that there will be no more new Frenchmen welcome in this town. Jus' read that note."

"This will be our last warning, no more new Frenchmen moving in as of June 1868."

"Who does he think he is?" Louie is amazed; never did he imagine such a welcome his first night back home in good old Red River Settlement!

Smitty jumps up from the circle and grabs a rifle off the wall, "Where are your bullets Madame Julie?"

"Just a minute Smitty, don't get excited, we will not lift a hand until we 'ave spoken to h'our people." Louie has not even uncrossed his legs.

"I suppose you are right, my friend. But that riled up my blood, I am just trembling."

"Well, duh first t'ing Pierre told me when I entered duh villiage was not to worry about Scott; he says he is h'all talk. Tomorrow we will meet at Henri Coutu's house and make a plan," …with that Louie continues saying goodnight to his siblings and offering a blessing upon each of them.

*Glossary

Footnotes:

1 '...duh fire'- In 1863 a fire destroyed the large Cathedral where all Catholics attended Mass. By 1869 a magnificent Cathedral had been built in its place. It was believed that a renegade faction of 'Orangemen', who were Metis-haters, had set the fire.

Chapter Twenty Three

Ontario Orange Elite, Red River: 1870…

The following day Smitty and Louie ride out to L'Ambitieaux's to get Pierre's advice on what they should do.

True to his style, Smitty talks all the way, filling Louie in on some of the Red River trouble-makers.

"Well Chawam, the first thing you need to know is…" He lifts his scruffy cowboy hat, scratches his head, then continues "…there are decent white settlers living here now… and there are the greedy rich ones that you can't trust no-how. The trick is to get wise right quick to which ones are which."

He fills Louie in on the behaviors of Schultz, Mair, Scott and MacDougall:

"I reckon the biggest trouble-maker is Thomas Scott. Good thing you ran into him right away, that saves us from tryin' to get you to see just how hard he is to deal with. 'Do unto others' is a foreign language with that guy." Louie is looking at Smitty long and hard, *I guess I need to listen; this is going to be a critical undertaking by the sound of it.*

In the distance he can see the main street and some of the businesses he has been hearing about, "I cannot believe this is the same old Red River!" Louie kicks his horse into a trot.

"Sorry my friend, but we will be circling the town; we'll stick to this old wagon trail close to the trees." Smitty leads Louie off on a small trail and continues his exposé on the local culprits who have tormented the Metis people.

"Mair is also dangerous as a political opponent. He is educated, writes very convincingly and is in the newspaper business. At least you are a competent match for him; you may stand a chance with him in a war of words. You may even want to respond to his racist comments that appear in an editorial in *Le Nouveau Monde,** from time to time."

Soon they connect back onto the main road; Smitty continues with his local politics.

"Even though these guys sound intimidating, my friend, the one you will need to look out for is Dr. Schultz. He has very powerful connections in the east from the Orangemen and has a devoted following by these three fellows and several more in the community who have been looking for favors. He struggles with winning over the white settlers; they have been treated well by the Metis and have not forgotten about the broken promises of the 'Canadians', under John A. McDonald.

One that is not trusted by either Protestants or Catholics is MacDougall, he acts like his orders come from England. He would go over John A's head if he had to; he wants to be our new ruler in Rupert's land, once it is signed over.

Now these are the most vicious local politicians, the ones you will likely be dealing with from time to time. The one who is pulling the strings of all these political puppets is the one and only John A. MacDonald who operates out of Ottawa; he is the true antagonist, as you likely should know from your eastern experiences."

Louie raises his round-brimmed black hat and scratches his head, "Yes, yes, my friend. I have had a glimpse of him but have never met him. We do have a mutual friend who is Georges Cartier; he was very accommodating to me in my past life h'as a circuit speaker. I had connections with influencial people and he needed their support in various political situations. Unfortunately when I needed his support in acquiring a decent job in his bureaucracy he would not get back to me. One of my lawyer friends in Chicago told me Cartier was afraid to ruffle MacDonald's conservative collars as he had heard rumors d'at my gifts in public speaking intimidated him." Louie lifts his hat and scratches his head, "Now why would an old died in the wool conservative with all the Orangemen in Ontario behind him, be afraid of a little old Metis boy from Red River?" Ambroise turns and grins at Louie,

"There's another fellow who you will meet soon, his name is Bannatyne; he owns a fairly successful line of stores and warehouses right on King's street, right next to the businesses owned by his father-in-law, Andrew McDermot. They are both married to Metis women and their children fan out across the valley to create a network of successful Metis farmers or freighters. To give you an idea about the significance of the Metis women in the Red River settlement you need to hear about Annie Bannatyne.

Not long ago our esteemed Charlie Mair wrote a scathing account of the differences between the white women and the Metis women in the Nor'wester, a local paper run by Schultz. Nothing strange about slander towards the Metis in that paper...but it was even picked up by the Toronto Globe:

"...many wealthy people are married to half-breed women, who, having no coat of arms but a totem to look to, they make up for the deficiency by biting at the backs of their 'white' sisters..." (Siggins, pg. 87*)*.

Well, I'll tell you my friend, Annie is a fysty metis woman, married to Bannatyne, one of our wealthiest citizens in the valley. She was boiling mad because she had hosted the bugger and treated him royally when he first got to town, before he moved in with 'King Schultz', then like a snake, he turned on her and run her down in the paper."

"Now that is low, my friend, he must have no conscience." Louie is shaking his head back and forth.

"Well, he got his Red River justice a few days later. Annie waited for him at the post office on Saturday; a true Orangeman, he showed up, like always, right at 4:00 p.m.; Annie was waiting for him. She grabbed him by the nose, pulled him over near the wicket, where the crowd was gathered trying to smother their laughter. Then she opened up her shawl and grabbed her leather quirt* and she went to whippin' him over the back. I guess everyone roared with laughter. She told him she would show him what metis women thought of him."

They were both bent over their saddlehorns laughing, when suddenly they saw the outline of a lone rider coming toward them…it was Pierre L'Ambitieaux, on his way back from Benjamin Lagimodiere's house.

"What's up Smitty, you look all stirred up?" Pierre reins his horse in and leans on the saddle horn for what he thinks is a visit.

"Well, what would you do, mon chawam, if the Orangemen sailed a big rock through your window?" Smitty's eyes are still big as saucers.

"Slow down, mon ami; what 'appened?" He looks over at Louie, for his version.

"Dats exactly what 'appened, mon Chawam; dere was a note tied to duh rock saying dey are not h'allowing any new Frenchmen in Red River."

"Well now dere h'ar a helluva lot 'o Frenchmen 'ere already! Did he forget dat? Duh las' count dere was over 10,000 Metis people living 'ere, most 'o dem h'ar French Metis."

"That's right Pierre and the other ones who are not French… half 'o dem side with us, they are married to Metis people."

"Tapway, Smitty, 'alf 'o dem h'ar Irish Catholics, so what is he talkin' h'about? I tink he better pull in his horns."

"Ya, before they get lopped off." Smitty is still puffing.

"What do you say Louie?" Pierre is looking straight at Louie…he waits for an answer.

"How fast is your muster-power?" Louie pulls on his moustache.

"You would be surprised, sir, how fast we can gadder a crowd." Pierre raises all his fingers in the air, then, rams a fist into his palm.

"C'est, bon, mon ami! We will have a general meeting at the Cathedral tomorrow night at seven o'clock. Tonight we will meet at Henri Coutu's house to strategize with your Leaders. We need to have the most effective presentation for our people that we can possibly plan." He finishes their exchange in pure French.

Louie turns his horse around in the direction of the Coutu farm. He looks back at Pierre.

Pierre lifts his old cowboy hat from his curly mop of dark hair and uses the same hand to slowly scratch his head. He sets his hat down firmly on his head and studies Louie for a minute.

"You go ahead on over to Henri's, Louie. We will bring our Captains over in one hour…'ave duh tea made!" Pierre's horse turns so fast he rare's back into a squat before he gallops off; Louie can hear him hollering orders to Smitty as he rides away.

"Stay on this trail, my friend; it is only a couple of miles to the Coutu sign. If you see any riders go back in the trees until they pass." Smitty turns in the direction of Proulx' farm as Pierre had instructed.

Louie feels a bit uneasy, riding alone in the Red River settlement he once knew so well. As he looks around everything suddenly seems strange; he gives his horse a little kick and he breaks into a trot.

Well, it looks like Pierre means business. I believe the Orangemen have bitten off more than they bargained for…Dear Lord Jesus, Joseph and

Mary…I beseech you…send a host of your holy angels to guide and protect our people.

Something that always amazed me about Henri's…even his meat market; they never stink. Mama's never stinks either but how often does she butcher, twice a year? She uses a lot of lye but Henri's has a different smell…I just know that it smells clean. A dim light appears in the distance.

Soon he spots a sign by the road, 'Coutu's Meats'. *That must be the farm where they do the slaughtering.*

Thank God they are at home! He trots his horse up to the veranda, jumps off and ties him to the hitching rail.

Louie runs up to the door and knocks, the door flies open and Henri Coutu is standing there staring at Louie.

"Bon soir, mon ami!" Louie reaches out his hand to an aging Henri…a very close friend to his Papa.

"You are Louie Riel Jr.?" He reaches for Louie's outstretched hand, "What a pleasant surprise! Fix him some tea, ma Cheri!"

"How wonderful to see you again, cousin Henri! I used to think of you often when I was in Montreal. And you, my cousin Marie, you are looking beautiful!" He kisses Henri's wife, Marie Catherine, on each cheek; she is beaming.

"You have your Papa's features, my boy," Henri speaks in Mechif. "What brings you out this late? Apih.*" He pulls two chairs out from the table and motions for Louie to sit on one. They immediately begin an intimate exchange, finally he asks, "I used to wonder how your place never stunk; what did you use, if I may be so bold."

"Back then, we used an old Indian remedy and boiled up lots of spruce branches; that brine makes the best disinfectant you can find anywhere.

It only takes apsis, (he indicates a half a finger), or it gets sticky. Now we can buy Creolin right over at Bannatyne's General Store."

"You will soon be hearing the hoofbeats of many horses, mon ami…we have a situation with Thomas Scott and his friends; I h'am very sorry to disturb you, Henri."

"Do not apologize, my boy, we have been ignoring many potential uprisings. Pierre and Smitty have told us to be patient until you h'arrive to provide us with some expertise in law and politics."

"Pierre never put it quite that bluntly; however, he has indicated several times that I was not to look forward to the old Red River…and to be prepared for trouble."

"We always counted on your Papa to guide us in our political negotiations, as you know…your Papa and I remained very close. He schooled me in politics and passed on much of his knowledge to several of h'us before he died. We 'ave been waiting for you to h'arrive to take us furder wit' our struggle for land rights."

"I have taken much Law in my studies; however, in the study of Land Acquisition, I have some very recent publications that will be arriving shortly from St. Joseph. We may find some helpful information in them. I believe I can hear hoofbeats turning into your lane."

"Tapway, make the big teapot, Mama."

"Tapway, my man, praise be to God, Louie…I have been praying for your return." Marie pats Louie's shoulder as she makes her way to the cook-stove and lifts the heavy lid to stuff in two sticks of dry wood. She moves the big blue tea kettle to the front of the stove where it will quickly be brought back to the boil.

"Merci, Madame, I am so honored to be of help. I will be putting my faith in God to guide us as we submit claims for our properties."

Outside there is a loud commotion as the Metis 'Captains of the Hunt'*, all descend on Monsieur Coutu's front yard, they are now wearing the blue capotes received in a ceremony at training camp.

There is a quick "knock, knock... knock, a secret knock of the Metis militia; Henri pulls the door open to a crowd of familiar faces, "Petikway*, mes ami!"

Henri is shaking hands as they all file by. Their capotes and hats are all hung on heavy spikes by the door in the foyer; then, they seat themselves around the table.

Madame Coutu greets them all by name and gives them their first cup of tea. She has waited on all of them back at their shop in town since they were little boys. She always kept a barrel of fresh apples in a big barrel by the counter. As soon as they would begin to lose their shine she would peel them and make freshly baked apple pies to her baked goods on display next to the cheese wheel.*

Before long Smitty will teach Louie all the secret signals that have been passed on to the annual new recruits attending the fall men's training camp each year. There are several bird sounds, signals using fingers, hands or arms, depending on the distance between the quiet communicators.

When the chairs and benches are all taken up, they wrestle for who gets to sit on the long wire couch. It has a mattress that is stuffed with straw and is covered with a cozy feather quilt.

Paul Proulx and Ambroise Lépine are locked in a 'hold', when old Pierre Poitras takes Paul by the nape of the neck and sits him straight, "Muh, now be still!"

Both boys sit up and settle down as Pierre L'Ambitieaux makes introductions.

"Well, here we are Louie, just like I said. We have rounded up all the Captains from each clan; in some cases I see there are two from each clan. Most of you will remember Louie Riel junior as a young lad, back in '58, before he went off to Montreal. Did we miss anything?" Pierre is speaking his best French.

"I am astounded, Pierre, I should have timed you, but I thought everyone would be dribbling in until midnight." Louie is shaking his head, "So, who is your leader?" He prefers to speak in French when doing business.

"We generally decide dat h'evry fall; Ambroise brudder, Maxime was elected last November but he is on a freight run to St. Paul dis week. Who will chair dis election tonight?" Pierre looks around, "Ambroise, would you take duh chair? I will nominate you for duh firs' business of duh election, sil vous plait."

"Oui, I have chaired before." Ambroise Lepine is a clown but is very dedicated if there is a job to be done.

"What do you say? Raise your hands for a yes." All are in favour of Ambroise to take the chair.

Ambroise settles into the chair Henri is offering him, at the head of the table. He proceeds with nominations for the President and Secretary.

In a matter of moments John Bruce has taken pen in hand and Henri sets him up with ink and a scribbler; he will serve tomorrow night as Secretary. Louie has been elected President of the Metis National Committee, by acclamation.

Louis takes over the chair from Ambroise and conducts the first order of business, which is, passing on to John Bruce, items for the evening agenda.

Ambroise limps back to his seat acting the usual fool, wiping his eyes as though losing his position has wounded his pride. Pierre shakes his head and has a chuckle; then, he quickly suggests the first agenda item:

"I would like to suggest dat we set duh agenda h'up to ratify our new h'executive first."

"Merci, Pierre." Louie continues to conduct the rest of the meeting in French. He points to John Bruce, who quickly documents Pierre's agenda item.

"That sounds good for our first agenda item, Pierre, merci. Now, I would like any other suggestions for tonight's agenda."

Henri Coutu raises his hand; Louie acknowledges him, "Merci, Monsieur Presidente, I would like to suggest that we have a word from our President as the next item on the agenda."

Louie looks around, Ambroise is at his side waving his hand like a drowning sailor, "Scusé,* mon ami, I could not see you, yes?"

"Sir, I would like to second Henri's motion; then, further move to have a motion for our Election results to go into the local papers."

Before long they have finished with the business of the evening and Louie is asking for a motion to adjourn the meeting.

"First, mes ami, could we have a few more words from our President before we adjourn?" The entire room breaks into a cheer, "...we are so pleased to have you among us again, mon ami!"

"Merci, merci, mes ami, I am very honored to be here and to have an opportunity to serve you." Louie then takes a deep bow, "Merci, I appreciate your confidence so much," he says softly.

Louie suggests that an agenda for tomorrow's meeting be brought to the Committee from those present; other items may arise from the floor. He also suggests a motion at that time to approve door to door visits, as he and Ambroise take a census of the Metis community.

"I must select an Adjutant General for myself if the community sanctions my nomination as President. The role is critical and requires a dedicated administrative person. Someone who understands the importance of following direction, who takes confidential Committee strategies seriously, but most of all...they must be faithful to the cause...at all costs.

Our vision should be clear. I would suggest that we begin negotiations to secure Land entitlements and recognition as equal partners in the Confederation as a province.

You may have more suggestions for a solid Committee; if you are not ready to share them tonight, bring them to the Assembly tomorrow night at St. Boniface.

I would also suggest Ambroise Lépine to the position of Adjutant General; if Monsieur Lépine will accept this appointment, I would ask for a motion to that effect, sil vous plait." He takes a squeaky pull off his Papa's pipe and watches the smoke as it slowly wafts upward.

John Bruce finishes taking minutes for the appointment and Louie asks for a motion to adjourn, all are in favor.

Henri Couti gives Marie a hand with the tea and the men begin lighting their pipes. A short visit follows; then Louie asks for silence while he asks a blessing on their meeting tomorrow night and gives thanks for the expedition of a good meeting this evening.

"Merci, mon ami, we appreciate your support; we have waited for your return anxiously; I already am beginning to feel better, eh mes ami?" Henri asks the men as he pours their tea. "Tapway, tapway, oui, Henri, merci, we appreciate you sharing your home."

Pierre takes Henri's guitar down off the wall while Keiren begins to play softly on his harmonica; Louie sits back in the corner with his legs crossed, taking short puffs on his Papa's old pipe; he contemplates the actions of the evening,

It is so sweet to be home, and yet my stomach tingles with the same excitement I recall before the wedding of my youth...an excitement that exploded into a

nightmare… I cannot shake off this feeling of impending doom…even so, Lord God, in the words of your Son, "Thy will be done".

*Glossary

Footnotes:

Chapter Twenty Four

St. Boniface, Red River: 1869...

Word has spread quickly by 'moccasin telegraph' as people begin arriving at St. Boniface Cathedral, the following evening. Louie has driven his Papa's team and wagon with the women and children. The rest of the family has ridden their ponies and are tieing them up to the hitching rail when Louie and Julie pull up,

"There are already a lot of people tied up all around the Cathedral." Julie says in French as she motions with her lips towards all the horses down both sides of the stone path leading up to the Cathedral stairs.

"Oui, Mama, there is a large crowd gathering." Louie wraps his reins around the peg on the wagon box; then, he jumps down and runs around to Julie's side and helps her from the wagon.

"My boy, you remind me of your Papa, he always helped me down. I had to get used to driving and climbing up and down myself. It is very nice, merci, my boy."

Louie has worn one of his outfits he would wear in Montreal to his speaking engagements. He had thought twice before donning his top hat; then, he defiantly put it on and straightened his bow-tie. *I must dress becomingly, for the sake of my people and my Lord.*

He takes his mother's hand in his left hand and grabs his valise with the other hand. He had spent several hours praying and writing, upon rising that morning, while the rest of the family went about their morning chores.

True to his word, Ambroise is waiting at the top of the stairs with an open door to receive Louie and his Mama into the Cathedral. Father Noel-Joseph Ritchot stands just inside the door.

He welcomes them in the rich Montreal French to which Louie had become accustomed, "Bon soir, Monsieur Riel and Madame Julie; I have heard much about you Louie, if I may address you as such."

"Most certainly, Father, I am so sorry the reports you have heard were not always honorable." Louie has removed his hat and bows as he takes Father Ritchot's hand.

"My boy, I am not your judge, besides, most of my reports have come from your mother." They all join in together in a pleasant round of laughter.

As they step inside there is more laughter. Keiren, Pierre, Paul Proulx all stand together in a ring, arms flying in typical Metis fashion, their laughter rings off the rafters and Keiren is doubling over.

Now this doesn't look like what you would expect from your typical oppressed, downtrodden, terrorized people of an inferior race. Louie stands with his hands in his pockets surveying the half-dozen little groups of Metis men sprinkled around the edges of the Cathedral. He reaches into his vest pocket and takes out a beautifully decorated golden watch fob, hanging from a golden chain.

Stuffing it back into his pocket he scans the room, eyes penetrating the growing crowd beneath a set of eyebrows that are slightly furrowed, much like his Papa's would be at such a gathering.

He pulls at his meticulously trimmed moustache and takes in, for the first time, the grand statues that have replaced the precious white statues he would dust adoringly, as a young boy.

They are beautiful but they will never replace the figurines I used to cherish as a child. Such a disastrous fire, had I been here...it would have broken my heart.

He watches as Ambroise delivers his mother to a seat in the front row; there she will pray for her son.

The lights in the chapel grow dim as three men on each side move along with a long handled snuffer* and 'slock'* every second light. Up on the beautifully decorated stage stands a pulpit with a slim table on each side bearing bronze candellas. A larger table in the rear contains the Communion elements carefully covered with white clothes; a large statue of Christ on a huge wooden Cross hangs above them.

As if on que, the crowd quietens down during the lighting of another, much larger Candella, off to the side of the pulpit.

Father Ritchot steps up to the pulpit, he clears his throat and everyone goes silent, "Merci mes ami, I do that in the absence of Bishop Taché, who is in Paris and could not be here tonight. It does work though, does it not?" The crowd has a little laugh then quickly settles down.

"We have gathered here on a very serious note; our homeland is being invaded and we are at risk of losing the rich farmland we have grown to love. Our people are in fear and have been unsuccessful in several attempts to negotiate with the Canadian Government; that is why we are here tonight.

Now, without further adieu I would like to invite your newly elected President and Secretary up here to begin the election of a Metis National Committee. Please give a big hand to Monsieur John Bruce, your Secretary-elect, and Monsieur Louie Riel Jr., your President-elect.

The entire assembly rises to their feet and begins what turns out to be a minute long applause. Ambroise brings Louie up to the pulpit then takes a chair behind him. Louie motions for them to be seated; then, taking a clean white handkerchief from his vest pocket he wipes his eyes and blows his nose.

He begins in French and uses very little English throughout the evening; the occasional Cree is thrown in for added flavour.

"I am so pleased to be home, please excuse my tears, it has been a long time, and I have missed you all so very, very much." He blows his nose once more.

"If it please the assembly, I would like to call Father Ritchot back up to begin our evening proper, with a prayer. Father, sil vous plait?" He steps back and folds his hands behind his back.

A request is made from the assembly to have a word from Louie Riel which is met with a thundering applause.

"I have to say that I am honored for your confidence to have me speak on your behalf with the Government, merci, merci boucoup." He takes a gentle bow to each side of the large, fully occupied chapel, then continues,

"Our needs have already been very well articulated by Father Ritchot. I might add to that, the need to stand united under a faithful God. We must be guided by the Holy Spirit and be ready to walk in His strength and power." The assembly broke into a mumble of "Tapways, Ouis, Ayes and Amens" then settled back down.

Following a quick bow, Louie turns back to Father Ritchot, "My apologies Father, you may proceed with a prayer."

After a prayer of thanksgiving and a request for guidance and blessings upon the meeting and the assembly, a blessing is returned from the parishoners and the Father takes a seat beside Ambroise Lépine.

Louie begins again, "Once the business of the elections has been completed, I wish to speak at that time, regarding our need for a census to be conducted, house to house. Monsieur Lepine has agreed to assist Monsieur Bruce and myself, as we cover demographics of all four quadrants in the community. I will be happy to speak to you then."

Business of the agenda moves along smoothly, elected Executives from the previous meeting are ratified and within the next half hour they have elected a full slate of counsellors: President: Louie Riel, Secretary, John Bruce: Adjutant-General: Ambroise Lepine. Counsellors: Charles Larocque, Pierre Delorme, Thomas Bunn, Xavier Pagée, Ambroise Lépine, Baptiste Tourond, Thomas Spence, Pierre Poitras, John Bruce, François Dauphinais and Paul Proulx.

When election business is complete, they call for Louie to speak once more.

"I would like to take this time to thank all those who have supported my family since the passing of my Papa. She wrote to me often throughout my years of absence and she always mentioned the kindness of our people in Red River."

He speaks at great length to the legal ramifications of establishing a Council that may appear to be in opposition to the Council of Assinaboine. He makes himself very clear that order must be maintained within the jurisdiction of the settlement.

"Both French and English must be respectfully elected as Members of Parliament to represent the needs of both Catholic and Protestant. We have a serious situation arising as the influx of settlers continues; we must have a means of protecting our land and language rights.

The sovereignty that has been enjoyed by the Metis for hundreds of years must be recognized and respected by the Canadian government."

As the son of Louie Riel Sr. articulates, in both English and French, the vision he sees for his people, the faces of his audience glow with pride, men can be seen making the sign of the cross as he bows to end his speech.

"Once again, merci, mes ami; the blessings of the Father, Son and the Holy Spirit be upon you."

The crowd rises to their feet and after a second round of applause, Louie begins another fifteen minute exposé on what a framework for their submission for Rights may look like. He expounds on the immediate need for river plots to be registered with Governor Mactavish…. when dealing with land acquisition. At the same time, he briefly mentions the importance of sovereign rights, which should ultimately include Language rights.

In closing, he speaks of possible Metis policing strategies that may need to be developed by the National Committee to deal with local Terrorists.

The next meeting of the Council is to be held at St. Norbert in two weeks at which time Louie will report on their progress with the Census.

Father Ritchot announces that he will put up a sign on the door of his Chapel. Ten Captains are assigned to provide security around the Chapel for the next large assembly.

"When we have had discussion around a new submission, we will bring a document back to this assembly to be modified or ratified before it is sent to the Government.

It has been a pleasure to be with you all tonight, mes ami…merci, merci."

After a motion for adjournment, the meeting is closed by Father Ritchot with a prayer of thanks.

"I have been informed by Madame Riel that there will be a homecoming supper on Sunday evening at the Riel farm. As is the tradition for your gatherings I expect those who attend will bring canned meat, vegetables or berries. Would this be correct Madame Julie?" Julie smiles and gives a nod.

Louie takes a deep bow to the assembly once more; then, he steps down to meet with his Mama. She rises from the front pew and reaches out with tear-filled eyes to hug the son she has missed so much…her heart is swelled with pride and gratitude to her Lord. The old Red River people are so proud of their handsome and articulate young politician; he and Julie are kept busy shaking hands for fifteen minutes; even so, they are greeted by Amroise with a big smile, he has brought their wagon up to the steps.

"I would say our first assembly has been a success, mon ami." Louie's smile is his only response.

***

The following Sunday, wagons begin lining up at the edge of the lane leading into the front yard of the white-washed, two-story log home of the Riels.

Julie's girls have helped her bake and prepare food the day before and now Julie and her beloved son sit on the front veranda ready to receive their guests. Chairs and benches line the veranda and as folks arrive the greet Louie and Julie then find a seat or gather out on family blankets to smoke and visit. Most are smoking kinikinik in hand-made pipes, including some of the women.

Before long the men have moved the large heavy tables out onto the grass and the women have covered them with clean sheets. Children are being washed up in the big washtub, as the young girls help to get all the food set out onto the tables.

Soon the guests gather around the tables as Father Ritchot offers up a prayer of thanksgiving for the safe return of Louie Jr. and for a joyful evening of feasting and dancing, then he blesses the food. There is an abundance of meats, gravies, potatoes and vegetables. The women of the valley pride themselves in their French pastries and breads, including a variety of berrie pies and bannocks. The Scottish and Irish halfbreed women try to outdo one another with their tasty honey biscuits, cream puffs and potatoe dishes while the French metis women cook a lot of chicken and use a lot of eggs, cream and maple syrup in their dessert recipes, both use a lot of molasses but not in the summertime.

The young boys dish up the Elders and serve them where they are seated on their blankets. Once the Elders are served, the children are dished up and taken to the blanket of their family.

After much feasting and visiting the young women gather up the dishes and the mothers cover the food for more feasting later.

As the women are busy cleaning up the young boys get the chairs set in a half-circle for the musicians. Soon the air is filled with the sounds of fiddles and guitars, all tuning up to Paul Proulx on his Papa's old Concertina.

Guests include mostly members of the Riel, Lagimodiere and L'Ambitieaux clans who are all within a fifteen mile radius.

As the musicians warm up with a gentle old waltz Louie takes his Mama by the hand and bows before her, "If I request a French Minuet would you do me the honors, my sweet Mama?" Gabriel L'Ambitieaux is listening as Madame Julie gives her consent in French…when the fiddler hears, "Oui…" he immediately begins to play the French Minuet and Louie takes his Mama out to dance on the grass. Even though they are not dressed in their finery they look grand as they bow and glide around on the grass; Julie's pretty cotton house-dress looks fine as it sweeps back and forth across her little beaded moccassins.

Everyone claps and cheers, then Julie and Louie are joined by several couples who fill up the front yard with a colorful display of Frenchy Minuet.

As the evening wears on children are put to bed. The men have set up tents under the trees in the front yard along the edge of the lane.

The music and dancing carries on into the night until Keiren calls out for Red River Jig; which is generally considered the signal that ends the evening as everyone knows that Red River Jig is saved for the grand finale.

Couples begin to line up by the rhythm guitar, played by Joseph L'Ambitieaux, who calls out the names of the dancers and asks the crowd for a generous applause for each dance team.

Louie is still quite intimidated by all the good dancers so Keiren helps him by grabbing Madeleine and her beautiful daughter Marie by their wrists and getting into the line-up together; Joseph catches on to Keiren's strategy to get Louie dancing and accommodates him by calling out, "Give a big hand, ladies and gentlemen for, Madeleine and Keiren O'Brien and Marie Lamito and our own honorable Louie Riel!"

A great round of applause echoes across the Riel farm so that the dogs all begin to bark. Louie is feeling so energized that his feet move faster than ever before; he looks mighty fine with his slim body held erect, red sash flying and one big curl bouncing on his forehead.

Marie L'Ambitieaux has been keeping an eye on Louie; when he finally bows and takes her hand and raises her up for the 'French Minuet', she curtsies with a broad beautiful smile. *This girl really knows her stuff...such a beauty! I feel like I am back in Montreal.*

As Louie crawls into bed that night he reflects on the evening, *I am so thankful, precious Jesus, Mary and Joseph, for your love towards our family and for the joy of gathering. Forgive me for feeling so warm towards Marie...I had to take her for a walk by the river...she is so beautiful; she reminds me of my sweet Julie but...she is so learned! Oh well...the Lord giveth and the Lord taketh away...*the next moment, Louie is snoring.

***

Louie's life takes on a whole new flavour as he answers to the requests of his Mama once more; however, Julie is very cognizant of the changing responsililities of her darling son. She recognizes that the community looks upon Louie as their long returning political and spiritual leader, much like his Papa.

It is difficult for Julie to see Louie becoming so deeply involved in their community as it becomes embroiled in the grip of of a bitter feud, fueled by John A. MacDonald, who finds the Metis people 'despicable and an obstacle to progress'. (See footnote by Siggins.)

The growing conflict is between a large majority of Metis and a small but ferocious contingent of English speaking citizens under the tenacious and well-financed leadership of Colonal Donald Smith.

Louie continues to become more deeply involved as the surveyors move into the colony with their chains and sextants*; Metis people grow concerned as they set up on their hay meadows.

On August 20th, 1869, as they begin moving their long metal chain along the edge of Edouard Marion's property, Louie's cousin André Nault is tending his cattle as they graze a strip borrowed from Marion. Alarmed at the boldness of the intruders, Nault rides over to get a closer look, sure enough! They carry on unconcerned, even after Nault yells out in French, "This is the property of Edouard Marion!" Turning his saddle horse abruptly he gallops all the way to Riel's farm.

Louie and Smitty saddle up immediately, as they ride past the neighbors they shout for them to follow. They waste no time getting to Marion's; as they ride up to the surveyors they yell out in French, "What are you doing?"

The surveyors are surprised at the boldness of these Indians, "Get to hell outta here you nosy bastards!" Riel rides right up to them; the others follow.

"Just what do you t'ink you are doing? Dis is duh property of H'edouard Marion and you are trespassing!"

They continue to stretch out their chain, "Do you hear?"

He jumps off his horse and steps on the chain,"

Despite her anxiety, Julie gradually grows accustomed to Louie's overnight stays at the home of Henri Coutu.

She was particularly proud of Louie as he went off with Smitty and Pierre to the annual Training camp held in an unrevealed location. He came home looking robust and happy; he looked so much like his Papa!

"I have never in my life experienced such a well-organized event. Mama, I do not exaggerate, there were three hundred and eighty men all under the command of Maxime Lépine, Ambroise's older brother; everyone was so well-trained! They all obeyed their Captains who took orders from Commander Lépine. It was incredible, they all knew their roles and their wives fed us like royalty, each clan contributed food and some of our men were cooks, they prepared the meals and rang a bell at meal-time.

Mama, we swear an oath to not reveal the whereabouts of our camp. We are not to discuss this event. We were not preparing for the buffalo camp we are going on next week, like they told us." He looks around to be sure no-one is listening, then he whispers, "...it is actually a military camp... for training and exceptional Metis Militia." Julie smiles at her son, "I know, my boy...your Papa attended it faithfully every year. They are all sharp-shooters."

Louie shakes his head back and forth,"I know Mama. I myself am trained to shoot the eye out of a crow at quite a distance." He looks back at Julie, "I am now, a 'crackshot', they call it...all the while hoping I never need to shoot anyone."

Louie looks forward to his next exciting experience, the annual buffalo hunt. He remembers as a four year old child the tons and tons of dry meat tightly bound into bales and tied with wet strips of hide 'edges', the tough part of the cured hides. Strong men could pull very hard on them and they would never break.

The exciting part was seeing everyone, listening to them visit and playing games. He remembers the last evening as men raced their saddle horses to win lovely beaded vests and jackets. Even though Louie was not experienced at many of the events, he became very popular and well-acquainted with the Metis members of the local militia.

Louie and his brother Charles had left with Smitty to go meet up with Lagimodieres and L'Ambitieauxs; they are gone for ten days.

***

Julie and the children look forward to their return; she regrets the inevitable disappointment of the boys upon their return. She has watched every year as the hunts gradually become less and less productive.

When the dogs begin to bark excitedly, they all go out onto the veranda to await the arrival of the hunters.

As the hunters come into view, they turn the corner and head down the lane, they all begin to wave, the children shout and the dogs bark.

Julie can already see a trace of disappointment on Louie's face. Smitty drives the team and cart around to the back to unload the pitifully small harvest of buffalo meat.

As Louie and Charles dismount, Julie and the girls are ready with hugs and kisses, "Welcome back, my boys!" Julie is turning her cheeks to receive her traditional kiss on each cheek.

"I am ashamed to tell you, Mama. We brought a small amount of dry meat to you, but…it is so sad. I heard stories of Bill Cody and his slaughter of millions of buffalo to feed the U.S. army and the waste of so much of the meat and hides. Mama, it is a crime…there are barely any buffalo left."

"I know, my boy." Julie turns and leaves for her kitchen; life at the old Red River will never be the same again.

Nevertheless, Louie never has time to regret what used to be; his life will now be filled with preparing for the cold winters in the valley. He is ever so thankful for the farming experience he received as he worked for his Papa's old friend Antoine Gringas at St. Joseph Mission. His family is impressed at what a good farmer he is.

As winter sets in he will be spending hours with Father Ritchot, Governor MacTavish and his faithful friend, Louie Schmidt, who is recognized in the community as being educated; he is honored to be able to help his old friend, Louie, as they work together developing submissions to be endorsed by the Council and sent on to Ottawa.

The Council of Assinabois is in such a weakened condition that their administrative authority diminishes with every proposal submitted by Riel's committee; nothing ever becomes of their efforts.

When the committee diminishes to three members, the committee becomes dormant.

Louie realizes the people of Red River are right; they do not have a government.

*Glossary

Footnotes: There are no Footnotes in this chapter.

Chapter Twenty Five

St. Vital, Red River: 1869...

A chilling revelation begins to manifest itself, as Louie notes the remarks and senses the tone of his people...*Mama tried to warn me of the unrest that is happening around our old homeland.*

He and Smitty spend time during the rest of September helping Julie get the rest of her garden into the cellar; the other chores are generally done up by Joe and Charlie before breakfast.

Julie fixes a nice breakfast for everyone each morning, while the girls make lunches with home-made bread, biscuits or bannock.

Julie will need to can wild goose, beef and chicken this fall...again there will be no shelves of canned buffalo meat in her cellar.

Alexandre is delighted to be the new owner of Madame, who wags her tail happily as Louie hands his companion over to his little brother.

Charles is very proud of Blackie, his new horse, who Louie has replaced with a fast little mare he purchased from Pierre L'Ambitieaux.

"I like my little Chérie but Blackie has been a faithful friend for many miles, little brother; take good care of him," Louie gently instructs young Charles in his usual quiet French manner.

"Oui, my brother, merci … merci, beaucoup; I cannot believe how much you sound like my Papa." Charlie says quietly as he smooths Blackie's thick black mane.

"He was my Papa also," Louie says with a little wink.

The excitement of finally having their big brother home has given Julie's family a new energy and Julie sings one of her Mama's favourite old French songs as she happily cleans up after breakfast.

Louie pokes his head into the house for a moment to say good-bye.

"The boys are off to work Mama; Smitty and I will continue our travels around the Northwest quadrant of the settlement. Please say a prayer for us, I will be praying for your safety also. God willing, Smitty and I will be home for supper; if we have not finished our census, Ambroise will be with us and we should be able to complete our manifest tomorrow."

Julie continues wiping down her kitchen stove with a grease rag, now that it has cooled down a bit. It turns a shiny black and is looking like new. She returns the cloth back to its place in the corner of the warming oven.

She nods to Louie as she closes the warming oven and begins to wipe down the cream-colored enamel of the warming oven and the oven door, *I love my stove; it is my final gift from Louie... before his death.*

"We will be fine, my boy; Madeleine will be here soon to take me to town for supplies."

Julie loves to travel with Madeliene O'Brien, the wife of Louie's little Irish buddy, Keiren.

She has no fear of anyone, not even Thomas Scott. Julie smiles when she recalls Madeliene pulling out her rifle and shooting the hat off Scott's head, when he tried to run her off the road one time.

When she told the story to Louie he laughed so hard he had tears in his eyes. As Julie finished the story in her quick French, "He took off down the road like a skinned rabbit!" Louie laughed all the harder.

The familiar fragrance of blue bells mingled with the smell of the old Red River gives Louie a feeling of gratitude as he fixes his cowboy hat into his thick waves. *I am so thankful to be with my family once more, I will cherish this cowboy hat forever, it is Papa's 'good' cowboy hat. The one he was wearing when we said our last good-bye, and the beaded moccassins she made him. …it is all I can do to keep from crying sometime…especially when I hear the voice of Mama singing her old songs. Praise be to God!*

He heads back out to the barnyard with a spring in his step to help Smitty saddle up.

Louie's young mare is giving Smitty a rough time as he throws the saddle over her; she lets her rear down and the saddle slides off again.

Louie has a little giggle as his horse acts up with Smitty, "Now settle down, ma Chérie. Let see dat saddle Smitty."

Louie straightens out her red saddle blanket. He was recently presented with a 'Red Blanket', "…the official red saddle blanket of the Metis Cavalry," Henri Coutu had put it in French, as he, a respected Metis Elder*, made the presentation, at Louie's 'Homecoming Feast'.

Smitty grins at Louie as the little black mare settles down to her master's touch.

Soon they are on their way over to the home of John Bruce on the south-west corner of the Settlement.

They hope to finish the west side right up to Kildonan Anglican Parish. John has committed himself to travel as a scribe and respected Elder to assist Louie; they have been documenting all the names and ages of each household.

Ambroise Lépine rides with them also, to provide introductions and casual social interaction; he is well-liked by most of the English speaking community.

Louie had shaken most of their hands at St. Boniface Cathedral, after their first meeting, but he tells Ambroise in French, "...but then, their faces were a blur and I would not remember all their names. Little did I know then that I would be stepping into a fast moving attempt by the Canadian Party to take over Red River."

Smitty pulls his horse over a little closer, so as to catch Louie's response as he admits something that he has been aware of for some time:

"Well, my friend, we tried to warn you. The Canadian Party is obviously gaining momentum and will soon be a power to reckon with as more Orangemen set up shop here in Red River. The word is out that they are dedicated to destroying Louie Riel and his Metis National Committee. They say that even John A. is afraid of you, Chawam. He thinks you have intention of creating a Liberal force in the west."

Smitty peeks at Louie for a reaction; Louie has lit his pipe and is smoking peacefully.

Smitty goes on, "I have been hearing our people speak of you as if you would be just what they have needed to protect them from a take-over, almost like a long awaited messiah."*

Louie throws his head back and lets out a high peal of laughter; it warbles its way down to settle on his regular giggle, "Heh, heh, heh. It sure feels good to laugh; little do dey all know dat my service to my people is an assignment dat I h'approach wit' major trepidation; I must call on duh Father, duh Christ, and as many saints or angels as dey can spare. It will h'all work out, I have been shown in a vision dat I mus' remain humble and depend upon our Creator...just like David of old, as he prepared for war wit' duh Philistines*." 2 Samuel KJV

“That’s what I mean, your words give us faith to keep moving ahead.” Smitty glances at Ambroise; Smitty could see his head nodding with his periferral vision.

“Merci, my friend, I will be needing all duh h’encouragement I can get… including a miracle of God, I might say. It is one t’ing to be knowledgable in duh law; it is another t’ing, unfortunately, to ‘ave duh personal grit and strength to implement it. Always keep in mind, my friends, dat under Section 92 of duh British Nort’ America Act, duh Provinces of Canada control d‘heir own Lands and Forests. D’erefore it is h’our responsibility to gain recognition as a provincial government in h’order to maintain control of land registration. H’our timing is right; Governor MacTavish would gladly hand over duh reins, he knows ‘ow greedy and crooked Schultz and his followers h’are. Duh writing is on duh wall.”

Louie takes every opportunity to enlighten his comrades of the political climate in the east, while they fill him in on all the Red River politics.

Sometimes there are a few miles between the farms of the Anglo*-residents which gives them ample time for discussion.

“There is now a lot of talk in the saloons about Colonal Donald Smith and his quiet, underhanded recruitment of the white settlers to build a British militia; he is offering money or land to anyone who will join his militia. Apparently not too many want to take a chance on him. I guess there are too many settlers that have been helped by the Metis; they don’t forget their kindness.”

Smitty gives a little chuckle, “Besides half of them have Metis wives who have family in our militia.” He cackles some more, enjoying the sheer confusion of it all.

Smitty is relieved to pour out more and more of Red River’s tragic tale to someone who cares and understands.

He speaks as though it is all very secretive, known only to the Orangemen who run the popular O’malley’s Saloon. He swears that there is something strange about Sir John A. hand-picking William McDougall for Governor. McDougall has been waiting in the wings for December 1st. to arrive. At that time, the Queen will issue her notice of the sale of Rupert's Land to Canada, in an official proclamation.

MacDougall believes he can then officially replace the sickly Governor MacTavish, who still presides over Red River under the authority of the Hudson's Bay Company*.

Smitty pokes a 'chaw' of tobacco into his cheek and continues, "He has even purchased fine furnishings for his mansion, including a majestic Governor's chair for his parlor. That sneaky Dr. Schultz is another one waiting; he is apparently in close connection to the Orangemen of Ontario."

MacDougall is so blindly determined to reach his goal, that the newly developed Metis National Committee is forced to issue a formal Declaration for his removal in order to complete the process necessary to establish their rights, preferably without interference:

> *Dated at St. Norbert, Red River, this 21st day of October, 1869.*
>
> *Sir,*
>
> *The National Committee of the Metis of Red River orders William MacDougall not to enter the Territory of the North West without special permission from the above mentioned committee.*
>
> *By order of the President, John Bruce*
>
> *Louie Riel, Secretary.* 'Strange Empire', Joseph Kinsey Howard, New York, 1952.

"You know Chawam, it's as though he don't see the Metis as human beings; he see's us like those big herds of buffalo they've been gettin' rid of, to make room for duh railroad. I recall a statement made by John A. in a newspaper a year or so ago; it made my blood boil, he referred to us as the 'feral'* of the west. You know that the wages of that road gang were paid in 'chits' valued only at Schultz' store."

"Tapway, dat's what you call crooked!" Ambroise laughs and shakes his head.

Each time they arrive at another home, Smitty stays with the horses and provides look-out for the ten or twenty minutes it takes for Louie to get acquainted, do a quick census, and in most cases, charm the family into supporting the recently formed Provisional Government.

Louie informs them of their intentions to submit a Bill to the Council of Assiniboia that will begin proceedings for provincial inclusion into the Canadian Confederacy.

"We will need both French and English speaking residents to agree to a Bill of Rights that will guarantee both our Land and Language rights. I am quite sure that Governor Mactavish will agree to a peaceful solution such as this. We have an h'element of our community who is buying up land and are beginning to re-survey some of our ancient lands."

Louie takes a long sip of tea that has been prepared for him, John Bruce and Ambroise Lépine by Mrs. Sutherland, the moment they arrived, "Excellent Madame!" Louie raises his cup to the lady of the house; she smiles in return.

James, her husband is sitting quietly at the head of the table. He begins to speak, his voice cracks with emotion as he shares his concerns.

"We know what you are sayin' Mr. Riel, many of us from this Anglican Parish are very nervous when we hear what is going on with Boulton, Mair, Schultz and Scott. Our women don't even want to go to town for supplies. We don't know who is our friends and who is our enemy. Even some of our kinfolks are joining with them; they give them a piece of land and say they will get them a deed for it."

Louie sets down his cup, "Well my friend, you can be assured that they will not process your registration. H'as a matter of fact, we h'as a Provisional Government, will now 'ave more authority than they have, as long as we 'ave our full Metis membership and a majority of English speaking residents supporting h'us. Father Richot will be hand delivering our Bill of Rights; then we will know they have received it."

Sutherland reaches for Louie's hand as he rises from his chair, "Thank you Mr. Riel; you sound like a smart fella and a might more honest then some 'o these so-called leaders around here," he crisply rolls his 'rs', sounding very decisive.

"We will be 'appy to see you h'at duh next meeting in two weeks," Louie lays his hand on Sutherland's shoulder as he shakes his hand.

"Sounds good to me, we will tell both our sons, they are both married to Metis women," Sutherland says, his 'rs' rolling like the rapids on the Red River.

***

On October 27th, 1869, the long grueling census began to take fruition as most of the Metis citizens of Red River descended upon St. Norbert parish; surprisingly, there was a decent representation of Anglo Saxon from the North-west quadrant of the census and even a few interested Indian people of the Sioux nation.

By meetings end, most are in favour of dispelling McDougall from the edge of the Settlement.

On the fourth day, after the large gathering at St. Norbert, Riel and his men are summoned by André Nault, a cousin of Louie's, to Edouard Marion's. He is the owner of a hay meadow where Nault's stock has been pasturing.

They arrive there just in time to see three surveyors pounding stakes in the ground on Marion's meadow.

The followers of Riel ride in at a gallop. Louie reins in his fast little two-year old mare and comes to a stop so close to the men one of them falls over backwards as they quickly jump back.

Riel dismounts and steps up to a stake, jerks it out and says, "You go no further!" as he places his mocassined foot upon the steel chain that is stretched across the grass.

The men begin to swear at Louie and again he says, "You go no further, this land belongs to Monsieur Marion."

He lowers his tone and fixes his gaze on the head surveyor. Janvier Ritchot looms up behind Louie and places his huge moccasin on the chain behind Louie's, the surveyors scatter to their horses.

Nault rides over and shakes hands with Louie and his men, "Those idiots do not understand a word of French…they totally ignored me so I had to gallop my horse all the way to town." He speaks neither Cree nor English and is obviously exasperated as he spills his frustrations on Riel in a torrent of French.

As Louie shakes his hand he thanks him for reporting the tresspassers. "This is only the beginning, my friend. We must now be prepared for anything."

Things will get tougher throughout the next year, as the Provisional Government prepares the necessary documents for submission of a Bill of Rights.

The Metis Militia keeps a vigilant watch as they make their way back to town.

Louie will continue to help Julie and the boys with the farming, while also rescuing traditional property from greedy landgrabbers. But the majority of his time is devoted to politics… his heart is still set on serving God and his people.

The Executive committee continues to meet regularly.

***

Members of the Executive committee begin to arrive at St. Norbert shortly before six o'clock…the Security brigade can be seen in the distance as they separate to encircle the Mission grounds.

"That was ingenious of you Ambroise, to remind us that the Orangemen are so steeped in tradition that everything grinds to a halt for their precise meal times. I bet you see these habitual differences with the Half-breeds many times."

Louie has taken out his pocket watch; the Father has not arrived to open the door.

"You bet, mon ami!" Ambroise checks the bullets in his sidearm, "… we have been known to have conflict because of their loyalty to British tradition."

Ambroise continues to inform Louie of happenings during his absence using his Red River French.

"They will stand behind their 'Okimows'*, regardless. Look at that crooked preacher of theirs; they will defend him no matter what. He got a young girl pregnant then gave her an operation to remove the baby. The Justice of the Peace sentencenced him to four years …and they broke him out of jail! I never saw anything like it;... my God!" Ambroise is shaking his head back and forth.

"Well, you know that Oscar Malmros; he was so nice to you, all the while thinking that he could get you to back him in his quest to have our settlement annexed into the American states. He was so crooked; he had to mount his horse backwards."

He had a few chuckles, enjoying his own joke; however, it was very shocking to the Metis people to see another bigoted, landgrabber added to the Council of Assinibois.

"You do have a point, mon ami…but here comes Father Ritchot; we would do well to not judge and keep our attitudes focused on the assignment at hand." He reins his horse over to the hitching rail, jumps down and gives Blackie a loose rein again so he can resume his nibbling on the grass, the crunching can be heard until the Father rides up.

"Bon soir, mes ami! I will have the door open shortly. I had company and tried my best not to be rude." He slides his long black robe down from the saddle and Ambroise takes his reins, "You go ahead Father, I will care for your horse."

As Father Ritchot unlocks the chapel door he tells Louie, "You have yourself a good Adjutant General, my boy. He is very faithful and kind, just do not get him angry or drunk. Heh, heh."

Ambroise has himself a little giggle, "Well Father, does that not apply to all Frenchmen?" They both have a little laugh.

Louie adds his usual analytical observation, "Particularly to those of a generous Indian mix, I might add. I have studied the Indian alcohol dilemma a bit… there is apparently no tolerance in the make-up of the Indian to physically break down the chemistry of alcohol. Give them a century or so and they may catch up to the European people who have traditionally had their daily drinks, in one form or another. I thank the Lord… He has protected me from the clutches of 'Demon alcohol': Two glasses of wine or two snifters of brandy is my limit and by the grace of God …that is where it shall remain."

He steps up to the Holy water, dips his finger and makes the sign of the Cross, bows to the statue of Christ before stepping across the isle to wait beside Father Ritchot.

The rest of the Committee has arrived and Father Ritchot takes them down a hallway that leads to a long narrow room. A large framed painting of the Last Supper hangs on the wall under a round stained-glass window.

"You boys get comfortable and I will go and request a large pot of tea from the sisters."

"Merci, Father. But, could you offer a blessing on our meeting before you leave, sil vous plait?" Louie is being careful not to appear as a dictator, *I shall be pleased to pray when it is appropriate.*

"You are still missing some committee members, my boy, shall we wait until everyone has arrived?"

"Oiu, Father. I see we are missing Charles Larocque, Thomas Spence and Thomas Bunn, mon ami. We must remember to accommodate the English speakers with simple but accurate translation. I am sure Spence and Bunn are sincere but they have relatives who may try to dissuade them from being involved."

Louie clutches at his curls, "… I pray the Lord will protect Bunn and Spence, their people could make it rough for them and they represent the halfbreed people of our community. It is critical that we have them on the committee simply to establish respect from the Federal government. Perhaps someday we will have equal representation."

Suddenly the door flies open and Charlie Larocque comes in, "I am sorry if we h'ar late, We figured this must be the place wit h'all dose horses h'outside, den Magnus Duret rose down from his security post and told us. It is 'ard to see, set back in duh trees."

The meeting moves along quickly, now that Louie and John Bruce have officially traded positions. Louie was finding it very difficult to sit back and listen to the meeting being led in all different directions by men who continued to bring up meaningful issues at inappropriate times. Louie, on many occasions would laugh goodnaturedly, while calling '…point of order', then the Committee would have a laugh while a motion was made to get the issue on the agenda.

"'Scusé, mon ami, we will never get finished if we do not stay focused. I agree, these issues are of grave importance but try to remember...these minutes may some day be read by the 'Canadians'as business of our Provincial legislature, there is no room for sloppiness." Louie had risen from his seat and tapped his walking stick on the floor to bring the meeting to order after a discussion around the mail, newspapers and illegal activity.

"You are beginning to look like old Pukeface!" Paul Proulx never fails to get the men laughing and making fun of old pukeface, (which, of course, makes reference to the honorable, John A), one of his favourites, if Keiren does not beat him.

Louie lifts up the pocket of his long, knee-length jacket. Everyone roars, "'Scusé, but we need to stay in order, mes ami!" Louie grins and sits back down.

"Well, Louie is absolutely right!" Pierre takes a swab of chewing tobacco and sticks it in his lip, "...I have a wife waiting at home; for some reason she will not go to bed until I get d'ere. So I move dat Monsieur Bruce replace Monsieur Riel as Secretary. Den someone can make a motion for Louie to go back to serving as our President. No offence John, but Louie keeps us on track."

After dealing with a few new agenda items, they reach the final agenda item... the Militia Training camp, an exciting annual event which is followed by the fall buffalo hunt.

***

The meetings of the Provincial Committee will now stay focused and much progress will be made under the leadership of Louie Riel.

A special sub-committee is appointed to develop submissions to the Committee of Assinaboia consisting of Louie, Smitty, Ambroise, an Elder, generally Henri Coutu, and a Priest, generally Father Ritchot. They will soon be submitting a very well-developed List of Rights:

*Glossary

Footnotes:

1 'Awaited Messiah' – Smitty informs Louie of the high expectations of the Red River people, 2 'Philistines'- Louie draws a parallel to his assignment to fight for his people with King David's fight with Goliath. 2 Samuel, Old Testament-KJV.
2 'ferals' – John A. Macdonald's reference to the Metis people comparing them to 'untamed animals'.

Chapter Twenty Six

Fort Garry, Red River: 1870...

Louie has travelled the entire Red River community being received very cordially by the majority of the Metis, with the exception of a few who have had their land registered under the Hudson Bay, even these people however, have had enough of the Schultz and Mair regime.

Louie, being gifted in discernment, quickly picked up on the aloof behavior of some of the halfbreeds who have obviously crossed over to align themselves with Schultz, Mair and their Loyalist followers.

These men, incidently, had been very busy the past few months buying the loyalty of any halfbreeds who would listen to them. Those inclined to accept the bribes of Schultz's men are generally married to halfbreed women with strong ties to the Angloes.

October 6th, 1869, Louie summons his Provisional Committee together for an emergency meeting.

"Mes ami, we have gathered here to deal with grave concerns; our homeland is in deep trouble. During the past year our people have been living in terror; we cannot wait any longer." He stands aside as Father Ritchot offers up a prayer for protection and guidance.

Louie begins the meeting by welcoming everyone and calling the meeting to order in English, then continuing in French, he calls upon Lépine to interpret.

"I am so sorry to disrupt your evening; thank you for your prompt attendance; however, we are now dealing with a very serious problem. Most of you are aware of recent acts of harassment escalating into open warfare coming, of course,… from the same hateful element that has been wreaking havoc with the families of this committee for over a year." He clears his throat.

Louie is speaking French and is obviously irritated. He tugs at his hair while Ambroise translates Louie's announcement into English.

Thomas Spence is very annoyed, "How many times do I have to tell you. Thomas Scott and Major Charles Boulton do not represent the majority of the English speaking community. They listen to everthing Mair and Schultz* tell them; they are radicals and trouble-makers. Their intention is to remove the French-speaking people from the community! You know as well as I do, that is not only ridiculous…but impossible!"

Ambroise Lepine is speaking through clenched teeth, "We 'ave ignored and forgiven dese guys for a year and dey 'ave terrorized our people with threats, fires and constant harassment! Now dey 'ave broke into Henri Coutu's place, looking for Louie. Dey even tore up duh home of Madame Riel! Nobody feels safe h'anymore!"

He speaks in his clearest English, "Women h'ar in danger; dere h'ar rumors of young girls pulled into parties who are made to drink an' dance for duh Orangemen, den some h'ar raped. Which girls dey h'ar …we h'ar not told, udder wise we would ask who done h'it. Prob'ly duh same one who beat Eleazir Goulet to death! Dis 'as to stop somewhere!" Ambroise is speaking English…there is no time for translation.

He leans forward, "Louie, you 'ave to send our Security squad out and arrest duh leaders of dis group. No telling what will come next!"

Kieren is appalled at the actions of his people, he pulls his six-shooter from the holster and lays it on the table, "Dis is what dey need! I makes a motion to back up Lapine's suggestion!"

John Bruce slams down his pen, "I second that motion, monsieur President. Our women are afraid to go to the store for coal-oil; they are sewing by a bitch-lamp* at nights!" Bruce's words have generated a loud response from a half-dozen committee members, "Oui, oui! Dey h'ar out of control!" …resounds around the table.

"We have all suffered the abuse of Mair, Schultz and Scott's vicious words, whether in the newspapers or by their unruly tongues; now our women are under attack and suffering from the fear of more violence. Oui, oui, mes ami, something must be done!" Louie is grasping at his curls, speaking his Montreal French slowly but forcefully in low tones, every one goes silent as they watch Louie rise slowly, not taking his gaze off the six-shooter lying on the table.

"How many are in favor of arresting these men? You must also agree to sieze Fort Garry as our stronghold and command centre. Metis control has to be established in Red River to bring about some sort of order, before the Orangemen push us right out of here and take over our land. They apparently have a swarm of white settlers just waiting for the take-over from MacTavish, the old Hudson Bay Governor." Speaking in a more assertive and powerful mode of French, Louie is now standing as he awaits the translation of Ambroise Lépine.

All hands are raised in favour of a militant take-over of Fort Garry. The assembly has suddenly grown calm and composed.

"Merci, Ambroise. Now, we will need Father Ritchot to be summoned for prayer, mon ami, if you please." Riel sits back down as Ambroise quickly leaves to call the Father back from the residence attached to the rear of the Mission.

Louie takes out his little green prayer book and glances through Proverbs Chapter 3 verses 5 to 12 *, as if to ground himself for what is about to happen, ...*it always settles me down when I remember those words: Trust in the Lord with all your heart and lean not unto your own understanding...* He tucks his little book back into his vest pocket, then turns his attention to Pierre,

"Mon ami, I will be calling on your mustering skills once more. We will close the meeting with prayer once you have had a few minutes with our Captains. They are very proficient in summoning their clans. You can be very proud of a Militia that boasts such a quick response."

He leans back in his chair and folds his arms as if to prepare to watch Pierre in action, he is rather taken aback when all Pierre says is, "Sil vous plait, all Captains report to Riel's barnyard at sunrise tomorrow... Ambroise will get word to his brother, General Maxime Lépine... have your brigades in tow with water and weapons, tapway?"

"Tapway!" says Keiren, as echos of, "Tapway, oui, aye-huh," echo around the table, "We will eat our breakfasts tonight!" says Smitty which brings loud laughter from all the Council. A good laugh will always cool the nerves.

As much as Louie is enjoying the laughter of his comrades, he raises his hand for silence, "I love your laughter, mes ami; it is music to my ears. However, we must collect our thoughts and close our meeting in prayer, Father Ritchot, sil vous plait?"

Father Ritchot offers a prayer of thanksgiving for protection and guidance throughout the recent upheavals. Then he asks a special prayer for safety and wisdom during the coming events. Everyone makes the sign of the cross to the statue of Jesus before leaving.

***

On the ride back to Riel's, Smitty begins to comment on the information brought forth this evening,

"You know, Chawam, it sounds like Captain Dennis is on assignment to bring the Metis Militia down, He is bragging around town that he has three hundred and sixty white Protestant settlers behind him. We will need to be one jump ahead of them."

Louie has his new little mare trotting at an even lope, his voice breaks with every bounce,

"You will notice dat d'ere has been a shift in duh behaviors of Schultz's party since our letter to William MacDougall was received. D'ere h'are now rumors of Schultz setting up a stronghold. Dey even 'ave Colonal Dennis moving into Red River to recruit as many Half-breeds and Indians as possible; apparently McDougall will provide arms and ammunition. He was obviously surprised to receive an order from our Provisional Government to stay away from Red River."

Smitty shakes his head back and forth, "You know Chawam, McDougall never believed we were serious about our boundaries. Even though he was sent back to Pembina under Metis armed guard, he still didn't catch on. He lives in a dream world; all he can think of is his promise from John A. to rule our land as Lieutenant Governor once the Canadian Party has purchased it from Queen Victoria."

Louie gives his Cherie a little nudge with his right knee as they turn and head up the lane to the Riel farm,

"Oui, if God is willing, we will 'ave dem under our control by tomorrow night. I would prefer if our conversation around Mama tonight would not be alarming."

"I agree that we should speak quietly, not to wake up the house; but, Louie we are approaching a showdown and Madame Julie will not be surprised. She may not speak that much English but she knows exactly what is going on." Ambroise is speaking straight French to Louie and Smitty is not getting it.

"What in duh hell are you talking about Lépine?" Nerves are getting raw as they are nearing the tree-lined lane at Riel's. Madam is barking and wagging her tail.

"Oh settle down Smitty, I just said dat Madam Julie doesn't miss a t'ing; she knows dis is coming, any time now."

"Okay guys, I just don't want us to burst in on her and shock her wit what is 'appening in duh morning. You are correct. She knows what is going on."

"Let me take your horse, mon ami. You go 'ave a talk wit' your Mama." Ambroise takes Louie's mare by the bridle while Louie swings down to the ground, "Merci, my friend. It sounds like duh boys h'are still h'up; d'ere is quite a racket going h'on."

As Louie enters the kitchen, he removes his hat and looks around, Julie is sitting in her chair crying; Eulalie is sweeping up broken glass and the two little ones are hugging their Mama.

"Waz 'appenin', Charlie?" Louie can see the terror in his eyes.

"They attacked us again; they are out to kill you Louie!" Charlie is bent over the fireplace laying a dry log on the red coals and a green one on top; he is shivering in his long underwear.

Julie is holding Henriette on her lap smoothing her hair and rocking her back and forth; she begins to cry even harder when Louie entered, "Come here my girl, come to big brother. What did they look like Mama?"

By now Smitty is in the house; they begin to speak in English, "Dey 'ad scarves tied around d'ere faces; dey spoke English wit' a Scottish accent," Julie says with a very heavy French accent.

Smitty lets out a curse, "...sorry Madame, it sounds like Scott and some of his scoundrels."

"You are likely correct Smitty, but right now we better pack up Mama and duh little ones and get dem over to duh L'Ambitieaux farm; Pierre will likely have duh heater going in duh bunkhouse. You boys keep duh chores done; dey will not bodder you if I h'am elsewhere. Please hitch Mama's buggy Joseph; you h'and Smitty can follow her on horseback and keep watch. I shall be 'ere awaiting Ambroise h'and Pierre's arrival at daybreak wit' d'ere Metis troops. We will pray for duh occupation of Fort Garry wit'out blood-shed."

Smitty crams his old woolen touque on his head and jokingly tells Louie, "I reckon I need to grab a piece of Madame's bannock for my breakfast. We'll get to Pierre's in time to have a wink of sleep, rest and water the horses and head back here for muster, we need to take it easy on our horses tonight. If they get too exhausted they might stumble in the dark."

Louie manages a grin, "Oui, my friend, I 'reckon' you will need your breakfast. Duh more you keep company wit' Kieren, duh more you h'are beginning to sound like 'im. No doubt Madeleine and duh children will continue to stay at duh L'Ambitieaux farm until dese scoundrels are caught."

"I will stay at the Residence and help out the sisters," Eulalie is already packed and is now busy helping Julie to pack a bag.

"If all goes well Mama, we will see you in a few days." Louie hugs Julie and Henriette together as he carries his little sister out to the buggy, now parked out front; Smitty's horse is still saddled and tied to the rear of the buggy.

***

At the crack of dawn Louie is awakened by Julie's old white rooster...*this is one time when I am thankful for that crazy old rooster...I'm scared to death of the old bugger but have never admitted it, heh, heh, heh... today could be the last day of my life...what am I laughing about?* As Louie climbs into his clothes he is overcome by a feeling of dire responsibility...*How did I manage to get myself into a crucial life or death situation, again.* He reaches for his red sash and neckerchief; somehow he feels a strange power surging through his body. He is suddenly energized...*I think I know how David felt when he was facing the Philistine army...This Battle is the Lord's also!* I am not alone*...he ties the handkerchief loosely around his neck and adjusts the knot on his sash, *I have the power of the Holy Spirit with me; besides, I have an army of well-trained men behind me. They are gifted with sharp eyes and ears and they have no fear. Praise God for that, Precious Mary, Joseph and Jesus...keep us safe this day...I commit this mission into your hands. Praise be to God.*

Louie has just reached the bottom of the stairs when he begins to hear the sound of hoofbeats coming closer, and closer. Suddenly there are three sharp knocks on the door, knock, knock...knock. Louie recognizes the secret code and quickly opens the door.

He greets them quietly as they all file in, "Bon jour, mes ami, quietly be seated sil vous plait. Do not eat this until everyone is in; some will need to stand."

As they file by Louie breaks off a piece of bannock and hands them, then shakes their hand, "Api,* mon ami." He moves to the next one in, he speaks a bit louder... "When we are all here I will pray the holy prayer of the sacraments, Henri Couti will bring around this jar of Saskatoon juice representing the blood of Christ. Madame Julie left us with this huge bannock which is strangely nothing but an act of Divine providence; therefore, we shall begin the sharing of the Sacrements of our Lord."

He hands Henri Coutu the jar of saskatoon juice and begins the prayer, everyone makes the sign of the cross.

After Louie has closed with a blessing on all the men, he turns to Maxime Lépine, who has headed up the Training camp with Pierre, his Lieutenant, "I will now turn things over to General Lépine."

"Merci, mon ami, I can feel the importance of this mission in my bones, can you?" Maxime looks to the crowd... everyone responds with a, "Oui, oui."

"We have begun this day in a most powerful way, do you all remember the hand signals?" They all respond with a, "Oui, oui."

"That means to me that no one will do anything without a signal from your Captains, most important the discharging of any rifles, oui?" They all respond again with "Oui, oui!"

"I will now meet with all our Captains, our Elder, Henri Coutu and Monsieur Riel out in the corral for a few moments."

Pierre mounts his horse and reins him around toward the barnyard. He joins the circle where General Maxime Lépine has just reined his nervous mount in to a circle of Captains …they are also holding their mounts on the spot.

Louie Riel begins a prayer in English, he asks for"… guidance and protection for all, from the sacred Mother, Joseph and our Lord, Jesus Christ. Then he gives thanks for a wonderful land and asks for a successful campaign to protect the rights of the Metis Nation without the shedding of blood." Henri Coutu, their respected Elder repeats Riel's prayer in the French language.

Maxime Lépine is a well respected General who has been in charge, up to now, of several scourmages with the Fenian rebels who have crossed the border a few times, in an attempt to claim territory. His good-natured style, but, tough military measures have been very effective during his years of heading the annual buffalo hunts. Due to the growth of attendance, the hunts measuring in the two thousands, discipline and control had become inperative.

He still provides much of the training in the fall, even though the American Cavalry have depleted the buffalo herds to near distinction, it is still necessary for the hunts to remain organized.

Their fall training session is now being put to the test as General Lepine heads up the Troops.

His orders begin in English, then move into French, "Gentlemen, prepare to move out! In the meantime, everyone check your gear and prepare for the ride over to Fort Garry. There we will finally begin to claim our land, God protect Red River! Oui?" Everyone yells, "Oui! Oui!" They all begin to chant, "God protect Red River! God protect Red River!"

When the Captains all mount up, they raise their hands and all is silent, except for the pawing of the horses hooves. Continuing in French, the Captains bring down their arms and point toward the barnyard gate, General Lépine yells out the command, "Forward Ho! Double file, sil vous plait!"

In a matter of moments they are an army riding off to war. The Red River Rebellion has officially begun!

*Glossary

Footnotes:

1 Mair and Schultz – They are two of the leading Orangemen who are taking over Red River. Mair, the publisher of his own newspaper, is informing the coming pioneers in Ontario of the land of 'milk and honey' awaiting them. He uses the opportunity to slander the lifestyles of the Metis at the same time. Dr. Schultz, the only local Physician, is biding his time awaiting a position in Government.

2 'bitch-lamp' – a pet name for the dim light provided by a braided rag sitting in a tin pan of grease which is lit on fire. Generally used on 'the trail' but used also when there is no fuel for the coal oil lamp.

Chapter Twenty Seven

Fort Garry, Red River: 1870...

As hundreds of thundering hoofs approach the old Fort, a splendid red streak in the east begins to widen and Louie makes the sign of the cross as he keeps an eye on the breathtaking scene before him...the outline of the Fort, set against a bright red sky. It begins to loom closer and closer.

He glances behind him at all the faces of the Metis Mititia as they ride in a swift trot, their eyes set on the walls of the Fort.

General Lépine stops exactly on a previously planned strategic spot and raises his hand. Everyone halts, "We shall do our utmost to commandeer these headquarters without bloodshed."

Lépine orders his two lead Captains, François Marion and André Nault, to make the initial entry.

Marion is first; he enters through the back door of the Fort. He glances around; all is quiet. He quickly removes his red militia neckerchief from around his neck and waves it back and forth.

In a matter of moments, twenty armed Metis Militia men, their red sashes flying, ride into the Fort and begin dismounting, strapping their reins to a sturdy hitching rail outside the Hudson Bay Post.

At the same time, another hundred soldiers marching three abreast move in to take command of all the lookouts.

Meanwhile, Riel is inside the Governor's Mansion, not far from the Fort. Nearby, is the Anglican Cathedral, not quite as large as the St. Boniface Cathedral, across the river on the east side.

The favor of entering Governor Mactavish's bedroom is left to Riel and two armed guards, Pierre L'Ambitieaux and Keiren O'brien.

They enter the Governor's Mansion cautiously; everyone seems to be asleep; suddenly a deep raspy cough comes from an open door down the hall; Riel and his comrades walk quickly toward the open door.

Mactavish's health has deteriorated since Riel's last visit and Dr. Cowan is on duty caring for him, a temporary mat lay on the floor beside the Governor's lavishly draped bed.

Cowan jumps to his feet, "What are you doing here?" he says with an astonished look on his face.

"We are here to guard zuh fort." Riel says, dropping his patois like a hot potato.

"Against whom?" Cowan queries, stuffing his shirt-tail into his trousers.

"Against a danger which I have reason to believe, threatens it, but which I cannot explain to you at present. You have no reason to fear that my men will molest your people in any way, nor will they disturb private property. Be assured zat our intentions are honorable, any provisions taken to provide our subsistence will be listed and compensated by the National Committee under which we serve."

Louie walks over and shakes Governor Mactavish's hand, he looks up at Louie with tears in his eyes, "I am not surprised at your appearance; we have been hearing that the Schultz Regime was about to take over the Fort.

As of today there is no ruling authority, the Council of Assinaboia is now dormant and will be replaced upon the official Transfer on December 1st., 1869." Governor MacTavish is speaking quickly, as though the angel of death is leaning in the doorway; his Scottish brogue is clipping his words like a sharp set of shears.

The old man stops to take a breath, he begins to cough, "Take your time, mon ami." Riel sits next to the bed, his fur cap on his lap.

"I'm afraid I will not be around much longer, my boy, my hope is for peace to this community." The old man turns his head to the wall and begins again to cough weakly. "I will fetch him some water," says Keiren O'Brien.

"Zat is h'our wish also, Monsieur. Our intent has never been to harm anyone. We simply need to be acknowledged by the Canada Party h'as a people wiz rights. Unfortunately z'at will require us to compenscate zee files from your headquarters; zey should contain evidence of zuh many unanswered requests of zuh Red River people. You shall not be implicated in any wrong-doing, my friend."

Riel and his comrades leave after they have checked the cabinets for all relevant correspondence.

***

A large house facing the Assiniboine River will provide offices and a council chamber. Another large building called Bachelor's Hill, will be lodging for the sentries. All bookkeeping files, lands and forests documents, arms and ammunition are confiscated.

By nightfall the National Committee have full control of Winnipeg and the entire Red River settlement.[*1]

The Colony is laid out in the formation of a cross with St. Boniface on the east side of the quadrant to Portage la Prairie and a meandering settlement of English-speaking halfbreeds to the west.

Initially, when the Hudson Bay took possession of old Fort Gibralter, which belonged to the Northwest Company, the Fort contained most of the necessary immenities of a colonial infrastructure.

Although the grounds cover a mere four acres, there are still facilities sufficient to house all the administrative clerks and officers needed to support a frontier community.

A wide wooden sidewalk frames the buildings that still line the walls of the Fort. The trading post houses a well-used public store, graneries, a livery stable with a corral off to the side, a blacksmith shop, a carpentry shop, a court-house and a jail.

"I would like for a small detail of four to inspect the jail; it must be secure," says Maxime Lépine, as they tour the facilities.

***

Meanwhile, as Riel is busy dealing with MacTavish, the Lépine brothers ride back and forth at the head of three columns of soldiers that have entered the commandeered Fort; not a shot has been fired.

"Captains step forward!" Maxime calls out as he points out the Officers quarters, "…there is a meeting area in here. The Captains will gather there to be kept informed on our plans. So far there are no disturbances."

General Lépine then takes out a 'chawbag'*, breaks off a chunk of tobacco and hands it to his brother Ambroise; then, he pokes a generous chunk into his cheek and carries on in French, his loud voice booming across the grounds.

"While the Captains are gathering, bring your horses into the corral and feed and water them, sil vous plait. Captains will send their cooks to the cookhouse next to the barracks; look to your Captains for translation, merci." He finishes in English; then, he rides with Ambroise over to the stables.

By high noon everyone has settled into the barracks; when the bell rings at the mess hall*, there is a rush for the door,

"Hold it!" Maxime stands up and raises his hand in the air, "You look like a herd of buffalo, now, resume formation!"

The men resume triple file, then march toward the cookhouse.

Although they are not decked out like the U.S. Cavalry, they are still a fine looking bunch with the usual Metis trousers, beaded vests and red bandanas hanging in a loose knot around their necks. The traditional red sash of the voyageurs swings proudly at their sides. Captains of the hunt now wear blue capotes which were presented at this fall's training camp.

As they reach the door they break into single file, stomp the mud from their riding boots; then, they remove their touques or hats as they enter the building.

It has never been acceptable for metis men to enter a room with their hats on. Boys are taught at an early age that headgear is removed, even upon entering a tent or a tipi.

Similar to the system on buffalo hunts, the Captains eat at one of the shorter tables in order to review, plan and communicate in general; their brigades sit together at longer tables.

After a lunch of bannock and soup, the Captains disperse to the tables of their respective brigades, "Kitchen detail, omah!"

With that, in French and English, two men from each brigade are ordered to rise up and move toward the kitchen to provide clean-up.

General Lépine remains standing as he gives instructions for the arrest of Schultz, Mair, Boulton and Scott; "...they will be housed in the jail until further notice."

Riel does not stay at the fort but retires to the home of his old friend Henri Coutu each evening, with security provided by the L'Ambitieaux men.

***

The take-over of Fort Garry now precipitates a series of events that will cause the entire community of Red River to become enveloped in a state of shock and near hysteria.

The English speaking half-breeds are tossed to and fro emotionally as they deal with divided loyalties... they are torn between siding with their Metis relatives or the Canadians led by Donald Smith, most will chose their families.

Smith had been sent in by John A. to make promises of land and money, if they will align themselves with the Canadian party, who are set to oust the "... miserable 'halfbreed' insurgents." [*2]

The Metis, on the other hand, are soley committed to the leadership of Louie Riel, who has surrounded himself with politically savvy people. They are equipped and ready to do whatever it takes to establish law and order to a floundering community, ungoverned since the collapse of the Council of Assinaboia.

Metis men are now leaving their wives and children behind to ride with the Metis Militia; ...all they can do is pray for their safe return.

Everyone in the community is aware that December 1st. is the date that has been set by John A. for the official take-over of Rupert's Land from the Hudson's Bay Company; all that is required is the Royal Proclamation from Queen Victoria.

Hoards of Orangemen from the east await this Proclamation with bated breath. Schultz, Mair, Smith and other greedy land grabbers boast of all the opportunities in the west through their jointly owned weekly papers, *Le Nouveau Monde, and the Nor'Wester.*

In the meantime, McDougall is losing patience awaiting the Royal position of Lieutenant Governor, promised by John A.

On October 30th, 1869, Riel meets up with McDougall's 'royal' entourage; he hand delivers a written Declaration that he is not to enter the Northwest Territory without special permission from the Council, signed by the Officers of Riel's government.[*1]

> *Dated at St. Norbert, this 21st day of October, 1869*
>
> *Sir,*
>
> *The National Committee of the Metis of Red River orders William McDougall not to enter the Territory of the North West without special permission of the above mentioned Committee.*
>
> *By order of the President John Bruce.*
>
> *Louis Riel, Secretary.* Pg. 106, "Riel', Maggie Siggins, 1994

He is shocked and apalled at the very thought of occupying a small log structure, along with his servants, in the ancient Metis villiage of Pembina. He finds it incredible that he should be subjected to such a lowly lifestyle, unfitting to a man of his stature.

After two letters on November 6th and 7th in an attempt to bully ex-Governor MacTavish into ordering his return to the Colony, McDougall sends another letter; yet another complaint that MacTavish is not taking authority over the Metis who have commandeered Fort Garry.

Finally, on November 9th, Governor MacTavish sends his final response; essentially…" The Council of Assinaboia has no authority over the Metis National Committee.

Riel has virtually managed a bloodless and successful war strategy, or coup*, by capturing the leaders of the Terrorist group, disarming them and preventing the outbreak of a civil war in the Red River valley.

Finally, McDougall has endured as much Metis hospitality as he can stand. He drafts an official-looking replica of the Queen's proclamation, signs her signature to it and has his messenger, Colonal Dennis deliver it to Riel.

He arrives, after riding all night, in the middle of a large meeting; it is the third in a series of attempts to unite the French and English in order to have an equally represented Provincial Government in the west.

The meeting is well attended, 24 French and 24 English are ready to unite and support the latest Bill of Rights.

It is a well articulated document addressing all the major issues in laying the fundamental groundwork for a Provincial Government.[*2]

Suddenly, Colonal Dennis' messenger bursts into the room, waving a document that has been hand-delivered… from McDougall.

After Dennis has ridden all night from Pembina; he hurries and has copies made up at the printing press of the local *Nor'Wester,* for distribution all over the settlement.

The messenger holds the document high in the air, he reads: *The proclamation of Queen Victoria from the United Kingdom of Great Britain; "The transfer of Rupert's Land to Canada has taken place. William McDougall will now take over the Red River settlement as Lieutenant Governor of Rupert's Land."* All heads turned to Riel

Riel is speechless… the people await his response; he has been tricked before by the Canadians. In a moment he gains his composure and rises up from his chair.

"Point of Order! We shall adjourn this meeting until tomorrow at the same time." The unannounced stranger looks on in amazement as the meeting is adjourned before his eyes.

The astonished Convention of Twenty Four file out the front door, as Riel summons his Executive together to a back room.

"We have seen the hand of the Canadians move in the past; this is no different. They are a crooked and perverse entity. You shall see; that proclamation is a fraud."

Maxime Lépine also rises to his feet, he shouts in French, "Monsieur, sil vous plait, that is a very bold conjecture!"

Riel gathers his papers and begins to put on his coat, as he buttons his coat he looks over at Lépine with a steady gaze and speaking quietly in French; he says, "Lépine, mark my words, that document is a fraud. Now we shall make several moves to protect our government. First we shall commandeer all the arms and ammunition outlets in town. Then we shall overtake Fort Schultz, arrest them all and confiscate their arms..." He turns to leave, "...and pork."

He winks at Ambroise Lépine who puts his hand over his mouth and smothers a laugh before translating.

Maxime shakes his head; he knows that he will be responsible for conveying this command to his Captains, "I will need a detail of one hundred men."

Although he is shocked at Riel's confidence, in such a brave move, he is also very proud of him.

"Remember now, we shall give receipts to all the vendors, with a promise to reimburse. Above all, we shall refrain from any shooting or injury, if at all possible."

Riel scratches his head and pulls his winter fur-lined touque over his thick curls, "...I shall meet you all over at the Fort as you arrive with your quarry."

Orders barked out in French and translated by Ambroise Lépine fade into the distance while Louie and John Bruce mount their saddle horses and ride over to the Fort with Louie Schmidt and four Security scouts from the L'Ambitieaux clan.

It is bitterly cold; steam flies up from the horse's nostrils and Louie chews on the frost gathered on his mustache.

No-one speaks. The sound of horse hoofs crunching on the snow creates a strong feeling of unity among the Executive.

Louie mentally reviews the latest happenings that have escalated the need for law and order. *Sweet Mary, Mother of our Lord, give us strength and wisdom as we set out on an even more precarious mission...the people we are dealing with are not the average sort. The forging of our monarch's signature is a sign of greed for power that is out of control. The sudden recruitment of a military force by Colonal Dennis has brought our peaceful brothers back into a state of unrest, possibly the revival of a forgotten warpath. Have mercy on us, Oh precious Mother of God. We are now dealing with the tyranny of Dr. Schultz, as he sets up his own command post, this is none other than the beginnings of a Civil War...we will need all the help we can get, sil vous plait...send a host of your holy angels, dear Lord.* He makes the sign of the Cross

They arrive at the Fort, a strange feeling fills the air. Sentries have been posted outside the old jail; Metis military are moving up and down the old wooden side-walk. The smell of wood smoke fills the air; the sunshine seems to have made it even colder.

Riel's body is rigid as he dismounts; he clears his throat, "Mes ami, let us refresh ourselves with some hot food and drinks...what do you say?"

"Oui, oui!"... echos throughout the brigade. They all dismount and turn their horses in to the stable hands for food and water.

In no time they are all gathered around the big iron heater, rubbing their hands and shivering. "I would hate to be Colonal Dennis riding all night to deliver that piece of bullshit," Smitty is stomping his feet to get the feeling back into his toes.

"Tapway, mon ami; but he is getting paid well!" says Keiren O'Brien. They all chime in, "Tapway, tapway!" Everyone is laughing and stamping their feet.

"Astum, metsu," the cooks are setting out pots of hot bean soup with pork; a large bannock is cut and stacked at the end of each table.

"Wuh wah! What a good smell!" Smitty is the first to the table, "Oh, sorry, my friend." They all remove their headgear as Riel says a blessing.

After the meal Louie summons them over by the stove for a quick and quiet meeting.

"Captains will deploy their brigades to various points for constant surveillance." Lépine speaks in a quiet whisper as a precaution to keeping their plans secure.

Along with the Royal Proclamation, Dennis is carrying a commission from William McDougall for the immediate recruitment of English settlers, half-breeds and Indians. This is shown only to the settlers as he rides throughout the northwest quadrant in a futile attempt to raise an army against Riel's Government.

To his dismay there are only a few men who will sign up for his military. Many are relatives of the Metis and the settlers have not forgotten the kind treatment they had received from the Metis during the droughts.

They would have starved had it not been for the moosemeat, berries and wild rice harvested by the Metis. They also have no use for Schultz and his crooked Orangemen who failed to come through with their promises.

The only thing accomplished by Dennis' efforts was to disturb the peaceful Cree and Sioux people.

When word reaches Riel he immediately sends for Maxime Lépine who is instructed to take a party of his troops into Winnipeg and seize all the weapons and ammunition from the store. They are also given receipts for confiscated goods and a promise for payment from his government.

When Riel is questioned about his authority he is quick to answer, "There is no other authority existing in Red River; someone must enforce Law and Order."

He states that it is a legitimate take-over, "Without a doubt, order must be restored before we end up with a civil war."

The next day on December 8th, 1869, Riel declares a Provisional Government in a proclamation signed by: John Bruce-President and Louis Riel-Secretary.

Steps must now be taken to establish a solid authority in Red River.*[2]

*Glossary

Footnotes:

1 Declaration – Riel follows up on a motion from the Metis National Committee and drafts a declaration forbidding McDougall entry into Red River. Quote from "Louis Riel" pg. 449, by Maggie Siggins.

2 '...a solid authority in Red River' - The commandeering of Fort Garry and the establishing of a 'command centre'by the Provision Government of the Metis Nation. Principles taken from, "A Cold Wind Foretold" by Frank Anderson, beginning at pg. 49.

Chapter Twenty Eight

Fort Garry, Red River 1870 . . .

The type-setters at the *Nor'Wester* refuse to print Riel's announcement, forcing the hand of Riel to commandeer the publishing office. He has his men lock the typesetters in a closet and puts his own printers in to set the type. Soon the new Government has been announced throughout the settlement.

John A. pronounced that they (the government in Ottawa) had no jurisdiction over the Territoties.

On December 7th, Ambroise Lépine brings word to Fort Garry that McDougall's declaration was indeed...a fraud. Also, John A. has made public that there would be no transfer until the uproar at Red River had settled down.

The only remaining opposition is by the formidable Dr. Schultz, and about fifty men. Riel's guards are freezing in the sub-zero weather, keeping a constant surveillance over Fort Schultz. The guards are beginning to complain bitterly; there is no alternative but to apprehend Schultz' party.

Riel then dispatches his peacemaker, Alexander Bannantyne to go to 'Fort Schultz' with a message to disband surrender their arms, and return to their homes.

The message from Schultz comes back loud and clear, "Tell Riel to try and make us."

Riel has no alternative but to give his Commander permission to surround the house with three cannons and 100 men, then to give the insurgents 15 minutes to surrender.

General Lépine then gathers their firearms and tells them they will be detained overnight. In the morning they will be interviewed by Riel and his council.

Once the Schultz's house has been vacated, Riel and his gaurds proceed to search the premises, besides all the pickled pork that Schultz had hidden from the poorly fed road crew; they quickly find a chilling discovery.

Within the fifteen minutes before surrender, the prisoners had stuffed all the chimnys, stove-pipes and crevices with gun-powder.

One lit match would have blown them sky high.

"Thank God we didn't stop for a smoke!" says Pierre L'Ambitieaux after they had moved the gun-powder to a safer place of storage.

It has been a nerve-wracking ordeal and when it is finished Riel's guards take to laughing.

Keiren twirls around, slapping his winter cap on his knee. The rest of them stand in a circle, laughing their heads off.

Riel raises his hand to calm them down, "Well, mes ami, I believe you deserve a big bowl of hot soup and some bannock and hot tea. We will see if they have some jam to go with it."

After they have all eaten, Riel rises to his feet, "Now, we shall all go over to the jail and greet our new guests. Let us keep our heads, and remain professional."

As they enter the outer office of the jail, Louie asks the guard quietly in French, "Where are they being held?"

"I will take you there...you will hear them long before you see them."

As they begin the walk down the hallway, the first voice they hear is Thomas Scott's, "Ye've done it now Riel; yer troubles are jist aboot ta start. Now turn us loose from this rotton jail I'm tellin' ye!"

The guards are having a hard time to control their tempers. Security at the jail is made up mostly of members from the Oulette and Lavalleé clans. They are no-nonsense descendants of the renowned voyageurs. They are known to have a few remedies for dealing with big mouths.

They grit their teeth and follow Riel's orders for peaceful measures if possble.

"Monsieur Riel, dese fellows 'ave been cursing us and calling h'us dirty names...dey h'ar getting 'ard to take." Joe Oulette is raising his fist to Thomas Scott.

Scott's voice is loud and raspy, "Ye will not be so tough if I get me 'ands on ye. Let us out of here Riel; yer men are nuthin' but a bunch of stinken' breeds. Ye will all be sorry when we are free; our Canadian government will 'ave ye fer treason, Ye should all be hung, ye sons-a-bitches!"

"Settle down now if you want supper." With that Riel walks out leaving orders to feed only those men who are quiet.

"We shall have them appear before an inquiry in the morning...ten o'clock at the courthouse."

In the morning the men are brought in one at a time, John Bruce is taking notes.

Each man is given the opportunity to sign a peace bond; whereupon, they will be released to go home to their families. Only sixteen sign the oath and are released; the rest of the men are either too stubborn or too intimidated by their leaders to sign.

By December 9th, it is clear to Colonal Dennis that his plans for ushering in 'McDougall's reign' has been a failure. The fraudulent proclamation now revealed; Natives and settlers begin to settle down.

The last sighting of Dennis is by freighters as he, in disguise, (posing as an old 'squaw'*[1] wrapped in a blanket), begs for a ride to Pembina.

McDougall makes one final effort on December 13th, 1869 to meet with Riel; after all the deceit and treachery he has caused, Riel ignores his appeal.

Soon it is told abroad that he has loaded his servants and 'royal furniture' onto a train of oxen and headed east.

Still, there remains the issue of Donald Smith, District Manager of the Hudson Bay Company.

He is in a position to gain untold wealth should the Hudson Bay Co. complete negotiations successfully with the Crown, in the sale of Rupert's land.

He is so determined that he goes to great length attempting to get John A.'s approval of sending him with troops out to put down Riel's government.

MacDonald, however disturbed as he might be by Riel's opposition to colonization, is wise enough to know that with the strenghth of Riel's loyal following in Red River, sending in troops at this point would not be the answer.

On December 10th John A. MacDonald finally gives in to Smith and agrees to finance his trip out west to investigate the upheaval in Red River. His success depends on the transfer of Rupert's Land; this historic transaction would perpetuate an explosion in the value of his shares from the transfer.

Riel is suspicious of Smith but needs evidence to justify his expulsion from Red River. He asks for his credentials, which Smith is unable to produce.

He tells Riel that his credentials have been left in Pembina for safe-keeping. Riel asks him to go and get them; he will be expected to read them to all the people of Red River at a mass meeting on January 19th, 1870.

Smith arrives back at the settlement with a letter from Governor General, John Young, appointing Smith as Special Commissioner to prepare Red River for the transfer.

Upon his arrival, Riel greets Smith cordially; he checks the credentials which are to be read to the people of the colony.

He goes so far as to grant him permission to travel the colony. He is to speak to the English settlers of the rewards of a speedy transfer, a 'good will tour', so to speak.

Riel is gracious to a certain extent; however, he cautions Smith that he may travel freely among the settlers... with one condition; he is to speak respectfully of the Provisional Government and to cause no harm to the growing unity between French and English.

***

Smith begins immediately to undermine Riel's government among the English speaking settlers. He causes a split among the people with bribes for some and jealousy among others. He also causes a split among the councillors of the Metis National Committee.

He stirs up the prisoners and before long there is an attempted escape, all but two are caught; one of them is Thomas Scott.

Soon John Bruce resigns as President and Riel takes his place on January 8th, 1870.

In the meantime Donald Smith is back; he has been commissioned to bring a letter to Red River from John Young, Governor General, the only one Smith could find who would agree to write such a letter.

The entire community has gathered to listen to Smith as he reads his credentials; there is no building large enough to accommodate such a gathering, so regaredless of the sub-zero weather, the meeting is held outside in the large courtyard of the Fort. The people are buiding small fires to stay warm in the 40 degree weather.

After two days of stomping their feet to keep their feet from freezing, they are growing restless from listening to Smith's endless rhetoric. He has appointed Riel to interpret to French and Reverend Henry Cochran translates to Cree, it is a long procedure. Finally, Riel suggests a vote for equal representation of both English and French.

After some discussion, a consensus is eventually struck to form a Convention of Forty. Riel opens nominations for twenty English and twenty French representatives from the community to be elected to the Convention.

On January 25th, 1870, a vote is carried to establish a Convention of 40 and everyone is happy to go home.

Meanwhile, on January 23rd. John Schultz is lowered down from the prison window by a rope made of strips of buffalo hide. He escapes to St. Peters and begins to spread tales of cruel treatment to the prisoners at the jail, by Riel. (If the truth were to be known, Schultz' wife brought his prepared meals in every day and she was also allowed to bring in fresh underclothes.)

Soon word is out that Schultz and the Canadians are about to attack Fort Garry. News of the impending attack causes a stir among the prisoners, but the attack never comes.

From January 25th to February 10th, days are filled with meetings of the Convention; eventually a committee is struck to fine tune the List of Rights and to deliver the new 'Bill of Rights' to Ottawa.

During this time, Thomas Scott and Dr. Schultz are trying to organize a military force of English Settlers who are extremely opposed to the idea.

Even their attempts to recruit Major Boulton are met with disdain. How would he look? …a professional Military man heading up a group of 60 ill-equipped farmers trudging through the snow?

In desperation, the Preacher from the Anglican Parish leads a group of people to head them off between Portage la Prairie and Fort Garry, but their pleas go ignored, Thomas Scott is determined to take Riel, dead or alive.

Reaching Winnipeg on February 15th, they search for Riel; …they want his scalp. Trudging through the deep snow, they suddenly meet up with a company of Canadians. They have several hundred armed men from town, mostly Irish Saloon-owners and their patrons. They have one cannon; now to locate Riel.

Riel is receiving reports of their movements from a bunker within the Fort. There are six-hundred men armed and ready inside Fort Garry.

He is reading his Mama's little green prayer book, *Dearest Mary, Mother of God, grant us safety and wisdom as we deal with these evil men. Give my Mama the …peace that passes all understanding. They have ravaged the homes of both Mama and Henri Coutu in their search for me. They are prepared to hang me, shoot me or take my scalp. Grant me. Oh Lord, the confidence of your salvation, that I may be prepared to meet you at any time, merci, O Holy Father, amen.*

Louie makes the sign of the cross; then, he tucks his little green prayer book back into his vest pocket… *Thanks be to God for the comforting promise of eternity…it will be a joy to see my Papa again.*

There is a light knock at the door, he straightens his tie. "We have a lady here wishing to speak with you, monsieur. She says she has a solution for you so that you may release the prisoners."

"Let her in Ambroise, merci." Riel is hoping for a miraculous move of God.

Ambroise ushers in a very pretty young Metis lady by the name of Miss Victoria McVicor, he makes introductions, then seats her in front of Riel's desk, "Do you wish for me to stay, sir?", Riel nods, and Lépine, his Adjutant General stands beside the door.

"Now, what do you have in mind, Miss McVicor?" Riel is friendly, but slightly aloof, he recognizes her as a distant cousin from the Lagimodiere side.

She has a message from Major Boulton, "All the Canadians want is to have the prisoners released and there would no longer be a threat of attack."

"I am sorry Madamoiselle; that is impossible. You see, the Canadians may agree; however, we are not dealing with the Canadians. We are dealing with an element who have proven to be highly unscrupulous; they refuse to sign an oath to keep the peace. Once the prisoners are released they will immediately take up arms against us."

"Thank you sir, I will take your message to Major Boulton." Ambroise opens the door and the young lady is gone.

In less than an hour she is back; she has a good friend of Riel's with her, Alexander Bannatyne, he has served as moderator and peacemaker many times in the community.

He presents a strategy which Riel receives with curiosity.

"You know Bannatyne, you could have a point; they are either too proud, too ornery or too intimidated by their peers to sign the oath. It may be worth a try. We will give you a private interview room in which to speak alone with each prisoner."

Finally, by break of day, all the prisoners have been privately interviewed, have signed the oath and have been released to go home.

In the mean time, to Riel's amazement, the Canadians send in a messenger saying, "You are being ordered to surrender the Fort, release the prisoners and provide amnesty to Dr. Schultz by your Government."

> Riel had the messenger take a seat while he wrote a letter back,
>
> *"Be informed: The prisoners have all signed oaths, swearing to keep the peace and have gone home.*
>
> *We are following the instructions of Governor MacTavish to form a government and keep order before there is a civil war. Hudson Bay will back up our Government." Signed-Louis Riel* Maggie Siggins, 1994.

On February 17th, 1870, Mr. Sutherland arrives asking for the release of the prisoners. When Riel informs him that the prisoners are all gone home, Sutherland excitedly leaves to spread the news.

He rides home to the other side of the river and sends his son, Hugh Sutherland, to cross over the river to take the news to the camp of the Canadians.

No one ever suspected the horror that awaited him.

Just at that time Parsiens, a half-wit being used by the Canadians as a spy, sees Hugh and thinking he was after him, he shoots him in the head. A group of Canadians surround the two young men; Thomas Scott strikes Parsiens in the head with a hatchet, he falls to the ground; then ... several begin to beat him.

Major Boulton arrives and puts a stop to the horrifying scene. The two boys are then carried to the Anglican Church and cared for by Dr. Schultz.

Everyone is in shock at the viciousness of the attack; grown men hang their heads in shame. Weeks of strained nerves have taken their toll on the Canadians and they have finally snapped.

Dr. Schultz is suddenly acting as a Doctor; he does what he can but the Sutherland boy is dead in a matter of minutes.

The Parsiens boy hangs on for two weeks; his struggle for life has changed the tough attitudes of many of the men.

Riel is struggling with his responsibility as President; his guards are extremely restless and are watching Riel closely to see what he is going to do to bring justice to the families involved in the tragedy.

He has not been able to eat for days. Sleep comes in dreams that end abruptly in a cold sweat.

The troops and guards are saying someone should be held responsible for the deaths of the two young boys.

If Riel does not take a stand…they feel that they will have to take the matter into their own hands.

As Major Boulton and Thomas Scott speed their way home with a small brigade of troops, they are suddenly surrounded by a group of armed, mounted Metis troops, led by Maxime Lépine.

Boulton orders his men to drop their weapons in the snow. They are arrested and taken to jail; four of them are court-marshalled.

Later that evening, the Sutherlands arrive with Miss McVicor; they plead for the men to be spared, particularly Major Boulton. "He begged for the soldiers to leave the boys alone," they told Riel.

"Major Boulton and two of his men may go; Scott must stay."

As Riel was about to leave, he encounters Donald Smith coming up the steps of the jail, "Riel, I am here to beg the life of Major Boulton." Riel is suddenly taken up with a crazy, slightly humorous notion, "Yes, Mr. Smith…I would be willing to let Boulton go, if you will spread the message of the good intentions of our Government."

"Most certainly, Mr Riel, I will begin immediately; you may take my word and release Boulton tonight, agreed?"

"Yes, sir, we will see to it immediately." He shakes Smith's hand and sends him on his way. Watching out the window, Ambroise, Smitty and Riel get a great kick out of Smith as he unties the reins from around the hitching rail outside the jail.

He mounts his horse and speeds away; unaware that Boulton has been released and has left the jail an hour ago.

The prisoners are obviously in a subservient position to Schultz and Scott; they crouch on their bunks, hanging on Schultz' every word, "You watch, these people are sneaky and dangerous. They travel in packs…like wolves, if you see one, you know that there are more close by. They are always smiling, even in times of confrontation."

One of the prisoners, who is enjoying the doctor's eerie description of the nature of the Metis, leans forward, "Sounds bloody scary, Doc; a fella wouldn't know what in the hell they are thinkin'!"

"You bet your boots; I hear they're hell to play poker with. Just when you think they are getting scared, or losing…they'll burst out laughing like a hyena and throw out a Straight! I've seen them, it can be unnerving, they are sneakier than hell!"

Just then, a guard steps out from the shadows. "See what I mean?" Schultz says.

Oulette grins at Schultz, "We are not sneaky, Dr. Schultz, we h'are jus' cautious."

From morning to night, the intermittent grating of Scott's voice can be heard throughout the jail. He has a burning hatred for the Metis and he will not let up his constant ranting and raving at the guards, "Ye rotton, stinken' halfbreeds…ye are all a bunch o' cowards."

Finally, they are calling for Scott to be hung, "...ye don't have the guts; I'll break out agin and hunt ye all down."

The guards are finding it almost unbearable to deal with the stench. Buckets of Creolin are thrown into the cells, to be mopped up by the prisoners. The guards are kept busy emptying chamber pails of smelly waste.

For a while they assign two gaurds to accompany prisoners to the Courthouse latrines where they are cleaned with Creolin and kept sanitary for the Judges. Unfortunately, the prisoners begin using this as an opportunity to break away and escape.

Thomas Scott escapes three times, as he overpowers the two guards with sheer bull strength, in a fit of violent anger, "Let him go; he is not worth having black eyes and broken fingers!"

Riel seems reluctant to punish Scott but he can see that he will have to assert the authority of his Government if they expect to gain some respect.

The guards are losing confidence in Riel...the situation is grave, and Riel knows... it is his turn to move; he can feel it in his bones.

The next morning one of his councillors is at his door, "Monsieur, we are going to have to do something about Scott. The men are saying you need to show your authority. They are restraining themselves; he is calling them a bunch of cowards. He dares them to shoot him."

Riel calls his council together, they discuss the situation and later on that day they decide that Scott should be given a court martial trial to decide his fate.

The court consists of seven jurors who listen to a long list of charges:

- He has demonstrated insubordination and has broken out of jail six times.

- He is fighting each day with the guards, threatening more breakouts and revenge.

-He has defied the laws of the Provisional Government and made threats to take down their 'phony' Government.

- He has insulted the President and physically assaulted him.

Upon hearing all the evidence, all the Jurors find him guilty. Five of them call for the death sentence; two of the Jurors call for Scott's exile to the United States. They are using the same justice system used during Buffalo hunts.

After much deliberation regarding Scott's exile he yells out to them, "If ye exile me to the United States, I'll beat ye back to Red River."

His refusal to agree to his only alternative to the death sentence leaves only one option.

Scott's death penalty would be carried out the next morning, March 4th, 1870, at ten o'clock, with death by firing squad.

Scott still did not believe they would carry out an execution. As he walked past Riel, he struck him in the face with his handcuffs.

The following morning Scott is beginning to realize the execution is set to happen. In a final attempt to plead for his life he has a Protestant minister, a Catholic Priest and Donald Smith speak to Riel in the hope of a retraction.

"At dis point, I h'am not prepare to renege on duh sentence 'anded down. If Scott were pardoned now, after his refusal for exile, my people would lose faith in our Government and dere President."

Scott is brought out to a room overlooking the courtyard; the room is suddenly eerily silent; armed guards surround the room. Cards are dealt out to twelve guards...those with clubs or spades will serve on the firing squad.

Scott is allowed a period of time to say his good-byes to a few Orangemen. He drags it out until noon. Riel is seated at a small table with Smitty and the Lépine brothers.

Shortly before noon Riel speaks quietly to Maxime Lépine. General Lepine rises to his feet, "Take the prisoner to the post, sil vous plait!"

Four guards march the struggling Scott out to the courtyard. His hands are tied behind his back; he kicks and curses the guards as they tie his feet and arms with a rope stretched tightly around a pole. They slip a black hood over his head, the guards step back four paces, then stand with feet apart and arms behind their backs.

Six guards march out to form a line; Their Captain, Andre Nault gives the command; they raise their rifles, fire…and it is over.

March 5th, 1870, upon the execution of Thomas Scott, the Metis Provisional Government has excersised its authority and established law and order in Red River.

Riel rises from his chair; his knees are weak; he turns and walks out into the hall; four security guards follow him, one of them is Smitty, his life-long friend.

Smitty has been watching Riel, he is sweating and pawing at his hair; he is as pale as a ghost, "Are you going to faint, mon Chawam?"

Riel grabs the door post, "Non, mon ami, I am going to t'row h'up."

Smitty takes his arm as he enters the latrine*. "I'll stay with you, my friend." They disappear into the latrine.

***

When Riel awakens; he is lying in his little room at Henri Coutu's, "Mama, I have been going through hell."

Julie wipes his face with a damp cloth, "I know, my boy. You have been very sick for more than two weeks. Father Richot has been with us day and night; you have been dilerious and trying to call out; but you have been too weak. I am so thankful that you finally woke up; the guards will be so happy, my boy." Julie's old French is a comfort to Louie; he can feel some strength returning.

Every time there is a changing of the guards, we feed them; they have been well-fed." Julie gives her funny little musical laugh, "Henri and your auntie Marie have been very kind."

Smitty appears in the doorway, "My friend, it's so good to see you awake! And it's so good to hear your laugh, Madame Julie."

He pulls up a chair to the bedside and reaches for Riel's hand. He goes to shake it and it is so weak and white, Smitty almost lets go. He gives it a gentle shake, then turns to Julie, he is holding his touque in one hand and scratching at his red curls with the other, he looks very puzzled and worried.

"Can you tell me what's wrong with him, Madame Julie?" Smitty is almost in tears. Louie has closed his eyes again.

"We 'ave no Doctor in town Smitty, we could not use Schultz, so we 'ave 'ad an old Cree lady treating him with honey and balsam tea along with sweetgrass ceremonies; she knows lots about her medicines. She says he is suffering from curses put upon him. Once his fever is down we h'are to bring a singer, a drummer; and a fiddler h'in to treat him wit' prayers and music"

"That sounds good Madam Julie; we can do that, you bet we can!" Smitty is smiling with tears in his eyes.

"Tell him I'll get back shortly; see you semak*, Madame Julie." As Smitty goes out the door he is stopped by Madame Coutu who is cooking breakfast in the kitchen,

"Come back and h'eat, Smitty, breakfast h'it is h'almos' ready! Julie says duh Lavallé boys h'are coming right away. Dey will 'ave good music for Louie's healing."

"Merci, Marie, I am so happy to see my boy getting better…thanks be to God." Julie fixes a cup of hot tea and honey for Louie and when he has finished drinking a half a cup, he falls into a peaceful sleep. She pours a cup for herself and Marie.

"Oui, Henri and I are also relieved and thankful…it looked like we were going to lose him there for a while."

Marie and Julie have always enjoyed their energetic and animated visits in French, as long as there is no English company. They try to remember to speak English when Smitty, Keiren or halfbreed relatives are around.

With prayer from the Father Richot and Elders, and music to soothe his soul, Riel is soon up sitting in a chair; Julie's quilt around his shoulders.

The Lavallee boys are staying out behind the back of the old Coutu farmhouse; their horses are pastured close by and along with a few forks of hay they had thrown into the back of the sleigh, they are also fnding a bit of grass, now that there are a few patches of melted snow.

It has been a mild day and the water is dripping from the roof, "Boy, does dat ol' spring air ever smell good, eh Chawam?" Young Jean Lavallee, the fiddler, smiles at Smitty as he steps up onto the veranda with an armful of wood for Madame Coutu's woodbox.

"Yeah, it has been a nice day. I think Louie has been really enjoying your music…he's lookin' better every day."

"Well, h'as long as dese women keep feedin' h'us we'll keep a'playin'." They both have a good laugh as Smitty opens the door for Jean and his large armful of wood.

Bishop Taché arrives to administer the sacrements to Louie and others from the Coutu household. "You are looking much better, my boy. You may not recall, but my last visit was to administer your last rites; no-one expected you to live.

It was not long before Louie is back working on the Bill of Rights; this time he has Bishop Taché, Henri Coutu and one of his Councilors working with him. Due to all the threats coming in from the east, Riel is having a new clause put into the Bill, claiming amnesty for the people of the Red River Provisional Government who participated in the uprisings.

Schultz is now back in business spreading poisonous accusations in his paper, accusing Riel of, "*the murder of Thomas Scott, one of their members of the Loyal Order of the Orange, Lodge #404.*"

List of Rights

(As drawn by the Executive of the Provisional Government)

I. That the Territories heretofore known as Rupert's Land and North-West, shall not enter into the Confederation of the Dominion of Canada, except as a Province; to be styled and known as the Province of Assiniboia, and with all the rights and privileges common to the different Provinces of the Dominion.

II. That we have two Representatives in the Senate, and four in the House of Commons of Canada, until such time as an increase of population entitle the Province to a greater Representation.

III. That the Province of Assiniboia shall not be held liable at any time for any portion of the Public debt of the Dominion contracted before the date the said Province shall have entered the Confederation, unless the said Province shall have first received from the Dominion the full amount for which the said Province is to be held liable.

IV. That the sum of Eighty Thousand ($80,000.00) dollars be paid annually by the Dominion Government to the local Legislature of this Province.

V. That all properties, rights and privileges engaged [sic: enjoyed] by the people of this Province, up to the date of our entering into the Confederation, be respected; and that the arrangement and confirmation of all customs, usages and privileges be left exclusively to the local Legislature.

VI. That during the term of five years, the Province of Assiniboia shall not be subjected to any direct taxation, except such as may be imposed by local Legislature, for municipal or local purposes.

VII. That a sum of money equal to .80 cents per head of the population of this Province, be paid annually by the Canadian Government to the local Legislature of the said Province; until such time as the said population shall have reached six hundred thousand.

VIII. That the local Legislature shall have the right to determine the qualification of members to represent this Province in the Parliament of Canada and in the local Legislature.

IX. That in this Province, with the exception of uncivilised and unsettled Indians, every male native citizen who has attained the age of twenty one years, and every foreigner, other than a British subject, who has resided here during the same period, being a householder and having taken the oath of allegiance, shall be entitled to vote at the election of members for the local Legislature and for the Canadian Parliament. It being understood that this article be subject to amendment exclusively by the local Legislature.

X. That the bargain of the Hudson Bay Company with respect to the transfer of the Government of this country to the Dominion of Canada, be annulled; so far as it interferes with the rights of the people of Assiniboia, and so far as it would affect our future relations with Canada.

XI. That the local Legislature of the Province of Assiniboia shall have full control over all the public lands of the

Province and the right to annul all acts or arrangements made, or entered into, with reference to the public lands of Rupert's Land, and the North-West now called the Province of Assisiboia.

XII. That the Government of Canada appoint a commission of Engineers to explore the various districts of the Province of Assiniboia, and to lay before the local Legislature a report of the mineral wealth of the Province, within five years from the date of our entering into Confederation.

XIII. That treaties be concluded between Canada and the different Indian tribes of the Province of Assiniboia, by and with the advice and cooperation of the local Legislature of this Province.

XIV. That an uninterrupted steam communication from Lake Superior to Fort Garry be guaranteed, to be completed within the space of five years.

XV. That all public buildings, bridges, roads and other public works, be at the cost of the Dominion Treasury.

XVI. That the English and French languages be common in the Legislature and in the Courts, and that all public documents, as well as acts of the Legislature be published in both languages.

XVII. That whereas the French and English speaking people of Assiniboia are so equally divided as to number, yet so united in their interests and so connected by commerce, family connections and other political and social relations, that it has, happily, been found impossible to bring them into hostile collision-although repeated attempts have been made by designing strangers, for reasons known to themselves, to bring about so ruinous an event-and whereas after all the troubles and apparent dissensions of the past-the result of misunderstanding among themselves; they have-as soon as the evil agencies referred to above were removed-become as united and friendly as ever-therefore, as a means to strengthen this unionand friendly feeling among all classes, we deem it and advisable-that

the Lieutenant-Governor, who may be appointed to the Province of Assiniboia, should be familiar with both the French and English languages.

XVIII. That the Judge of the Supreme Court speak the English and French languages.

XIX. That all debts contracted by the Provincial Government of the Territory of the Northwest, now called Assiniboia, in consequence of the illegal and inconsiderate measure adopted by the Canadian officials to bring about a civil war in our midst, be paid out of the Dominion Treasury; and that none of the members of the Provisional Government, or any of those acting under them, be in any way held liable or responsible with regard to the movement, or any of the actions which led to the present negotiations.

XX. That in view of the present exceptional position of Assiniboia, duties upon goods imported into the province, shall, except in the case of spirituous liquors, continue as at present for the first three years from the date of our entering the Confederation and for such further time as may elapse until there be uninterrupted railroad communication between Winnipeg and St. Paul and also steam communication between Winnipeg and Lake Superior.

March 24th, Bishop Taché and a member of the Provisional Government of Red River, set out for Ottawa to deliver the new revised Bill of Rights. Louie waits for word; there is nothing.

Suddenly, everything begins to happen at once. Riel receives news that the delegation sent to Ottawa has been arrested and charged with aiding and abetting in the execution of Thomas Scott; at the same time, he is shown an article in the Toronto Star. The news article is saying that there is a reward being offered for his capture, dead or alive! Orangemen want his scalp, they have posted a $5000 reward.

Louie can feel it in his bones, his emotions are up and down, good things are happening at Red River, now that things have settled down; but,...

Louie can see dark clouds looming on the horizon. A self imposed exile is inevitable.

His heart is aching as he thanks the Coutus and bids farewell to his buddy, Smitty, and, once again… to his beloved Mama, "I have packed a very small bag Mama…Ambroise and I will appreciate that bannock and dry meat. We have to travel light. Pierre is our guide and he says in order for us to take a hidden back road, it will be at least a good week to get to St. Joseph. You can send my mail to Antoine Gringas' address. If the Canadians are only a few miles away, we had better get going."

He kisses his Mama on each cheek as he steps down from the veranda… Ambroise has his horse closeby; he hands Louie the reins.

Pierre steadies Louie's horse, who is chomping at the bit, "Well, mon Chawam, we h'are back on the trail again, this time we cannot say when we will be back."

In a few moments Julie is sobbing, her teary eyes are fixed on the blurry sight of Louie's back as they ride out of sight. She makes the sign of the cross and whispers quietly, "*Dear St. Joseph, precious mother Mary and our Lord, Jesus Christ, sil vous plait…take good care of my boy…merci, thanks be to God.*"

She steps inside and closes the heavy kitchen door behind her.

*Glossary

Footnotes:

1 'squaw' - A term used liberally to mean 'Indian woman', it gradually evolved to squaw, the meaning eventually taking on a derogatory meaning. The proper term is 'esquao', meaning 'native lady' in Cree.

Chapter Twenty Nine

St. Norbert, Red River, 1870...

They follow the trail of the cattle down to the river behind Coutu's farm, where all the stock go to drink. Once Pierre feels their tracks are impossible to find, they venture further into the thick woods.

"Tapway, mon ami. It is good to be travelling with you again, and I must say, when your life lies in the balance...there is no one I would rather be travelling with than my good friend, Pierre." Louie grins over at Ambroise,

"I agree, totally, mon ami. If we are on the run from threats of assassination, travelling under cover of night at times, better we should be with someone who knows the territory. Then of course we have Louie to pray for us...me, I'm just along for the ride." Ambroise lets out a squeaky giggle.

"Nevermind, you can do the cooking." Ambroise covers his mouth with one hand, and squeeks out a few more giggles...peeking at Louie, his shoulders are going up and down in the traditional Metis laugh.

Everything is silent for a ways, then Pierre makes a sobering remark, "Unless we are deep in the woods we will need to stay extra vigilant and quiet. Once we are on our secret trail it won't be quite so bad."

Louie nods his head, "You are right Pierre, we could get picked off pretty easy out here in this patchy wood. We will soon be back in the thick woods again, by the looks of it." Ambroise blocks the sun from his eyes with his hand and looks off in the distance.

Pierre looks back over his shoulder at the two outlaws, the way they look tickles Pierre. Both are humped up peeking constantly from one side to the other, with the occasional glance over their shoulders, "Just remember to watch your horses ears; they should flick if there's danger."

"Merci, Pierre, we will just say our prayers and watch your ears." Ambroise winks at Louie.

"Not mine, the horse's, you crazy ass!"

"Thank God for you and Ambroise' sense of humor…me, I'm not good at jokes but I am a good laugher. Heh, heh, heh!"

Their journey takes them through miles of muskeg and bush…Pierre is always aware of their proximity to the Red River. Each night the horses are watered and left with front hobbles, on a patch of nice grass.

Pierre is so shocked and disgusted when he awakens to discover that their horses have disappeared, he automatically lets out a string of curses, "… sorry, mon Chawam; but, we are only half way there and we are now on foot."

Louie is not surprised in the least at Pierre's language; they are miles from no-where…*looks like a good time to be saying our prayers.* He takes his little green book out of his vest pocket and looks for a good Psalm to read…*I am sure we cannot go wrong with Psalm 23…* meanwhile, Amroise gathers wood for a fire and Pierre takes the tea pail down to the river.

Louie is shivering beside a small fire, "I wish we could make a bigger fire, mon Chawam, but it would be too dangerous. Nuh*, have some hot tea." Pierre hands him a steaming cup of tea.

Ambroise lays his heavy horse blanket over Louie's back, "This will help take the chill out of you. When we reach Antoine's ranch he will have some brandy… we'll make you a nice hot drink."

Louie looks around at the darkened woods surrounding them, "Good t'ing we h'are hidden deep in duh woods wit all dis racket!" With that, they all burst into a good belly laugh, then they get ready for the night.

"…I can't believe how far we got down duh river before our raft fell apart. We would still be pluggin' h'along if duh horses didn't get away duh udder night."

"Oui, mom ami, you could almost call it a blessing." Loiue is snuggling down under his horseblanket, "Good t'ing you got a good wing on you Pierre, I could never t'row dose blankets all duh way to duh shore. We would be still drying blankets!" Pierre gives a little giggle, "D'ey sail pretty damn good tied h'around a rifle butt." He gives another little giggle.

"You h'are so right Louie!" Ambroise has a little chuckle, "We woudda been twisting dem h'around a tree and wringin' dem out like a hide!"

"Don't remind me of tanning hides, Ambroise, dat's duh hardest work in duh world! I had to help Kookum. Wah wah! Know wonder dat little ol' woman is so tough!"

Pierre always has to go through the motions with his fists and shoulders when he tells something; somehow things seem hilarious… "I will take duh first watch."

Antoine Gringas is so pleased to see them all huddled in the darkened doorway, he grabs Louie and gives him a big bear hug, "Wah wah, you are soaking wet, my boy!"

Then he shakes hands with Pierre and Ambroise, "You boys are welcome to stay as long as you want. I 'ave kept abreast of h'all duh goings on down dere in Red River. We will keep a close watch on what is said in town and your presence here is our business only…dat's right eh, Mama? Dey are h'after your hide, tapway?" Louie is now shivering uncontrollably, "Oui, oui, Monsieur." His teeth are chattering with every word.

Madame Gingras is a wonderful cook and hostess but she is a lady of few words, she nods her head in agreement with Antoine's comment regarding Louie's secret hideaway.

"Get your shirts, Antoine." That is the extent of Madame Gingras' comments, speaking quickly in French…she can see that the boys are soaked to the skin, it has rained for two days. Louie is again on the verge of pneumonia.

After a wonderful meal of fried chicken, mashed potatoes, gravy and bannock, fresh out of the oven, they all retire to the parlor.

"Madame, your chicken was fabulous. My apologies for eating so lightly, one drumstick was nearly too much, merci, merci."

"That is the most I have seen Louie eat in two months, Madame. He has been gravely ill; we nearly lost him at Red River. Then when our raft fell apart he had to swim to shore. I don't think that helped any, eh, mon ami?" Ambroise is happy to speak French with Madame Gringas; she speaks little English and is very shy.

"We will keep an eye on Louie and treat that croupy cough; the river still has bits of ice floating on it, you know." Pierre continues, "…well, I would like to thank you both for everything. The three of us will do just fine at that little cabin by the river. There's lots of bush for us to cut wood and once Louie and Ambroise are settled I will be heading home to my family. Merci, merci, mes ami."

With that, Pierre stands up and stretches, "Bon soir, Antoine, I am beat, we will feed duh 'orses and go warm up dat cabin, if you can spare a bit of Brandy and honey, Antoine, we will doctor up our friend before he goes to bed tonight."

Later when their cabin is warmed up, Pierre gives Louie his nightcap…it quickly begins to kick in. Louie has been writing poetry again; he sits on the edge of the bed, tapping his feet in time to a funny song.

Ambroise and Pierre bend over in laughter as Louie's songs get funnier. Songs about their trek through the woods and their trip down the river on the raft…Pierre gets right into it on his harmonica. "Wah wah, you fellahs, you can really put on a show!"

Ambroise claps his hands and clicks his feet in time to Louie's lively songs; to make them even funnier, Louie has to stop to cough once in a while, then he immediately starts in again, not cracking a smile.

Pierre spends a few days helping Louie and Ambroise break a couple of saddle horses given to them by Antoine, "Dat is very kind for Antoine to get you two fellahs rigged with saddles and 'orses. I will get him to drive me in to St. Joseph in a day or so to catch one of those freight barges heading for Red River. Antoine says he will pick up newspapers and your mail. I am sure your Mama will have written you by now, Louie."

The boys are using mostly French or Mechif and will now be using it habitually. For weeks their only company is Antoine Gingras.

"As a matter of fact I have two letters ready to be mailed to Joseph Debuc and Mama on Antoine's next trip to St. Joseph or St. Paul."

Louie is pulling off the boots, given to him by Father LaFloch, "It was so good to see my confessor once again. I could have cried when Father LeFloch walked in. He knows that it is too dangerous for me to leave the cabin to attend Mass, so he will come out to minister our sacrements, Ambroise."

"Merci, Louie. I appreciate you getting him to come out; that will be great!"

Louie looks over with a grin, "Oui, my friend, you will especially appreciate the grubstake he is bringing out. We shall be feasting on beans and salt pork!"

"Praise be to God!" Ambroise looks over at Louie, with a cheeky look, as he mocks Louie.

"Oui, mon ami, you are beginning to sound like Louie Riel," says Louie, as he grins and winks at Pierre.

"Well for my part, he could do worse." Pierre has not lost any respect for Louie and he has seen him through many rough times. "To be honest, I think we can be truly t'ankful; we've been t'rough a helluva ordeal!" Pierre is suddenly talking as though he is speaking to Kieren.

Ambroise digs a pint of brandy from his bag, "Orders from Monsieur Gingras, Louie. You are to drink two fingers with honey and hot water, every night. That is what Madame Gingras has been giving you at night. Are you getting any stronger, my friend?"

"Oui, I will be fine. It helps me to sleep…I can doze off without hearing breathing outside this window." He takes the hot drink from Ambroise, "Merci, my friend."

Soon they are all dozing off as they listen to the crackling of the fire.

On November 7th, 1870, Antoine brings Riel a letter from the citizens of St. Vital. They are asking him to let his name stand as a candidate for the Manitoba Legislative Assembly.

He lies down on his little wooden bunk *…do they forget the horror that our family endured during Schultz' reign of terror? I know that I must try to forgive and forget but…just the thought of returning to Red River gives me stomach cramps.* He immediately sends a letter of decline.

Little do they know, I will be making a break for Keeseville soon…Praise be to God, I was so delighted to get a letter back from Evelina…she says her brother, Fabien, wants me down there right away, before something happens to me.

Marie has recently arrived from St. Vital to keep house for her big brother, "Louie, I can't believe that you are so confined, you might as well be in jail." She gently drops some bannock dough into a frying pan of hot tallow.

"Do not fret, my girl, I am feeling blessed to be alive."

As Marie sets a plate of steaming, golden brown bannock on the table she asks her brother to bless their meal. He makes the sign of the cross:

"Precious Lord Jesus, Mother Marie, hear our prayers:

We thank you and praise you for all that you have been doing for us, Thank you for sending Marie to bring a ray of sunshine into our lives, and thank you for Charles for bringing all those newspapers from the east. We put our trust in you, heavenly Father, as we hide from the bloodthirsty Orangemen who are hot on our trail. If you provide a way for me to go, I will know that I should leave soon for Keeseville. Bless Pierre as he goes home to his family. Also be with Ambroise' wife and children as they come up to stay a while in the cabin next to us. It will be so good to see children once more. Please bless my siblings, and most of all, my sweet Mama. Thank you for the food...praise be to God, amen." They all make the sign of the cross.

"Marie you have turned out to be a great cook, just like our Mama." Louie reaches out and takes the plate of bannock from Charlie as he hands it to him.

Although Louie has been taking soup and a bit of bannock and beans, he is still very thin and frail, "Have some more bannock, my brother. You need to get some meat on your bones."

"Merci, my sister; you are so kind. That is all I can take in, mewasin; you cook like Mama."

"Merci, Louie, it is a pleasure to spend time with you. Our visiting time in St. Vital was so limited; me, I was always working and you were busy with our people, fighting to keep their land. You have done well, my brother. I hear that some of the land applications are being approved now and most of all…our homeland now has a name, Manitoba. You have done well, my brother."

"You are so kind Marie. I wish Ambroise and Charlie were not down at the river fishing…Ambroise needs to hear that. He needs to know that our suffering has not all been in vain. I received a letter from Father Richot saying our Bill of Rights has been passed in the House of Commons. My sister, our province of Manitoba is now the fourth Province in the Canadian Confederation, Praise be to God!"

Louie keeps a shoebox by his bed, in it are packages of letters tied with string; they keep coming in. Many are from family: His sisters, Sara, Marie, Henriette and Eulalie and his loving Mama. Several are from faithful political supporters, a few are from spiritual friends and colleagues from the Priesthood who still hold him in high regard.

Louie has always been diligent with his correspondence, unless he is going through something or… he is not well. There is a need for regular letters to his Mama, who worries if she hears nothing for a while.

"Congratulations Louie, I am so proud of you!" Marie wipes down the little wooden table and spreads a pretty, round blue, crocheted table cloth over it and sets a coal oil lamp in the middle of it.

After she straightens the quilts on the little wooden cots, she removes her long, calico* apron and hangs it on a little clothesline where she has hung her wet dish towel. She opens the small shutters wide and says, "Come on Louie, let's go for a walk through the woods down to the river. We'll meet up with Charlie and Ambroise and bring them some bannock for lunch."

"Yes my sister, they will be happy to see us. I will take my walking stick and walk behind you…don't go too fast or I will play out."

"Wonderful, my sweet Louie, you need the fresh air." Louie loves to hear Marie's French, she speaks like her Mama…she even has the same kind of voice…soft and musical.

What makes her visit even more pleasant is her singing, she sings the same French songs as Julie...even the quick comical songs from old Quebec.

The secret Metis knock is heard and Marie answers the door, "Come on in, Monsieur Gingras, we were about to make a pot of tea."

Antoine thanks Marie for the invitation "...I am just back from town and need to unload...merci, merci." he hands Marie the mail and turns and leaves.

"I see Ambroise has a letter from his wife." Marie lays the mail on the table and Louie takes his mail and sits down.

Letters from Father Fabien Barnabe are coming regularly; he is very concerned for Louie's life. He lies on his little bunk reading a note that has been tucked into Father Barnabe's letter; it is a short little letter from Evelina, his soul mate from his Priesthood past, *I need to see Evelina; she has always been medicine for my soul. This will surely get me to Keeseville with some to spare...my trouble will be keeping incognito on the streets of St. Paul as I cash this and get to the Train Depot.*

Louie and Ambroise are getting the traditional springtime'itchy feet' of the Metis, when on April 28th, 1871, a huge fire breaks out in the middle of the night at the Hotel Montreal, in St. Paul. Louie and Ambroise hop in the wagon box with Antoine, as they all head in the direction of the fire.

As they pull up they can hear the roar of the fire; people are scrambling every direction; a bucket brigade is in full swing, frantically throwing water onto the buidings on each side of the Hotel Montreal.

They tie the team to a hitching rail in front of the bank and run toward a crowd that is spell-bound, staring up into the flames as they send sparks reaching high into the sky.

Louie and Ambroise are like two coyotes glancing around at strange faces glowing red in the dark; they have not ventured into public since the last assassination attempt. It was a traumatizing event that neither Riel nor Lépine will soon forget.

Two shadowy figures had been seen looking up at the window of the second story room they were renting... in the boarding house that is now ablaze.

Tonight they are bravely moving in closer. They stop behind two bearded men; they turn and spit once in a while. Gobs of tobacco juice are landing on each side of them, "This ol' place shore went up fast! They kep' it from spreadin' to the other buildings, that was about it."

His partner looks at him and grins, "Loyal Order #404. They were aimin' to burn up the outlaws, Riel and Lépine...could be a might crisp by now."

"It's about time someone torched that place any how; they say that you needn't go in there lessen you speak French...they'd be worth catchin'."

His scruffy companion rubs his beard, "You betcha, last I heard they're worth five grand, dead or alive!"

Their voices fade as Louie and Ambroise circle around the block and sneak up to the wagon. They climb in under the straw and stay there until they hear Antoine untying the team. "We are down here Antoine; they think we're in that fire!"

"My God! Let's get the hell outta here!" Antoine takes it as gently as he can until he gets to the outskirts of St. Paul, then he slaps them into a gallop.

"That is enough for me; I am heading home Louie. I care less if they arrest me...I need to see my wife and family!" Ambroise is smearing the tears out of his eyes with his fists. "I cannot take it anymore Louie, I am sorry to pull out on you."

Louie sits with his face in his hands, "I do not blame you my friend. I hated to see Pierre leave also, but..." Louie's shoulders begin to heave up and down. After a moment, he straightens his shoulders, "I must go east now...

to the little Canadas in the northern states. There is much support over there for an amnesty from the Metis communities along the St. Lawrence, also the Oblate Fathers, according to Father Lafloche."

Antoine is sitting at their little wooden table, taking it all in, "I am so sorry, mes ami. If you like, I will drive you to catch a barge at St. Paul, Ambroise."

Antoine looks at Louie; he heaves a sigh, "…and you, mon ami, I will take you to catch the 7:00 a.m. train. I will miss you both but I want what is best for you both. I will go get the horses watered while you both get packed.

Chapter Thirty

Keeseville, New York, 1872 ...

Louie catches a glimpse of the old Keeseville water tower as he feels the train slowing down. There is a new buggy parked out at the side of the platform ...*it has been nearly six years since I left Keeseville, I suppose there would be a different cab driver by now. I cannot get over the houses and businesses that have gone up since I left here.*

Before long the buggy is pulling up in Barnabe's yard behind the rectory; Evelina is looking out the door to see why the dog is barking so hard.

The old driver steps down and opens the back door for Louie to lift out his bags. While Louie is paying the driver Evelina comes running, "Oh Louie, you made it; you're finally back!"

She hugs him around the neck and Louie kisses her on both cheeks, "Evelina! It is so good to see you h'again, my girl!" Evelina giggles and Louie is reminded of her infatuation with his extremely sophisticated French accent. Even he can hear the difference as he reverts from Red River patois to the accent of the Montreal elite.

"Come on in; I'll help you with your bags. Rags! Get down; keep quiet!" Evelina's little black and white collie is excited with this company that appears to be so important.

"Mother, guess who is here!" Evelina sets his bags in the foirer, "I guess you can remember where to hang your coat and hat." She grins toward the same old coat rack and hat shelf Louie was so familiar with back in 1866.

"My dear, it seems like a 'undred years h'ago. I h'appreciated your kindness and 'ospitality back zen and now zat I h'am a wanted man…h'accused of murder and treason…I h'appreciate it even more," his voice is beginning to crack.

He looks at Evelina, try as he might, he cannot stop the tears, she pulls out a chair at the kitchen table, "Louie, please sit, you look ready to fall."

"I h'am so sorry, it seems h'as zo… I finally feel safe." His shoulders are moving up and down as he heaves great wracking sobs.

"Don't try to speak Louie, I know you are too kind to murder anyone; we have been reading all kinds of things about you. We only believe half of what we hear…now we will hear your version."

"So much 'as transpired in such a short time; Manitoba is now recognized as zuh fourth province in Confederation. …But there has been hell to pay in the process.

As a people we submitted several h'appeals for recognition of h'our basic rights, like Land, H'education, Language, Religion, both Protestant and Catholic. Our citizens also need a voice h'in Parliament, remember dear Evelina…zis 'as been zuh 'omeland of zuh Fur Trade people since zuh 1600's, h'our roots go very deep."

Evelina is wide-eyed… she has not seen Louie expressing his passion for his people for several years…nothing has changed, except she can hear a note of intensity in his voice…maybe even despair.

"You have done well, Louie. But I can see that you are mentally and physically exhausted…you must rest. We will do nothing but relax and get some food into you."

Louie smiles, but carries on…"You likely know zat I h'am despised by zuh Loyal Order of zuh Orange…zey are literally offering $5000.00 for my scalp. One of z'eir Grand Masters 'as offered $5000.00 for my h'entire head… brought to 'im in a sack, mind you."

"Oh Louie, I know, we've heard that. You can tell us more after supper; I hear mother coming up the walk to start her chicken. She makes wonderful fried chicken, better than mine. I make great mashed potatoes and I have apple pies cooling in the window."

"I h'am so sorry, H'evelina, I h'already was sniffing h'and drooling when I h'entered. H'as I remember, your fried chicken was delicious and I could smell your pies as we came up zuh walk, so much for zuh surprise." Louie rubs his pitifully sunken belly and gives a little giggle.

The door opens and Evelina's mother enters with a big smile for Louie, "You are every bit as handsome as they tell me; I am so pleased to finally meet you, Louie."

Louie rises and gently holds her little hands, as he kisses her sweetly on each cheek. "I have only seen your picture Madame and I must say; it does not do you justice. You are nearly as beautiful as your daughter."

Madame Barnabe is blushing, but loving it, "Now I must do a good job of this chicken while you sit with Evelina and have tea. She has her potatoes peeled and on the stove already; I will take care of things now. She can set the table in about twenty minutes. Put the kettle on, my girl."

"Where have you been hiding Louie?" Evelina asks, as she stokes the fire in the cook-stove and puts in a couple of dry sticks of wood.

"My fugitive friend, Ambroise Lépine h'and I, 'ave spent most of our time wis' an old employee from my stay at St. Joseph and St. Paul back in '67-'68. Zey h'are very good people; zey employ all Metis men at logging and lumber operations. Zuh Gingras family are also big farmers wis' crops and gardens so zuh people 'ave chickens and animals of z'eir own; zey 'ave zere own h'eggs an' milk. Zere little farms are strung h'all along zuh Red River;

zat serves zem very well for shipment and freighting. Zey build z'eir 'omes and barns for one anozzer h'as a community.

We felt quite safe as long as we stayed away from town; we received zuh very best in security. Metis people can become very tight-lipped in order to protect one anuzzer, one of z'eir expressions during z'ose times h'is, '…h'ask me no questions and I will tell you no lies'. Zat is h'after …so zey can laugh.

Zuh mission sent out food h'and we even 'ad our Mass brought to us; but, as wonderful as zat may sound…we 'ave been very lonesome for h'our people. Ambroise was desperately lonesome for his joyful little wife and his sweet little children. He finally could take it no longer, he said, 'I don't care if I go to jail; I've had it, I am going home to my family!' and he did."

Evelina looks sadly at Louie, "Can you blame him?" Louie is shaking his head as Madame Barnabe calls for the table to be set.

"I have to go Louie, but after supper tell me what Ambroise is doing now: is he o.k.?" Louie gets up and stretches, "As far h'as I know H'evelina; I 'ave no word on 'im lately." Louie heads for the outdoor toilet and Evelina begins to set the table.

***

Bright and early finds Louie out taking care of the stock with a friendly old black man who lives out by the garden with his wife; she helps him with the family garden.

"Evelina is taking me along zuh border to zuh Canadian villages where I shall visit some of my old French h'acquaintances today. Noah! Merci, my man, you h'are so kind to 'elp me. We h'are ready to go! Heh heh heh, zat was fast! Heh heh heh!"

Noah joins in his laughter, "I nevah took notice, sir; I bin doin' dis so long! Hee, hee, hee!"

"What's so funny, you two?" Evelina is carrying a picnic basket.

"We are jus' plain havin' fun, ma'am!" Noah says, chuckling.

"We 'arnessed and hooked up zis team before you could blink twice, H'evelina." Louie is enjoying his freedom from fear…for the moment at least.

A cool breeze is blowing as they head east to Plattsburg where Louie is hoping to find an old friend who has been concerned about him for some time. "My dear friend Fazzer Lafloch has never ceased in his support of me; he knows my heart. Correspondence between the Fazzers of zee Oblate and zuh Priests h'out west has been pregnant w'is concern for my life. He tells me zat I h'am in z'eir prayers and even z'ough z'ey h'are sorry for my change in careers, z'ey have remained faitful to my cause.

Fazzer Lafloch has kept me informed of z'eir concern. He has encouraged me z'at z'ey remember my genuine spirit of dedication to zuh Catholic Church."

Evelina is always impressed with Louie's honesty, "Louie it's such a treat to hear your voice again, and your cute French accent. You know my heart too, Louie, and you know that I won't consider you being immodest when you tell me how devoted you are to your faith. You are so sweet Louie; I can't believe that I'm actually sitting next to you…just riding along enjoying the sunshine."

Louie is still feeling safe as he spends time with the Oblates; Evelina keeps busy with the sisters in the kitchen; she enjoys light chatter about the trip over from Keeseville, "It's been a beautiful trip; we stopped once by the river for a chance to stretch our legs and have a couple of sandwiches."

Sister Bernice is drying dishes for Evelina, "Something I remember about Louie Riel, when he stayed with us one time; he loved birds and trees. He would sit under a tree out back for hours, just reading and feeding bread to the birds."

"Yes Sister, he has a tree out back at our place too. He told me that he had a favourite tree when he was growing up; he called it his 'thinking tree'."

They have a little laugh as they begin setting up trays to take out to the Priests for their lunch, Louie will be joining them.

Before long they are back home and Madame Barnabe has prepared sauerkraut, roast pork and warmed over mashed potatoes and onions.

After Louie finishes one piece of pork and a small helping of mashed potatoes and gravy, he moves "I could become very spoiled, Madame; your meal was superb." Louie sits back and rubs his tummy.

"Oh, Louie! You eat like a bird!" Evelina is giggling in her usually infectous laughter.

"I would love to 'ave more but I h'am full; believe it or not. I 'ave been 'aving too many sick spells nd am suffering from a very rare condition, not common among my people… a shrunken stomach."

Evelina throws her head back and laughs, quite loudly for the 'cultured' women of the day.

"I believe zat my constant state of worrying about my people losing z'eir farms, h'and my family back home with no provider. Zese and zuh increasing torment of zuh daily feeling of impending doom 'as disturbed my entire system. Only zuh love of God keeps me carrying h'on. I 'ave 'ad a few nervous breakdowns but h'our beloved Mary, Joseph and Jesus always bring me back."

"You have many people kneeling in prayer for you, brother Louie…never feel alone." Father Barnabe adores Louie and is always happy to see him and Evelina enjoying each other's company. "I wish you would have some pie, Louie. It would do you good and Evelina's pies are hard to beat."

"Yes, I do h'agree, my friend. I believe I will 'ave a piece of pie later...before bedtime." In the back of his mind he sees a pleasant picture...he and his Papa, as they eat apple pie and enjoy their last evening together.

Louie has been in touchwith Madame Masson and she sends her regards to the Barnabes and sends enough money for Louie to purchase new clothes and give Barnabes some money for Room and Board.

"Can you believe it H'evelina? She is paying for her son to come down here for a visit. I cannot believe she is h'allowing him to leave University for awhile and go to Red River. He is apparently all h'excited about researching Red River politics to write a Thesis for his degree. He should be h'arriving h'any day now."

Evelina is overwhelmed with the generosity of Madame Masson, "We will treat him well, Louie...does he speak English?"

Louie is amused at her question, "My dear H'evelina, he has been living in H'england most of his life...he speaks H'english much better than I. Heh, heh, heh." Evelina jumps on his lap and mussles his hair, "You are so adorable Louie, I could just eat you up..." she begins to chew on his ear. Suddenly Louie is overcome...it has been so long since he has touched a woman like this, she whispers in his ear, "...you know, we could have some pie in your cabin."

Louie jumps up so fast Evelina falls on the floor, she begins to laugh and Louie helps her up, "I would be 'appy to 'ave some pie w'it you. You carry zuh lantern h'and I will carry zuh tea tray."

"No, you carry the lantern, I'll carry the tea tray; you're too clumsy!" Louie is laughing, "Okay, have your way; I will carry zuh lantern. Good t'ing your folks are gone; we sound like a bunch of noisy children."

Louie leads the way down the path to his cabin; Evelina follows close behind with a tray bearing two cups, a little pot of tea and two pieces of apple pie, "...slow down, and stop swinging that light; we're not flagging a train." This only causes Louie to laugh all the harder, "H'evelina, you h'are giving me zuh giggles, heh, heh, heh."

He finally gets the door unlocked and opens the door wide for Evelina to get safely in with the tray. He sets the lantern on the night stand and Evelina sets the tray on the table, then she pushes Louie over onto the bed, "Hey what are doing?"

She blows out the light and says, "I'm gonna have some pie!" They both role around on the bed laughing until Louie finds her lips…he feels her body suddenly go limp.

Days are pleasant at the Barnabe's and Louie is just beginning to get his strength built up when he receives an urgent letter from Father Ritchot…his people need him to run in the election for the constituency of Provencher, which takes in most of the Lagimodiere farms. "You will be provided with heavy security from the moment you disembark. Your expenses are enclosed, merci, merci, my boy."

Louie sits back in Fabien's old chair…the smell of leather poofs out from behind him reminding him of the smell of his saddle, as he rode off to an uncertain exile. *Dear heavenly Father, guide my steps, sil vous plait, and sweet Jesus and Joseph, protect me as I enter the political arena once again…* his heart is racing and his mouth is dry.

"Louie, is it bad news?" Evelina can see the color leaving his face.

"You might say zat, my dear, zen again h'it could be considered wonderful news! I have been asked to offer my name for nomination in the fall election. H'it is nearly August and if I h'agree z'ere will be a 'eavy campaign ahead of me."

Evelina smiles, "As much as I hate to see you go, Louie, I have been watching your old self coming to life lately. It looked to me like you were campaigning at those gatherings at the little Canadas along the river."

"Yes, you could say zat, I have solicited some fine support, especially from zuh Priests. Zey h'are willing to promote zuh cause of zuh western French Metis. Z'ere are likely a few letters and articles being written as we speak."

"Yes Louie, I know that they have relatives in Quebec just waiting for your instructions, I could hear the concern in their voices."

"You h'are so correct, my dear; zey h'are very anxious for John A. MacDonald to fulfill his commitments to zuh people of zuh Red River in response to h'our Declaration of Rights, Bill of Rights and in particular, zee Amnesty he promised to zuh people involved in zuh resistence in 1869, many 'ave relatives h'in Quebec. Our Military 'ad every right to rise up h'under a new Government with the fall of the Hudson Bay Company rule, zat is zuh beauty of 'aving a legal background. Heh, heh, heh."

"I totally admire your knowledge on these issues; I'm so sorry I hardly understand what you are talking about, but all power to you!"

"Merci, merci, my dear, we get very little encouragement from anyone, you know. One issue zat h'is understood very well by h'our people is zat we h'ar living under zuh constant t'reat of a take-over. If not by zee Orange elite from zuh east, zen it is zuh American resistance from zuh sou't zat is always in zuh wings offering annexation to America."

Louie accepts a cup of tea from Evelina and begins to fill his pipe, "Please continue Louie, I'll have a cup of tea with you and enjoy the smell of your pipe."

"Merci, my dear, I love zee h'aroma of kinikinik* also; h'it reminds me of my dear Papa. Well, zee only reprieve we seem to 'ave at Red River, is a strong peaceful relationship wi's our native bruzzers from zuh west; zey h'are generally supportive to h'our cause. We always h'include zem h'in h'our negotiations; we know zat zey are also suffering zuh loss of z'ier hunting grounds and being pushed around zuh same h'as our Metis and halfbreeds. Zere leadership was aware of our strategy and would 'ave 'elped us had we needed zem."

"Oh, Louie, no wonder you are suffering. All I can say is, thank the good Lord, you have Him on your side." Evelina is wiping tears away as she speaks. She is always so cheerful and full of fun, it bothers Louie to see her weep over his burdens.

"Please, my sweet H'evelina, do not weep…zese s'ings shall pass. Zuh Word of zuh Lord says, '…I will never leave you nor forsake you, even unto zee h'end of zuh world…' I believe zat, H'evelina, I may take my leave from Him for a time but He never leaves me."

***

*Glossary

Footnotes: There are no footnotes in this chapter.

Chapter Thirty One

St. Norbert, Manitoba: 1872...

After a teary farewell at the Train Station in Keeseville, New York State, Louie boards the train for St. Paul.

Father Ritchot has given his word of safe passage from St. Paul Train Depot to the northern border of Minnesota. He will be sending out a brigade of security to escort him all the way from St. Paul and over the border to St. Norbert... there his family will be waiting to welcome him.

Praise be to God, it feels so good to be going home...unfortunately I am not that naïve to think that all is well.

He makes himself comfortable on an empty seat, using his folded coat for a pillow, his hat shielding his eyes. *I will miss H'evelina for awhile but my lonliness is usually crowded out by every kind of disturbance you can imagine. I sure enjoyed that visit from Rodrigue Masson; he is a real gentleman, sophisticated but funny...very adaptable I would say...what they usually refer to as a cameleon. Not a thing wrong with that...you have to be a cameleon to survive these days.*

I really needed these new clothes that Rodrigue, Evelina and I picked up in town. They are not quite as extravagant as what Sophie would have chosen to buy for me, back in Montreal, but they are chic and smart...they will make my people proud.

This old train sounds so good. There is something strange about the feeling of the train, adventure, intrigue, privacy? … I will soon be sound asleep…I have checked all the cars and there are no suspicious looking people on board, nice family people…little kids…

Louie is awakened by the sound of boxcars bumping into one another, he rears up and looks out the window *…I cannot believe it…we are in Chicago! Oh well, that is good, I am so excited to see my family…especially my sweet Mama. They are all so special in their own way. I do not see much of Sara but she writes wherever I go…she is so faithful…Marie and Charlie are especially close to me, likely because they came and helped me through my toughest times in St. Joseph.*

He rises and visits the nearest latrine. When he returns he is washed, hair is combed and beard is even trimmed a bit …now, *I feels like a picture out of the Toronto Star,* he smoothes out his beard, *Heh, heh, heh. I may as well begin sounding like Kieren now, heh, heh.*

I will order my lunch and stay right here and mind my own business; I love to watch people…their behaviors puzzle me and keep me analyzing them…very entertaining, I might say.

… I would go visit Laflamme but he will want me to stayin Chicago for a while. I am very anxious to get to Red River, now …Dear Heavenly Father, keep me safe… also my friend Lépine; please send your Holy angels to watch over our families, merci, merci. His eyes are getting heavy…*I believe I shall purchase my berth now; it will give me some piece of mind; God only knows who will be boarding in Chicago…those Orangemen are all over the continent.*

***

Soon Louie is waking up in the stock yards of St. Paul, Minnesota, *I wondered what that ungodly smell was…I had better be watching for Pierre and Kieren; I am sure they will be leading the pack for my security… to get me back to Red River. I will gather my luggage…there is more luggage now after my dear Sophie dressed me up, '…for your new career' she says…if she only knew. It is not so glamorous.*

As the train slows, Louie's heart races; he can see the city coming to life in the early morning sun. Traffic begins to appear in changing modes as they move into the heart of St. Paul.

Louie notices saddle horses tied to hitching rails in front of several establishments...*I know how those boys operate...as soon as they hear the train they will mount up and decsend on the railroad station from all directions.*

Sure enough, as the Conductor yells out, "St. Paul, Minnesoootaaaa!" he sees two riders headed for the station...*praise be to God! ...there goes my security.*

Louie reaches up and takes down his hat; he brushes it off, runs his fingers through his thick waves and pulls it on. He gives it a little twist, a habit of Metis cowboys before they ride. His bags are a little heavier now with his new outfit he purchased for speaking engagements...*I can see them approaching in pairs, wah wah, there is Pierre and Kieren! This outta be a side-show...if I do not get shot right quick, heh, heh, heh.* Louie can feel himself coming under the influence of the Metis culture; it is a relief.

Only Pierre and Kieren board the train; the other six riders have been strategically posted around the paremeter of the Station grounds; they are all sharpshooters, trained for lookout duties.

As Pierre swings up into the train, Louie appears at the door, "What a sight for sore eyes!" Pierre grabs him and lifts him in the air, "Watch my ribs, Chawam, they might break!" Pierre sets him back down, "Yore not kidding, mon ami, your ribs are like a chicadee's! Wah wah, we will need to fatten you h'up, my friend."

"If you t'ink I h'am skinny now, you should have seen me before H'evelina fed me like a market hog. I was very ill; I am just now getting my strength back; praise be to God."

"Well, let's get h'our arses on duh trail; yore Mama sent some bacon and bannock for h'our first breakfast togedder. We'll make about five miles h'along duh river first. Here's h'our man, Kieren!"

Kieren grabs Louie and hugs him around the neck, "You made it, you bugger. It's so good ta see ya, me friend!"

Louie shakes his hand and says, "You h'are a blessed sight, my friend; dat's my bag also." He points to another bag just inside the doorway of the train, "I can tie dat on behin' me Louie," Kieren says, as he grabs it and heaves it over his shoulder.

Before long they are emerging from the woods to go down the steep riverbank to water their horses, "We'll hobble h'our horses here in duh grass while we cook h'our breakfast."

Louie has dismounted and is grinning at Pierre, "Jus' make sure dat you 'ave dem tied right; we do not need anudder nightmare like 'appened on duh way to St. Joseph dat time, back in '70."

"Oh! Don't even mention dat trip, mon ami. Dat was a disaster!" Peirre doubles over laughing and Louie joins in. "We will tell you dat story tonight, before we go to sleep; it's funny but it's frightful also." Louie continues laughing.

Pierre is letting down his horse's head to drink from the river, "Chawam, dat story is funnier d'an hell; but it was nearly duh h'end of you, my friend."

"Oui, oui, I am still suffering from bouts of consumption h'occasionally; usually if I am under severe duress."

"What is dat, my frien'?" Pierre says, as they take the horses to a patch of grass. "Well, I guess you could say it is worry." Louie says with a shrug.

"Well, hell, dat's prob'ly half duh time," Pierre says with a giggle.

"Tapway, mon ami … tapway."

After a strong prayer of blessing and thanksgiving by Louie, they enjoy a wonderful meal of bacon and bannock, "Do you t'ink dose buggers could smell dis bacon, if dey are following?" Kieren asks Pierre.

"Hell no, h'if dey h'are following dey will be a long ways off. H'our men are scoping duh horizon from tree-tops h'every mile or so." Louie can feel his body relaxing as they discuss their security tactics…Louie grins, "W'it duh comforting h'expertise of you all and duh good Lord looking down…I should feel quite safe."

They hold up once in a while as a couple of boys, generally the Lavallee brothers, go to a farmhouse and notify them of the gathering at St. Norbert on August 21st.

Louie is sitting under a tree smoking his pipe as the boys take the news to another family along the river, "I feel badly to not go and greet d'ose folks, h'it will be good to see d'em." He takes another little drag from his pipe.

"Don't worry about d'at, my frien'; you need to stay outta d'is h'until h'after camping day, when we gadder at duh church, d'ere h'at St. Norbert. Dey can greet you d'en; you will need your rest h'until den…sorry Chief." Pierre gives a little giggle.

The Lavallee boys can be seen coming into view, "I don't recall ever seein' you with any more d'an a moustache before, Chawam," Kieren says, "I never woulda reconized you, w'it d'at curly beard."

"I shall give h'it a good trim before I do any public speaking," Louie grins.

"Well, you do look like an old trapper!" says Kieren.

"I need to look half decent to go h'around doing my campaigning; I might frighten all d'ose little children, heh, heh, heh. How many will I 'ave for security when I travel h'around, Pierre?"

"We will need to put out two spotters in front and two in duh rear…you will be safe, my friend." Pierre makes a fist and grabs it with his other hand.

"D'en, o' course, you will need a scribe h'again, maybe Smitty or Ambroise, eh?" Pierre looks questioningly at Louie.

Louie taps the dead ashes out of his pipe onto his tree trunk "… I would prefer both, if Ambroise is doing well, d'ey h'are h'after 'im pretty bad also…poor fella, he has been so faithful."

"I know Louie, he came home like a whipped hound, he wouldn't leave his bedroom for a long time. His kids stayed on duh bed wit' 'im most o' duh time…poor bugger. Our men keep a constant watch on his house, dey will climb a tree, den scope duh horizon wit' a spyglass, den everyt'ing in between. We've 'ad to fire a few shots at tresspassers, a couple o' times. Dat makes dem skin d'ere h'asses outta d'ere, heh, heh, heh."

"All is clear!" Louie can hear the Nault boys galloping their way back from the St. Norbert mission. They holler first in French, then in English.

"It looks like we can carry on Louie," Pierre begins to roll up the blanket he has been resting his head on. He stands up, stretches, then scratches his head, "How about giving our horses another drink and having a good wash?"

"Sounds like a heck of an idea, Pierre!" Louie sets his hat on his head and begins the short walk over to the horses; they are all feeding not too far from the river, Pierre never forgets how fussy Louie is about his personal grooming.

Before long they are all freshened up, including the security. Hair combed, neckerchiefs clean and wet around their necks…they even wash out their sashes and tie them around their waists.

They ride along the trail to St. Norbert, three riders joining the trail every half mile, so as not to descend upon the encampment in a suspicious party of nine. Each rider heads toward their own family camp as they ride through the camp.

Pierre speaks quietly to Louie, in French, "Remember, my friend, Kieren and I will not leave you until you are safely at home after the gathering... then the Nault brothers will take over until you are ready to begin your rounds, for some reason, there has been no physical attacks on your family. About all I have heard of is shots fired once in a while and they tore up the garden a couple of times."

"I believe God protects them, Pierre. My heart is pounding, mon ami…I see my family by d'ere tents, now, d'ey do not see me, yet."

As he gets closer to his Mama's tent, his youngest brother, Alexandre, spots him, he yells, "Mama!" Louie raises his finger to his lips…the way his Papa always quietened the children.

They ride around to the rear of the tent and tie their horses to a tree branch. Alexandre runs around to hug his brother as soon as he is down from the saddle, "Hello, my dear little brother; you have grown so much!" Louie gives him a big bear hug; then, they go around and enter the tent.

"My Boy!" Julie is overwhelmed, "I have been waiting for you; we did not expect you until dark!" Louie hugs his Mama, rocking her back and forth, she wipes her tears with her apron.

Pierre and Kieren take turns kissing her cheeks, Pierre says, "You would be surprised at how secure this camp is, Madame Julie, we would like for Louie to have a quiet rest before the people begin their rough and noisy welcome, you know how we are, Madame, he will likely be swollen and bruised by tomorrow, heh, heh, heh."

Pierre and Kieren leave for the L'Ambitieaux camp once they have greeted all Louie's family. There is much ado at the Riel camp and after they have finished supper Louie listens to all the latest news until his eyes are getting heavy, "As much as I am enjoying all of you, I must retire."

"Of course, my boy, you must be exhausted! Charles could you light a lantern and help your brothers get moved over to your tent, sil vous plait?"

"Oui, oui, ma mere, we will have our beds made semak*, eh, Joseph?"

"Louie bids the women a joyful. 'Bon soir', and crawls into a fresh bed upon a straw mattress...*thanks be to God; this mattress smells heavenly...it must have been the first earthly aroma smelled by our Lord in that manger long ago...* he thanks his brothers and is asleep almost immediately.

The day is wearing on as folks drift back and forth between camps visiting with friends and relatives. The exciting smell of campfire smoke fills the air; dogs are barking and wagging their tails as children meet up with their cousins squealing with glee.

"Does this not remind you of our good old hunting camps, Madeleine?" Julie and Henriette, Louie's younger sister meet up with Pierre's wife as they unload food onto a large table where people will dish up and go sit on a blanket to eat. "Oui, Madame Julie, it brings back memories of happier times. But we will enjoy the return of your son; he is a welcome sight. Also, my feet are itching to dance," she gives a little jig,

"I will give Louie a run for his money after his debate with old Clark tonight. He will need a good jig after that, word that's out says Clark is a tough one to run against."

Julie begins to unfold blankets and hand them to her daughters to spread on the ground, "You know what that means, Maddie; we must be in prayer as Louie goes to the schoolroom after our feast." Julie gives Maddie one of her nods that tells Madeleine... they are dealing with serious business. She is speaking in old French... that gives her words all the more power.

Maddie answers her in Mechif, "Tapway, Madame, tapway."

The women spread a dozen blankets on the ground and the young boys carry all the food out to a huge blanketed feasting table, all set out on the ground. Fiddles and guitars are playing off and on until Henri Coutu stands at the head of the feast and claps his hands to get everyone's attention; he calls Louie over, speaking in French,

"We are so proud and happy to have our boy, Louie Riel back home with us," everyone cheers and claps, "…you may have something to say Louie and you are also welcome to bless our Feast."

Louie stands beside Henri Coutu, "My dear Henri, I am so thrilled to be here amongst my people once again." He bows in each direction, "…Merci, merci, I was so happy to receive your invitation; it would be my pleasure to let my name stand for nomination to serve you under our new Provincial Government, merci, merci.

I would like to call my good friends Ambroise Lépine and Louie Schmidt forward; we spoke earlier and they are willing to travel with me and to serve as my faithful scribes once more; we are overwhelmed to be together once more, he shakes their hands as they come forward, Ambroise embraces him with tears in his eyes. Everyone stands and cheers…

"Ambroise and I have suffered a lonely exile together; please continue to pray for our Canadian government to grant us an amnesty soon, that we may finally be recognized as servants of our people. We are very tired of being seen as criminals; pray that the Orange Canadians may be rendered powerless and that we may serve our people in peace. I do pray for a mighty blessing upon our gathering but… it would give me much pleasure to hear the prayers of our faithful Father Ritchot."

The crowd responds with a roar of applause and Father Ritchot steps forward to pray.

After the feast is over the fiddles and guitars begin their lively rendition of "Joys of Quebec".

Later in the evening a delegation of voters arrive at the St. Norbert school with Steven Clark…conversations around the camp trickle to a quiet and formidable silence as they realize the new arrivals are nothing less than… Clark with his own private security of Orangemen.

There is an awkward silence as seats are taken by Metis men, a few English speaking halfbreeds and local Orangemen…all are armed.

The debate had been arranged by Governor Archibald who also fills the role of moderator.

Clark is surprisingly pleasant and is treated respectfully in return. Both men speak of the need for equal participation in government; however, as the evening wears on it becomes very obvious that Riel has mesmerized Clark with his easy flowing manner. His knowledge of political law and his articulate delivery have had an intimidating effect on Clark. Each time Riel makes a profound and effective point, the crowd goes into another round of applause; soon Clark is gathering up his papers and stuffing them into a valise; he has had enough.

The debate wraps up and Steven Clark's delegation rides off.

Moments later the sound of the drums of the Elders can be heard warming up for a traditional Round dance. The families all begin to get into a circle around the fire to dance together and Honor the Creator.

After a busy day it will be nice to wind down before the children are taken back to their tents to be tucked in.

Louie's people are glowing with pride; they have no idea that a twist of fate is about to throw Riel out of the race…even with an obvious victory in the wind.

Nothing in the little constituency of Provencer will be able to stop the grinding political wheels in Ottawa.

Riel is well aware of the seething hatred Sir John A. MacDonald holds for the Metis; he makes no effort to hide his distrust for the widespread 'ferals' of the prairies who are standing in the way of progress.

He is also aware that Sir John holds George-Ettiénne Cartier tightly at his disposal; this is his ticket to retain Quebecois votes. Riel rarely speaks of his history with John A. and a series of subtle blows he has endured in the past.

While attending St. Sulspice seminary in Montreal, he had earned a reputation as a lecturer on a variety of subjects such as French, Greek and British history. He had learned to handle hecklers very gracefully; however, it was also no secret that John A. already viewed Riel as a threat.

Hecklers were soon forgotten, but when George Cartier turned his back on him, when he needed the job he had offered him…Louie was devastated.

Cartier had befriended Riel for political gain, until he realized John A's extreme dislike for him.

Louie had written several letters to Cartier hoping for one of the positions as a government bureaucrat, promised to Riel during one of their long conversations in a popular hangout in downtown Montreal.

It had taken years for Louie to deal with the betrayal of a good friend. Now he needs to choose between winning a seat by acclamation to serve his people, or to decline in order to accommodate Cartier.

Cartier, who had lost his Quebec seat, is now prepared to accommodate Red River with amnesties for those who participated in the Resistance of 1870. John A. needs to maintain Cartier's seat in the House of Commons in order to insure his Quebec support, at this point he is totally in favour of granting an amnesty.

Riel has not come this close to amnesty before, and although there is no mention of amnesty for Riel and Lépine, they assume they are included.

The only demand Riel made upon Cartier, as he promised to take up 'the cause', was that he also take up the responsibility of insuring the allocation of lands promised to the Metis people under the Manitoba Act…a promise being ignored by John A, who looked upon the Metis as "…ferals* of the west who need to be subdued." Pg. 11, 'The Riel Rebellion-1885', Frank Anderson 1984.

Word begins to spread that amnesty is forthcoming and "…there is hardly a soul in the French parishes of Red River who do not believe that 'the cause' includes amnesty for Louie Riel and Ambroise Lépine." Siggins, pg. 215.

Louie spends precious time with his Mama, sisters Marie and Eulalie, and his three brothers. He also takes time to receive folks from the community who need help with their applications under the Manitoba Lands Act.

Before Louie flees back, under cover, to St. Joseph, he spends time with Louie Schmidt and Ambroise Lépine doing an outline for a documentary on the Red River uprising, "...people need to understand that our intentions have always been honorable and that we have never deviated from our loyalty to the Queen."

Louie slides his chair back from the table out of the glare of the coal oil lamp, he heaves a long sigh and continues, "...Ambroise, my friend, no one will ever know how we have suffered in exile from our people. You know the truth and you may get some relief by telling your perspective and getting some of this burden off your chest. I have written much and I promise, my friend, you will find some relief."

Ambroise turns to Smitty, "The best way dat I can translate dis is ...dat we 'ave suffered greatly...sometimes duh fear is like being smuddered wit' a pillow..." his voice breaks and he cannot go on. He lays his head on the table and Julie brings him a cup of steaming tea, she speaks very gently to him in French, "My boy, drink this slowly, it has honey and ginger in it."

They are all sitting around the table drinking tea when Charlie and Joseph burst in, "Louie! You 'ave to leave...now! Dey h'are coming h'up duh road, about rwo miles back...dey h'are coming to h'arrest you!"

*Glossary

There are no Footnotes in this chapter.

Chapter Thirty Two

St. Joseph/St. Vital 1873

Louie has been sitting down by his favourite tree hidden up on the riverbank. He is reading his little green prayer book. The winter traffic passes back and forth on the Red River highway of snow, someone has dragged it again and the snowbanks are higher today.

*I feel so safe here watching the freight sleighs as they pass by. They have no idea that someone is watching them…this old buffalo robe is so warm; I feel like taking a nap…but, I better get back to the cabin…Antoine will soon be bringing my mail…*He does not realize that he will soon be opening a letter from Father Taché that will shatter his world.

Louie rises from his nest under the branches of a large pine tree; he lifts the large heavy buffalo robe as high as he can, then swings it around the tree trunk. As it smacks against the bark, snow flies up and takes Louie's breath away. He gives it one more shake and neatly folds it into four… *now, I will be played out when I get back, for sure. Smitty will think I have been hiking, heh, heh, heh. I sure hope he has the kettle on to boil…I could use a hot cup of tea.*

As he enters the house he sees a set of fresh tracks, *well, I see Antoine has arrived with the mail, he must be staying for tea.* He opens the door and Antoine greets him with a handshake, "Merci, Antoine, are you staying for tea?"

Antoine removes the fur hat from his matted head, "I was going to get back to splitting wood but dat sounds good!"

Smitty takes that as a hint and sets the kettle on to boil, "Now I told you Antoine, I can chop your wood, I'll follow you back up the trail to your woodpile." Smitty pulls up his sleeve and flexes his bi-ceps, "Gotta keep these babies up you know, Antoine."

"Merci, Smitty, dat will be real nice, my boy."

Louie begins reading his mail, "My God! No, no!" He falls back on his cot and begins to cough and choke.

Smitty grabs the letter he has been reading…it's from Father Taché, "My God! It's his sister Marie, she died a week ago!"

"Oh for God's sake! What next? Smitty, fix him a hot drink of honey and brandy, quick!"

"You bet, sir, here, put this pillow under his head."

Louie chokes out a few more words, "Tell me… dere is a mistake… Antoine, read dat again… sil vous plait." Antoine hands the letter to Smitty. "I can't read dis fancy writing Smitty, sorry."

Smitty takes the letter and reads the first sentence, "My boy, it is with deepest regret that I bring you this news, your Mama is in bed very ill, suffering with the shock of Marie's death today, she died of the influenza."

"I am so sorry, my friend, but I guess it's true." Smitty hands the letter back to Louie and goes to make a pot of tea and fix a small hot drink.

Antoine is at a loss for words for a moment, then, "I am so sorry Louie, what can I do for you? I can hitch the team to the sleigh and have Smitty light the heater in the caravan." Louie takes the letter and squeezes it in his hand as though he can squeeze the life from those horrible words.

"Monsieur, merci, merci, whatever you say." He rolls over and begins to sob into the pillow.

Soon after the funeral of his beloved sister Marie, Louie decides it is time... his heart is telling him that he must do the retreat he has been postponing. He must face up to the uncertainty of his destiny. He kneels at the side of his bed, in an upstairs loft at his Mama's...

Is he meant to resume the religious commitment he once had with God? Or is he meant to serve his people in a more secular discipline...perhaps politics or teaching...*It has been nearly ten years since I left the priesthood...I remember asking God to allow me ten years in the world...during this time I am to seek God's will for my life...I know that God would forgive me... and accept me back into the priesthood...I feel so bad when I see my poor Mama suffering such grief at the loss of our dear Marie...I wish I could help her...my heart aches to be able to work again and help her raise her little orphans...she is so ill, her headaches are so severe she dare not raise her head from her pillow... Oh, dear Lord Jesus, have pity on her. I will spend the next two weeks in a retreat. St. Boniface would be perfect...I will be in close touch with Mama, yet I will be in the safety of the Mission. Merci, sweet Mother Mary, Joseph and Lord Jesus...thank you for your guidance in my time of torment.*

Louie rises up from his knees and combs his hair before going downstairs to greet his sisters, Henriette and Eulalie, who are in the kitchen preparing the evening meal. *I will write a letter to our dear sister Sara, it will break her heart to not be with us at this time, but...she is betrothed to God and her busy life at the Ile-a-la-Crosse Mission will help to heal her heart.*

The girls have fixed a cot for Julie to sleep on downstairs; Louie spends some time sitting on a chair beside her, holding her hand. "Mama, you are looking stronger today. Keep drinking your tea and you will soon be back on your feet."

Louie checks Julie's supply of red willow that sits in a basket under the window in the parlor where Julie has been convalescing. She is recovering slowly by drinking red willow tea, "If there is anything I can do for you Mama, send word to St. Boniface Mission with the boys, sil vous plait. I will be doing my retreat there; when I am finished I will come home for a while and get ready to go where the Lord leads me."

During his second week at St. Boniface, Louie has a peculiar night, he is restless and has been having dreams of his Papa and his sister Marie. They are sweet dreams but, so short…too short.

He rises at 6:00 a.m. and goes downstairs; there, Sister Thérese is sitting by the fireplace, her face aglow in the dark, from the reflection of the flames coming off the burning logs.

She speaks pure French, "Good morning, Louie! How are you today?"

Louie has had his morning wash and is combing his hair; he pushes the waves back into his thick hair and pinches his moustache into place, "Good morning to you Sister Thérese. I am feeling better today, since I broke my fast. I have been too ill for the past two years to attempt a fast…my stomach had shrunk until I could barely take food. Yesterday, as you may have noticed, I ate very lightly until supper; then suddenly at suppertime I was hungry."

Sister Thérese began to laugh, "Yes, my boy, you were hungry! That is what happens when you spend precious time with the Lord…things suddenly do begin to improve!" She continues to laugh "…that is good Louie; you needed that. You are looking better today…when you arrived you looked awful, I am sorry to say."

"I agree Sister, you should know me quite well." Louie is remembering the trip to Montreal with Sister Thérèse, back in 1858, he was only fourteen.

"Louie, please do not be angry with me; I have something very special for you, it has been impossible to catch up to you. But now …Louie, I think it is time."

"What is it, Sister Thérèse?" Louie has sat down by the little greying nun.

"It is a blessing left for you by your father back in 1864, I was with him as he lay dying on his deathbed...he had a hard time speaking, but...I understood his every word."

Louie grabs at his hair, "Sister, what are you saying?"

The little nun looks at him, "Are you prepared for this Louie?"

"Yes, yes! What must I do?" He removes his fingers from his hair and pushes it back into place.

"If you please, Louie, kneel there by your chair and I shall pronounce the blessing upon you."

"Yes, yes, my dear sister, I shall." He kneels down immediately, folds his hands...and waits.

"Your Papa told me, 'Sister, I am dying, please... I must leave a blessing for my son in Montreal. Tell him that God has given me a wonderful blessing for him...he will be very gifted and will be a blessing to his people. He will suffer many afflictions, but God will deliver him out of them all. Whether he chooses to serve through church or state; God will be with him.' It was not long Louie, but it was very powerful."

Louie begins to sob. He sobs uncontrollably for a few moments; then, suddenly he is silent. His hands are trembling slightly as he presses his palms onto the sides of his chair and arises to his feet. He brushes the knees of his trousers, as if by habit; then, offers his hand to Sister Thérèse. She gently takes Louie's hand and rubs it with the other one, "Please forgive me Louie for taking so long to deliver your father's final words."

Louie smiles at the little nun and shakes his head, "Never give it another thought Sister; I am sure you know that God's timing is not the same as ours...obviously it was not time... until now."

As they speak, an unusual turn of events is taking place in London England. No one would have suspected that Louie Riel's life was about to take a sudden turn…a turn that would shake up Canada, the events of which are still resounding to this day.

The moment the news of Sir George Cartier's death in London hits the streets of Winnipeg…the race is on to fill his empty seat in the House of Commons.

Campaigning begins immediately. Louie, with his entourage of security, sets out on the campaign trail. He visits all the parishes in the constituency of Provencer. Support for Louie is so strong that neighbors come out to work the Riel property and get the crops into the ground.

By August it is common knowledge that Riel's chances to win by acclamation are fairly certain. His old enemy, John Schultz, is not happy with the way the election seems to be going; Henry Clarke is even unhappier.

Clarke summons up all his resources and plots for a final takedown of Riel "…and Lépine will go down with him," he tells his circle of supporters.

They all meet in the law office of Francis Cornish in downtown Winnipeg, cigar and pipesmoke fills the air.

William Farmer is appointed to draft arrest warrants for murder, "I can prepare your documents for an immediate arrest of both Riel and Lépine, for the murder of Thomas Scott…it will be up to you to find someone to sign them," Farmer says with a sneer, looking around the room. His eyes rest upon Dr. O'Donnell.

"Don't look at me, you bastard, you're the one who served time in his prison,… sign it yourself!"

"Hold on now, O'Donnell, you are the only Justice of the Peace in town; it's your duty to sign these warrants!"

"I will lose all my patients in the valley; my practice will be ruined!" With that John Schultz comes and stands towering over him, "Come on O'Donnell, you can leave town for a few months, by that time I will be too busy in Ottawa serving in Cartier's seat and you can have all my military patients…besides any other's of the Loyal Order; you'll be busier than hell!" O'Donnell signs the warrants grabs his hat and leaves.

Later that night the warrants are handed over to two policemen who immediately set out with a well-paid translator, Léon Dupont, to deliver the warrant of Louis Riel. It is not going to be that easy…suddenly there is a torrential rain; the three men get bogged down in black muskeg, they plug along in the pitch black night when suddenly they see a dim light… it is the lamplight of a French farmer. Dupont orders them to stay.

They take refuge in a darkened barn. Shivering with the cold rain they set out again in the early dawn, "Dere is duh Riel farm, straight ahead. I will stay back h'unless you wave me h'in."

Soon the two policemen return, their hats have been lost and their hair is full of shavings, "What the 'ell 'appened to you?" Dupont is doubled over in laughter.

"Go ahead and laugh you maniac! We fell through the ceiling. The son-uva…is not even there! Take us to Lépine, and hurry; before someone tips him off too!"

…….I have been watching that branch now for two days…still no sign of Charlie's necktie. He said he would leave it hanging close to a bush where he will hide food and messages. There is no traffic on the river to speak of… one freighter and a canoe. Why would he be afraid to cross the river? I am so thankful for the small buffalo robe with bread and boiled eggs tied in it that Octavie shoved at me as I ran out the back door…

Louie gathers a wad of moss and squeezes a piece of it in the bottom of a tobacco can, *…no one will ever see this little stream of smoke, but when I say prayers over it I can feel all the mosquitos, knats and evil spirits leaving this canoe…then I can lie on my robe and read Mama's little prayer book in peace.*

He starts his little smudge and blows down into the can to get it going. *This canoe is light as a feather…good thing I am not heavy…I sleep real good in it…*

if any animals try to get rough with me I have Papa's old rifle to protect myself. I am not used to all this fresh air...thank the good Lord I get sleepy real easy...

The third morning, Louie rises up and steps out of the canoe, his mocassins sink into the moss. He looks around, the birds are singing in the trees and a soft breeze sends him a wonderful fragrance *...I love the smell of those blueberries... Praise be to God, I can see Charlie's necktie hanging from that limb.*

He looks carefully up and down the banks of the Red River, it looks beautiful with rich green foliage along it's edges...*I love this old river...*he lovingly scoops out his first drink of the day and washes up happily, using his red neckerchief for a towel. *I am so anxious to get a note from my family. Please be with them and protect them Mary, Joseph and Lord Jesus, amen, praise be to God.*

He makes his way through the thick bush to the trunk of the tree that holds the necktie, he parts a green clump of undergrowth and picks up a dishtowel that is tied into a bundle. Then he sits and snuggles his back up against the trunk of the tree, *Aha, look at the buns, butter and ham...oh, praise be to God! Now, what is in this note?* He opens the little note paper and reads: *We hope this finds you well, my boy. I am sorry to tell you that Ambroise Lépine has been arrested for the murder of Thomas Scott. Please do not worry; God does have good plans for you. I believe your blessing from Papa, you are destined to serve your people.*

We will watch for the sign that you have received this. Charlie says to leave it in a half–hitch, take care my boy, we love you dearly, Mother and family.

Louie buries his face in the note...*Dear God, they have taken Ambroise, please take care of him, and his family...*He sobs into the note, then folds it neatly and tucks it into an inside pocket in his beaded vest.

I shall not move until they tell me it is safe...in the meantime I shall spend a lot of time in Mama's little green prayer book...I shall keep myself busy reading the Proverbs of Solomen and the Psalms of my beloved David.

Julie, knowing her son very well, has left him the stub of a pencil and a few sheets of paper. He puts it to good use:*[1]

...I will lie down in the cold.

Sad and alone in the woods.

The wind I hear always murmuring.

It seems to me your voice, my beloved country!

It seems to me your voice, my adorable sweetheart.

The day I find is not so long.

Though I experience the most profound Sorrow.

Yet my soul is charmed... Siggins, Louis Riel, 1994

There seems to be much comfort coming to Louie by the writing of poems, it has always provided a solace. He dreams of King David and his parallel life of sins, sorrows and repentence. *...Even the fears and sorrows of my present 'hiding out in the bush' reminds me of David as he hides out in a cave, in fear of the Philistines. I should praise God for the honor of hiding in the comfort of these bushes. If the mosquitoes get bad I just rub mud on my face.*

It is Louie's fourty-fifth day of hiding when he finally gets a note saying it is safe to come home, everyone is gathered there and they are ready to celebrate Louie's victory. He has been elected by acclamation to serve in the House of Commons!

Louie emerges from the bush, his face covered in mud, his teeth shining white, wearing the smile of victory. His friends and family wait on the other side of the river, smiling, shouting and waving!

Louie buries his face in the river, washes his face and hair and soon he is as handsome as ever, He paddles at top speed to get to the other side.

Julie is given room to hug Louie first, then the hugs and handshaking begins, finally Louie excuses himself to take his mother up to the house. She is still rather weak and Louie does not mind walking slowly up the slope… then through the barnyard and up to the house. The women rush on ahead to put all the food out for a celebration feast.

Blankets are spread out on the ground and the Elders, after the smudging ceremony is done, begin to sit down on the blankets. They chatter in Cree, laughing and joking. Then they are dished up and served by all the young men.

Everyone gathers around the blankets in a large circle; Father Richot prays a blessing upon Louie and his new role in Ottawa; then he pronounces a blessing upon the food.

After the meal, the instruments come out and the dancing begins. Women wearing long full skirts covered with aprons are held firmly by their men as they are propelled across the grass, mocassins and riding boots step lightly to the sound of energetic, traditional fiddle music.

Women and children dance in the kitchen; children are laughing and dogs are barking around their little moccasined feet. Great joy has come to the Riel family!

*Glossary

Footnotes:

1 'Provincer' - The constituency in Red River where Louis Riel was elected to a seat in the House of Commons.

Chapter Thirty Three

Ottawa/Montreal, 1874

October 21st, 1873, Louie leaves for Ottawa. Family and friends have gathered up enough money to pay Louie's expenses with some left over for Julie, including $100.00 from Bishop Taché, who is slowly beginning to accept Louie's change in vocations.

Louie is accompanied by two bodyguards who map out a short cut that will by-pass St. Paul, a stronghold for deviants from the Orange Order in the east.

Riel is met in Montreal by Honoré Mercier who becomes an instant fan. He is a thirty three year-old Lawyer who has followed the legends of Riel in Quebec; he immediately introduces him to Alphonse Desjardins, a lawyer and the editor of *Le Nouveau Monde,* the paper that has been speaking in defence of the Red River Resistance ever since it began in 1869.

Louie's powerful and articulate response to the slanderous and racist letter of Mair in Red River, was proudly published by Desjardins, now he gets to shake Riel's hand, the author of this letter that set the Ontario elite on their heels.

Mercier and Desjardins seem to be oblivious to the dangers Riel keeps reminding them of; they are anxiously impatient to show him off in the House of Commons.

Soon they are settled in at the home of Jean Duret, a friend of Mercier and Desjardins, a mere stone's throw from Hull Quebec, which is directly across the river from Ottawa. To Riel's amazement…a long-time spiritual icon Bishop Bourget, lives just around the corner.

When Louie has investigated the validity of this incredible neighbor, he finds that his hero has been very ill, he is seventy-five years of age... *I must visit this man, I have spent years hearing of his historical feats in restoring the credibility of the papal Diocese here in Montreal, after the shattering destruction of the French Revolution. He will surely be a powerful force to reckon with in our struggle to obtain an amnesty for our people. We need to move fast…my dear friend Ambroise Lépine's life is on the line. Now that he has been charged with the crime of murder… he is a constant visitor in my nightmares.*

His imagination runs wild as he stands at the large window facing the Hull bridge that divides Upper and Lower Canada,

The thought of Bishop Bourget's palace being so close-by, is causing Riel to be more than anxious to meet him…*Could this man help me to heal from my paranoia?*

Louie can see the new and intimidating government buildings on the other side of the river. He has lost his nerve, again. I cannot enter that building without a blessing from God.

I will take a cab to the Bishop's mansion…tomorrow.

As he pays for the cab, he looks up at the intimidating, large building… *I must make it up those steps…*He steps onto the cobblestone plateau; he still has to walk across to the huge double doors.

He takes out a fresh handkerchief and presses it across his brow, careful not to disturb his unruly hair that is combed in his favourite style. He straightens his tie.

Guards stand on each side of the ornate doorway, in pure French he asks, "Could you tell me what is the protocol used in seeing the Bishop?"

The guard on the right replies in French, "I am sorry, sir, the Bishop is at Hotel- Dieu, you must take a cab and when you are inside, go straight to the Nurses Station. They will make Bishop Bourget aware of your request."

Riel bows to each guard, touching the brim of his flat-brimmed hat, "Merci, merci."

Before long Louie is stepping in the door of the Bishop's dazzling hospital room. Candelabras and statues are reminders of the Bishop's holy state, "Come in Louie Riel, it is a pleasure to meet you."

Louie steps forward and bows low before the Bishop, "It is my pleasure, sir. I have heard much about your endeavors and your accomplishments in the past thirty years of your term, you are an amazing man. I am very honored to make your acquiantance."

Louie is beginning to feel dizzy, he goes down on his knees, "Dear Bishop, I have been elected to the seat of our dearly departed George Cartier. I must confess…I have been very ill…I do not have the strength to enter the House of Commons…where there are men of hatred ready to take my head."

"You are in need of a spiritual renewal, my boy. You must visit the Oblates and perform a novena. Now, rise up and reclaim your faith, your health and your position in Christ. Do what your Doctor prescribes you."

Louie rises and Bishop Bourget makes the sign of the cross upon him, "I bless the medicines that are given you."

Louie tucks his hat under his arm and bows once more, "Merci, Merci." He crosses himself and smiles before taking his leave.

Louie makes his way back to his current abode, *I feel a great relief, now, I must get into bed…I believe I will sleep for two days…*

***

Madam Masson has been on his mind, he decides to visit the Terrebonne Estate; he knows Madame Sophie will be happy to see him.

The gates are locked at the mansion and Louie is investigating the security lock when a voice calls out from behind the hedge and stone wall, "Who goes de'ya?"

"Moses! Z'is is Louie Riel, remember me?" He steps back from the gate as he hears the footsteps of Moses on the cobblestone entrance, he pulls open the gate; Louie is amazed, it still sounds the same, a grinding squeak. Moses has become a bit greyer but his smile is still captivating.

"Of course I remembers you, sir. Come on in, Miss Sophie will be thrilled to see you and so will Miss Millie!" He grabs Louie's hand and pumps it up and down. Louie takes his shoulders and plants a traditional French kiss on each cheek.

Madame Sophie is overwhelmed. She heard the fuss out in the foyer, but stayed and waited in her chair by the fireplace.

"We has a surprise for you Miss Sophie," Moses steps aside and lets Louie through the door, "It's Mastah Louie Ma'am, he's come home for a visit!"

Louie kisses her cheeks; then, takes her in his arms, "Please, forgive me Madame." Sophie is dabbing at her eyes with a small hankie, "There is nothing to forgive, my boy."

After two days of celebrating and shopping, Louie is played out; he asks Madame Sophie if he can spend one day alone in his old guest house, "Of course, my boy, you can stay as long as you want."

Louie pulls on his long jacket and slips into his shiny new boots, "I would love to Madame Sophie, but I must get some rest then be on my way to spend some time with my beloved Oblates. Then, when I get strong enough, I will take my seat in the House." Louie is enjoying the old French he has always used when speaking with Madame Sophie.

Crawling into the large four poster bed he has a few passing thoughts of his first love; then, he drifts off to sleep.

His dreams are busy, moving in and out, back and forth, from Red River to Montreal.

He awakens to find that Moses has been in and out, leaving him with a decanter of hot coffee and a small plate of crépettes. *I am enjoying this visit but my brain needs a rest…even in a safe place like this…I still feel threatened.*

After visiting the outhouse he pours some water into the large basin and washes up.

He leans back in his large padded chair and sips at the familiar strong sweet coffee, *I am so happy to finally be acquainted with Madame Sophie's son, Rodrigue Masson; what a fine young gentleman. He was always attending University in London when I stayed here before…I cannot believe that he is willing to travel to Red River and meet my constituents. He said he would visit as many as he could and let them know that I have solicited a lot of support for an amnesty for the people of Red River. It will be so helpful for him to write a report on his findings.*

Rodrigue is also going to defend poor Ambroise in his upcoming trial.

It was like old times, dealing with a tailor who will be delivering my two new suits tomorrow…Praise be to God, I am so thankful for His care.

After supper and a teary good-bye with Sophie and Millie, Moses drives Louie over to Mile End to spend the evening with Uncle John and Auntie Lucie.

Moses helps him up to the house with his bags, "Now you take care 'o yersef Mastah Louie, you looks good but Moses know yous not well at all. Promise ol' Moses, you'll see a Doctor right away." He sets down the bags, "Yes Moses, I promise."

He tips his hat to Aunt Lucie as she opens the door, "Oh, my God! John, it's Louie! Come on in, my boy, give me your bags, here, take off your coat." Louie kisses her cheeks and hands her his coat.

He steps into the dining room where Uncle John is having his tea and cigar, "For God's sake, Louie! Where have you been hiding? They are still after your head in a sack you know!"

Shaking hands with his uncle he explains to him that he has body gaurds who see him to his cabs when he goes anywhere, "I hardly go out Uncle, I have been spending a couple of days with Madame Sophie and..." Uncle John, as uncouth as ever, buts in "...Well I can see that by your new clothes!"

"I am about to go to Plattsburg for a couple of weeks. There is a hellish ordeal taking place with Sir John A. I doubt if things will settle down for a while, even with this Mackenzie, who is about to replace him, if he has to resign."

"Now isn't that just like the Conservatives, trying to scoop money from the Railroad stockholders...they're all alike, even the Liberals...you'll find out. They're all out for the money, you mark my words!"

"Oh please John, let the boy alone, you're making him nervous. Would you like a coffee, my boy?"

"Why yes, Auntie I have been fighting off another bout of the influenza. You know, my dear sister Marie died from the influenza just last winter... it broke my heart, Auntie."

"I am sure it did, my boy." Lucie hands him a cup of coffee, he begins to scoop spoons of sugar into it...three spoons and he begins to stir, stir... Lucie looks at John and John shakes his head.

"You know Louie, it will be nice to have you stay the night but I don't trust those Orangemen, they have a hatred for the French and even moreso if they are part Indian. They could have spies looking in our window right now. I don't trust them one bit."

"Oh John, lets go into the parlor and sit by the fire; Louie needs to relax."

"Come on Louie, grab your coffee, we'll have a smoke by the fire."

"Yes Uncle, I will get my pipe. You know I could catch the midnight train if you would take me to the station Uncle." Louie sits down with his pipe and takes a long drink of his coffee.

"That sounds like a good idea, my boy. So let's smoke, you can tell me about your family. They rarely stop by, you know, your Papa's brothers come every once in a while to visit Lucie."

By eleven oclock Louie has had enough of Uncle John's bragging, "Well Uncle, I can move my bags out back and help you hitch up your carriage."

"That sounds good Louie; you can say your good-byes to your Auntie while I hitch up."

Louie can feel himself slipping into that dreaded cloud of paranioa, he has lost his appetite again and has been visiting one of Desjardin's doctors, he begins to chatter nervously with his uncle on the way to the station, "… he is supposed to be highly recommended by people in government who suffer from the stress of politics, Desjardins tells me." Uncle John is only half listening… soon they arrive at the huge Montreal Train Station.

Now I am being treated like I have a dreaded plague…by my own uncle.

I have wished to go to Keeseville at times…Evelina is comforting to be around…but I am not fit company at the moment. Perhaps on my return from Plattsburg, I shall stop and see her and Father Fabien.

Now, I must get well…how can I be of help to my people when I am too paranoid to enter the House of Commons?

Soon Louie is settled on the train, back in the safety of his favourite seat. As the clacking of the train speeds up, he leans back with his hat over his eyes. The carefree sound of children's laughter in the seat behind him gives him great comfort…soon he is sound asleep.

*Glossary

Footnotes: There are no Footnotes in this chapter.

Chapter Thirty Four

Keeseville, New York State/Ottawa 1873

After a two-week stay at Plattsburg, Louie begins to regain some strength. He has been having a quiet and blessed retreat with the Oblates… enjoying the warmth of their company.

He has now grown a full beard and is back to dressing in the chic wardrobes chosen by the fashion conscious, Madam Masson and her son, Rodrigue.

As the steam blasts from the front wheels of the huge train engine, Louie hears the welcome sound of the conductor's loud and long, "All aboo… ooard!"

He swings his walking stick up onto the second, strong, metal step. With one quick twist of his wrist he has pulled his skinny frame up into the passenger car, a friendly Porter greets him, "Allow me, sir!"

Louie hands him his bags and struts along behind him, glancing back and forth, from side to side, *They all look fairly normal to me,* "I shall be seated near the lavatories, if you please." *I always feel safe sitting with families who are keeping their children close to the lavatories.*

"Next stop, Kee…eesville!" The conductor sings out the familiar words; soon he is disembarking at Keeseville Station. Two carriages are parked waiting for passengers, *This little place just keeps on growing little by little, not quite like St. Paul, it seemed to blossom into a city overnight.*

Soon the driver is slowing his carriage down, "Whoa, whoa, Prince, take it easy. If you need another ride back to the train, I kin come back, sir."

"Yes, I will need a ride in three days, in time for the evening train, with extra time to get my other bag from storage." Louie can hear Rags barking and Evelina is coming down the sidewalk to the gate.

"You bet, sir. I will be here!" He pockets his generous tip and turns his team around and trots them back down the tree lined lane.

Once again, Miss Sophie has sponsored Louie with a generous gift.

He looks around, *Not much seems to ever change at the School Mission across the street; but, Barnabe's two-story home now has a three-story addition by the looks of it.* He looks around at the impressive balconies that surround the house. *I bet Evelina is still teaching those little Mohawk girls to sew. Now wouldn't I look if she has acquired a husband. I haven't written to her since I was elected.*

"Louie, Louie! Why haven't you written?" She throws her arms around his neck; Rags is barking and jumping up on Louie's freshly pressed pants. "Down Rags! Oh, Louie, it's so good to see you, you are so thin. Come on in and have some breakfast."

Louie picks up his bag, "No, no, my dear. Don't be troubling yourself."

"Oh it's no trouble Louie, there are left over sausages and pancakes, I could even cook eggs."

"No H'evelina, sausages and pancakes sound wonderful!"

As usual, Louie is given the royal treatment for the next two days, he now has a bedroom to himself that has a balcony overlooking the growing city. He fills Evelina and Father Fabien in on the political happenings.

"Now Louie, you need to get in there and expedite that amnesty, now that you are in that sort of a position!"

Evelina's mother is a bit more sensitive to Louie's condition, "Oh Fabien, he's not well, don't be pressuring him!"

"Well, there is an old saying, 'You've got to strike while the iron is hot!' You know what I mean Louie, get yourself some good medicine and get on with it!"

"Please Fabien, you have always had high expectations of Louie, and that's good, but the man is suffering. He hasn't had time to grieve for his sweet sister Marie." Evelina breaks into tears and Louie puts his arm around her shoulder.

"That's okay, Evelina, Fabien is right. Time is wasting while I wimp around feeling sorry for myself. Fabien has a way of making me realize how blessed I am. You are absolutely correct Fabien, it is back to good old Proverbs 3:5, 'Trust in the Lord with all your heart and lean not on your own understanding.' I am getting too high on myself Fabien. Once again, I thank you for setting me straight,"

"Well, my friend, I believe you are right to go to the Oblates for a spiritual renewal, but the time comes when you need to take yourself by the nap of the neck and get with it!"

"I do h'appreciate your advice, brother Fabien, you 'ave always been honest wi's me. Now it is time for my cab to h'arrive and I shall be off to Montreal. May God give me zuh strength and protection to accomplish what He has set me out to do."

"Amen, when things settle down and you are feeling better, come and stay with us for a while. I realize Keeseville is not the same, since the fire.*" pg.275, Siggins.

"Merci, Fabien, and H'evelina, I do miss you and think of you often; someday I may ask you to marry me, if you remain single...you h'are a very good friend…take care…I must go, my cab is here." Louie holds Evelina in his arms, then kisses her cheeks. He wipes away the tears from under her big blue eyes.

Once he is settled on the train he begins to doze off…*Evelina is always like a good tonic to me…I can't forget how good it felt to hear her sing, once again…I surprised her when I jumped up and jigged to her piano playing…it sounded so good…I need to go back to my homeland…where there is laughter and music, like 'Turkey in the…'*

***

Back in Montreal, things are heating up in the back room meetings of the Canadian Pacific Railway. By November 5th, 1873, Sir John A. has resigned from his post as Prime Minister of Canada. He has fled the scene as he is being investigated for fraud…he heads for North Carolina where his wife is staying with family.

For Louie Riel the upheaval is a convenience. He is not feeling like forcing himself into public …*I am fine right here writing poetry and letters back home; the doctor has prescribed me the right medicine…I am not fearful anymore. I just feel like staying out of the line of fire…hell, why should I offer myself up for someone's target practice…let them all squabble, heh, heh, heh. I have written so many letters that I have a hard time keeping up with reading my replies. Might as well enjoy life for a change. Now that Mackenzie is running the show and chosen a bigot like himself for a right hand man, I shall just lay low.*

January 17th, 1874, Prime Minister Mackenzie calls an election for February 13th…immediately Louie is bombarded by mail from home asking him to let his name stand again.

'Le Metis' is strongly supporting him, and a plan has been arranged that Louie will take a seat right next to his friend, Alphonse Desjardins, one of the more prestigious members of Parliament.

In Red River, the opposition to Riel is Joseph Hamelin who brought in 68 votes to Riel's 195, a surprising victory for a candidate who is *in absentia.*

Riel is elated with the loyalty of his people, but now he must appear in the House to sign the register of new Members of Parliament.

Merci, merci, Mother Mary, Joseph and Jesus, Son of God. If you believe in me, then I must believe in you...you all will be there as I sign that register...I will do it ...so help me God. He makes the sign of the cross.

Thankfully, Louie is totally unaware that, upon the news of his victory, the city is suddenly flooded with headhunters, all armed with guns and arrest warrants for the famed revolutionary.

At 1:30, March 26th, 1874, Louie Riel saunters around the lobby of the House of Commons, dressed and groomed meticulously. Moustache trimmed in the latest style and hair trimmed in a handsome cut, he moves about wearing an elaborate suit and a new name, during introductions... he is seemingly at ease.

He moves in the general direction of the registration desk with his assistant Jean-Baptiste-Romauld Fiset, who leads the dashing young politician into the office of the chief clerk, Alfred Patrick, "Sir, I have with me a young member of Parliament who wishes to register."

Fiset stands aside; Patrick, a thirty year veteran of the House, glances quickly over the spectacles hanging on his nose, as he reaches for the Registration Book.

Then he administers the oath ... Riel quietly responds. The Register is pushed in front of him and Riel scribbles his famous ineligible signature.

"Thank you sir," says the clerk, and as Riel and Fiset leave out a side door, Riel turns at the door and bows...the clerk sees his face and jumps up yelling frantically for the Minister of Justice, who is mingling in the crowd nearby.

When the news breaks, all hell tears loose … the whole city of Ottawa goes into an uproar.

Every detective and policeman in town is armed with a gun and a warrant for the arrest of the fugitive, Louie Riel.

While the haters of Riel are abuzz with stories, both true and false, the supporters of Riel quickly begin to rally. The media has a heyday as the city parts like the Red Sea.

In the House of Commons both sides boldly take their stands and even though Louie's seat is glaringly empty, his supporters rise to his defence.

First the eloquent son of Madame Masson, Rodrigue, delivers a very well researched exposé on the well-intentioned Red River resistance.

He drives home his points regarding Riel's stubborn loyalty to the Queen. First he notes the the attempted take-over of the Fenians and the immediate response of the Metis, in answer to to the Governor's request for aid.

Next, he expounds on Riel's guidance and legal expertise while establishing the Provisional Government.

Finally, even though Riel spoke of a new province within the Canadian confederation, steps had to be taken immediately to protect the people against the rising terrorism of the Orange rebels.

Tyranny was the order of the day; women were being abducted and raped, he reports. Anyone who resisted the 'so-called' Canadians, were threatened, beaten or killed.

Terror ruled the streets of the Red River community; women were afraid to go to town without protection; even the men rode in packs.

The ring leader was a man named Thomas Scott. He was arrested immediately, along with several other renegade Orangemen, upon the bloodless takeover of Fort Garry by the Metis.

Scott turned out to be a nightmare for the guards of the Fort Garry prison. Every waking hour was spent degrading the 'dispicable authority' by threatening, cursing the Metis guards and yelling out racial slurs.

Still, he was not formally charged until his third jail-break.

"Louie Riel was assaulted, cursed, spit upon and attacked by Scott with his fists. Finally, after consistently stirring up hatred among the prisoners, he was charged with insubordination and treason ... I have personally interviewed a large cross-section of Red River residents and whether the testimony is from Angloes or Metis, the story is the same. His leadership was impeccable and honorable.

Joseph-Alfred Mousseau also delivers a strong case for the amnesty of those involved in the resistance, particularly on behalf of Riel and Lépine. He gave a clear definition of the responsibility of the sovereign right to rule and restore order, in the absence of Hudson Bay rule.

Mousseau then makes a motion calling for a full amnesty for the Metis leaders; the motion is quickly defeated by a large majority of Orangemen.

Mackenzie Bowell, a grand master of the North Hastings Lodge and an extreme bigot, rises in the House and calls for a motion that, "...the exact legal status of Louis Riel be established..." The motion is carried.

The House then adjourns.

The visitor's gallery is full to capacity and as the Speaker adjourns the House, a hush falls over the crowd...which is followed by a giant cascade of disappointed moans and groans.

The next day, when Parliament resumes, Louie's bitter enemy and the Attorney General of Manitoba, Henry Clarke, arises and presents an indictment against Louis Riel... for the murder of Thomas Scott. "He is nothing less than a fugitive from justice."

Mackenzie Bowell then insists that Riel be ordered to attend the House session the next day, which brings a smile to the face of Dr. John Schultz, M.P. for Selkirk. This is an incredible 'catch 22'; if Louie doesn't take his seat, he will be expelled. If he does appear, he will be arrested.

April 2nd, 1874, the House and Gallery are all filled to overflowing again and people scan the House, many carrying photos of the mysterious M.P.

Riel does not appear; everyone is devastated. The House is adjourned for one week.

One week later when Parliament reconvenes, the seat beside Desjardins is still empty; a motion for expulsion is put forward by Mackenzie Bowell, "... Louis Riel, having fled from justice and having failed to obey an Order of this House, that he should attend in his place, Thursday, 9th day of April, 1874, be expelled by this House." (Siggins, pg. 231.)

The motion is passed 124 to 68. Dr. John Schultz, M.P. for Selkirk, is smiling with glee.

Although Riel is devastated, his supporters quickly remind him that, along with the expulsion, a committee is struck to hear evidence relating to the amnesty.

Riel is haunted by two strong desires: the longing to see his family and the heart-ache of being in constant prayer for the comfort of his compatriot, Ambroise Lépine, who is languishing in shackles, being fed bread and water.

He spends many sleepless nights praying for God's intervention...*dear Father in Heaven, grant that you may save Lépine from his death sentence.*

Riel resumes his two year vendetta, travelling by rail on the Northern Pacific Railway; he speaks at many rallies on behalf of the Manitoba 'cause'. The 'little Canadas' strung along the shores of the Au Sable River, welcome Riel as a hero.

The little French-speaking communities that line the border from New York State to New England are filled with many Ojibwe and Mohawk men from Quebec. They are hardworking loggers, construction and iron-workers who have left their little farms in Quebec for higher wages in the industrial northern States.

He writes his Mama a pleasant letter on July 20th, 1874 informing her of his recent turn of events …for once his expectations are promising. "… everyone is for us wherever I go…"

His exuberance is short-lived. To his honor and distress, his faithful countrymen nominate him to run in a by-election; by August he is back in Montreal.

Dr. Lachapelle, an old classmate, sends $50.00 to pay for his election deposit and Rodrigue again travels to Red River to campaign for the disenchanted Louie.

He is not excited about subjecting himself to the emotional abuse of another election…he is even more dissolusioned when he is again elected… *Sweet Mary, Joseph and precious Lord Jesus, I have worked so hard to help my dear Ambroise to be set free, guide me and direct my paths, sil vous plait, Praise be to God.*

Louie decises he would be foolish to attempt to take his seat in the House. He develops another plan of action; he will meet with as many highly influential Members of Parliament as possible.

His prayer is to maintain a consistant rapport with these people of influence, as they pressure the government toward granting an amnesty.

His first visit is with his old teacher of Latin and Greek, Father LaFlèche, who is now the Bishop of Trois Rivières. He prays for guidance as he approaches several of his supporters who may be of a Liberal influence, including a young liberal M.P. by the name of Wilfred Laurier.

In October Riel is successful in obtaining two excellent defence lawyers for the long-awaited trial of Ambroise Lépine, Joseph Royal of Red River, and Joseph-Adolphe Chapleau of Montreal, one of Riel's old classmates.

The trial lasts three excruciating weeks and although the team delivers an excellent arguement, with many ups and downs, the final blow is delivered...the jury delivers a guilty verdict and Lépine is sentenced to death by hanging. Riel is devastated.

After several weeks of sleeping, prescriptions of his special nerve tonic, and prayer, Riel emerges from his convalescence at the Masson Estate.

Once again he is determined to continue his fight for an amnesty; he returns to Keeseville to resume his speaking engagements throughout the little Canadas, "...the sound of Lépine and Nault's chains have aroused the sympathies of every French Canadian and every Catholic..." Riel continues.

Louie has sent most of Madame Sophie's sponsorship funds to help out his mother. For now he will be depending on the kindness of Barnabe's for room and board. Small donations collected at his speaking engagements help with expenses for a while; however, the majority of his audiences in attendance are not wealthy sponsors any more.

Finally, in January, 1875, Riel receives his miracle, a reprieve is offered by Governor General Lord Dufferin...Lépine's death sentence is revoked and he will be released October 26th, 1876, four days before his execution date.

Like many miracles, Riel receives his own amnesty but not without sorrow...he must be banished from Canada for five years.

Louie is crushed; he visits his Doctor for more medicine and begins to work on a new plan of action.

He must try to accept the fact that his life, over in his precious homeland of Red River ... is now on hold. *How will I be able to help my Mama? I must sell a plot of land to pay up some of her debts and provide food for the family.*

Louie recalls an offer he once received from Monsieur Ballantyne; he will write his Mama a letter of permission to sell the land.

News from home has not been good.

According to his brother Joseph and his good friend Smitty, Governor Morris has been proving to be blatently cruel to all Indians and Metis. He has no interest in meeting with most Treaty commitments.

There has been a steady exodus of Metis from the Red River settlement. They are gradually migrating west to meet with their relatives near the confluence of the North and South Saskatchewan rivers.

Riel is becoming very disturbed that his people, the mixed bloods, Metis and Indians, who number more than 48,000 in the region of Rupert's Land, are being so mistreated they are reported to be 'seething with discontent'.

His relationships with the Priests of New York State and New England are strong and his hope is to promote some good will amongst the network of Catholics spread from Montreal to Red River. They wield a strong influence over the politicians in Ottawa.

There seems to be nothing else Riel can do to help… while he is in exile.

*Glossary

Footnotes:

There are no Footnotes in this chapter.

Chapter Thirty Five

Longue-Pointe Assylum, 1876

Louie has spent the summer of '75 travelling throughout the little Canadas and he has grown very close to the Priests in each parish.

His home base is the home of the Barnabes and although he is physically exhausted many times, he returns home to catch up on his correspondence and to spend time with the lovely Evelina.

"H'evelina! I am back; where are you?" Louie's voice echos throughout the large home of the Barnabe's; he climbs the stairs up to his bedroom.

"I'm out here on the balcony Louie; grab a cup of tea and come sit out here with me."

Louie pours himself a cup of tea, drops three teaspoons of sugar into it and takes his spoon with him, "You look lovely my dear; your hair shines like gold in zuh sunlight."

He seats himself at the little table, breathing in the fresh air as he sets his tea down and begins to stir.

"Louie, my brother Fabien received this letter from Bishop Taché out in Winnipeg. He says not to give it to you without staying with you as you read it."

She hands the letter to Louie. He looks at her suspiciously, "Now what h'on eart' is going h'on?" He takes the letter from Evelina's hand; he lays down his spoon, then, he begins to gasp… "H'evelina, did you know? Why… why would Charlie just h'up and die? …I am banned from entering Canada!" His fingers automatically grab at his hair, "… I cannot go home to be with Mama... oh my God!"

He slumps forward, his face resting on his arms… his teacup goes over and slowly, like a slow moving tide, the tea spreads a brown stain over the white linen tablecloth.

A young Mohawk boy is working in the garden out back; Evelina leans over the balcony, "Sylvain, Silvain! Hurry up here and help me with Mr. Riel!"

As the young man enters the bedroom Evelina yells, "Out here on the balcony Sylvain, I think he has fainted."

She is mopping his brow with a wet facecloth, "Take and lay him on that bed, then ride as fast as you can to Dr. Marsh's, tell him it is urgent!"

The young Mohawk man, who works in a Sawmill upriver, picks Louie up like a child and gently lays him on the bed; he curls up like a worm on the patchwork quilt.

After several days Louie begins to move around the bedroom using his walking stick, "Louie, don't you be trying to walk when I am not up there!" Evelina is yelling up the stairs; she can hear him moving about.

He is now having new dreams; he keeps hearing the words of his brother Joseph's recent letter, "…Charlie became very ill while working on the tracks for Northern Pacific Railway…" Brother-in-law Louie Lavalle writes, "…he languished in pain …he was well prepared for death and died quietly, like a little child." Siggins, pg. 252.

Louie lies back down and stretches out on the large patchwork quilt, *I must go home; Mama will be broken-hearted again. Oh…my sweet sister Sara, away up in Ile-a-la-Cross, she will be missing another tragic funeral…*

dear Father in Heaven, send a host of your Holy angels to comfort our family... Praise be to God.

Louie rolls over; presses his face into a pillow, and sobs. *Dear Mother of God, have mercy on me, I am so weak...I must remember Psalm 34:19 '... many are the afflictions of the righteous... but the Lord shall deliver them out of them all...' Praise be to God, have mercy on my poor Mama...* Evelina brings him a drink of water and gives him a tablespoon of his medicine... soon he drifts off to sleep.

Louie continues to sleep in fits and nightmares. Evelina is deeply concerned, "Fabien, I don't know what to do; he's running out of medicine, I've been giving him double doses like the doctor told me to. He says he can bring more but, maybe we should try to get him to his family," she searches her brother's face for an answer.

"I agree Evelina, we will pack him up and get him ready to travel on the train back to Montreal. Hopefully his uncle John will take him. He's upsetting the whole household and Mother is not well to have to be subjected to Louie's erratic behavior. There's nothing else we can do."

Father Barnabe is at his wit's end. He wires John Lee to come and get his nephew. He agrees, but at the same time, he makes arrangements for a carriage to pick them up at St. Lambert, to avoid drawing attention at the massive Bonaventure Station in downtown Montreal, which is crawling with security.

John Lee is not about to risk his neck by being an accomplice to a felony; he is well aware that entering Canada would be a contravention of Louie's exile order.

Louie's poor Aunt Lucie was aghast at Riel's appearance. Her handsome nephew seemed like a stranger. He ranted and raved that he was being forbidden to attend mass.

John Lee did not show mercy on him and told him he could not take him into public, as he was acting crazy, "No I am not crazy! Never say I am crazy! I have a mission to perform and I am a prophet…I am sent by God!"*[1] Footnote: Siggins, pg. 257.

He had shared his recent revelations with Father Primeau, who was his confessor at Worcester and was criticized in a letter to another disappointed follower:

> *…the poor child! When I told him that some of these things were impossible illusions, he started to weep and said, "But we have to do miracles!"*
>
> *In my view nothing but a miracle will restore him to his normal state-very probably his role is finished-May God lead him to an honorable and Christian end.* Siggins, pg.256.

When he first arrived at Lee's, he frightened his poor auntie twisting and stiffening like a man in an epileptic seizure; they were so frightened they locked him in his room.

Finally, when he stopped ranting and raving, they took him to Mass at St. Jean Baptist Church. He went from one extreme to another. First he was filled with joy, raising his hands in worship…then he went into a fit of weeping. John Lee was very embarrassed.

His behaviors continued to go from one extreme to the other. Finally, John Lee tricked him into 'going for a ride' to visit an old school friend, Dr. Lachapelle. Immediately upon entering the gates of Dr. Lachapelle's workplace, Louie realized he was being committed to Hospice of St. Jean de Dieu, an asylum for the insane.

Conditions at the asylum are so horrifying that Louie becomes an uncontrollable handful.

His behaviors began as they dragged him up to the door. The plump old porter wheezed and sweated as he carried his end of the limp sack which was only recently… a Member of Parliament. They never would have guessed that the smile pasted on a face hiding its persona behind tightly closed eyes was alertly aware...*' heave away you old fart'...if he breathes any harder, I shall stand straight up on my feet and open my eyes heh, heh, heh. Then again the old bugger may still go into cardiac...my God...what else can possibly happen...*

He is prescribed to walk several miles a day to play him out so he will sleep; they take him out back where he has to walk under guard, back and forth, back and forth, chains around his feet and hands.

Soon Louie takes to sitting still in one place from meal to meal; his only deviation from the routine is to visit a chamber pail[*1], then he returns immediately to the same position. He is able to see two of his favourite things from this window; a steeple containing a cross stands high above all other tall buildings in Quebec City. He is able to see a small portion of a beautiful cathedral below... an architectural splendor. Then, in direct linear perspective, stands Louie's precious tree with a huge trunk shaded by a mighty canopy of strong thick branches... pregnant with lush, colorful maple leaves... *one day soon, I shall sit beneath that beautiful creature...for now I will continue petitioning those nuns for my prayer book...*

He becomes furious when the mean nun ransacks his precious suitcase; he has carried it every where.

It was filled with his most precious writings and letters from home; the mean-spirited nun, has cut it open and taken all his things. He is beside himself; to settle him down they stripped him naked and put him in a strait-jacket.

The only thing he found any comfort in was taking in mass, but even that became a problem. The chapel was as filthy as the rest of the institution and it broke Louie's heart to see the figurines, windows, and candelabras covered in grime. When he spoke up they again placed him in solitary confinement. *I only wanted to clean those figurines...too bad I had to pop that porter alongside the head...maybe next time I will be treated a little more respectfully, heh, heh, heh.*

Once more, he resisted by going on a hunger strike. After four days they decided they did not want a major scandal if he happened to die; they began to fear that he was suicidal.

He opposed the cruel behavior of some of the nuns and suffered the consequences of their punishment. Many times he cried out to God to save him from this despicable place. He finds great solace* in reciting Psalms:

1. *Blessed is he that considereth the poor; the Lord will deliver him in time of trouble.*

2. *The Lord will preserve him, and keep him alive; and he shall be blessed upon the earth; and Thou wilt not deliver him unto the will of his enemies.*

3. *The Lord will strengthen him upon the bed of languishing; Thou wilt make all his bed in his sickness.*

4. *I said, Lord, be merciful unto me; heal my soul, for I have sinned against Thee.*

5. *Mine enemies speak evil of me, When shall he die, and his name perish?* Psalm 41:1-5, KJV.

He misses his little green prayer book so...*I am amazed at how many Psalms I can recall...I have now forgiven that wicked nun who tormented me; taking away my mama's prayer book! Obviously God used her to develop my patience; I rarely see her now...*

He begins to recite Psalm 150, his favourite psalm of praises. As he finishes the last line he is so overcome by a feeling of joy that he begins to dance...*I shall 'dance before the Lord with all my might'...just like King David!* ...suddenly he strips down to his little summer underwears..."Now I have a revelation of the joy of David...he will not mind if I take his name into my own...Louie ...David...Riel..."

He is running out of breath when suddenly, the door flies open…*Oh no! It would have to be her! I thought I had seen the last of her, heh, heh.* He ceases his spiritual choreography and stares at the nun as wide-eyed as she, "What in zuh hell h'ar you looking at?"

The nun quickly grabs his clothes off the bed and throws them at him, "You are despicable!"

"You 'ave no business walking into my room." Louie is quickly pulling everything on at once.

"You sounded like a maniac! We shall see about this!"

Ironically, it is the Orangemen who can be credited for his transfer to the St. Michele-Archange Asylum at Beauport from Longue-Pointe…they have gotten wind of Riel staying there and are threatening to burn it down.

His stay at Beauport Asylum is not much better; he writes constantly to Bishop Bourget and becomes a strong admirer of Bourget's ultramontane ideology as he receives letters of encouragement from him.

Louie goes through times of deep depression but when he pours his heart out to the Lord, he finds himself being filled with joy…like King David. He takes off all his clothes except for his shorts…*I shall dance before the Lord with all my might…just like King David when he gave a dance offering unto the Lord…*2nd Samuel, KJV.

About that time two nuns enter the room, the mean one calls for help and they send him back down to solitary for another four days on bread and water.

He rarely receives letters from home and he limits his writing to Bishop Bourget and the production of much poetry, he feels that his people will not value his opinions coming from an asylum, *…my Mama would not appreciate revelations of a new world system; or of Priests marrying. I believe what St. Paul teaches, "…it is better to marry than to burn…"* First Corinthians 7:9, KJV. Louie continues his reflections… *the new system* *would allow Priests to marry but only to suitable and dedicated nuns. Someday I will ask Father Lafloch what he thinks.*

Riel begs Bishop Bourget to "...get me out of here!"

Finally, after much torment and suffering he writes to Father Ritchot who makes people aware of his sane and sensible letter.

He also makes Julie aware of where her son has been for the past year. Louie immediately receives a letter from his Mama; it breaks his heart.

She says she has not heard from him for a year and that they did not know where he was...before long he is being discharged from Beauport Asylum.

On January 29th, 1878, regardless of the income they would be losing, the moment they found out that they had been harboring a fugitive from exile they wanted to wash their hands of him.

Officials from the Asylum quickly escort him to the American Border.

He had received a short letter from Father Barnabe that upon his release he would be welcome to spend a year with them, until his exile was complete... *I must accept Fabien's generous invitation...it will keep me going until I decide what I want to do...Father in heaven, protect me and guide me as I set out in a new direction...Praise be to God.*

Riel is ecstatic to be free; his arrival at Keeseville is filled with joy. The women make a feast while Louie catches up on local news with Father Barnabe. He shares with him his desire to farm a little place in Nebraska, "You know Fabien, I h'own six plots of farmland h'in Red River but I cannot go near z'em."

While the women are in the kitchen, they visit in French; Evelina and her mother do not understand very much French.

"We are just beginning to come out of an economic tragedy here Louie, you must not have heard about the Keeseville fire. We lost a few businesses and a couple of neighborhoods; everyone has been pitching in and helping one another get back on their feet. I hate to say it but our churches have doubled in membership since the fire."

"So what you are saying is the tragedy has turned out to be a blessing?" Louie leans back in his wicker chair as he gazes off into the distance at the tree-lined fields.

"Yes, it is a well-known fact that tragedy brings a community together, Louie, you likely can think of an example."

"In a way, yes. Our Metis community in Red River has really been pulling together since they have been inundated with newcomers, according to Mama's letters. As you know, there are a few very powerful, wealthy Orangemen buying up the land; however, once they have sold them land they have no compassion for their hardships. The settlers are very thankful for the Metis community and their kindness. They have suffered with floods and droughts but they have not given up. The Metis people have helped them to survive through some very hard times. Apparently, the Settlers are also being let down by the Canadians. Some of them have also been moving west with the Metis, into Saskatchewan. I guess having to put up with the new regime is just not worth it."

Before long Louie has a small loan from Barnabe and he is waiting for money to arrive from Julie for seed and horses.

Louie had to mail an affidavit assigning power of attorney over to his mother. The sale of one piece of property will give her the money to live on for a while and to send Louie the money he needs to get started farming.

Before too long it becomes obvious that not all the Barnabe's are thrilled with his presence.

Louie once was admired by Evelina's mother but since she witnessed his descent into severe depression, she is now very opposed to Evelina's infatuation with the good-looking politician, "Mother... Louie is back to his old self. I wish you weren't so rude to him; someday he could be your son-in-law you know."

Evelina shines the cookstove with a grease rag; then, she puts it away into the warming oven.

"Oh please, Evelina! Don't be so foolish, he may look fine now but… 'Still waters run deep' you know." She lifts the stove-lid and pokes in a stick of wood; then, she puts water in the kettle and sets it on the front lid.

Louie rents three acres of farm land from Fabien's neighbor for ten dollars an acre and has money left over for seed and the medicine prescribed by his doctor.

The following warm autumn, Louie is putting away his corn and potatoes, his crop has not yielded well…*if this is any kind of a sign I would guess it is time for me to move on…*

Louie is getting very anxious to see his family and he is feeling very put off by Evelina's mother, "I want to thank you for all your help, Fabien. Here is the money I owe you and I have saved enough to get home and see my family."

They are sitting out on the veranda and the fragrance of fresh cut grass fills the air as Silvain, their Mohawk handiman, cuts the grass for the last time before winter.

"Louie, we will miss you, I'm sure, but I understand your devotion to your mother. Our mother is not well and is cranky at times, but she means well."

She means well alright, she means she wants my ass out of here…"Well, I haven't said too much to Evelina yet, but I will tell her when she gets back from teaching her sewing class over at the Residential School."

"She will be upset Louie, I know, but you must do what you need to do."

By the time Evelina gets back from the school, Louie is all packed and ready to go, she walks in, takes off her hat, pokes the long pin* through it and sets it up on the shelf. She looks over at Louie with a puzzled look on her face, "Sorry my dear, z'ere h'is no use in prolonging zee agony…I must go, I am h'all packed and ready to load zuh carriage."

Evelina runs over and throws her arms around Louie's neck, "Louie, Louie, when will you be back?" She sobs and kisses his cheeks.

"I 'ate to go, my dear, but I 'ave been putting it off until I 'ave finished h'all my business 'ere. I will come back when winter is over; I have a job at St. Joseph wis' zuh Gingras family, for zuh winter."

Louie's farewell at the Keeseville Train Station is strangely different from other partings he has had with Evelina. As he settles into a comfortable seat, he feels the tension leaving his body…*perhaps I should not feel this way, but it is somewhat like the feeling I had leaving Beaumont Asylum, the only difference is my role at Beaumont was to play the part of an insane man, which I played quite well, if I must say, heh, heh, heh, …now I am escaping the role of a man in love… I do not enjoy being fickle…God deliver me from a spirit of callousness. Evelina will always have a soft spot in my heart.*

Although Louie has grown accustomed to 'riding the rails', he has not lost that original 'spirit of adventure'; he still enjoys the feeling of excitement as he speeds across the prairies to his beloved homeland.

As the train enters the depot in St. Paul, Louie begins to feel those cold fingers of fear runnind down his spine…*I have nothing to fear; I am of no political value in a foreign land…I am no longer a threat to anyone…no threat, no sweat, heh, heh.*

As Louie disembarks from the train, he scans his surroundings, the livery stable is a short walk… *I shall rent a cab to take me out to St. Joseph, no Metis sharp-shooters on guard duty this time.*

When he arrives at the Gingras ranch and trading post he notices a few changes; the trees that line the driveway are getting higher and the old house has another addition built onto it…*that old place must be very roomy now; there are additions on three sides… heh, heh.*

Louie's brother-in-law has written to him a few weeks ago and let him know of Antoine Gingras' passing…*that broke my heart when I read it…I had no-one to share my grief with so I wrote Mama to pass on my condolences to the three boys…I see Norman and his old brown dog 'Curly' coming out to greet us…*

"Bon Jour, mon ami. Good to see you Norman!" Louie jumps down from the surrey and grabs his bags from the back seat. As he sets them down he reaches in his pocket and takes out his fare, "Merci, my man. That was a fast ride."

"Louie, my friend, it is so good to see you! You see how smooth our roads are now? They drag them every week or so, depending on the weather. How have you been, some of the stories in the papers are incredible. They cannot decide whether you and Lépine are heroes or criminals, heh, heh, heh." They shake and hug.

"Tapway, my friend, both of us have been through hell; but, someday it will all be good." Louie pets old Curly before he picks up his bags.

"Here Louie let me take one of those. You have to meet my wife and children, they are a lot of fun. I miss Papa still; but, thank God for a good family. The other two boys run the store in Winnipeg; we took over the saw-mill, the ranching and the Trading Post."

"I was very saddened to hear of Antoine's death; he was like my Papa. They were both real good business heads."

As they enter the foyer and set the luggage to the side, both children come running, "Uncle Louie, uncle Louie!" They both hug his legs. Sally comes in and shakes Louie's hand, "Welcome, Louie! The children have been all excited waiting for your arrival!"

"You h'are very welcome, mon ami,; make yourself at home just like you did when Papa was h'alive. Mama is in duh kitchen. We will get your luggage upstairs to duh t'ird bedroom h'up in duh loft; I t'ink we will have time for tea and one pipeful before we h'eat." They are teaching the children some English so they generally alternate their French and English.

"Do you have something you want me to do tomorrow, my friend? I would like to spend an afternoon with Father Lafloch sometime soon. He has been my confessor for many years. I can still remember my first confession when I took an apple from the apple barrel in Couti's Meat Market. I went and ate it out side, heh, heh, heh. I always felt better after a visit with Father Lafloch."

"Oui, my friend, Sally and I have been going to mass with him since before we were married; he even performed our ceremony and christened our children."

"I 'ave no h'idea 'ow old he is, Norman. I would reckon he would be close to eighty." Louie has been outside doing chores and is pouring himself a cup of warm tea.

"Oui, I know he is over 70...he still gets around duh community to eat wit' each family. See what you are missing, Chawam?"

"I know, my friend, don't rub it in. I am now getting very keen on learning more about duh h'outdoor life. Joseph says he will introduce me to duh great wildwest. We have taken a couple of trips out west."

"Now dat sounds good, Louie. No, dere is nutting special tomorrow...jus' cutting winter wood and duh chores."

After a good visit with Father Lafloch, Louie gets himself very busy helping with the fall chores. They chat about Louie's folks who are only two or three days away, now with good roads. The railroad will soon be finished and travel will be much easier...but they have come a long way since Louie rode with Pierre's oxen brigade back in '58.

"What do you think of having Julie and your family up here for Christmas, Louie?"

Louie breaks out into a big smile, "I think that sounds great, Chawam! What does Sally think of that?"

Norman takes a bucket of water from Louie, who is standing up on the stoneboat dipping river water from a rainbarrel*.

"She loves the idea, you know how she loves to cook and dance; Mama is looking forward to seeing your Mama also."

"You have me so excited, Chawam, I feel like yelling!"

"You go right ahead and yell, my friend."

Louie throws his flat brimmed cowboy hat in the air, "Aaaaeeeee!" He stirs up the chickens and they all run in circles squawking and flapping their wings…old Curly begins barking and Sally runs out onto the veranda, "Hey, What are you doing down d'ere you guys?"

Louie is looking down at Norman wearing a big grin, "Christmas is sounding better and better all the time …Merci, merci, mon ami."

*Glossary

Footnotes:

1 Father Bourget is priming Louie for his role in the New Catholic system in the New World. He envisions a cleansing of the old Catholic Church, which had grown corrupt in the old world. Under his 'Ultramomtane' ideology there would be a new Pope and a system that would allow Priests to marry Nuns in order to address sexual deviancy which was said to be rampant in the old world.

2 chamber pail –a blue granite pail with a lid, kept in the bedroom, used for an indoor toilet, taken out to be dumped down the 'large' toilet hole. There are generally two holes in the toilet seat; one is 'small', specifically for the children

Chapter Thirty Six

St. Joseph/Dakotas, 1879/80

Louie is so busy that time flies and soon a blanket of snow spreads itself quietly over the prairies and the Gingras ranch takes on a fresh new look.

This is one winter I am going to enjoy...I have no threats hanging over my head and the landscape holds a special beauty you cannot see in the summertime.

As Louie descends the steps up to the loft he smells the awesome fragrance of Sally's crepes drifting through the air, as he settles into his place at the table Norman passes him the platter, "'ow do you like duh surprise we woke h'up to, Chawam?"

"Well, mon ami, you cannot beat duh smell of Sally's crepes." Louie takes his crepes and passes the platter to Madame Gingras.

"I h'agree mon ami, but I am talking h'about duh snow. Could you ask the blessing Louie, sil vous plait?"

"Most certainly, but you know, I t'ought I could smell snow in duh h'air last night when I went out to shut duh door on duh chicken 'ouse."

Then, Louie bows his head and asks a blessing upon their meal and the new day...they all make the sign of the cross and begin to eat.

"Mama says she 'as told all duh children and Pierre and Kieren; dey will h'all come for Christmas. Dey will be 'ere on duh 22nd or 23rd of duh mont'; she says dat gives h'us time to get ready. As long as duh ice road is ready on duh river." Louie has settled into his old patois, now that he is no longer a public speaker.

Madame Gingras, though she is usually quiet, is delighted to hear that Julie is coming for Christmas, "I am so 'appy to 'ave Julie coming. We used to be very close when we would meet at duh annual hunts."

Back in those days there were millions of buffalo roaming the prairies in large herds, tents and teepees lined the river for as far as you could see.

"Dose were duh days, eh Mama? Dey say dere were millions of buffalo roaming duh prairies in large herds." Norman looks tenderly over at his Mama.

"Aye huh*, we visited lots back den, kyas, mana*, duh tents and teepees lined duh rivers for miles, tapway." Madame Gingras smiles thinking of the old days.

In a few days, Louie and Norman are down at the river with a stoneboat* pulled by old 'Grey', filling a barrel with water from the river. Norman has chopped the hole back out to make it large enough for the milk pails to fit in, "Chawam, does dat look like some sleighs way down by dat bend?" Norman, leaning on the axe-handle, lifts his touque and scratches his head with the same hand, as he looks up river.

Louie shades his eyes from the sun and gazes up the frozen ice-road. Hoar frost hangs on every limb and branch, making the old Red River look like a wonderland. "You know, my friend, I t'ink you h'are right. Dat looks like more dan one sleigh."

"Tapway, Louie, I can see it now, it is a winter caravan. Oui, it is t'ree sleighs."

"Yes, I can see t'ree stove-pipes; it's got to be dem!"

"Come on, Chawam, let's get d'is water up to duh house and water duh h'animals."

By the time the troughs have been filled, Louie can hear the sounds of sleigh runners coming up the ice road, squeaking over the snow. He unhitches the horse from the singletree; then, he unharnesses Norman's old Clydesdale.

As he is hanging the harness up on the barn wall, he hears the first sleigh turn and come up the slope to the house.

By the time he gets up to the house, Norman, his Mama and Sally are all out greeting everyone, as they pile out the back of the covered wagon, "Phew! It was gettin' a might hot in dere!" Kieren helps Madeliene down from the sleigh, then their little son Bennie jumps down, "I can get down Papa, stan' back!"

Pierre helps Julie down and steers her in the direction of Louie.

"Oh, mon garçon*, mon garçon!" Louie takes her in his arms and rocks her back and forth as they both weep, "Mama, Mama, it is so good to see you!" He unfolds a clean white handkerchief, and wipes the tears from her eyes.

Once the greetings are complete they all head into Norman's big sitting room and sit in a circle around the fireplace; all the children sit on the floor.

Louie is beaming as he looks around the circle; all his sisters and their husbands are here, except for Sara, who is still at the Ille a la Cross Mission. His brothers Joseph and Alexandre are both there …Louie suddenly feels a pang of grief as he notices the absence of Charlie and Marie.

Norman sits down beside Louie and begins by saying a big welcome to all in French and then in English, "I 'ope you h'all make yourselves at 'ome, bote in duh 'ouse and in duh cookhouse, where dere is a big dining hall for dancing and visiting.

Across duh way, you will see a goodsized bunk-house wit' a couple of bedrooms for dressing wit' doors on dem. Dere's a couple more bedrooms partitioned off wit no doors. We will 'ave lots of room; dere's also a couple of extra bedrooms in duh 'ouse.

Most of you know where duh woodpile and duh toilets are; Louie and I 'ave shovelled most of duh paths out already. If we get a snowfall d'ere h'are shovels in duh shed. Heh, heh, heh."

Pierre thanks Norman, Madame Gingras and Sally for all their preparations, "Now don't you be worryin' h'about anyt'ing, my friend; everyt'ing looks wonderful. I see you fellows 'ave a couple of Christmas trees cut down. We'll hep you bring dem in an' set dem h'up."

The next two days are busy as the women finish up their Christmas baking and the men are kept busy outside or over at the cookhouse where the women are cooking and feeding most of the family in the dining hall next to the kitchen.

There is plenty for the children to do outside all day long; they have brought their sleds and tobbogans; they barely stop long enough to eat.

The evenings are filled with sitting around the stoves, visiting, snacking and playing music, "It is so hard to believe that I am seeing all the people I have been missing for so long."

Julie can hear the emotion in Louie's voice; she rubs the back of his hand, "I am having a hard time also, my boy. I am so happy and yet I miss the ones who are not here…we will all be together in Paradise, my boy. That will be a time of rejoicing." She speaks softly… in the special French that Louie loves so dearly.

Louie looks at his Mama; her beautiful face is beginning to show signs of age, "I know that you are right Mama; but, I also wish the others were here…it is a wonderful gathering…praise be to God."

On Christmas Eve, several sleighloads leave together and travel over to St. Joseph Cathedral for Mid-night Mass.

After Mass, on their way out, Norman and Sally invite Father Ritchot and Father Lafloch for Christmas Dinner the next day.

Once the women and girls have set all the food out on tables, the families lay blankets on the floor and everyone sits in the floor. The older people sit on benches around a table where the younger boys will dish them up and bring them their food.

Louie is asked to pray a prayer of thanksgiving while Gabriel smudges the food and the people with sweetgrass. Then the blessing is offered by Father Ritchot.

Christmas dinner is wonderful with roasts of young venison, turkey, potatoes and gravy, dressing, mashed turnips and carrots…a feast fit for a king!

The women have baked shortbread, berrie pies and fresh bannock. Traditional delicasies are set out for snacking… moosenose*, tripe*, dry meat and neck-bones are covered and left on a table with the punch bowl for later.

Before long the women are cleaning up and doing dishes while the men are tuning up their instruments.

Father Ritchot leans over and asks Father Lafloch if he's tired, "I will drive home if you will stay for a while longer."

Father Lafloch turns to him and says, "Are you joking? I would not miss the jigging for anything. That is the best part of the night!" They both laugh!

The fiddlers take turns playing all the old tunes. Many Metis traditional songs are from a Sottish or Irish influence and of course, one of the favourites is … the 'French Minuet'*!

Once the dancers have waltzed off their dinner they begin taking partners for 'Square Dances', 'Reel of eight', 'Duck Dance' and finally, the 'Red River' jig.

Joseph has arrived just before dinner with his two friends, the Marion sisters, Louise-Anne and her younger sister, Marie-Rose, who is obviously sweet on young Joseph.

As the jiggers line up, Keiren O'Brien takes a little nip from a small flask of moonshine, then tucks it back into his vest pocket,

"Good evening ladies and gentlemen, we shall now be treated to duh highlight o' duh evenin', duh Red River jig! Everybody cheers. The fiddlers are applying a double dose of 'paguh'* to their fiddle-bows. (Foot-note for 'puguh', which is resin, from spruce pitch.)

"Gabe L'Ambitieaux is our first fiddler and Louie Lavallee will be a-spellin' him off.... take it away Gabe!"

Suddenly the sound of Gabe's strong intro in the key of "A" sounds out across the floor; "Please give a hand to Joseph Riel and Marie-Rose Marion...St. Joseph, Minnesoootaaaa!" Everyone claps again.

Joseph and Marie-Rose go for one change*; then, when Gabe switches into the second change, in the key of "D", Keiren yells out, "aaaaeeee!"...on the third change Joseph yells out, "Astom my brudder, nimetuh!*" ...and he waves Louie and Louise-Anne up onto the floor. As Louie and Louise-Anne jig out to the middle, Joseph and Marie-Rose jig back to the edge; everyone claps.

The men look great keeping good time with their feet, chests out, shoulders back and sashes flying. When someone whistles and waves at them, Louie gives them a quick bow and carries on; everyone is keeping time clapping. The girls are lovely in fancy ribbon blouses, wide waist- bands on full-length skirts, mocassins or wrap-arounds beaded profusely in brightly colored floral patterns.

The music sounds great, both fiddlers are going with two rhythm guitars, a mandolin and Proulx's consortina are backing them up.

When the last team of jiggers dances to the edge and Kieren yells, "Everybody dance!"...the floor fills up and the ones who are not dancing keep time clapping their hands. The clapping gives the dancers energy... as the teams tire and drop out, they begin to jig backwards to the edge of the crowd. The remaining jiggers go several more changes until the fiddlers nod to their backup and end the song.

Everyone is clapping and yelling. Specially beaded gifts are handed out to the jiggers who are still on the floor.

When the evening winds down and everyone is either going to bed or making a last cup of tea for the evening, Joseph turns to Louie, "How would you like to drive me and the girls back over to Marions? Then I'll have company on the way home."

Louie answers him back in French, "Well of course I will keep you company," he winks at Pierre who gives his little giggle.

"Don't be long now you boys." Pierre is teasing them, sounding like the 'big brother'. He can see already that Louie is interested in Louise-Anne.

In the morning, after a huge breakfast in the dining hall, Pierre, Kieren and Louie sit around the table drinking coffee. They still have some catching up to do before they pack up in the morning and get ready to head north back to St. Vital.

"It sounds like t'ings h'at Red River are not going to ever be duh same again, eh Chawam?" Louie taps a little wad of tobacco into his pipe.

"Dat could be true, mon ami, but don't ever feel like what you did was not wort'while. Many good t'ings 'ave come out of it."

"Tapway, my friend, dere is open talks going along wit' Ottawa an' every year it gets a little better." Kieren says, nodding his head.

"Oiu, mostly when dere is some kind of h'election. For many of us its not bad. Dose of h'us who 'ave been close to duh Hudson Bay for a long time, some of h'us 'ave very old property. Like your Mama, she is treated good, so are duh Lagimodieres. But even some of dose relations 'ave 'eaded west. I 'ear Coutu's are even leaving."

"Well, you know why. Many of duh younger generations are sick and tired of duh lies of John A. He tells dem dey got land and duh next t'ing you know, duh Canadians 'ave a new set 'o surveyors out measurin' more o' duh land fer duh Railway. Dey say you might as well use dat 'scrip'* fer asswipe."

They all have a good laugh and Louie says, "Well, it sounds like dey are settling in duh west wit' relatives quite 'appily. It 'as taken me a long time to get h'over John A's treatment of h'our people. I was pleased wit' Fadder Ritchot when he put Macdonald in his place…he knew all duh lies dat were told to us, especially regarding h'our h'amnesties. God bless 'is heart; he would not give up. His negotiations carried on for t'ree days, until he finally received duh promise of an h'amnesty for h'our people. He insisted dat dey recognize Section 92 of h'our Bill of Rights, dat Red River Settlement be entered into Confederation as a Province. T'ank duh Lord; John A. did not renege on dat. Many of 'is lies were bribes to get votes. Cartier also knew of his lies, but he was caught between promises to h'our people and pressure from duh railway people. When h'it h'all collapsed on John A. I had to keep wiping my mout'. Duh smile would not come off!"

Kieren slaps his knee with his cap and Pierre rares back howling, as they have a good laugh. Louie is wound up; just like the good old days!

"Tapway, dat's a good one! But we do 'ave to t'ink different now, before long we'll be able to 'op on a train and be visiting over in Batoche duh same night."

Louie finds it hard to say good-bye to everyone, as they wave good-bye and watch the winter caravan disappear around the river bend, Louie thinks to himself…*it never fails, when I say good bye, it is not long before someone else from the family dies…*

Joseph continues to work along with Louie doing winter chores on the Gingras Ranch. Louie is itching to get out west looking for new adventures; always keeping in mind his commitment to his people and to God.

By March they have made several trips out to meet with the Metis people of the west and any Indian tribes in close proximity to the Metis camps. Louie is well-liked by those they meet; Joseph is pleased and proud of his brother's knowledge of so many Indian languages.

The Marion sisters have been fun to travel with, now and again until... suddenly, they admit to the Riel boys, their 'betrothal'* to boyfriends who are trapping up north.

They bid the girls good-bye... when they learn that the men will soon be coming back down south with their furs, after a winter of trapping.

Joseph is now ready to pay attention to Louie's ambitions and they make plans to head west.

Louie is anxious to launch into a new adventure, but not without a pang of guilt. He is reminded of his parting words to Evelina...*please forgive me precious Mother, I did not mean to be heartless and fickle...I feel at this time in my life that, Evelina cannot fit in...she is too fragile...her brother Fabien informed me at Christmas time, she is failing from Tuberculosis...God bless her and keep her from suffering. I believe God still has a mission for me among my people...please guide me and protect me dear Jesus and Joseph, sil vous plait... amen. Praise be to God.*

Before long, Louie and Joseph have hooked up with a band of Metis who are camped at the farm of André Martineau.

Martineau has been employing Louie and Joseph from time to time when they are not busy at Norman's. Soon his summer employees will be returning with their furs, ready to begin working the fields.

On a warm spring day, Riel is down at the corral behind Martineau's barn when Joseph comes around the corner of the barn with a strange Metis fellow Louie has never seen before.

"Louie, can you leave your horses for awhile?" They both climb up on the rail fence.

"Oui, it is time for a break anyway." Louie takes the scarf from around his neck and wipes the sweat from his brow.

"Dis 'ere is Patrice Bellehumeur from Wood Mountain Montana; he 'as been anxious to meet you, mon ami."

"I am pleased to meet you, Patrice. I 'ave seen you h'around duh camp a few times; no one ever boddered to introduce h'us." Louie reaches out and shakes Patrice's hand.

"Pleased to meet you, Monsieur Riel, we talk about you a lot among duh 'alfbreed people of duh west. Wait 'til I tell mon Papa, Jean-Baptiste. Better yet, I would like to take you to meet mon Papa…he is a fine man."

Joseph is leaning on the top rail of the corral,"You know, my brudder, I would love to go wit you but I am going to 'elp Mama h'at 'ome, she needs me for spring work h'and our young brudder H'alexandre needs someone to kick 'is h'ass once in a while."

"I can not h'imagine travelling wit'out my brudder Joseph…let me t'ink about it Patrice. I shall tell you tomorrow."

"Well, let's go and metsu*, Louie, you 'ave worked h'all day with nut'ing but bannock and tea."

Early the next day Louie and Joseph are having coffee, beans and bannock along with their boss, Monsieur Martineau. He is coming in from the tents by the road where he has been paying the brushing crew, mostly with bullets and tobacco, a few dollars and several bags of beans and flour.

He speaks mostly French, "The boys seemed to be quite happy with their pay; they are loading their tents into the covered wagon now, getting ready to go."

Louie is squirming in his seat, he hates to leave his brother behind, "What do you think of the Bellehumeur people, sir?"

Martineau, looks straight at Riel, "You are a man of very high standards, I have observed; you will find that the old man, Jean-Baptiste, is a man of integrity. He is also dedicated to the Catholic faith. I believe you will like him and his family."

Louie is taking it all in, "Merci, merci, monsieur Martineau, you have been very helpful. So my brother, I will go and quickly give Patrice my answer and get back here to pack my things."

Louie comes back into the house and packs up his few clothes that have not been left at the Gingras Ranch.

As he lifts his bag up into the covered wagon, Joseph is tightening down his bedding and capote under a canvas behind his saddle. He tosses the reins up to Louie and bids him farewell, "Dis rifle shoots dead on, brudder, "He taps the butt down good, "'ave you got lots of bullets and tobacco?"

"You bet, I got my pay from Martineau, bought a slab of salt pork from him and I have my prayer book right here." He is speaking in his 'excited' French as he pats his vest pocket.

"Tapway, 'ave a good trip, my brudder, see you in duh fall!" Joseph lifts his hat and waves at Louie.

Louie nods at Joseph, then knees his little black mare into a trot. *...dear Saint Joseph, be with me and my family as we travel different roads...thank you dear Jesus and sweet Mary...Praise be to God.*

*Glossary:

Footnotes:

There are no Footnotes

Chapter Thirty Seven

Wood Mountain, Montana, 1880/'81

The sun is beginning to set as the small pack of Half-breeds reaches the brow of a hill. Patrice waves them over to a clump of bushes on a plateau; here there is a panoramic view of the Musselshell River and the confluence of Flatbed Creek; it appears to be peaceful and clear for three-hundred and sixty degrees. The hills in the distance are only a faint haze, like a painting craving for even a small dip of the brush.

Louie has soon realized that Patrice is the Captain of the brigade, after he watches him; he makes clear the rudimentary rules during their first stop. He sits forward on his horse.

As they survey the landscape for miles around Patrice raises his hand to silence the chatter, "We will begin a patrol h'after we eat. Duh one dat gets duh long straw will begin by riding to duh left, keeping our usual surveillance to duh left… h'all around duh circumference of duh bluff. H'after you 'ave circled t'ree times you may sleep. Den your relief takes over and does duh nex' t'ree rounds, omuh*… For dose who are here for dere first time, dis h'is your signal for alarm," …he raises his finger to his throat and makes the sound of a nightingale, twice. "…dat is h'it, you gadder at the wagon, semak,* where h'our horses h'are 'obbled close by."

Twelve riders have squatted on the ground, all eyes are on Patrice; they are paying close attention to the instruction of their leader. He twirls his dark curly beard as he delivers his instructions in a mixture of French and English…with a Cree expression injected, here or there.

The chuckwagon is set up at the bottom of the incline and the old 'Cookee', Pierre Poitras, sets up his little stove and gets his beans boiling, once the water arrives.

A creek runs conveniently along the bottom of the bluff. Ben Larocque and Bill Flamand are sent for water.

There are signs of a comfortable old ancient camp-site all around. Rock fire pits, a small rail corral, badly in need of repair, old lard pails still hanging from small branches.

Old bent over willows knarled into a half-circle, stand just around the bend. Faded old weathered prayer clothes still hang dutifully on branches nearby… evidence of a sacred sweat, used repeatedly for years as a of worship and prayer.

Louie hobbles his horse, Prince, after he has taken him to the creek for a drink. He lays his bedroll out under a little tree and leans back to watch the sun setting in the west as he waits for the sound of Cookie's dinner bell…a few taps on his skillet.

He has pulled his little prayer book from his vest pocket and is reading Proverbs chapter three for the umpteenth time, as Patrice sets himself down beside him.

"It is so beautiful out here you know, Louie. But if you do come home with me you will see…it is more beautiful the closer you get to Canada." Patrice and Louie have been down at the creek having a drink of water and washing up before 'chow'.

They are back up on the creek bank, combing their hair, "Duh more you talk about Wood Mountain, duh more I am convinced to go home wit' you. Your Papa sounds so much like mine…I can 'ardly wait to meet 'im. You 'ave been taught to keep yourself well-groomed; my Papa taught me duh same way. You 'ave been taught to take good care of your animals… feed dem first, you know, and make sure dey 'ave water. He taught us duh same way."

He ties his clean washed neckerchief around his neck; just as he places his cowboy hat back on his head, the supper bell rings.

***

Travelling with a band of rough Metis buffalo hunters has opened Louie's eyes to the type of lifestyle he has always escaped; whether it was avoided or simply not convenient, he is not sure. *There are some experiences I am proud to finally be a part of, then there are some things I would rather leave to others.*

Louie is thinking about some of the terrifying adventures he has endured in the past few months. He never seems to be able to slip in and out of gatherings without being noticed. The tranquility of the outdoors seems to overpower any anxieties that might arise during unfamiliar experiences.

They have stopped and camped with several Metis or Sioux parties along the trail south to the Missouri River. His mannerisms and charisma just naturally make him stand out in a crowd; regardless of any attempts he has made to maintain a low profile. *No matter where I go, people ask me questions; I think that they just like to hear me talk heh, heh, heh... God knows, I have not abandoned my commitment to do whatever He wants me to do for my people…even if it is just setting an example of living in a Christian manner, treating everyone equal, loving those who are not exactly loveable, staying calm in stressful conditions…praise be to God…*

"I am h'always impressed wit' you Louie; jus' when I t'ink I know a lot about you, we run into a band of Sioux, Blackfoot or Metis den 'bang,'… you know one o' dem or you can speak dere language.!" He throws his head back and laughs, as he rams his fist into the palm of his hand.

Louie always gets a kick out of Patrice's animated remarks, it reminds him of Pierre, "Well remember, mon ami, I travelled back and fort' to duh Missouri wit' my brudder Joseph for duh last couple of years. I met a lot of Joe's trading friends and he found it darn handy when I knew dere language. I grew up speaking dose languages listening to my Papa and his trading friends, back at Fort Garry, kayas*."

"Well, I jus' h'about fell off my horse first time we met h'up wit some Indians. First of h'all, dere wasn't a sign of fear as you rode h'up to dem!" Patrice is bouncing up and down on his invisible horse.

Louie makes the sign of the cross, "Mon ami, if you had been t'rough what I 'ave been t'rough…you also would not be h'afraid."

Patrice pours himself one last cup of coffee before he turns in for the night, "Do you mind tellin' h'us what you been t'rough?" The guys are all sitting around the fire…now they sit up and pay attention. Some of them are slightly acquainted with his story.

Louie looks up at the star filled sky, "Look h'up guys, see dose stars? Dat's just a little bit of duh wonders o' God h'almighty. Dat is what 'as kept me going…t'rough h'every kind of trials h'and tribulations you can h'imagine. Dere is not much dat frightens me h'anymore.

Dat raging river we crossed back dere, t'ree times I went h'under…h'it was ten minutes before I got a good breat' of air. I did not feel panic al'dough I did try to get a breat' of air…heh, heh…I felt duh protection of duh Holy Mudder Mary. I do not brag, I tell you dis because you asked.

I 'ave been shot at several times, hunted down like a cougar, hid in duh bush for fourty days, nearly t'rown off a moving train…and I mean… moving, heh, heh, heh."

He sits with his legs crossed, his hat on his knee…a fallen tree for a bench. He stares into the fire, "I wish I could say I was not scared but back den, h'it scared duh hell out of me, heh, heh, I drove dee old Red River h'elbow so 'ard into duh guy's ribs dat you could 'ear duh air come out of 'im… den I kicked 'im backward off duh train. I used to t'ink h'about 'im once in a while…I h'even said a prayer for duh bugger, I doubt if he died, but he would 'ave 'ad some h'awful scrapes from duh gravel, heh, heh, heh."

They all have a good laugh, "Tell us h'about your exile and some of dose times dey tried to assassinate you, my friend."

"H'it would take me h'all night to tell you what I 'ave been t'rough, I am sorry to say…I would radder forget some of dose s'ings."

"We h'are jus' being nosy now I t'ink, my friend. H'its time to turn in h'anyways, eh guys?" The men begin to rise and head for their bedrolls.

"T'anks, mon ami, dese boys crave entertainment in duh evenings, you know."

After the men are satisfied that they have finished with their trading out in the west, they begin making plans to head back to St. Paul with their cargo of furs.

"Bengimen, h'are you still ready to take care of duh boys on dere way home?" Patrice is all packed and ready to begin heading north to Wood Mountain.

"We'll be fine Monsieur Patrice, it has been good travellin' wit' you, mes ami." The men begin to come forward to shake hands with Louie and Patrice, "It has been a long haul but you boys 'ave been good to travel wit', merci, merci."

***

As they begin the journey north to Wood Mountain, Louie feels that familiar tickle in the pit of his stomach…*Praise be to God, I feel like my life is about to change once more…I pray that it would be your will, heavenly Father…send your precious saints to check on us daily; thank you for giving me health and strength. It is wonderful to be living in the outdoors, merci, merci…praise be to God.* Using the French of his dear mother, he whispers a prayer of protection on his mother and siblings…*I do not wish to be pessimistic but it is so hard…after the loss of Charles and Marie, just when I was least expecting it. Whenever I begin a new journey…I seem to be met with another tragedy…dear Mary, Joseph and Jesus, protect us, sil vous plait, praise be to God.*

***

The sun is beginning to set as Louie and Patrice arrive at Wilder's Landing, "You will enjoy the final leg of our journey, my friend. We will sell these last furs for enough money to get us onto the steamboat that will take us to Wolf point. After that it's not a very long ride to my Papa's; sometimes you can make it most of the way catching freight barges."

"That would be wonderful, my friend; I would like to take it easy on Prince and have him ride down the river some more. Now that he is used to the water we can sail down these rivers and enjoy our journey."

"Yes, my friend, our poor horses have been through some tough trails; they need a rest." Patrice rubs his horses neck and smooths out his mane. "They are damn good horses, Louie; they deserve the best of care."

"Tapway, my friend, we are blessed to have such nice saddle horses. Well, there are a few houses showing up; it looks like a busy little place." Louie is relieved to see a bit of civilization.

They have spoken mostly French since the halfbreed boys left them to head east to their camp. "You will like it here, Louie. There are some very nice Catholic people living here, they speak mostly French except for a few halfbreed folks. There are also some wild old freighters who are having a hard time to find work, now that the steamers come up and down the rivers regularly. You won't see much of dem unless you go to the tavern."

They pull up to a Trading Post that offers most of their services, a freight/post office, general store and a restaurant. "Let's go in and sell h'our furs."

They both dismount and tie their horses with a half-hitch at the hitching rail. Louie grabs his twin bales that hang over his bedroll.

They are cordially welcomed by a husky Metis man with curly thick hair and a curly moustache stretched over a big smile, "Greetings Patrice, who is your friend?"

"Good to see you Edouard, Dis is Louie Riel from St. Joseph, Minnesota." Louie offers his hand with a smile. "We have travelled with a couple of Durets for a short while dis summer."

"Yes, dat is likely my brudder and his son Charlie. Dey were going home to Flat Willow Creek, Oui?"

Louie nods his head, "Oui. Dey 'ad been trapping and drying fish from duh Mussel Shell River." Edouard nods his head, "Oui, oui."

Once the furs are sold, they purchase their tobacco and check for mail. Louie has not stayed in one place long enough to post a letter home. *The first thing I will do when I get to Fort Belknap is write Mama a letter; she will give the address to those I correspond with. My life is so different now; my Mama will not believe how rough I live*, he counts his money and stuffs it into his little 'muskemut*' that hangs next to his precious knife scabbard... *my Papa would be so pleased to see how much I have learned to use his old knife. God bless Evelina for taking good care of my things while I languished in those incredible asylums.* A shudder goes through his body at the thought of it.

He walks over to one of the little tables in the corner of the store. The floor is old, scrubbed gray with lye; wide crooked cracks lead him up to the table. He hangs his tattered black, knee-length frock coat over the back of his chair, then he removes his cowboy hat and keeps it on his knee until they are ready to go.

"Are you as hungry as I am, Chawam?" Patrice goes through the same motions as Louie, even placing his hat on his knee.

"Tapway, I am starved, mon ami!" Louie keeps his voice low but responds with gusto, rubbing his tummy.

"Oui, I could h'eat duh h'ass-end outta a live bear!"

His voice is not as quiet as Louie's and he gets a good laugh from the old fellow behind the counter. The place is empty and very quiet. "Astom, Marie, quayaho! Dese guys are starving!"

A short plump lady comes quickly through a curtained doorway; one long dark braid hangs down her back. She steps along quickly, a long skirt and apron nearly covering her beaded wrap-arounds "Bon jour, mes ami, what will you 'ave, bannock and stew or side-pork h'and beans?"

"Bannock definitely sounds good for starters, h'and a good hot cup of tea. I will take your stew, we are beaned out h'after two months on duh trail, stew sounds wonderful, merci."

"I agree, my friend; I will 'ave duh same, merci."

"'ave you seen Francois Duret lately, Edouard?" Patrice is obviously very familiar with the community.

"Oui, my friend, he comes in every udder day…der's not much to do dis time of year. Dey bought some seeds and he is 'elping 'is wife wit a garden. He stopped in las' week h'and picked h'up some bullets…true to 'is word, he brought me some deer meat yesterday and paid for 'is bullets."

Marie brings two cups and a plate of hot fry-bannock, "Merci, Marie, dis is good, meewasin paquasigan*…yes Francois is very honest. He always finds room for me and my companions to stay…even in his barn, dat makes for a comfortable bed in dat hay."

"You bet, dat is very comfortable, Patrice. Long as he is 'ome you will be fine."

Soon the men are finished their stew and bannock, they put on their coats and hats and walk over to the counter, "Meewasin, merci, merci." Louie pays for the meal and shakes Edouard's burly hand.

"'ave a nice trip 'ome Patrice, give our regards to your Papa."

***

Patrice is right, once the horses are safely in the belly of the steam-boat, they relax up on the deck, a great calm comes over Louie, as he smells the fragrance of the old Missouri River filling the air. *...all I need to do is close my eyes and I am back sitting under my old tree by the Red River...I had better take this opportunity to write a letter to my Mama...praise be to God!*

Patrice comes to sit in the chair next to Louie, "Didn't I tell you, Chawam? Dis is what you call peaceful."

Louie is leaning back in his chair, hands folded behind his head, eyes closed, "You were so right, my friend...dis is peaceful. I feel like a little boy sitting by duh old Red River."

"H'it won't be long and we will be h'at duh bow of duh Missouri where we pass duh Mussel Shell River, dere h'is a bit of a rough spot dere at duh forks. Den h'it gets smooth again until we reach Wolf Point where we stop at a landing, wait for duh next boat nort' and load our horses again to head nort' up duh Milk River."

"How far do we go h'up duh Milk River to your Papa's, my friend?" Louie has taken out his pipe and is stuffing it with tobacco.

"I would guess it to be about t'ree pipefuls from Wolf Point to Fort Belknap, h'up duh Milk River. Dat's where you said you want to mail your letter to your Mama." Patrice is also lighting his pipe, "H'it is not too far of a ride to Frenchman's Creek to my Papa's settlement."

"Yes, my friend, we will just take h'our time and stop once in a while and rest h'our horses."

"Dat's right, Chawam. We will pick h'up a few t'ings to take 'ome to my Mama and also get a little grub for duh road, eh?"

"Sounds good to me, my friend, tapway." Louie takes a good drag from his pipe; then, he watches the smoke twirl upward and off to the west, as they chug on towards the forks at Wolf Point. He gazes to the northern shore and beyond; the skies are a rich blue fading into a haze of cloudy mountains in the west. Louie finds himself thinking like kid, *...I wonder how far away we are from our destination...* He checks on Patrice, he is also relaxed and enjoying the scenery, "It is hard to believe all we have been t'rough, my friend...you made a lot of new friends...well me too, I made a lot of new friends also. People I 'ave run into before but, t'ank God, you opened up a lot of new trading circles, jabbering h'away in dose languages. Heh, heh, heh."

"'Ow far away from your 'ome are we, mon ami?" Louie is still gazing out over the beauty of the wide-open west. He kills the sparks in his pipe with his index finger and sets it to rest and cool off, down by his chair leg; they are on the 'brow' of the boat, where the view is the best. Other passengers have gone down into the dining room for supper.

"It will be a while before we get to Wolf Point, then we go in a north-easterly direction to Fort Belknap. You are looking in that direction, Chawam, if we could go the way the crow flies we would be there tonight, heh, heh, heh." He speaks in French until they get into the dining room, then he resumes his broken English, "Somet'ing smells good, mon ami, is it fish, you t'ink?"

"Louie sniffs the air, I t'ink you h'ar rightt, mon ami, it smells like fish."

***

As they settle onto the next steamboat, they begin to head in a northerly direction, Louie whispers in French, "This boat is carrying a lot of booze, they are gambling next door and a lot swearing is going on. That must be why you don't see any women and children."

Patrice answers back quietly, "Well, you know by now, my friend, it is not always rosy out here in the west."

Louie breaks into a grin, "I know that, my friend, I just got a little spoiled on that last boat, heh, heh, heh. It was so peaceful and beautiful."

They have spent the night at the home of Monsieur Lemere's. They have been good friends with the Bellehumere's for many years.

Papa Romain is very happy to see Patrice, "My boy, are you going home this soon? Who is your friend?" He looks Louie up and down, Pulling at his long bristly beard. Louie gives him his winning smile, "I am Louie Riel, sir. I am so pleased to make your acquaintance, Patrice has been telling me about your wonderful family."

The Lemeres make them very welcome; the old man is immediately impressed with Louie's French and keeps him talking as long as he can. Louie ducks and dives quite cordially through a series of fairly sensitive questions.

After Madame Lemere has given them a breakfast of biscuits and gravy, they bid them good-bye.

Plans have been made around the breakfast table to meet up with the hunters near Cypress Hills for the hunt.

After the Blackfoot people have chased the buffalo south and finished their hunt for the season, they can still manage a few buffalo. They are now drying more deer for the winter; the buffalo are very scarce.

They load their grub and gifts onto their horses and head for the ferry on the Milk River; soon they will be home, "Next time we are down here on the Missouri I will show you a classy Fort…you will be surprised at the collection of Indian crafts, fancy household stuff, any thing you want… you will find it at Fort Assiniboine. Even their buildings are made of the best materials. I guess after Custer's big failure the government decided to build a secure headquarters out here."

"Tapway, the U.S. has more pride than the Canadians…if they make a big mistake, they never try to make up for it, not John A.…they just carry on like it never happened, heh, heh, heh."

"Well, it looks to me like Canada has British policy to blame things on; down here if we make a mistake… it is our own fault and we have to fix it, heh, heh, heh."

"So, where is this magnificent fort?" Louie is always curious about U.S. policies.

"You know when we were at Fort Belknap, it was only about one pipeful down the Missouri river from Fort Assinaboine."

"Sounds like a good trip to me; it should be not far from Fort Benton, the way the crow flies."

Tapway, Louie. You can go across with carts and oxen but I hear it is pretty rough."

"Oui, and look at the beautiful trip on the river you would miss."

"Aye huh*, Patrice, I am happy we took the river."

"We will stop up here at Frenchman's Creek and have a rest." Louie nods, "You bet, we can have a can of beans while our horses drink and chew on some grass…they will like that; I only need a drink; no beans for me. For one thing, my belt is getting tight again; and furthermore, I am so anxious to meet your family…I do not care to be farting around there, shaking hands…you know what I mean."

"Yes Louie, I know what you mean, heh heh, heh. I would not be surprised if you put on your 'gentleman' outfit."

"You are getting to know me Patrice. While you are swelling your stomach, I shall be washing up, including my hair, and changing my shirt. How does that sound?"

"It sounds mighty fine. I might wash up a bit myself. Heh, heh, heh. We are only about five miles from my Mama's stove, heh, heh."

As they reach the edge of the woods they break into a clearing. Several log huts stand in a circle, most have sod roofs and a have a 'camp' tent sitting out back with drying racks standing empty.

A community corral made of sturdy peeled rails sits to the west of the little villiage. Each house has a toilet out back with a well-worn path leading up to it.

Louie is mezmerized by the community spirit; the typically Metis villiage, sitting away out in the middle of nowhere. There are kids and dogs everywhere you look.

Patrice leads the way to one of the larger huts that has a veranda out front with a hitching rail, one of the few. A couple of people are watching them ride up; the man and the woman are sitting on rocking chairs; their hair is showing signs of grey. A dog comes toward Patrice wagging his tail. Suddenly they recognize Patrice, "Look Jean-Baptiste, it is our son, omuh!"

Jean-Baptiste rises from his chair and steps off the little veranda as Patrice bails out of the saddle, "Papa, Papa, it is so good to see you, pascutz*! And Mama, you are so thin...but you are beautiful!"

Patrice hugs his Papa; then, he lifts Mama Marie in the air and swings her around, "My boy, my boy...put me down, you will break my bones! Here comes your sister; you can swing her around, moochowin!*"

They are all laughing and Louie is standing taking it all in feeling suddenly very homesick. Patrice is jabbering so fast in French that Louie is losing him, trying desperately to sort out the idioms in Patrice's western dialect, "Mon ami, I am so sorry, I should have introduced you...this is my sweet Mama Marie, my Papa, Jean-Baptiste, I have spoken of so often...and my beautiful sister, Marguerite." She stands very straight with a thick dark braid reaching the waistband of her long skirt. Her teeth are white as she gives Louie a shy smile...*I bet my teeth are brown!*

Louie, in his uaual charming way, shakes hands with each one, in order, "Madame, Patrice loves you dearly, as I love my own sweet Mama. Monsieur Jean-Baptiste, I have waited patiently to meet you, Patrice speaks of you very honorably…and Madamoiselle Marguerite, I am so sorry that I often heard Patrice mention his siblings, but never could I have imagined he had a sister like you…. It so confused me as now I know that his sister, 'Chickie' was you also." He gives Margeurite his most handsome smile as he kisses her hand, "I am so pleased to make your acquaintance." He gives a low bow with his hat in one hand; holding her hand in the other. When he straightens up he looks into her eyes…he can hear the others talking but he is drowning in the most beautiful brown eyes, "Louie, do you want me to take your horse…I'll put them in the pasture after they have a drink… do you want your bridle and saddle brought in?"

"Uh… oui, mon ami… I will come with you." *What is wrong with me; I am acting like a young boy…worse yet, a dumb boy…*

Once they are out of earshot, and the horse's hoofs are drowning out the whispers, Louie jabs Patrice in the ribs, "Why didn't you tell me about your sister Marguerite?"

"What are you talking about? She's just a girl, I guess she is good looking, that is what they say, anyway…Chawam, I really don't want you to think your stuff is not safe in our community. There are bands of renegade Metis, Blackfoot and Sioux that drop by from time to time. We call them 'night raiders'; they are banned from their own people because of theft, but we don't consider them dangerous…we shoot over their heads and they shoot over ours…it is what we call a 'coup', if we catch them quick enough they ride off empty-handed."

Louie is still trembling from his encounter with the most beautiful girl he has ever seen…"Tapway, mon ami, I do treasure my saddle, it was made by an old Elder who works with leather, Mooshum Cardinal. It was given to me by Pierre L'Ambitieaux, my life-long friend from Red River."

By the time they get back to the house supper is on the table. Louie is still feeling nervous sitting next to Marguerite, "We will give thanks for our meal, then you may dish up first Louie."

Papa Jean-Baptiste asks a blessing and gives thanks; they all make the sign of the cross and Louie takes one potatoe, then a scoop of deer gravy with onions; he passes them on, reaches for a piece of bannock, *I can't believe how like my family these people are... in their manners. I suppose eating on the trail with those rowdy, ravenous trail bums made me forget how I was raised.*

The evening is pleasant with a relaxing exchange of family information, names, whereabouts, grandchildren and the community in general.

Louie is sneaking glances at Marguerite and once in a while...he catches her looking at him; they smile. *...is this what you had waiting for me, precious Mary, Joseph and Jesus? Praise be to God...*

**Glossary*

Footnotes:

No footnotes in this chapter.

Chapter Thirty Eight

Wood Mountain, Montana: 1881

As the sun is going down, Marguerite asks Patrice and Louie if they would like to go picking saskatoons down by the creek, "Now that sounds like a good idea, Madamoiselle; I have not picked berries since I lived in Red River."

Marguerite smiles back at Louie, "Please, call me Marguerite, or if you like, you may call me Margie, like my relatives and friends call me." Speaking nothing but French for weeks, Louie has a hard time saying Margie, with his heavy accent.

Louie is delighted; it feels like he has been accepted into their circle, "I will be happy to call you Margie; you are so pretty; you look like a Margie, heh, heh."

Louie was in his glory heading for a berry patch with a string if berry-pickers, Margie stopped and waited for her sisters, Christine and Cecile, who came bouncing out of their log huts, each with two children at their heels, happily swinging their berry pails. It is not far to the creek where saskatoons are hanging in clusters. Louie gathers some dry twigs and green grass and moss into a lard pail and lights it up,"I will hang this smudge between these two saskatoon bushes so the mosquitoes are kept from all of us."

Mama Marie has sent a sack of frybread and after an hour of picking they stop for a snack. The ground up on the riverbank is soft with moss; they sit and enjoy the sound of the creek rapids as they take a break and have their lunch.

Louie and Patrice are kept busy helping Papa Jean-Baptiste with all his summer projects, "I am so happy to have your help, you boys; Patrice's brothers are busy keeping up with whatever freighting they can find. It is sad how those big boats have left so many of our boys unemployed; there is just not enough freighting to go around. Many have moved into the larger towns and work in factories or they go to work in fisheries along the coast. Most of our boys from this community take their families and go brushing and picking rocks to clear land for the settlers as they move in. There is not much money, but they give them household supplies, including food."

Louie has brought up more clay from the riverbank and is mixing it up in a washtub* with some moss. Then he continues to fill the cracks in the logs on the outside walls. The logs shrink through the summer, the 'chinking'* gets dried out and has to be scooped out with a green stick. Then the crack is smeared full of fresh 'putty' and smoothed out with the same green stick; each time it is sharpened, "It sure makes a difference if you spend a winter without applying new putty. The year I arrived back home from Montreal, the children had only patched the cracks. I bet Mama burned twice as much wood that winter."

"Oui, oui, my boy, it does make a difference." The old man has taken a real liking to Louie and is not looking forward to seeing him and Patrice leave to join a hunting party that will soon be heading for Cypress hills. They will try to bring home one buffalo for each family.

"Back in the old days we could take our families and go up into the fall herds that were so big they would spread out for miles. Now the men leave their women at home and do their own butchering and drying. We are beginning to get used to it, but for the first few years… it was disgusting and disgraceful to not have the women with us to do meat. Not only that, it is lonely now, I miss all the visiting with the other families…and all the children. Many romances began on those fall hunts, heh, heh, heh. Our children were marrying trappers and freighters from away up river!"

"Tapway, Monsieur, my Mama is still talking about the old days, how they would all gather from the four directions and set up tents along the Saskatchewan River as far as the eye could see. They would gather in small crowds with relatives each day, then, they would have a big pow-wow, fiddling, jigging and feasting, all sorts of games for the children the last day. I even remember how we would get in a circle before we all parted to go our own directions. We would sing, drum and round dance. Mama says that the last few round dances…everyone would be weeping… there were hardly any buffalo left, she said."

Old Bellehumeur has no problem agreeing with Louie and adding more to the story, "We are doing our best to survive but you know, my boy, we need to learn to stay home and be farmers…we will survive if we can get a little land, a few tools and some farm animals. You know, my boy… like cows, pigs, sheep and chickens. With good gardens, we will survive, my boy. We just need a little bit of land."

Here we go again…I can feel that tugging on my heart and my spirit…God wants me to help my people again.

"If we only had someone to help us get some land and tools…" Louie is losing part of the old man's words… he is too deep in thought.

"I reckon I can talk Patrice into travelling with me this winter…he knows people we can stay with along the trail…I even lived in some of their camps with Joseph…I can get the attention of the U.S. Government…so help me God…I may need to have citizenship, hopefully not…

The old man reaches into Louie's tub and fills a lard pail with fresh mortar, "You do a good job of mixing, my boy."

"Well, I have to give credit to an old friend, Henri Coutu, in Red River; I helped him do his barn. He was very fussy about that recipe. He says if you use too much water it will shrink faster, and if you use too little, it will crack faster. So it needs to stick to your fingers a bit."

The old man throws his head back and laughs, "I remember when we had nothing but dried manure to mix with it; it is good to have moss nearby; the women are not too happy with the fumes when the heater is going in the wintertime, heh, heh."

Louie and Marguerite often come back to the riverbank and sit together sharing their family histories; it is not long before they are passionately in love.

Louie is happy just laying back on a mossy bed enjoying the closeness of Margie as she plays with his hair and kisses his eyes nose and mouth, "My sweet Margie, how would you like to travel with Patrice and I to Fort Assinaboine? I am feeling that God still wants me to help my people to develop a plan of action for the acquisition of land…please say you will come."

Marguerite is very quiet for a while before she speaks, "Louie nothing would make me happier; but, Mama and Papa…you need to talk to them…I am their baby; it will break their hearts."

The evening is heavy with emotion as Louie breaks the news to Jean-Baptiste, "I am not ignorant, my boy. I have been watching the love between you and our Chickie grow, I am not surprised…please, leave us to pray and talk about this. Go over and spend the night at Cecile's tonight. We will talk in the morning, Marguerite."

Louie has tossed and turned all night…*I have never noticed how hard this little mattess is on the floor until last night…if I was not about to leave I would definitely be looking for some new moss to build it up…wah wah, I feel like an old man, heh heh.* He begins to get into his clothes before Mama Marie gets up; while he is making a fire and getting the kettle on, Jean-Baptiste comes out of the little bedroom by the stove that is partitioned off with a curtain, "Good morning, my boy, I will make us some coffee and we will talk before the women come in."

"Good morning Jean-Baptiste, you look like you slept well." The old man gives him a quick grin, "You know, when I face these things I always say a little prayer that my Papa taught me, *'Trust in the Lord with all your heart, and lean not on your own understanding, in all your ways acknowledge Him, and He shall direct your path,'* that little verse has taken me through many perils, my boy."

Louie is sitting at the table, raking his fingers through his curls, "Merci, monsieur. That is what I needed to hear. God always reminds me of Proverbs chapter three, also…I am getting careless and running ahead of God. I need to slow down, humble myself, and wait on the Lord, hye-hye, Jean-Baptiste."

"I have to tell you, Louie, it is not you that I am concerned about. I am certain that you would take good care of Marguerite…it is the unknown that I am concerned about. The west is not what it used to be, before the lust for gold spread over the land like a dirty blanket. There are angry Indians, especially the renegades from Sitting Bull's camps, and you know how vicious some of the white men are, especially the cavalry brigades who are sent out to annialate the Indians. You know they get paid by the scalp." He sets two cups on the table; you can smell the coffee boiling.

"Sir, I hesitate to say this, but I am only too familiar with the terror being wrought by some of the white people. Sooner or later you would have found out," Louie pokes a pinch of kinikinik into his pipe, "…I have been a wanted man, by the Orangemen of Canada since 1870. Even though the government finally granted me an amnesty during my exile in the seventies, I still watch my back…they wanted my scalp. As a matter of fact…they were willing to pay $5000.00 … for my head in a sack."

"I am so sorry, my boy. You rarely receive a threat of that nature without being a political threat of some sort." Jean-Baptiste shakes his head as he fills their cups with steaming coffee.

Louie lights his pipe and takes a short puff and lets it out, "You have that correct sir. I will be honest with you…I believe God is laying it on my heart to once again take up the 'torch', so to speak, for my people. If they need their rights realized by the U.S. government in order to at least get homestead rights, I am feeling the call. Marguerite must know this. I know how badly she wants to travel with me, but the first thing I must do is apply for U.S.citizenship in order to insure my negotiating powers will be respected. Once that process begins, my friend, I cannot promise what form in which opposition will appear."

The old man lights his pipe, "...my boy, we need to pray for four days... then we will know."

"Yes sir, I will fast, that will help our prayers to be honored." He makes the sign of the cross.

"You know Louie, sometimes you almost sound like a Priest." The old man takes a careful sip from his hot coffee, all the while, looking Louie right in the eye.

"Please forgive me, I would have told you before...but the time was not right. I studied for six years at a seminary in Montreal...to be a priest. Please ...forgive me." He has taken a clean folded handkerchief from his vest pocket...tears are flowing freely. "My heart still aches, sir...it is hard to talk about. I dropped out when my Papa died...you so remind me of my Papa, Jean-Baptiste..." He says through deep wracking sobs, "...My Mama's Papa was also, Jean-Baptiste...Jean-Baptiste Lagimodiere."

"Oui, I remember him from the buffalo hunts... years ago. Your story is very intrigueing, my boy...it is almost too much for me...I do not know what to say. I am very sincere when I say, 'I wish you well', I will be praying now for four days. Mama Marie will be out soon, I hear her getting dressed."

"May I take my coffee and go waken Marguerite?" Louie is feeling strangely relieved after his confessions to Jean-Baptiste.

"Of course, you may as well share with her our morning conversation, my boy. Mama will likely have some crepes ready in about 20 minutes."

Louie gives him a wink and closes the door behind him. *Tomorrow will be Sunday and the Jesuits will be here to do Mass* ...that will be perfect...I will begin my fast in the morning before Mass.

Louie and Marguerite walk over to the little log chapel together. They have discussed everything regarding Louie's plans, "Louie, I am so happy to go to Mass before we begin trevelling together...we will ask the Jesuits for a blessing on our union." Marguerite is gently swinging Louie's hand as they stroll across the children's sand-pile and teeter-totter.

The little chapel is set back from the rest of the log buidings, in a little arbor of Aspen trees, people are streaming forth from their little homes, dogs and children following *...I suppose we may as well let everyone see us together, they will soon know, if they have not guessed...*

Margie looks around, the whole community of twenty-seven is out, twenty-eight counting Louie. "I will make a cake for supper tonight, Cecile has invited us for supper...she likes my cakes." Louie looks at her and smiles; she has confirmed his fast *...every time I have fasted it never fails...someone invites me to eat or I am tempted by one of my favourite foods.*

"Margie, could you please tell your sister, I am not afraid of her cooking, but I will not be having supper tonight. I must go down to the river to pray."

"Don't worry Louie, she knows you are a little strange. Heh, heh, heh."

"Now that is a wonderful compliment! In the Bible it says that 'we believers' are to be a 'peculiar people'. Heh, heh, heh." (KJV)

When the celebration of Mass has ended, everyone including the Jesuits go over to Cecile's to eat. Women can be seen walking across the playground carrying a pot of something or a berry pie of some sort.

Marguerite sits at the window watching the small opening in the trees, Louie left for Cypress Hills five days ago with Patrice, Jean-Baptiste and four other members of the community to hunt buffalo and deer. *...Patrice* *said they would be back in five days…no sign of them yet; it will soon be getting dark…*

"Come now, my girl, you better get used to waiting if you are marrying that Louie Riel. He will always be gone; mark my words. If he is a politician for Indian people he will have all kinds of enemies…even some of his own people, aspin*… your father is a good example. His own people were trying to kill him…they did not like that he was against drinking; your man is the same. The drinkers will hate him…at least when they are drunk." Mama Marie does not talk a lot, but she is very observant.

"He is a good man Mama; he is worth waiting for." Marguerite takes the tea towel and begins to dry dishes. "I am only trying to prepare you, my girl; your Father finally quit chasing dreams; if I was not so sick he would probably still be out there."

The dogs begin to bark, "Muh*, they are here, or else the Sioux are coming to take what little horses we have left, get your rifle my girl, just in case."

Marguerite takes her rifle down from the wall, slips her shawl over her shoulders and slides quickly out the door. There are several riders coming and soon she hears the chuckwagon coming behind. "Mama, it is the hunters! Praise be to God, they must have got away this morning; they beat the dark!"

As the riders follow the chuckwagon over to Poitras' Louie trots over to Marguerite; he takes his boot out of the stirrup and lets her step up and swing herself up to sit behind him. She throws her arms around his neck; they have a sweet kiss before Louie steers his horse over to Christine's. There they have pulled the chuckwagon up to a large heavy table where they unload the meat to be sorted; each family will take home what they need.

Marguerite jumps down from Louie's horse and takes the reins. She stands holding the reins while Louie helps Patrice and his Papa throw a few bags of dry meat over the saddle, "Welcome home Papa and Patrice; you never had any trouble?" Marguerite inquires.

"We had an excellent hunt, my girl, we even got an extra buffalo this fall, praise be to God." Papa nods toward Louie, "...your man claims it is so that you can take some with you on your trip south."

"Tapway, does that not make sense, Patrice?" Louie is wearing a big grin.

"Leave it to Louie to negotiate for his people. Heh, heh, heh. Aye huh, it makes sense to me. Heh, heh."

The women and children have got a fire started in the community fire pit and everyone is busy preparing for the 'Feast of the Harvest'.

Young boys are setting up benches around the fire, little children are bringing wood from their houses to stack by the fire, the older boys are carrying the lanterns.

Women are getting pans of tallow heated to deep fry bannock, strips if potatoes and strips of meat that have been cut ready for drying.

They have been brought home fresh for the fry pan ... the strips are cooked in moments...children are forbidden to go near the frying operation.

Blankets are being spread out on the ground and platters on one blanket, are being filled with steaming, golden brown bannock, thin strips of potatoes and meat that is cooked to perfection. Now, pies are beginning to appear on the blanket, "The singers are getting ready, Mama, everything looks good. When the Elders are done smudging could we ask Louie to give thanks also?" Mama Marie looks over at Jean-Baptiste, "What do you say Papa? There are no priests here."

"That is an excellent idea, I will give him a pipeful of kinikinik; where is he?"

"I believe he is having prayer and cleaning up; here he is, omuh, Louie you look very handsome; Papa needs to ask you something."

"My boy, it would give me much pleasure if you could offer a prayer of thanksgiving." He hands him a small pouch, Louie takes it and puts it in his vest pocket, "...Hye, hye, mon ami, it would be my honor."

The drummers suddenly give a call to order and everyone rises from their blankets; the men remove their hats. Old 'Mooswah' Makokis steps up to the circle and passes the smudge around, while one of the young men sweeps a sweetgrass smudge toward the food with an eagle feather.

The campfire gives an orange glow that dances upon all the faces around the fire; the children are giggling and happy...even the dogs are wagging their tails. Soon the sweetgrass ceremony is finished...

Jean-Baptiste moves into the light and makes a quiet announcement, "Mes ami most of you have met Louie Riel; I have asked him to say a blessing for us."

"Merci, hye, hye, mon ami, it is my pleasure to say a prayer of thanks for you. The hunters have been blessed with a successful hunt; it was my pleasure to travel with them. It has been an honor to stay in your camp and I will miss these wonderful Bellehumeur people when we leave.

He makes the sign of the cross and offers up a prayer '...Dear heavenly Father, we thank you for your kindness toward us, thank you for guiding and protecting us and thank you for the way you supply all our needs, bless this bountiful meal you have provided this evening, and thank you for a successful hunt this fall, Praise be to God... merci, hye, hye.' Everyone makes the sign of the cross and they begin their meal.

When they have eaten, Francois Desjarlais and Edouard Dumas, Pierre Poitra and Chuck Boyer bring out their fiddles and guitars. Soon the women have put away the food and Chuck and Francois are tuning their fiddles.

The evening ends earlier than usual; the men are exhausted after cleaning up their hunting camp, loading all the dry meat into 'puhgagan' bags and into the chuckwagon. Then upon arriving home they have to sort and deliver meat to each house.

While the women are getting the feast ready, they light their pipes and get their second wind … while they laugh about the events of the hunt.

Even the dogs are tired and happy. After giving a hand with the meat, the young boys get to take bones home to their dogs.

The young people enjoy a bit of Metis traditional dancing for about an hour, which ends in a lively round of the Red River jig.

When the jigging ends, they join hands and have the drummers sing a couple of songs as they do a round dance.

First, they have the honor song then, they put Patrice, Marguerite and Louie into the middle and they bless their journey with a round dance, moving in towards the fire where the travellers are standing, then they dance backwards to the edge, still yelling and laughing. The travellers are getting a big kick out of being honored.

Everyone bids the three travellers farewell and go off to their respective homes.

Back in the house, it is getting late and Louie and Marguerite say good-night and take their bedding out to sleep in the chuckwagon. We will be gone when you get up in the morning. I cleaned out the chuckwagon and the boys helped to load all our supplies."

"That is good, my girl, make sure and take extra quilts; it gets very cold out on the prairies at night." Patrice gives his Mama a hug, "Oui Mama, now, no worrying; we will be under the care of St. Joseph and his angels, eh Louie?"

"Tapway, Madame, we will be fine. God be with you two; we will be back in the spring." He shakes the strong hand of Jean-Baptiste, "We have enjoyed your stay with us, my boy…tie two extra horses behind your wagon; that lead team can get tired…especially if there are hills." Louie gives Marie a hug and they are gone.

*Glossary

Footnotes:

There is no footnotes.

Chapter Thirty Nine

Fort Benton, Montana/St, Patrick Mission: 1882/84

The sun is beginning to peek over the hill and cast an orange glow over the green shrubs that lead down to the landing on Milk river; there they will drive their covered wagon downhill onto an apron lowered down from the side of a steamboat.

The western traffic, heading for Fort Belknap generally appears about every hour. If there is no cargo space left, they will need to wait for the next steamboat.

In the mean time they park up on the riverbank to have breakfast. There is a grand view as they settle under a big leafy tree not too far from a ready-made fire pit.

Louie begins to build a fire while Patrick goes for water; Marguerite is stirring up a batch of crepes for when the skillet is hot.

As soon as Patrick puts the kettle on to boil, he carries on to unhitching the team and driving them down to the river in their harnesses. The first appearance of the steamboat negotiating the big bend, about one mile downriver, will still leave them enough time to load everything, hitch up the team, and get down to the river.

Hitching and loading a chuckwagon has developed into an exciting and competitive race, over the years. The speed of these Metis men as they execute this ancient skill has become a well-known feat. It could be said that it has saved many lives as the half-starved Indians would pursue any number of wagons for some of their food and ammunition, sometimes killing the drivers so as to gain control of the wagons. Trained renegade Metis and Indians, known as 'Indian war parties', could overpower Cavalry wagon trains that were loaded with rich trade goods.

They are just finishing breakfast when the sound of a steamboat whistle sends a cheery greeting over the water. The smokestack sends out a sycipated rhythm in time with the chug of the engine.

"There you go Bellehumeur, show us your skills. Heh, heh, heh!" Louie chuckles away, quickly putting out the fire, as Patrice jumps into action. Before you could count to ten the horses are hitched and parked by the gear that Louie and Margie have packed up, ready to toss into the wagon, "There you go, Riel, aspin, show us your skills! Heh, heh, heh."

Patrice lines up the wagon onto the landing… ready and aimed to drive onto the apron, once they stop and let it down. They all stare aghast as the Captain waves from the deck, "We are full! Anyone sick?" Patrice calls back, "No, carry on!"

As they watch the big boat sail on up the river, they look at one another, suddenly they all begin to laugh at once. "Now, that was a good one on us, heh, heh, heh!" Louie bends over holding his stomach; Patrice throws himself to the ground, and rolls over laughing!

Patrice unhitches the team and drives them up under the big tree. Louie and Margie toss a blanket on the ground under the tree. Louie sits down and leans his back up against the rough bark, "I am happy we get to sit here and watch the river, it is so calm this time of year." Margie snuggles up to Louie, "Ouie, and the leaves are turning just enough to be beautiful."

"Tapway, my darling." Louie lifts her chin and kisses the tip of her nose.

Patrice steps up to the tree, sits down, takes his harmonica from his shirt pocket and begins to play a beautiful melody…it suits the mood of the river. "Chawam, please play the Irish Washerwoman…now there is a good old tune!" Louie tries to tap his feet but he is sitting too low, so he joins Margie and they both clap their hands in time to the music.

***

As the big boat docks at Fort Belknap, Louie looks out over the little settlement; *I would guess that there would be about two hundred constituents living here.* Louie wastes no time putting his plan into action …*we will put up posters here for a gathering of halfbreeds wanting a proposal to Washington for land and tools. They must register for a halfbreed census. We will see how many will respond when we get back from Assinaboine in two weeks.*

"Patrice, where is the best place to meet here in Belknap?" Louie is untieing the two horses at the back of the chuckwagon to help Patrice take them all down to the river, "The best thing to do is get your posters made at the local newspaper, then they will tell you when and where is the best time and place." Louie gives him his wink of approval.

"Now, that is the kind of Adjutant General we need for the Committee that will appraoch the government with a proposal."

Margie is quiet; it amazes her to see these men in action, "You boys will make a powerful team."

"Merci, mon cheri; but, we need your encouragement."

After an evening sitting by the wagon watching the fire and making plans for Fort Assinaboine, everyone is ready to retire, "That was good gravy and bannock, my girl. You and Louie go and get settled in the wagon and I will check the hobbles on the horses and bring our things into the wagon." Patrice is not dumb; he knows that sweethearts need privacy.

The next day they are parked again at the landing, "That was a very successful stop, mon ami. We have old Edouard on board now; he says he will be explaining the poster hanging in his store. The date is set for two weeks from now for a big meeting at the local mission." Louie and Patrice are hanging over the deck enjoying the colorful fall shoreline. Louie can feel that old familiar fire beginning to burn once again in his soul, "Partice, my passion to help my people has never left…it has only been resting."

Patrice grins, "I know, I can see that, my friend."

Louie gazes on up the river, sandbars are beginning to appear, "I can see we are about to navigate a sharp bend…" At that, there is a loud screech from the fog horn, "…see, I told you, they have to warn anyone that is on the other side of the bend…there is no answer back."

"You seem to know your rivers, Louie, this old Milk River has a lot of sharp bends…it is crooked as a dog's hind leg."

Louie has a little laugh, "So, it will be a slow trip, I guess. How long before we get to Fort Assinaboine?"

Patrice shakes his head and pulls at his sparce curly beard, "No, my friend, it soon straightend out and we pick up speed; we will be their before high noon, I would think."

"Well, where do you think we should go first?" Louie is depending on Patrice for a bit of history, demographics and political background on Assinaboine in order to feel comfortable speaking with constituents.

"I think we should set up camp as close to town as possible, we can haul water if we have to, Chawam. We need Margie to be safe while we ride around the country drumming up support for a proposal to the government. They will not show if they have not heard what is the reason for the meeting."

"I agree, my friend, I am already praying for wisdom; that submission needs to be clear, short and to the point."

By the time they have spoken to a few people there is keen interest in a meeting in Fort Belknap. Local Metis are very impressed with Louie and his skills in speaking and answering questions in English, Cree, or French.

Before they pack up and go down to board the next steamboat, Louie has posters printed and Patrice puts them up at the Trading Post and Post Office, "I am glad now we decided to hold the meeting at Fort Belcamp; I see what you meant when you said there was no use riling up the white folks at Fort Assinaboine. That is an impressive Fort. I did not see many Metis in town…just those few camps we hit."

"Oui, my friend, Fort Belknap is nearly all Metis and they know a lot of Metis that are camped up and down the Missouri, both sides of Belknap. There are a few Half-breed camps also."

"Meewasin*, my friend, that sounds good! I will begin the submission tonight. You can help me. We will be forming a committee that will be reviewing it and making any changes before we submit it to Government. We will need as many signatures and x's as we can get even if we have to witness them ourselves."

When they have the document finished it says the following:

> *We ask the government to set apart a portion of land as a special reservation in this territory for the halfbreeds, as, scattered amongst other settlers, it becomes a very difficult matter for us to make a living and owing to our present limited means and want of experience in economy, we cannot compete with the majority of our fellow countrymen.*
>
> *Our want of legal knowledge has also been a stumbling block in our way, as often defrauded by tricky men, we have again been as individuals, to expense in the law courts use. This alone has rendered us often unable to remain more than four or five years at a time in our place without being completely impoverished.* Siggins, pg. 298: Harper Collins, 1995- Toronto, Canada.

Patrice is amazed at the momentum of Louie's campaign among the halfbreeds and Metis people along the Missouri, "My friend, you never cease to amaze me; people sit and soak up your every word; they are mezmerized."

"My dear brother; they are hungry for help. It does not hurt either, that I have learned to fast and pray in these situations." He grins and gives Patrice one of his famous winks.

Since his appointment by Marshal Botkin to the policing responsibilities of U.S. Marshal, life has picked up momentum and before he knows it, he is catapulted into a ring of controversy.

Before he knows it he is pulled into the centre of two impending court dates: March, 1884...a stunning charge against Simon Pepin, who had resisted all previous threats toward his profitable whiskey trade with Halfbreeds and Indians. Then, in April, 1884...he is set to appear on two counts of election fraud. These court appearances would send him into a grueling investigation for court evidence.

He is adored by a majority of the Metis and Halfbreed population; they are both opposed to his unabashed disdain for their abuse of whiskey and yet... fiercly proud of his defence of his people.

"Oh, my husband, I am so proud of you!" Margeurite hugs Louie around the neck. She has followed the two politicians as much as possible but since she has made friends with the nuns at St, Peter's Mission, she has become attached to the little log house they have put her into, she finally feels like they have a home.

The grounds of St. Peter's mission are beautiful; every cottage is surrounded by clumps of colorful flowers and as spring begins to bring forth life to the settlement, all kinds of berry bushes began to leaf out.

Louie takes a walk with Marguerite along the edge of a clearing that is surrounded with the little log homes of thirty two Metis families. The clearing is framed in by cottonwood trees, currant trees in bloom, and bristly bushes laden with wild roses. Each log cabin is home to two or three families.

They are being followed by a half dozen little Metis children with their dogs at their heels. When they meander off onto a path that leads down to a little babbling brook, the dogs and children take their leave.

A good-sized community garden is framed by a rail fence, and a similar rail fence surrounds a corral, where they herd horses or cattle that have been rounded up.

Chickens peck around at random and are free to roam. If they go out of bounds, or bother the gardens, they are soon brought to task by the nearest dogs.

Next to the corral is the main road that leads down to a landing on the Missouri River. Father Damiani drives his little buggy down to the landing every other day and waits for the mail.

Now that she is settled, Marguerite is willing to see her 'husband', in the country sense of the word, leaving for meetings at various points along Missouri River. He is, once again absorbed with fighting for the cause of his people.

They sit down on the bank of the creek and look up at the splendor of the mountains in the background, "Have you ever seen anything so beautiful, my love?" Marguerite rests her head on his shoulder, "Oui, my man, it is breathtaking."

The landscape to the west is a strange blue panorama of every shape of buttes you can imagine, "The people out here have a system of location that lines up with those buttes; they all have names. Your Papa has explained to me how they have provided a frame of reference.

"Louie, I have learned names of some of the buttes, like 'Priest's Frock Butte, Eagle Rock and Birdtail Rock...that long ridge."

"Oui, that is the way the trappers and voyageurs spoke of their locations... every landmark has a name of its own."

"How did you learn that, Louie?" Marguerite is always amazed at the scope of Louie's intelligence, "My dear, I scarcely remember it; my Papa told me stories of his days on the rivers. Being on these rivers and learning the names of some of these landmarks... is bringing it all back. I have thought of my Papa a lot since I met your Papa...they are basically the same type of Metis men...very thoughtful, faithful and ambitious. They are excellent story tellers and a lot of fun...but have very strong principles...tapway?"

Marguerite smiles, "Louie, it is wonderful how God has put us together."

"I am blessed to have you, my dear Chickie...not many women would wait on their man like you do; then when I return... you are willing to share my tales of victory or defeat." He takes her face in his hands and kisses her eyes and nose; then, they lie back on the moss, for a long sweet kiss...

Back at the cabin, Louie has an important announcement for Patrice, "My brother, you will never guess what has happened; we have had a miracle!" Patrice sits up on his little straw mattress, under the window, "What are you saying, did we get an answer from Botkin about our proposal?" Louie begins to laugh, he laughs and laughs until he gets the giggles, "Come on Riel, sober up, what is the miracle?"

Marguerite is sitting in their little Winnipeg cot, holding her stomach and laughing at another one of Louie's 'fits of joy', "My brother, I am pregnant, it is for sure!"

"Wuh wah! No wonder Louie is having a fit. That is fantastic, my sister! I will make us some tea...a baby for the Riels, wah wah!"

They spend the evening talking, "Father Damiani wants me to begin Teaching, we have a comfortable home, enough to eat...good clothes to wear, praise be to God! Tomorrow, mon cheri, let us go to Father Damiani and have a ceremony to bless our marriage...Praise be to God, great are our blessings!"

"I will be much happier with you teaching; it sounds like a safe job."

Patrice is still giggling about Louie's performance, "You bet, my sister. Any thing would be better than dodging bullets as a Marshal. You know my brother, I think Botkin gave you that job because you are not afraid of anything…no one else wanted it, heh, heh, heh."

"Well, my brother, if I have God's blessing, I have nothing to fear. It was a nice way to get the Metis on my side…they even slowed down drinking. But I swear, as soon as word got around that I was cracking down on crooked lawmen and whiskey traders, I soon could see who was for me and who was against me…it was like the parting of the 'Red Sea'*."

Patrice laughs at his analogy, "Chawam, it is a blessing that Simon Pepin and Sherrif Healy hate you so; you do not need that kind of treatment. It is time for you to settle down. The Metis have been organized, their requests are made known to the government, and the drinking has subsided with our Metis men. You have accomplished a lot; Marshal Botkin is on your side and will support the Metis; you have done well."

"Merci, merci…you are very kind, Chawam. I will continue to pray for our Metis people but…I will be so thankful when my trial is over. I feel that I will be exonerated; there was no criminal intent when I allowed those two Metis men, Louie Jerome and Urbain Delorme, from Canada to vote in the election. Those charges are just trumped up to get me out of the road; Healy is just educated enough to be dangerous. There are apparently documents in Pembina that they were both born in the U.S."

"Well at least you know now that your decision to receive U.S. citizenship was the right thing to do. Otherwise you would really be in a jackpot."

Settling into a sedentary life has been good for Louie. He has finally caught up with his correspondence and is now back in touch with most of his Canadian relatives.

Even Fabien Barnabe has written, albeit, his news is very sad, Evelina is finally over him, after reading of his marriage in a New York paper. Sadly enough, both Fabien and Evelina are now suffering from tuberculosis.

His Mama is very happy for him in his marriage to Marguerite. His brother Joseph thought he died in the western wilderness and was overwhelmed to get a letter from him. He insists that Louie comes home to Manitoba for the marriage of their sister Henriette to Louie Lavallee, it will mean the joining of four traditional bourgeoisie families, Riels, Lagimodieres, Poitras and Lavallees.

Louie begins to give serious thought to making a quick trip home for the wedding,

I would love to take my beautiful wife home with me, but it would be very hard on her with a babe in arms and another one on the way. Louie is sitting on a quilt in the shade, out behind their cabin; his baby boy is determined to go 'out of bounds' and get off the quilt.

He has just started to walk and Louie keeps an eye on him; he doesn't take too many steps before he lands on his deriere. But, he gets up and makes another attempt to reach a little clump of bush; a tiny black bird keeps landing on the bush; but, as soon as Jean comes toward him squealing… he flies away. Jean immediately sits down again, chortling… his little black curls bouncing off his forehead, "My boy, you are so much fun to watch!" Louie laughs and grabs Jean and swings him in the air, he squeals with joy…*what a handsome little rascal; if only I could take him to see my Mama…* Louie has not spoken any English to Jean yet; they rarely use English any more, unless he is out with the Scottish/Irish halfbreeds. They mix more Cree into their French conversations than English…*when he is a little older we will need to speak more English. I will write a poem about him tonight… he is like his Papa…always chasing an elusive dream, heh, heh, heh.*

In June of 1883 Louie is on his way down the Missouri River, heading for Manitoba… *it was hard to tear myself away from my family, but Marguerite is correct about what a long trip it will be. I am hoping to clear up some business while I am there; I will stop off in Pembina and have those documents sent to my Lawyer at Fort Benton...Healy's charges will be thrown out of court... If Mama is short on funds we will sell another plot of land. I cannot make enough money teaching school to support my family and also send money to Mama. Perhaps I shall spend some more time as a horse wrangler on that ranch...that will give us money until school begins again...* Louie is sitting up on the deck of the Steamer soaking up the splendor along the shores of the Missouri...soon he is fast asleep.

Louie's telegram to his brother Joseph, has obviously been acknowledged. As the train pulls into Winnipeg he is watching a crowd on the platform... *My God! Joseph must have broadcast my arrival time...half my relations are out there...I swear those are reporters carrying cameras!... Well, God help me, I am not ready for this...*

As he steps down from the train he is rushed by both relatives and reporters; he waves and smiles ...*Thank God I cleaned up in Pembina and put on my Sunday best, heh, heh, heh.*

Joseph is the first to give him a big bear hug, "Mama, is waiting at home, my brother; she is so excited!"

As Louie follows Joseph to his carriage, he is greeted by friends and relatives he hasn't seen in years. His greetings are sincere and teary eyed, alternating between English and Cree/Mechif. Not far from the carriage he is accosted by the Press and he takes time to politely answer a few questions; they snap photos while he is climbing into the carriage. He has kept it short... he had not planned on this, "I am very impressed wit' duh growt' h'and prosperity of h'our beloved Winnipeg. I 'ave been missing my family h'and could not pass h'up duh h'opportunity of attending duh wedding of my dear sister, Henriette ...thank you, thank you, I am teaching school in Montana...merci, thank you..." The wet curls dangling on Louie's forehead are evidence of his anxiety to get into the carriage.

"Wah wah, my brudder, dat was a circus, if I ever saw one! Holeh! ...heh, heh, heh." Joseph clicks his tongue a couple of times and gets the team trotting up to speed as he pulls off in the direction of St. Vital.

Julie and the family are standing out in the yard as Joseph pulls up to the hitching rail *...the old place looks very nice; it has been freshly whitewashed... oh Dear God...my Mama...she is looking old...but she is still beautiful to me.*

Louie cannot stop the flow of tears as he sees his Mama's face streaked with tears. "Mama, my Mama, I have waited for so long to see you..." He grabs her into his arms and they hug and sob for a few moments, "My boy, I have missed you so much!" Julie is overjoyed to see her darling son at last.

Everything is ready for the big wedding. They will all be gathering here at the Riel farm after the Mass and wedding tomorrow.

There is a lot of activity as more relatives arrive and set up camp. There are all kinds of tents and teepees set up out in the pasture. Each camp appears to have their own fire out in front of their tent...*it is like old times...praise be to God...*

Louie has made himself comfortable out on the veranda; he smokes his Papa's old pipe and rocks in his old rocking chair, "Now dis is as close to paradise h'as I will get for a while." His sister Henriette walks behind his chair and hugs him around the neck. "I 'ave to feast my eyes on you once in a while Louie; I still cannot believe you h'are 'ere."

"Oui, praise be to God...I h'am so t'ankful to be 'ere." Louie takes Henriette's hand from his shoulder and gently kisses it.

The wedding is beautiful and before long a series of traditional customs have moved them into the evening celebrations, "I cannot believe how everyone has changed; no doubt I have changed and have aged also."

Julie is seated next to Louie, and while the fiddles move from 'Joys of Quebec' to 'Reel of Eight', on and on, one familiar dance to the next, she enjoys every minute visiting in French, "Well, my boy, when you consider what we have endured, I believe we are doing very well. It blessed my heart today as you offered up that wonderful prayer for the marriage of your sister. "It has become my habit, Mama; if someone asks me to bless the food, I must capitalize on the opportunity to pray for any obvious needs, heh, heh, heh. It was a special treat to celebrate a smudging ceremony with uncle Henri Coutu also."

"You are exactly like your Papa; that was also his custom."

The evening wears on and Louie has not had to move; friends and relatives take turns stepping up and taking their turn at visiting Louie…he soaks it all up.

Louie remains beside his Mama throughout the evening as they enjoy all the traditional ceremonies taking place in the house.

Meanwhile, besides the fiddling and dancing in the kitchen, there are two other fiddlers, one on the front veranda and one on the rear veranda facing the river; dancers are making a circle to honor each fiddler.

Even though he is tired, Louie is energized by the love and blessings being bestowed upon him and his little family at home.

The celebrations have filled Louie with extreme happiness for several days in a row; however, as is generally the case, Louie's ecstacy is suddenly turned into terror as they receive the news that an assassination attempt is eminent. Word is out that "…there's a bullet made for Riel and by that bullet he will die…" The Orangemen of Winnipeg had gotten wind of Riel's arrival in St. Boniface.

Louie is soon winding his way home; he will be keeping a low profile.

***

After the long trip up the Missouri river, he arrives home and is greeted at the landing by Patrice, Marguerite and his little son.

'Little Jean' will not leave his side…it is a happy reunion, "Papa, Papa…" What a joy to feel the little fingers of his son, as he pulls at Louie's pantleg, "Astom, my boy…you speak very well, heh, heh…I 'ear you say, Papa, Papa…sit up 'ere, my boy; tell your Papa some stories!"

Louie takes his mouth organ from his pocket and plays a jig; he bounces little Jean on his knee.

Patrice and Marguerite clap in time, while Onclé Patrice sings, "Deedle dum deedle-dum, deedle deedle-deedle dum..."

What a party it is!

*Glossary

Footnotes:

1 'change moss' – In the days before diapers or pampers, the baby would be taken from the mossbag each day, the soiled moss would be thrown out and replaced by fresh clean moss. After a quick bath the baby is placed back onto a fresh bed of moss, swaddled and laced snuggly back into the mossbag, the moss contains healing properties that prevents rashes..

2 Country Marriage – A term used commonly in the fur-trade era in order to give respect to a couple awaiting the opportunity for a proper marriage.

Chapter Fourty

Batoche, N.W.T.: 1884/'85

A few weeks later...Marguerite gives birth to a beautiful baby girl! As friends and relatives drop by to see the new baby, comments are made about this little moonyasquasis* girl with tawny-brown hair, light complexion, and large brown eyes set in a little pixie face, the old ladies laugh at her cuteness.

Louie writes to his Mama "... she is loved and adored by all, Mama," Marie-Angelique is the pride of Louie's life. Finally... it seems that he has found true happiness... with a wonderful little family he can call his very own.

Father Damiani is pleased to have Louie back at Mass and to hear the good news of Louie's family, back in Red River.

"Are they doing better, my boy? You have said they were very poor."

"I must admit, at this time, they do not look poor. My personal feeling of guilt has magnified their state into a vision of poverty. Rest assured; that is not the case. Mama is very comfortable living in an average lifestyle. You may even say she has recovered the bourgeoisè social status of my dear Papa. The properties that I signed over to her have brought her back to a comfortable life-style. She was able to host the wedding festivities in grand style...of course the family contributes in many ways."

"Very well, very well, my boy. It sounds like it was a worth-while trip...I am very happy for you." He shakes Louie's hand again, just as Margeurite steps forward, "Please Father, we would like you to come for supper. Patrice has brought home a feed of venison."

By the end of summer, the men have travelled east to join the hunting camps; Marguerite is well cared for by the women in the villiage and sister Louise from the Mission.

She is also happy to have help with the children as they pick huckleberries and cranberries. She straps little Angelique onto her back in her moss-bag.*

Sister Louise helps to keep Jean safely out of the way while Marguerite scalds jars and cans berries, "I am so thankful for your help sister, I would be so afraid of scalding our little boy; it would be impossible to work with this scalding water without your help."

Sister Louise has been a lot of help and a lot of fun, "Now Marguerite, you know how I enjoy your family; besides I enjoy your berries in the winter-time, heh, heh, heh!" She takes little Jean and goes to the baby to change her moss*, "You hand me that fresh moss, my boy."

When the men return, they distribute the meat; then they begin cutting wood for the winter.

"It is so good to be back home even if we have to work hard getting ready before the snow flies. Once those blizzards hit we need to be prepared, eh Chawam? They can be a holy terror, heh, heh!"

Patrice is sawing blocks of wood from a dry aspen with a small cross-cut saw and Louie is splitting it as the blocks fall to the ground.

Once classes begin, Louie has his hands full every morning as he teaches twenty four lively young Metis boys. They are a charming lot and Louie enjoys them for the first while; however, after a few weeks, he is thankful for the peace and quiet he finds at home.

Even though he is responsible for teaching them reading, writing and arithmetic, his job also includes: helping the little ones remove their coats and put them back on, teaching them to hang their coats and touques on the hooks in the chapel cloakroom. Then he also helps them lace up their wrap-arounds. Meanwhile he must keep a good fire going in the stove… among many other menial duties.

It has turned into a demanding job and when he arrives back home at the end of the day… he is exhausted.

He takes a break for a few days at Christmas and enjoys the festivities at home with his family… he has no idea what is looming on the horizon.

Early in January, Father Damiani delivers a letter from Red River. Louie is holding little Jean on his lap while he opens his letter, "Oh look, my boy, it is a letter from your uncle Joseph!" He opens the letter; the color drains from his face…his precious sister Sara… she has died with tuberculosis. Louie is devastated.

Patrice lifts Jean from Louie's lap and calls for his sister, Chickie, astom! Your brother is passing out…bring some water!"

Marguerite comes quickly, just in time to see Louie slip from the chair onto the floor, "Bring a pillow Patrice…and a blanket." She wipes his face with a cold cloth, "This will be very hard on him, Patrice. He just had a letter from Sara; she was not well and she was going to try to go home… but she never made it…oh Patrice, this is the fourth family member he has lost now. He gets very ill every time. What will we do?"

Patrice says, "I know how this affects him; he told me about it one time; he falls into a deep depression. We will see how he feels… he's waking up."

"Are you alright my brother? You passed out for a few minutes. Here have a drink of water." Louie struggles to sit up, Marguerite gives him a drink of water. "Come, my man…we will help you to bed. You must get warm… you are trembling."

"I was about to write her a letter…now it is too late…" Marguerite pulls back the covers and helps him into bed.

A week passes by and Father Damiani stops by every day after he finishes teaching Louie's class, "Father, I so appreciate you taking over my boys. How are they doing?" The old priest takes a paper from his pocket and hands it to Louie, "Here is a letter from your boys; they are missing you."

Louie takes it and smiles at the Father, "I think I had better get back to work. It has been hard on my family and I will not recover lying around. I wish that I could cry Father…I feel so guilty; I let her down so badly…she was so proud of me when I was pursuing the priesthood. We wrote to each other faithfully. Now I rarely ever write her and she was my favourite sister for many years. She just kind of faded out of my life…now she is gone."

Father Damiani takes the tea Marguerite has handed him and takes a sip, "You will see her in Paradise, my friend. But, I agree with you. It would be wise to go back to your boys and get busy again."

Time passes and Louie can hear the spring birds singing as he walks over to the mission, he has gone through a few very hard weeks, *Those little boys have no idea how I am suffering; I am as exhausted as I was back when my seat in Parliament was sitting vacant. Those poor little guys, they are so innocent; yet they are so noisy and full of energy…I try to be pleasant with them…God help me; it is so difficult.*

When he enters the house, little Jean comes running, "Papa, Papa!"

"Come, my boy…you are my little angel; you brighten my day…come dance on Papa's knee!" Louie sits down, takes out his mouth organ and begins to play, 'Turkey in the Straw,' then he dances Jean on his knee. He squeals and giggles as his little dark curls bounce off his forehead.

"Now it is your sister's turn." He sets Jean down and takes Angelique in his arms, he sings a French lullaby, "My sweet little girl, with the cute little smile, let me look at your eyes, let me hold you a while…" Angelique looks up at her Papa adoringly…this is what Louie has needed.

Marguerite also has something to help Louie feel better, "Here, my man, read this article from the *Helena Weekly,* I think it will make you smile."

> *"...Louis Riel has been said to be a gentleman and a scholar. He is an American citizen with as full rights and infinitely more character than his persecutors..."* Helena Weekly, March 1883. "Strange Empire"- Howard, Montana, 1952.

They are coming to his defence after the scathing article in the *Benton Record:*

> *"The majority of mankind would recognize Louis Riel for just what he is, a low scoundrel whose fox-like cunning has alone kept him out of jail for these many years..."* pp. 318-19, Siggins.

"Merci, ma Cheri, you are sweet, and yes, it is much better than what the *Benton Record* had to say. I will be so happy to put those trials behind me. The Simon Pepin trial is coming right up this month, and my two charges of election fraud are coming up on April 16th...then I will totally disassociate myself from my career as a U.S. Marshal."

"Oui, my man, I will be so relieved to be rid of that worry."

Before the end of March Louie is again buffeted from the trial of Simon Pepin, who was arrested by Louie on several charges of selling liquor to Indians.

The *Benton Record* reported on the court proceedings: '*...the witnesses subpenoed by Marshal Louis Riel are not from a Reserve. They are classified as 'Half-breeds' who are not prohibited from drinking. The charges are thrown out of court.'* The Benton Record: April, 1883. Siggins.

Louie writes a letter to his brother-in-law, Louie Lavallée: "My health, my occupation as a schoolteacher and study master, are overwhelming me..." pg. 321, Siggins. Once again Riel is slipping into that dreaded depression.

During his retreat he tells his confessor, Father Camillus Imoda: "I have not been well for weeks. My health suffers from the fatiguing regularity of having to look after children from 6 in the morning until 8 at night...I do not get enough rest..." pg.321, Siggins.

Louie has been in prayer daily and has scheduled a retreat during Easter week at which time he will be fasting for Divine guidance.

He has been wrestling with an evil foreboding spirit which is producing thoughts of worthlessness and bitter regret over his past. He tries to push away these evil thoughts but is squeezed into feeling like he would rather be in Paradise with his Papa and all his siblings. *I must remember that God has chosen me to lead my people in a good direction; I will read my favourite Psalm from my friend, King David:*

> *"The eyes of the Lord are upon the righteous, and His ears are open unto their cry.*
>
> *The face of the Lord is against them that do evil, to cut off the remembrance of them to the earth.*
>
> *The righteous cry and the Lord heareth, and delivereth them all out of their troubles.*
>
> *The Lord is nigh unto them that are of a broken heart; and saveth such as be of a contrite spirit.*
>
> *Many are the afflictions of the righteous; but the Lord delivereth them out of them all.* Psalm 34:15-19; KJV.

He begins a new journal; it will be a source of healing for him. He records his deepest thoughts and feelings.

He writes: *At my table I will have only what is strictly necessary-water or milk to drink, no dessert, no syrup.*

I do not even want to sit comfortably. I want to punish myself, mortify my self in everything.

Once again, Louie is caught up in episodes of deep depression, he prays for the safety of his family...*dear sweet Mary, Joseph and Jesus, send your holy angels to care for my loved ones...if you please, do not take them from me. It is I who has been disobedient...if I am allowed to live, give me the strength to do your will...*

He wrestles with thoughts of all his "failed missions', why does God allow him to be in positions of leadership? Why?

Margeurite takes the children over to visit Cecile and her children or over to spend time with Sister Louise at the Mission. Patrice assures her, "Do not be sad, my sister, pray to be cheerful, he has asked me to play my mouth-organ...he loves music. He says it cheers him as David cheered Saul with his harp, in his depression. Have faith, Chickie, it will soon pass."

Once again, Louie is experiencing a series of dreams, some of them are dreadful, some are joyful; he awakens with new courage. Could it be the fever? He reads his journal entries; he has had some beautiful and significant dreams. They do not feel like dilerious rantings...a strange visitor in the night speaks in French: *"...you must march out in front."...* words of exhortation. Two days later he hears the Latin words: *statue cum fudicia, "Believe with confidence."* Siggins, 1994, Riel: 'A life of Revolution'.

Both of these entries he took as signs of a new mission about to begin.

On April 16th, 1884, the trial of the Territory of Montana vs. Louis Riel convenes and documents are brought forward as evidence proving legal U.S. citizenship of the two voters who had been deemed as fraudulent non-resident voters.

Louie's trip into the Pembina court to search for birth certificates has paid off! The two charges of election fraud against Louis Riel are thrown out of court.

Finally, the dark cloud is beginning to lift; Louie attends a Mass at Fort Benton and lights a "most beautiful candle" to Saint Joseph, his protector. Pg. 321, Siggins.

On May 1st, Riels finally move into a new house, their own home at last! It is a beautiful log house, a bit larger than the previous 'cabin', with a separate bedroom instead of a partition made from a hanging quilt.

It sits near a babbling brook; a small footbridge arched just high enough to allow a canoe under it. It leads to a footpath that snakes around into the woods where clumps of huckleberries, gooseberries and cranberries abound.

Marguerite and Jean are so excited! Louie is happy but still very exhausted, he writes his brother Joseph, "…it is all very nice, but I am still exhausted, the never-ending teaching chores, the nerve-wracking legal battles, have taken their toll on me. I must congratulate you on your marriage to Eléonore Poitras; I wish we could attend…"

On June 2nd he writes: *"Leader of the Manitobans! You know that God is with the Métis; be meek and humble of heart. Be grateful to God in complete repentance, Jesus Christ wants to repay you for your labours. That is why He is leading you gradually along His way of the cross. Mortify yourself. Live as a saint, die as one of the elect.* Pg. 323, Siggins.

The lovely spring weather is beginning to bring him back to health.

On Sunday, June 4th, 1884, Louie attends Mass at St. Peters. While he is in deep prayer a message is brought to him by an old Métisse lady, her name is Madame Arcand. She whispers quietly to him that visitors have arrived.

Louie leaves the little church and goes outside. There, standing together, are four men. They are crusty, dusty and haggard looking. The stockiest of them comes forward with an outstretched hand; Louie takes it and holds onto it… as he searches his eyes.

"You are a man who has travelled far. I don't know you, but you seem to know me."

"Yes," the other replied, "...and I think you may know the name of Gabriel Dumont."

"Of course, quite well," answered Riel. "I know it well, it is good to see you but, if you will excuse me, I am going to hear the rest of the mass. Please go and wait for me at my home, over there," He points with his lips, "... the house near the small bridge. My wife is there and I will join you shortly." Pg. 324, Siggins.

Twenty minutes later, Riel comes through the door. He ducks his head, even though this doorway is built for his height; he removes his hat and holds it over his chest and extends his right hand to Gabriel Dumont. "You have met my wife, Madeleine?"

"Oui, oui, you have a beautiful family Monsieur Riel," His French accent is very western, with a muddle of Cree here and there. He carries on with introductions to James Isbister, Moise Ouelette and Michel Dumas; Marguerite gets Louie a cup and pours fresh tea for everyone. A platter of bannock in the centre of the table is badly mangled. Remnants of canned buffalo and raspberry jam are still evident.

"Patrice, Marguerite's brother, is over at the mission giving Father Damiani a hand with some heavy chores, he will be back soon."

"Now, Monsieur Riel," Louie interjects, "Please ...call me Louie." Gabriel continues, "I will get straight to the point. Our people are in deep distress, brought on by injustices from the Canadian Government. They are again losing their land as the surveyers come in and re-survey our river lots. We have been appointed by our communities, they include, Metis, Half-breeds and white settlers, to find help in dealing with the government. Your name keeps coming up as the most reliable help we could find."

"I am flattered, Monsieur Dumont," Gabriel interjects, "Please ... call me Gabriel or Gabe." Louie carries on, "...what you are asking could turn out to be a monumental undertaking…I am now a family man with a demanding job. I have, once before, experienced these negotiations. It was an all consuming nightmare."

"We have heard many stories about your battles with the government. You are a hero among our people."

Louie smiles and shakes his head back and forth, "Please, allow me one night to pray and speak with my wife, I will not detain you any longer; I will have an answer in the morning. Please make yourselves at home. I see Patrice coming now…he is a wonderful host."

Louie smokes his pipe and listens to the exchange throughtout the evening…they are about to retire to their tent when Louie excuses himself to go and attend to little Jean, who is crying on the other side of the partition, "Good night my friends; we will see you at breakfast when the sun is rising."

The next morning, the delegation comes in from sleeping in their tent; Louie is sitting at the table smoking his pipe.

He has spent the night sorting out his thoughts and he has concluded that… all signs he has been receiving from God, are leading to a new mission; he will again be leading his people to victory.

After they are settled down to a table of Marguerite's best breakfast food, Louie offers a blessing on the food and upon their day.

"I must be honest with you; there is a slightly selfish motive to my decision to attend to your request. I am one of the Red River residents that were never compensated for our land. The government owes me 240 acres of land; much like many of the people who vacated their homes in the 1870-'73 exodus. The 31st clause of the Manitoba Act has never been fulfilled.

The men from Batoche are astounded at the clear description Louie gives of the generally ambiguous history of the Red River Resistance in 1870.

"My wife and I have talked; she agrees that I must resume my commitments to God and to my people."

"I thank you both." Gabriel extends his hand. "Patrice is welcome to travel with us. We had a visit out by the fire this morning…he will come with us and help you as you travel back home after we have improvements happening with the government."

"Oui, I expect we will hear from them before fall. At that time I must be back here to resume classes with my boys. They are nerve-wracking…but I will miss them, heh, heh, heh. I must excuse myself today as I take care of business before we leave."

Gabriel lights a pipe with Louie, "Oui, my friend, you take your time, we have a camp and supplies so we will help you get ready and feed ourselves. We have brought plenty of supplies sent by the people…even the white store keeper is waiting for you, heh, heh, heh." Gabriel's shoulders bounce up and down in a typical Metis laugh.

Patrice comes in and joins them for breakfast, "Heh, heh, heh, Pascutz! They must really need you. Nestow, I have just returned from speaking with Father Damiani. They will pray for our journey and he will send off two telegrams: one to Red River for your brother Joseph, and one for my Papa at Fort Belknap." He takes three crepes, two eggs and a piece of bannock. "Umm, my sister, I hate to admit it, but you are a good cook!"

"Now watch it, my brother, this coffee is hot!" The men all have a good laugh; she is bringing the coffee pot to fill his cup and warm up the others.

"Heh, heh, heh, that is the kind of woman to take on a journey! Heh, heh, heh! Hye, hye, my girl." Gabe holds his cup up for Margie to fill.

"My wife is very efficient; she can have our covered wagon packed in no time, I must care for my business in the community before we leave. Patrice and I will load the water, hay and wood and get everything snubbed down as soon as we are ready to leave."

"You bet, Nestow…we will be camping at Cypress Hills by the new moon."

***

They set out on June 10th in their little caravan, Dumas, Ouellette and Isbister each driving their Red River carts and Louie and his family in a covered wagon.

Gabriel and Patrice are riding patrol on horseback; both are equipped with spyglasses, rifles and water canteens. They pull up for lunch wherever there is water. If there is no water, they have a reserve barrel on the wagon.

Each night Gabriel guides them into the camp site they had just used the week before. His camps are always beside a river or creek; wherever there is wood, water, grass and a decent look-out.

By sun-down everyone is ready to stretch and eat the food Margie has prepared, "Wah wah! We are getting spoiled with your wife's good cooking, my Nephew."Gabriel has bestowed an appropriate Metis title upon Louie.

The men are all back from watering and hobbling the horses for the night, "Tapway, Ogemow*, we had to eat some pretty tough bannock on the way down here!" Michel Dumas is looking at Margie's beautiful golden brown bannock cooking in a skillet of hot suet*, he rubs his belly and licks his lips.

The children have travelled well and their trip has been pleasant most of the way, with only one night of rain. Marguerite is a pleasant traveller and she takes over driving the team once in a while, as Louie has a rest and cares for the children.

The trip is rather uneventful and the only regular event that offers some reprieve from the boring landscape along their journey, is the sight of a lonely tumbleweed rolling across the prairie.

Then there is the occasional small herd of antelope. Quickly Gabriel disappears over a small rise without explanation. Moments later he re-appears with supper draped over the skirt of his saddle, "I must ask, my friend..." Louie is unabashedly praising God and Gabriel for the gift of a tasty feed of antelope, "...why is it that you only kill one...why not two?"

Gabriel gives Louie that mischievious grin; a cheeky twinkle sparkling in his eyes, "My friend, I hate to say this to a man of your faith; but ...God will still be around for the next herd. Heh, heh, heh."

Louie is gaining more respect for Gabriel every day...Gabriel is also beginning to know Louie. He sees a genuine devotion to his family, his faith and his people... soon, the respect is mutual.

The most stirring events that occur during their journey, is the occasional appearance of a band of Indians, suddenly and silently... silhouetting the skyline on a nearby rise. This is a sight that has taken the breath away from hundreds of adventurers who have traversed their way across the prairies... not Gabriel.

He waves and carries on. The Indians may come down and ride along beside the caravan, as Dumont visits with them in their language, or he may order one of his men to bring salt, flour and tea out to give to them. They may visit some more, laugh at Dumont's jokes, or just carry on.

Louie remembers back to when his brother Joseph was so proud of him for his linguistic abilities, as he visited with parties of Cree, Sioux, Ojibwe and Blackfoot people, during their travels out west.

Familiar names and faces appear as they pass through family camps throughout the Cypress Hills. Louie is pleased to exchange greetings with friends of his papa's who stayed behind with relatives who had lost their Red River lots. This buffalo hunt in the '60s which proved to be very disappointing, would be talked about for many years.[*1]

Now it is Louie who grins over at Patrice as Gabriel Dumont carries on conversations in the same languages, "Nestow, do you hear that man speak Blackfoot? He puts me to shame; he speaks all those languages also, but very well, eh? Heh, heh, heh. Wuh wahh!"

They approach Tourond's Coulee...Riel's visions and imaginations begin to become a reality...his heart begins to pound, "Marguerite, this is a very pretty little place...I imagined it to have a desolate appearance...may God be with us."

"Louie, look at the camp!" As they come over a rise carts and tents are set up all along a creek; in the distance they can see a river. "See that river Louie? It is much smaller than the Missouri...but it looks strong and beautiful...such a beautiful green river!"

Louie has slowed the team down, "That has to be the South Saskatchewan, my dear. I cannot believe the people down there...I wonder what is going on."

It has taken them 20 days to reach Tourond's Coulee which is only a stone's throw from Gabriel Dumont's home, finally...they are at Batoche!"

*Glossary

Footnotes:

1 The Cypress Hills became a refuge for many Metis people as Red River became more populated by British pioneers. Their mile long river lots, with half-mile river fronts, were now being surveyed into square plots with no consideration for water access. The Metis people, who had occupied the Red River for more than two centuries, began to pack their necessities into their carts and wagons to travel west. Many would meet up with their relatives who had relocated to St. Albert, Victoria Settlement, Meeting Creek or Cypress Hills.

Chapter Fourty One

Batoche, N.W.T./St. Vitale, Manitoba: 1884

Gabriel rides up to Louie's wagon, "Welcome to the community of Batoche mission…they have organized a welcome committee for us. Everyone is anxious to see you Louie! Heh, heh, heh." Gabriel is getting a kick out of the surprised look on their faces.

Louie wraps his reins around the wagon post; he lets the team saunter along while he combs his hair, "Marguerite, wipe the children's faces and comb your hairs."

Gabriel has another good laugh, "Louie, my friend, you have been travelling for 20 days…they know how you will look, heh, heh, heh."

As Louie's wagon reaches the edge of the crowd a roar goes up, "Welcome, Welcome, greetings, greetings!" a loud chorus of 'welcomes' come forth in Cree, French and English.

The whole crowd follows behind Gabriel as he brings in his 'trophy', they are singing the now famous, *'Pierre Falcon's Anthem'* "*…Ah, would you have seen these Englishmen…*"pg. 31, "Strange Empire", Joseph Kinsey Howard.

Gabriel leads them down to the edge of the creek where Michel Dumas unhooks the team and leads the tired horses down for a drink; the carts follow and their horses are also watered, by Ouelette and Isbister. The men all wash their faces in the creek, comb their hair and place their hats back on their heads.

Louie is thinking and smiling, *Gabriel explained this valley to me, it is named for the family who provided the secret meeting place at Norbert... for my election to the House of Commons in 1873. Gabe says they could not take the new, uncomfortable atmosphere in the 'new Red River'...they also joined the exodus to the Saskatchewan valley...*

Everyone is smiling and shaking hands with the new arrivals. Louie smiles and nods while quietly introducing his wife and children. He takes a closer look at the faces of the press as they wield their cameras. *...no sign of Charlie Mair...*a pleasant smile hides the apprehension Riel is feeling. He can see familiar faces of friends and relatives who have joined the exodus, those who have fled from the mass of greedy speculators taking over Red River.

As the crowd files by, the travellers have an opportunity to stretch, have a drink of water and meet a few folks who are thrilled to meet with the reknowned Louie Riel and family.

Gabriel Dumont is also a very welcome spectacle; he too receives a hero's welcome; he has fulfilled the wishes of his people and brought back their 'hero of the Red River Resistance'!

However, it is soon time to hitch up and finish the journey to Gabriel's place in the villiage of Batoche, just up the river from Fish Creek.

Madeleine Dumont makes Marguerite and her family very welcome, while all those who are following the cavalcade begin to set up camp out on Gabriel's property.

Madeleine and Marguerite become instant friends; as they scurry about making supper for the two families, they quickly become acquainted, "Gabriel and I have had no children," Madeleine begins in her chattery western French, spiced with Cree idioms, "...we are raising our niece

Angelique, but we call her Tantoo, so we won't mistake her for your Angelique. Gabriel and I love children so feel right at home here with us."

Marguerite is busy peeling potatoes, her French is much like Madeleine's, so they chatter as they work, "My husband has a great deal of respect for your Gabriel; they have struck up a deep friendship."

"You know Marguerite, my husband is very excited about having your husband Louie here to help him, Pascutz! He has had no-one to help him, even the Priests are afraid of the Government, wah wah!"

Marguerite sets the pot of potatoes on the stove, "Oh, my dear Madeleine, my husband is afraid of no-one, as long as he is well. He takes on too much sometime and aspin*, he gets very sick…then he is afraid of his own shadow."

Madeleine lifts the lid on the stove and pokes in two sticks of wood, "Oh, oh…we must pray for him…he is taking on a big job, pascutz! We don't mix our food until they have a gathering with a feast; everyone will be cooking for their own camps."

"Aye-huh*, my girl…we do the same. Then we have music and dancing."

"Tapway, us too, pascutz…sometime they go all night. Heh, heh, heh!"

"Oui, our men in Montana are the same. If someone gets too much to drink…the women tie them up, heh, heh, heh."

Soon the men are in washing up for supper, Gabriel is like an excited little boy, "My friend, you just make yourself right at home…you also Patrice, we are so happy to have you here. I would like to keep you here, but your cousin, Charles Nolin, says he wants you at his place; he is coming over tonight to invite you. He does have a big house, omuh."

"We are happy to be here Gabe, but if it takes the entire summer we may need to spread out. We can still visit… whatever Marguerite says."

As it turns out, they spend a few days with the Dumonts; then, they move to Nolin's. They stay there for three months; then, as the mission heats up, Louie moves his family back to Dumont's. The fifteen mile ride to Batoche has sometimes been inconvenient and time-consuming.

His first evening at Dumont's is spent questioning Gabriel, Ouelette, Isbister and Dumas about the political climate of Batoche, "We need to accomplish an assessment in the next few days. What are the needs? What have you done in the past to try to achieve your goals? Who is your support and who is your opposition?" Louie is pleased with their clear responses.

Gabriel is proud of Riel's exceptional French, his clear diction and his powerful delivery. His words cut right to the heart of the matter and he does not waste time explaining his position, "I have all the confidence in Gabriel as Leader; I am quite happy to be a spiritual and political advisor, if that is agreeable with everyone."

"Oui, oui, tapway, tapway!"… is heard all around the table.

Gabriel is anxious to begin the first item on their list of priorities, "I like your idea to gather the people, explain ourselves, and begin work on establishing a Bill of Rights for the people of Saskatchewan."

Riel nods toward Gabriel, "As Gabriel's father, Isadore Dumont accomplished in '71*, we shall do again. We need a legal framework from which to present our requests."

After supper there is a gathering outside at Dumont's; Gabriel summons the people the same way they do at buffalo hunts and training camps…a loud tapping on a cast iron skillet.

They are informed that they will be gathering at the new St. Antoine de Pudoue Church a half-mile from Batoche, the next day.

As word spreads, the crowd inside the new St. Antoine de Padoue church swells and they are forced to move outdoors onto a grassy slope.

Gabriel welcomes the people who have travelled from all the surrounding communities. He thanks them for coming out and welcomes his English speaking friend, Will Jackson, to interpret for half-breeds and white farmers who did not speak French. Jackson offered a short interpretation; then, Dumont carries on, "I have someone here today who understands our plight. You all have heard of his leadership in Red River as the Metis stood against the unfair treatment they were receiving from John A. Macdonald." Jackson paraphrases Dumont's statement. "Most of you were involved with our attempt in 1871 to help our people; today we will hear from the man who brought recognition to Manitoba…welcome, sil vous plait…Monsieur Louie Riel."

The crowd roars; Louie bows…they stand to their feet…Louie bows again, then he raises his hand pointing to the heavens, "…Praise be to God…I am your humble servant."

He thanks them for having faith in him and for bringing him and his little family to the beautiful land of St. Laurent. He has been treated very well by the wonderful people of the Batoche area.

"Your esteemed President, Monsieur Dumont, has graciously filled me in on your incredibly harsh treatment from the Macdonald government. It grieves my heart to hear of our starving brothers on these forgotten reserves. I am very proud of our people for giving them what they have, even though you are suffering the same devastation." Riel turns to Jackson for translation. Jackson is astounded by the extremely refined speaker.

The people are mesmerized by Riel's impressive speech; he makes no promises of himself. "…we will look to God almighty for direction and for deliverance from the oppression of an heartless government."

Riel closes twice… the people want to hear more. Nolan steps up close to Riel and speaks into his ear, above the noise of the crowd, "Tell them we will meet again on July 19th at Treston Hall in Prince Albert."

Once more Louie raises his hand for silence, "Sil vous plait, mes ami…we will be meeting again…"

He finishes the invitation, thanks them for listening, takes a bow and leaps up the steps onto Nolin's veranda. Marguerite brings him a drink of water, and he lights his pipe. The crowd is waving as they leave for their carts and wagons, Louie waves back. Little Jean is now on his Papa's lap and he is waving happily to the people. Gabriel and Charlie Nolan join him on the veranda, "Merci, my cousin…that will be good…July 19th." Louie lowers the brim of his flat brimmed cowboy hat and gazes out at the setting sun; he takes a drag from his pipe…*praise be to God…*

Immediately there were forces at work setting up roadblocks to sabbotage Louie's appearance at Prince Albert. Louie begins a fast and sets to work organizing a support system to strengthen him and work with him in laying the groundwork for his submissions to Government. *…if I never learned another thing from my past experiences, I have learned to surround myself with people I can trust…I must give Nolin a chance to prove himself…*

Louie has one major 'Goliath'*, as he refers to obstacles…John. A. is back in power…*now is my hour, I must rise up against John. A. in the power of God…as Jehosephat stood in the midst of his enemies…'stand ye still and see the salvation of the Lord…for the battle is not yours, but God's'.* 2 Chronicles, 15-17, KJV.

Ever since Gabriel's Provisional Government collapsed, back in '74, the people have shied away from organizing. They remember too well how Lawrence Clark, a known back-stabber, had interfered with Gabriel's enforcement of their by-laws when a rebellious clan continued to contravene a significant by-law. They were 'hunting out of order'. Clark had Dumont's security jailed for arresting the delinquent hunters. The security was devasted that their sovereignty was not respected, they soon disbanded.

Now they must regroup and rekindle that old enthusiasm to believe for their Rights to be established.

Riel is informed that petitions had begun to go into Ottawa from 1874 to 1884 with very little attention. The closest they came to a response was in 1878, when four Petitions were submitted at once from, St. Laurent, St.

Albert, Cypress Hills and Prince Albert. They strongly proposed that their farm lots be registered.

To their amazement surveyors were sent into Prince Albert to survey the farms of white settlers. When they arrived in the St. Laurent area they continued to survey in square plots. This went against everything the Metis believed in. They had settled on their river lots years before and were accustomed to the river front access with gardens and hayfields stretching back for two miles, like they were in Red River.

For Louie it was déja vu*, the Red River Resistance began when he stepped on the survey chain and said, "You go no further."

Rumours were circulating that a big 'Land Boom' was coming and they were about to be expropriated from their properties.

Riel could see that time was of the essence, he began to work nearly 'round the clock, with Will Jackson at his side, both of them to the point of exhaustion, preparing a Bill of Rights to be submitted as soon as possible.

At one point, Riel reiterated his intent to bill the federal government for his unpaid services at Red River, "I was honest from the beginning; I am now a family man and I will not stand aside from collecting my fees before I return to the U.S. My objectives will soon have been met and I will be ready to gather up my little family and return to work, teaching school in Montana." (Once in the wrong hands his remittance will become a bone of contention.)

The petition is finally ready and is submitted in classic form, It outlines all the previos submissions, the downhill spiral of their economy with the loss of the fur trade, the buffalo, the introduction of steam freighters, bringing a close to the Metis shipping and freighting industries...basically, both the Indians and Metis are destitute...and now the white settlers are destitute. Many signatures of all three factions are included in the proposal.

The land problem is not exclusively Metis; white settlers and English Halfbreeds are suffering the same anguish; no one is happy with the 'ignorance' of John A. Macdonald.

At times there was involvement of Treaty Indians; they are forbidden by law to leave their reserves to hunt and gather. Furthermore, their treaties have all been broken, Indian agents are selling their food and supplies and they cannot leave the reserve to find food. They are basically being iradicated by starvation and Smallpox; the petition also speaks on their behalf.

Metis, Halfbreeds and whites are looking to Riel to find the answers to their grievances and a stategy that will get attention from the east.

Many of them could recall the flashing performance of Riel, in particular, the Metis who remember with great pride, the accomplishments of the Red River Resistance and the historical mile-post achieved by the Manitoba Act.

***

Going back to May 24th, 1884 it had all begun when a ground-breaking meeting was held involving representation from all three social factions, Halfbreeds, white settlers and Metis. The meeting was Metis-driven and was well attended in a strategic location at the little Lindsay schoolhouse in Red Deer, situated halfway between the St. Laurent and St Albert Settlements.

Once more the name of Louie Riel is brought forward; when the people hear the name, a roar goes up. The unanimous agreement for Louis Riel to be fetched up from Montana had been voiced!

There is no doubt that Riel has full support from the Metis and Halfbreed communities; however, Louie is not comfortable with attending to invitations from the white people of Prince Albert.

Nonetheless, he sets his fears aside when in a few days a letter arrives with 84 signatures of white pioneers; he squares his shoulders, says a prayer and makes ready for his trip to Prince Albert...*the Lord hates a coward; I will speak to those people with the same zeal I have had for the Metis...so help me God!*

It is hard to refuse when he reads enticing words like: '...you must absolutely come; you are the most popular man in the country; everyone awaits you with impatience...with the exception of a few people...*I can imagine who the few people are; likely the same old faction is involved...and they are not 'apples', heh, heh, heh.*

His attendance in Prince Albert is overwhelming; the *Prince Albert Times* says it all:

> *'This was a mass meeting, such as Prince Albert has never seen; people came from the country to meet Mr. Riel, from everywhere, and they went back struck with the quiet and gentle way he spoke to them.'* Pg. 334, Siggins.

Even Father André is impressed. He had nothing good to say about Riel when he first arrived; he had a hard time swallowing the fact that Riel openly confronted the Priests as not being supportive to the Metis. Now he has nothing but praise for him. If he were to remain in opposition to Riel, he risked losing his following. After a series of meetings a new Council is set up and Louie knows from experience, it is imperitive that a good Executive be set in place.

One potential candidate for executive is William Jackson...Louie has been watching him. He is exceptionally skilled in writing proposals and has the freedom to serve as secretary.

Riel is wrestling with his loyalties, firstly, and most demanding, is the dissension between his beloved Metis people of Canada and their feelings of rejection from the local clergy. Then there is Marguerite, patient and loving, as she cares for Angelique and little Jean... and awaits his promise. Before they left home they agreed that they would do what they could to help the people of Canada; then, get back to their life in Montana.

Riel has tried to operate at 'arms length' in his role as political/spiritual advisor; therefore, his involvement in the appointment of a council has been in a temporary capacity. He has even discouraged them from publicly associating themselves with him, to the point of not using the name Provisional Government. He prefers to be seen as 'one of the flock'.

They will call themselves '*le petit provisoire*'; Louie will call them the 'Exovedate', Latin for '*those called out*'. He avoids jeopardizing their appeals by association with a known enemy of John A.'s.

When all is said and done, Gabriel is the 'Adjutant General'...head of the Army, Dumont, in turn, sets up a council of 20*, and Pierre Parenteau is named President.

Louie's diary entries begin to take on a deep and sometimes foreboding nature; he records his prayers:

> *Lord our God, through Jesus, Mary, Joseph and Saint John the Baptist, allow us in the month of March, in the year 1885, to take the same position as we did in '69; and to maintain it most gloriously for your sovereign domain, most honorably for religion, most favourably for the salvation of souls, advantageously for society, and most suitably to procure in this world and the next the greatest sum of happiness for all those...*
> pg. 370, Siggins

March 11th. 1885, the tone is set, a heavy cloud of suspicion falls over the Metis and the NWMP; everyone is jumpy.

Major Crozier, who once held a somewhat sympathetic stand towards the Metis and Indians, as he beheld their desperate situations, now begins to view them as a threat. With Lawrence Clark carrying tales back and forth, the relationship is becoming explosive. Clark has been pivotal in creating tension; the strain is as tight as a twine.

On March 11th, Lieutenant-Governor Dewdney receives a copy of Crozier's letter: "...a great deal of excitement has prevailed amongst the Halfbreeds for some days past. The leaders are continuously travelling about amongst their men and these are getting arms ready to use." He has decided to leave for Fort Carlton with a troop of fifty. Pg. 371, Siggins. "Louis Riel"

Dewdney sends the letter on to Ottawa with a condescending sneer, "Halfbreed rebellion likely to break out any moment. Troop must be largely reinforced. French Halfbreeds alone number seven hundred men. If Halfbreeds rise, Indians will join them."

The commander of the NWMP, Colonal A.G. Irvine, is ordered to lead a force of one-hundred men from Regina as soon as possible. Pg. 371, Siggins.

On March 17th, Michel Dumas, Napoleon Nault and a small party run into Lawrence Clark, the chief factor at Fort Carlton. They stop him and inquire as to the status of their Land Claims. He answers them in his usual domineering way that, "There are 500 armed men on their way to arrest 'the agitators'…the only answer they will get is bullets."

The 'agitators', meaning Riel and Dumont, have been holding a novena with all the Metis military… the news causes all Metis men to bolt into action, the novena would have to wait.

Nerves are raw; a confrontation breaks out Louie accuses Father André of not supporting the interests of the Metis people, he tosses his respect to the wind and openly scorns the tough and belligerent priest, "Take him out of here!" André is escorted out of the church. Then an open dispute erupts between Dumont and Bishop Grandin, who is mild-mannered and more inclined to civil negotiation, "I realize there is an offer pending from Sir John which I am not familiar with, please allow Monsieur Forget to give you the details."

Forget is not only the secretary for Lieutenant-Governor Dewdey, but is also the clerk of the Northwest Territorial Council, "Monsieur Riel, a fine offer has been put forward where you may be more influential in your dealings with the government. We are prepared to elect you to serve on the NWT council at $1,000.00 per annum salary. You also could very well be installed as a Senator."

Riel is infuriated, "Do you think I would dirty my name by accepting such an appointment? Do you think I do not know that those are both positions of neutrality?"

The very next day Dumont drops in to Joseph Vandal's house where Bishop Grandin is staying, "I am happy that you have come to see us, please excuse our honorable advisor. Monsieu Riel is not well and very exhausted; we need him here as our political leader. In other matters, I am still the chief." Bishop Grandin politely accepts Dumont's apology.

Dumont assures the Bishop and Forget that the mass meeting held recently, where several tribes of the west met, was not attended by Metis, "...however, they are our relatives and when they are starving they come to us for relief, and we have to feed them. The government is not doing right by them; we want the Indians fed and our rights recognized. We do not desire to create any disturbance." When Forget returned to Regina, he submitted a long report. He mentioned the discord happening with the Metis and the likelihood of the white settlers complaints simply owing to a dislike for the party in power. He 'forgot' to mention the disparity of the Indians and Metis.

The Church of St. Antoine de Purdoue is proclaimed a stronghold and a brigade of Metis troops follow Riel to the Kerr store, on the south side of Batoche.

History begins to repeat itself while stores are commandeered and guns, ammunition and food supplies are 'charged' to the 'petit provincoise'. Battle strategies are laid out by Dumont from the doorstep of the Church. Any opposing their actions are temporarily detained in the second floor of the Nault farmhouse.

Meanwhile, the NWMP are heading for Fort Carlton from the south, as Domont's troops make their way east to Fort Carlton via Duck Lake.

Superintendent Crozier happens to have a brother-in-law, Thomas McKay, who is itching for action; he coaxes Crozier to allow him to go and meet with Riel. Crozier finally agrees and McKay rides off, accompanied by

Hillyard Mitchell, to Batoche where the Exovedate has 'occupied' the church.

McKay is intercepted by two Metis sentries who redirect them to Norbert Delorme's little farmhouse, close to the church, where Riel is resting.

McKay knocks on the door. Riel opens it; he shakes hands with both the men and invites them in. They are just finishing the noon meal. McKay gets straight to the point, "There appears to be a great deal of excitement here, Mr. Riel."

Riel calmly replies, "There is no excitement; only a mere demonstration to redress the common grievances." McKay is not satisfied, he is vying for a showdown; soon his stubborn ignorance and Riel's sharp replies bring the men into a heated argument.

Gabriel Dumont is taking it all in, sitting on a wine keg, arms folded. He is not about to get involved, that is not his style...he throws his head back in laughter once in a while.

As the men carry on in a bitter dispute their arms are flailing about; suddenly McKay knocks over a small cup of bull's blood, used in a sausage or taken by spoon for Louie's severe anemia. Dumont finds it very funny... little does he know that the media will be using this story of bloodshed to turn Riel into a raving maniac involved in 'blood' rituals.[*1] Things quieten down and finally McKay suggests that Riel go over to Fort Carlton and meet with Crozier, "Now Monsieur McKay, do I look crazy to you; he is waiting to arrest me."

Riel writes a letter to Crozier suggesting a strong ultimatum:

> "*...you will be required to give up completely the situation which the Canadian government has placed you in...In case of acceptance, you and your men will be set free...In case of non-acceptance, we intend to attack you, when tomorrow, the Lord's day is over...*" pg. 380, Siggins.

Again, Louie throws caution to the wind and when the entire Exovedate has signed the document…he signs, *"Louie 'David' Riel, Exovede."*

Crozier does not respond to Riel's infuriating letter. There is no attack the following Monday; that was never his intension. He is hoping for a peaceful relolution…he is not aware of Crozier's tenacity and stubborness…it is not in his nature to surrender.

By now Dumont is ready for battle; he is set to do guerrilla warfare. A clever strategist; he is well-known in the west as a strong leader. He is a sharpshooter and his men have been trained with the same accuracy. He has had three attacks aborted by Riel. It is becoming a strain to hold back.

Riel has instructed Dumont of his dreams and visions from God…they are 'not to fire first.' Riel's spiritual guidance carries with it a strong influence and a great deal of respect.

Dumont's spies have brought back intelligence regarding Crozier's forces. He has 56 Mounties and 43 volunteers from Prince Albert; at this point Dumont is set up at Duck Lake with 27 Metis sharpshooters.

McKay is even more wound up than Dumont; he is ready to fight. Crozier allows him to accompany him on a ride out to meet with Dumont, who has taken with him, his brother Isadore and a Cree scout by the name of Assiyiwin.

What happens next will set in motion the Northwest Rebellion of 1885… the two parties meet. You could have 'cut the air with a knife', as an old saying goes.

Suddenly, there is a scuffle; Assiyiwin spots the movement of McKay's rifle…he lunges for it; McKay raises his rifle and shoots them both dead… Gabriel's brother is gone!

Dumont yells an order in French, the Canadians scatter and the battle is on![*1]

*Glossary

Footnotes:

1 Along with the 'blood ritual' story, the media also spins out a variety of bribery stories involving thousands of dollars.
2 There are many generous accounts of the battle of Batoche in several great History books, some appear in the Bibliography.

Chapter Fourty Two

Batoche, N.W.T. 1885

Pits have been dug in strategic locations, sharpshooters have been assigned positions and the women are busily stuffing the trousers and shirts that Dumont grabbed from one of the stores…when a comrade asks him what the brooms are for, he says, "Don't question me!"

Live sharpshooters will be free to leave their posts to sneak around through the bush and surround the Canadian troops, while dummies are set up with brooms for rifles, through the haze of gunfire they look very real. Dumont has received a painful headwound which only serves to spur him on…*for the sake of Isadore, we will prevail!…*

Crozier sends out for another 150 men to bolster his reconnaissance force who are now in fierce battle. For a while Crozier keeps up a relentless attack, while inching forward. Suddenly he surveys their positions and the Metis are behind them…closing in.

Crozier already has 12 men dead, and eleven wounded by the sharpshooters. Riel is riding around carrying a large crucifix and praying…not a bullet hits him in all the crossfire. He is shouting, "Fire, in the name of God the Almighty! Fire, in the name of God the Son! Fire, in the name of the Holy Spirit! Finally, Crozier gives the command to retreat!

The second battle takes place at Frog Lake on April 2nd. as Big Bear forces the evacuation of Fort Pitt; his braves have killed nine residents.

Riel and Dumont are still awaiting action at Fish Creek...Riel will not allow Dumont to storm the enemy, as he is itching to do.

On April 24th, another battle breaks out at Fish Creek, between the forces of Dumont and Middleton. Both sides are ready for battle; again, Dumont is held back by Riel...this precipitates a two week stalemate.

When the battle finally resumes, Dumont is not about to 'hold fire', as Riel is ordering...Dumont has been obeying Riel as his spiritual advisor and has been respectfully obeying the man he worships for his intelligence and spiritual direction from God.

"Had Dumont been the supreme authority, there would have been much more bloodshed, more victories for the Metis and possibly eventual success in the overall campaign." Pg. 69, Terrance Lusty, 'Lagimodiere', 1980.

Now Dumont has had enough, his plans to quash the new forces in their state of exhaustion, cut telegraph lines, blow up train tracks, confiscate food and ammunition, meant for the Canadian forces, is not going to happen. The success of Dumont's strategy may have changed history, some say; however, it is not meant to be.

None the less, Dumont finally loses patience and takes a stand against Riel's direction. Rapid gunfire erupts and a fierce battle ensues; deserters are dropping off from both sides. The Metis fight valiantly and brilliantly; what they lack in ammunition and numbers is compensated by their courage, tactics and skill. Middleton obviously believes they are losing ground as the fighting dwindles down to another stalemate.

In the meantime, on may 2nd. There is a violent scourmage between Colonial Otter with his force of 325 Canadian Militia, and Chief Poundmaker, with his force of 250 Indians, at Cutknife Hill. Colonal Otter is defeated.

By May 9th, everyone is on edge, then, finally...the battle of Batoche is touched off! They fight viciously for four days; as the Canadian forces, numbering 912 and Metis forces numbering 500, clash violently. Middleton has difficulty in assessing their position, believing the Metis forces to be stronger than what they really are. They are appearing from every direction.

As Metis reinforcements are slowing down and ammunition is running out, Dumont orders his men to set a line of fire across the battlefield. Thick smoke is now giving Dumont's men the advantage; they rush the front line, grabbing guns and ammunition from the fallen dead.

By now, deserters have decreased the numbers significantly and the ammunition is gone. Riel's prophetic dream had predicted that clear skies on Tuesday, May 12th, 1885 would mean Batoche's survival; if it was a cloudy day…the Metis cause would be doomed. As darkness turned to day, Riel, Dumont and Dumas stood outside the bullet riddled church, Riel's voice was hoarse with emotion as they looked skyward, "I am so sorry, my friend, we must bid our wives farewell; death is now on our doorstep."

"We fought a good fight, my friend. By the time the women wave the flag of truce we will be lost in a hidden trail of escape, heading north for bush country." Gabriel knows the terrain like the back of his hand.

They hug their wives; who will be catching the next train for Winnipeg where Julie is keeping the children. They tie up a blanket of necessities, toss them over their backs and head for the bush. Louie is exhausted; he grabs Dumont by the shoulder. "You and Michel go, as fast as you can…I will only slow you down…I must surrender." Riel is puffing.

Dumont begins to protest but Louie insists, "You will make it, without me…God be with you." There is no time to waste, they turn and leave… soon they are out of sight.

Riel is soon captured and taken to Regina NWMP barracks where he will be kept until his trial.

On July 28th, the trial commences; it will be the trial of the century. Riel is charged with high Treason and he is to be tried by a 'stipendary' magistrate for the N.W.T.; he is a known Member of of the Loyal Order of the Orangemen and has been chosen by his good Orangeman friend, Sir John A. Macdonald.

The jury is as questionable; it is made up of six Protestant, English-speaking men. One is from Red River and is still burning over being among Riel's detainees, who were held during the seizure of Fort Garry. Furthermore, a Jury of 12 is the legal slate of jurors to serve in a capital crime. As intelligent people, they would have seen this. It's what the Metis call, '…turning a blind eye'.

Another of the jurors is later interviewed by a Regina newspaper:

> *"…we tried Riel for Treason and he was hung for 'the murder of Thomas Scott'."* Pg. 70, Terrance Lusty, "Lagimodiere", 1980

Quote: "Richardson is said to have written his 'pre-judgements' toward Riel and the Metis. It is quite evident that the fiber of Riel's trial was legally and morally satiated with flaws." Pg.72, Terrance Lusty excerpt from, "Lagimodiere", 1980 by Hector Coutu.

Lawyers for the defence have decided that they must plead insanity as Riel's only defence. Riel is adamantly opposed. Riel does not feel that is necessary, they are missing the point *…this is not how God would want this honorable mission to be seen; he has bestowed this responsibility on my Papa, and now on me.*

Lawyers for the prosecution bring in two medical Doctors who are there soley to bring back a testimony that will leave Riel fully responsible for his actions.

Quote: Dumont has offered to testify his sole complicity for the Metis military operation, that the Exovedate, (12 man council), not Riel, had voted civil war. He insists that Riel's initial presence in Saskatchewan was of peaceful intent. Napoleon Nault offered similar testimony but the two dared not cross into Canada without promise of immunity: pp. 70 & 71, Lusty, "Louie Riel, the Humanitarian"

What many people do not realize is that Riel is a threat to Macdonald and he is now in a position to fulfill the wishes of the Orangemen who have long been waiting for Riel to be assassinated, one way or another.

On August 1st, 1885, the jury retires to deliberate; one hour and twenty minutes later they return with a verdict. Riel rises to face the jury, "We have found the accused to be guilty as charged; with a recommendation for mercy."

Letters begin to flood in from all over the world. The news has made international headlines and letters are coming in from the U.S., (where he is a citizen.), France and England. Many are bearing several hundred signatures; one letter has 1850 signatures.

Rodrigue Masson, the son of Sophie, Louie's old patron, is trying everything to save the Metis leader; he is now the Lieutenant Governor of Quebec and has no voice; his feelings cannot be made public. He discreetly approaches Sir. John and pleads with him to change his mind. Masson warns him of the possible consequences; this could create a movement in Quebec that could result in a Parti Nationale and the obliteration of the Conservative party in Quebec. Macdonald's reply has reverberated down throughout history, *"He shall hang though every dog in Quebec bark in his favour."*- Frank W. Anderson, 1984, 'The Riel Rebellion'.

Louie is visited in October by Julie, his Mama, and his brothers, Joseph and Alexandre, Marguerite has stayed in Winnipeg with the children.

Once Louie has emphasized his lawyer's recommendation for leniency, the visit takes on a more cheerful air, he kisses both cheeks of his Mama and reassures her in his gentle French, "Merci, Mama, your prayers are answered. I shall serve my time and be of service to God even in my incarceration, I will survive on Phillipians chapter 4, you remember that Mama." Julie smiles, "Oui, my boy; …I will remember." Louie watches them leave until a guard takes his arm and pulls him in the direction of his cell.

At 7:00 p.m. November 15th, a messenger sent by Ottawa, arrives at Regina.

Riel is told immediately that he will be executed the next day...construction on the scaffold begins and carries on throughout the night.

Louie is in shock; he begins a vigil of prayer...Father André visits him. He receives his prayers and then asks to be left alone while he writes to his darling Marguerite and to his precious Mama, "*...Dear Jesus, sweet Mary and Joseph...help me in this, my last night on this earth. I am ready to meet my Papa in eternity...all has been forgiven, I must comfort my loved ones who must stay behind... on this unkind earth."* His throat is as tight as a drum; finally he breaks into sobs...*the worst is not seeing my children grow up...I must leave them in the care of God*...he begins to write to Marguerite, she is so broken-hearted, so ill now. She will not last the winter...his letter is brief, as though he is already somewhat detached...*Dearly beloved Marguerite,*

> *I am writing to you early in the morning. It is scarcely 1:00 a.m. Today is the 16th. It is a remarkable day.*
>
> *I send you my best wishes. Take good care of your little children. Your children belong to God more than you.*
>
> *Write often to your good father, tell him that I do not forget him for a single day.*
>
> *Louie "David" Riel*
>
> *Your husband who loves you in our Savior*
>
> *...a word of kindness according to God, to my little, little Jean, a word of kindness to my little, little Marie-Angélique*
>
> *Take courage, I bless you.*
>
> *Your father, Louie "David" Riel*

> Final words to his Mama...*May you be blessed from generation to generation for having been so great a mother to me... I embrace you with the greatest affection...*
>
> *Dear Mother, I am your affectionate, submissive and obedient son,*
>
> *Louie "David" Riel* (Pg.444, Siggins)

For his last meal, Louie asks for 3 eggs and a glass of milk. He has listened to the hammers pounding all night as they erect the scaffold.

"It is 2:00 a.m. in the morning Good Father André comes again to my side, he cousels me to hold myself ready for tomorrow. I listen to him. The Lord is helping me to maintain a peaceful and a calm spirit, like the oil in a vase which cannot become agitated. My most profound prophesy has been given, Father André has taken it into his notes also: 'My people shall sleep for 100 years...then they will be awakened through the artists.' I am calm; I am not raving, my heart is soothed by the Holy Spirit. I am doing everything I can think of to be ready."

More notes: "...I embrace you all with the greatest affection. You, dear mother, I embrace you as a Christian...my dear little children, I embrace you as a Christian father...you my dear brothers and sisters, brother-in-laws and sister-in-laws, nephews and nieces, cousins and friends, I embrace you all withal the cordiality of which my heart is capable. Please, be joyful, Dear Mother...

Dawn has broken; outside it is cold and clear. The trees glitter with hoar frost in the morning sun. Sherrif Chapleau is in a wretched state; it is 8:00 o'clock and he refuses to carry out his role in this final tragedy of a French-Canadian compatriot.

Riel looks up at the Deputy Sherrif, as he unlocks the cell, "Mr. Gibson, you want me? I am ready."

Father André asks the condemned man, "Do you quit this life with regret?" Riel amswers, "No, I thank God for having given me the strength to die well. I am on the threshold of eternity and I do not want to turn back."

"For the love of God, do you forgive your enemies…?" The old priest is visably shaken. Reil replies, "I forgive them with all my heart, as I would ask God to forgive me."

"Have you nothing in your heart against anybody, and is your conscience at peace?"

"I die at peace with God and with man, and I thank all those who helped me in my misfortunes… also I thank the officers and the gaurds who have treated me with respect and compassion."* Louie arises from the little cot in his cell, the hangman approaches and binds his hands behind his back. The Father kisses Riel and walks with him to the scaffold, "Courage Father," Louie is calm; he shows no weakness. Father André is crying openly; the hood and rope are placed over his head.

"Say 'Our Father,'…Riel bows his head, the old preist is sobbing…finally they reach the words '…and deliver us from evil…'! It is all over!

The body is shipped by CNR to Winnipeg; there he is placed in St. Boniface Cathedral to lie in state.

The End

*Glossary

Footnotes:

1 There are meticulous accounts of the trial of Louis Riel to be found in "Louis Riel', by Maggie Siggins, also in "Strange Empire" by Joseph Kinsey Howard and perhaps others, which may not provide the same level of accuracy or detail. Above all, the fact remains... Louis Riel went to his death satisfied that he had served both his God... and his people.

2 There is a short account of the massive funeral held for Louis Riel in the Epilogue of this account; ...there is a more extensive account of "Louis Riel's funeral in the final chapter by Maggie Siggins.

About the author

Carrie Bouvette Mason was born at the beginning of WWII and was raised in several small Alberta towns.

Being the second from the eldest in a family of fourteen siblings, provided her with the opportunity to gather a wealth of real life experiences.

As a young girl Carrie showed signs of having some writing potential; this came through clearly when she would gather from some life experiences and tell stories to her post-war siblings, by the hour, embellishing the situation to keep the children drawn into the story.

This natural skill, complimented by a love for reading and writing, would lead to a post-retirement life-time dream coming true.

After having raised seven children and working at several jobs, she would finish her working career as the Executive Director of a 'not for profit' Native organization.

This job required her to write proposals and prepare presentations, which quickly demonstrated her natural writing skills.

This being her second published book, ("My Girl") being the first, makes those of us who know and love her, very proud of her accomplishments.

Like good wine, or an old fiddle, she just keeps getting better with age.

Ralph Bouvette (Brother)

Epilogue, "The man with no epitaph"

Did Louis Riel accomplish his Mission in life?

Like most aboriginal young people, I was led to believe that Louis Riel was a 'flash in the pan', who never accomplished a purpose and simply died young leaving behind a legacy of shame and disgrace. According to history, he was a tyrant who rose up against the Government leaving behind a confused following who abandoned him in the end.

My purpose in writing this book has been to view Louis Riel from a different perspective; to re-write his Legacy, so to speak.

We have had an opportunity to examine his mission and try to get a better understanding of his objectives.

In "The Incredible Adventures of Louis Riel", by Cat Klerks, 2004, she uses a most significant Sub-title on her front cover that says it all. Other authors may make similar remarks within the body of their works such as: ... his landmark success in having Manitoba placed within Canadian Confederation; some have gone so far as to say he is one of the Fathers of Confederation; Cat Klerks boldly declares, also on the front cover, that he is, "Canada's Most Famous Revolutionary".

His famous final statement and the incredible international media coverage had been kept quiet for decades, until recent years.

Apparently letters of protest flowed in to the Courthouse to protest the death sentence which had been pronounced upon Riel. Heavy opposition from the massive international Catholic Priesthood along with Quebec citizens and politicians flooded the courthouse in protest by mail and telegraphs. In response, the famous words of Sir John A. Macdonald rang out across Canada and throughout the ages "... Louis Riel will hang, though every dog in Quebec may bark in opposition!"

As his body was carried by train across the prairies back to his homeland, people began the trek to join the swelling crowds of Metis people who were in deep mourning. St. Boniface Cathedral could not hold the crowds who gathered to bid farewell to their faithful leader. A stream of Metis people followed Riel's coffin for five miles as it was born on the shoulders of grieving friends and family, to its final resting place at St. Vital. He had not been abandoned after all.

His desire to serve God and his people remained a priority throughout his short life; both objectives were met.

Cat Klerks penned the words appropriate for an epitaph that could be placed on his 'cold and empty' tombstone: "Canada's Most Famous Revolutionary".

Bibliography – "My Boy"

Anderson, Frank. *The Riel Rebellion-1885.* Surrey, B.C. Heritage House Publishing Company Ltd., 1984

Anderson, Frank. *The Riel Rebellion-1885.* Calgary, Alberta: Frontier Publishing Ltd.1965.

Campbell, Maria. *Half-breed.* Toronto, Ontario: Mc Lelland and Stewart Limited, 1973.

Champagne, Duane. *Native America, Portrait of the Peoples.* Washington, D.C.: Visible Ink Press, 1994.

Coutu, Hector et. al. *Lagimodiere and their Descendants. 1635-1885.* Edmonton, Alberta: Co-op Press Limited, 1980.

Gordon, Irene Ternier. *Marie-Anne Lagimodiere.* Canmore, Alberta: Altitude Publishing Canada Ltd., 2004.

Howard, Joseph Kinsey et. al. *Strange Empire.* New York: Toronto: George J McLeod, Limited, 1952.

Klerks, Cat. *The Incredible Adventures of Louie Riel.* Canmore, Alberta: Altitude Publishing, 2004.

Lefebvre, Georges, translated by Palmer, R.R. *The Coming of the French Revolution.* Princeton, New Jersey: Princeton University Press. 1947.

MacGregor, James G. *Blankets and Beads.* Edmonton, Alberta: The Institute of Applied Art, Ltd. 1949.

Mason, Carrie. *"My Girl, my baby girl".* Caroline, Alberta: Peekaboo Publishing, 2008.

Richards, David. *Soldier Boys.* Saskatoon, Sask: Thistledown Press Ltd. 1993

Silver, Alfred. *Lord of the Plains.* New York: Ballantine Books, a division of Randon House, Inc. and simultaneously in Canada by Random House of Canada Limited, Toronto, 1990.

Silver, Alfred. *Red River Story.* New York: Ballantine Books, a division of Random House, Inc. 1988.

Spague, D.N. *Canada and the Metis. 1869-1885.* Waterloo, Ontario: Wilfred Laurier University Press, 1988.

Woodcock, George. *Gabriel Dumont.* Edmonton, Alberta: Hurtig Publishers, 1975.

Smith, H. Murray. *Footprints in Time.* Toronto, Ontario: The House of Grant (Canada) Ltd. Toronto. 1962.

Siggins, Maggie. *Riel: A Life of Revolution.* Toronto, Canada: HarperCollins Publishers Ltd. 1994.

Boyden, Joseph. *Louie Riel & Gabriel Dumont.* Toronto, Ontario: Penguin Group (Canada), 2010.

Hunter, Robert & Calihoo, Robert. *Occupied Canada.* Toronto, Ontario: McClelland & Stewart Inc., 1991.

Forbes, Harry. *A Cold Wind Foretold.* Maple Creek, Saskatchewan: Self-published, 2009.

Glossary

Adieu	"Good Bye"- French
Aieeah!	A cry of horror!-Cree
Apih	"Sit down"-Cree
Aspin	An expression of excitement or amazement- Cree
Astom	"Come here"-Cree
Atim Gaurdienne	"Watchdog" - Mechif
Aussi	"Also" -French
Awas!	"Leave!" –Cree (dialect)
Awoos Keway	" Leave, get away!" -Cree
Ay-ee	A musical yell of joy –French/Cajun
Aye-huh	"Yes"-Cree
Back-house	An out-door toilet, made of wood, with two holes in the seat one large and one small, built in the back near the barn yard.
Bannock	Bread, may be baked, fried or wrapped on a stick and cooked over a fire- English/ Scottish
Beanie	Little round hat-English
Beaucoup	Lots- French
Beau-tanté	"...my pretty auntie"
Berth	Bed on a train or steam-boat-English
Bienvenue	"Welcome"- French
Bitch Lamp	Used in place of coal oil; a dish of grease is melted and a braided cloth is lit for a wick, providing enough light for a room

Bonjour	"Hello" or "Good day"- French
Bonsoir, vous allez bien?	"Good evening! Are doing well?"
Bourgeoisie	The 'middle-class', engaged in social mobility
Bowler	Fashionable small round-brimmed black hat
Brigade L'Rouge	"The Red Brigade", the trained Metis Militia-French
Buckboard	Wagon with a wooden seat up front
Buffalo chaps	Warm winter chaps made with the curly buffalo hide facing out.
Calico	Popular term for fabric in 1800's fashions.
Candelabra	A branched candlestick which holds several candles
Ca va et toi	"I am well, and you?"-French
Caucasians	Peoples who are identified as being 'white'
Ceace	A Mechif way of identifying someone as being deceased
Cést bon	"That's good!"-French
Chamber-pail	A pail with a lid, kept in the bedroom and emptied every other day into the out-door toilet in the back yard.
Chaps	Leather protectors for riding pants, held up with a belt, still, at the turn of the 19th Century, there were warm buffalo chaps among the Metis-English
Chasqwa	"Just a minute or just wait."-Cree
Chawah	"Joking!" Or an expression of slight disgust-Cree
Chawam	"Friend or buddy"-Cree
Chaw-bag	A small 'pugahkin (hide)' bag tightly closed to keep the chewing tobacco soft.
Chesterfield	British designed couch
Chic	(pronounced 'sheek'), well-dressed-French

Chicken Dance	A traditional dance to mock the prairie chicken
Chinking	The entire family helped with the 'chinking', old dry chinking was removed and fresh new 'putty'(made with grass and clay), was pressed tightly into each crack to dry and keep out the cold. Logs spread from the weather and from shrinking each year.
Chokkas	A nickname for "Charles"
Coal oil	A popular fuel, extracted from coal in 1800s
Cobbles	Large stones laid into a cement street
Compagnon	"Companion" –French
Comment allez vous	"How are you?" –French
Coup	A term used to describe a successful military maneuver.
Cordouroy	Metis men originated the cordouroy, a road built across muskeg by falling trees ahead of you as you move forward. Author of 'Vimy Ridge', Pierre Burton, tells how the Metis were sent in to make trail for troops to cross a formidable muskeg of quicksand in order to overtake the Nazi's with a surprise attack from the 'rear'. Burton gives credit to the Metis and First Nations for their role in many of the 'victories' in the second World War.
Cravat	A distinguishing white collar worn only by the highly educated.
Criminy	Short for 'criminiation', an exclamation-Irish
Deedle-deedle-dee	One of the many 'scat-type' dance words used by Metis musicians and dancers
Deficile	Difficult-French

Deja-vu	A sense that you have experienced this before.
Dejeuner	Breakfast-French
Demoisell d'honneur	'Matron of Honour' at a wedding-French
Door jamb	The frame around the inside of a door-way
Dove tail	A special notch used in the construction of log houses, chopped out with an axe, in the shape of a dove's tail, fits together to create tongue and groove tightness
Dormer	An upstairs window overlooking the front yard, generally set into a tile roof ; a matching alpine sloped roof provides a European detail. 'Dormer'- bedroom- French.
Equipage	"Team of Voyageurs, professional river men"-French
Exovedate	Those in charge.
Exseh!	"It is finished!"-Cree
Famille	"Family" –French
Fast	A time of self-restraint whereby you set aside food or other pleasures as an offering to the Lord, for a set period of time.
'Fazzer'	"Father" with a strong French accent-English
Feather 'tick'	A large mattress stuffed with feathers, ie: goose down and sometimes used as a quilt-English
Fenians	A break-away group from the American Irish who caused a stir in the 1800's.
First Change	Dance steps used in the first part of the "Red River Jig"-Metis
Flagroot	A popular medicine for pain and inflammation, also a relaxant
Flat irons	Small but heavy pointed irons heated on the wood stove to press wrinkles from

	clothes. Lifted from the stove, with a wooden spring-loaded handle
Fob	A fancy chain of gold or silver from which to hang a pocket watch
Fort de Prairie	Now known as Edmonton, Alberta
Fort Garry	Now known as Winnipeg, Manitoba
French Minuet	A sophisticated up-tempo ¾ time waltz brought over to Montreal from Paris.
Frocks	Loose gowns made with heavy fabric-English
Garçon	Boy-French
Genocide	The mass annihilation of a distinct people
Gingham	An heavy fabric used in the making of tablecloths, curtains, sometimes skirts, etc., generally plaid.
Goose down	The light fluffy feathers next to the goose's skin.
Grand Marriage	Big wedding-French
Grass Dance	A traditional camping dance to flatten the grass before setting up the tent. Some believe it to be a blessing
Grimm's Fairy Tales	Ancient European Tales which contain morals
H'old money	'old' money said with a French accent. An 'H' is used before a vowel.
H'our s'ird	The strong accent of the Nuns, "...our third...-English/French accent
'Habits'	Habits are head-gear worn by Nuns.
Half-breed	Aboriginals with some Caucasian heritage other than French
Half-hitch	A quick knot, half-tied
Hare & The Tortoise	Old fairy tale with a moral.
Hayrack	A large wooden rack on wheels for use in the summer; sleigh runners in the winter pulled by a team of horses to haul hay, straw, straw, etc.

HBC Blankets	Hudson's Bay Company blankets contaminated with Small Pox.
Hobbles	Rope tied loosely around front legs so the horse hops around and pastures.
Hye hye	"Thank you" -Cree
Je arbre de reflecher	"My thinking tree"
Je suis tres reconnaisant	"I am so thankful, etc., -French
Je suis navré	"I am terribly sorry."-French
K'moochiwin	"You are crazy!"-Cree
Kachisk	"Your ass", -Cree
Kayah!	"Stop it!"-Cree
Kayas	"A long time ago"-Cree
Keemooch	"To sneak" -Cree
Kookom	"Grandma" –Cree
Lagimodiere	The maiden name of Julie Riel, Louis' Sr's wife.
L'Ambitieaux	Fictitious family name meaning, "The ambitious"-French
Lamartine	Typical French name
Latrine	Meaning toilet-French
Latsee	Slang for "let's see"-Metis
Lavatory	Lavatoire (toilet)-French-English
Le Famille de L'Ambitieaux	"Of the L'amiteaux Family"-French
'Le Nouveau Monde'	'The New World', a newspaper that held a wide circulation
Le Soleil	The sun-French
Lye	A strong disinfectant.
M.B.	Made Beaver, the currency used during the fur trade era. (Equivalent to one beaver)1800s.
Mah	"Kidding!"
Mahtee	"Let me see" or "please" –Cree
Mais je preférer	"But I prefer…
Maskimut	"Medicine bag" -Cree

Mechif	An exclusive Canadian language which incorporates 3 languages.
Meewasin	"Good", -Cree
Mes ami	My friends - French
Mess Hall	A large military dining hall.
Metis Nation	A nation of exclusively Canadian people recognized in the Canadian Constitution along with Inuit Nation and First Nations.
Metsuh	To eat-Cree
Muskwasis	"A little bear" -Cree
Mixed company	Generally with reference to opposing views.
Mugyquay muskwah	"No bear!" –Cree
Mon ami	"My friend"-Cree
Mon fils	"My son" -French
Mon jeune fils	"My young son" -French
Mon petite fils	"My grandson" -French
Monsieur	"Sir or Master" -French
Moonyow	"Moonyow" a pet name bestowed upon Keiren. "White man"-Cree (French accent will pronounce it with accent at the end, ie. 'Moon/*yow*')
Mooshom	"Grandpa" -Cree
Mooshwah	A pet name for 'Moose'-Cree
Moose-nose	A prized delicacy, general given to the Elders; it is par-boiled, then immersed in cold water. The outer skin will then peel off easily. The light colored interior can then be finished in a variety of ways. Toasted on a stick and thinly sliced, it is a superb bannock topping.
Mot de la Jeur	"...word of the day"-French Game among Poets
Muh	"Quiet!"-Cree
Muskimut	Small bag

Namoyah	"No" –Cree
N'est ce pas toucher	"Don't you touch!"-French
Nestow	"Brother-in-law" -Cree
Nichywam	"Silly dog's name" -Cree
Nimituh	"Dance" -Cree
Nohkomis	"Uncle" -Cree
Northern Cree or Ojibwa	French with an influence of regional languages.
Nuh	"Here." Or "Take it!"-Cree
Olde	British for old.
Ogemow	"Boss" -Cree
Ohow	"Owl" -Cree
Omah	"Over there" –Cree
Orangemen	A large British organization who were progressive capitalists; some were extreme land grabbers.
Oui	"Yes." -French
Owyah	"Ow", an expression of pain –Cree
'ow	A heavy French accent where the 'h' is dropped before a vowel.
Pagahkin	"Soft naturally processed hide, either white or smoked" –Cree
Paguaysigan	Bread or bannock-Cree
Paskutz	"Gracious sakes" or "shame" –Cree
Patrois	A slang from your homeland-French. (Louie was overjoyed to hear Red River expressions being used in Montana, where he was teaching school and living in exile.)
Paguh	A dried piece of Spruce pitch used to resin the fiddle bow for increased accuracy and volume- Cree, Northern dialect.
Pemmican	Dried meat pounded between two rocks. Dried berries may be added-Cree
Petit dejeuner	Breakfast
Petigway	"Come in."-Cree

Pinafore	Worn over a fancy dress to protect the pleated fabric, like a long apron.
Planed	Lumber smoothed with a hand-plane.
Plaisantez	Pleasant-French
Portmonnaie	A safe place to carry your money-French
Protocol	Traditional procedures acceptable to the occasion
Provencer	The Constituency held by Riel when he was a Member of Parliament, largely French-speaking.
Pugooh	Hardened spruce gum, used to resin the fiddle bow-Metis
Quebec French	The regional French dialect spoken in Quebec, slightly different from the Paris dialect
Quayahoh	"Hurry!" –Cree
Quoi?	"What?"- French
Red River Carts	Wagons that were cut in half and shared with relatives; where they became two wheeled and were so convenient the Metis designed and built many of them
Red River Jig	An internationally renowned Mechif 'signature' dance song, sometimes referred to as the Metis National Anthem. Dance styles vary from region to region, but steps rarely change
Reservoir	A tank attached to stoves in the old days that was filled daily with snow or water to stay warm for cleaning
Resevoir	Slang for 'reservoir'-Metis
Rivet	A common screw used to clamp tightly. It was pounded on and would never come loose
Saddle notch	A special notch chipped out with an axe to create a 'round' tongue in groove – resembles a saddle

School Master	A term used for a 'school teacher', generally male, in the 1800's.
Scrip	An ambiguous government term used for the receipt that would claim Metis property.
Scow	A wooden platform that floats, used in the freighting business.
Scusé	"Excuse me." –English
Semak	"Right away!"-Cree
Shoe-shine boy	Very common in larger cities, set up for business on a Railroad platform to catch 'travelers'
Sil vous plait	"If you please" –French
Slock	To 'snuff out', as in a candle or wick
Soyez le bienvenu	"Welcome" -French
Spruce branches	Branches from the evergreen spruce tree, when heated they explode, they contain a powerful disinfectant
Spruce Gum	Rubbery gobs of pitch used for many purposes; tooth cleaner, gum for breath freshener, disinfecting the interior of a barn, resin for the fiddle bow, (after it hardens)
St. Paul	Major city in Minnesota.
Strainers	Sterilized funnels and cloths to strain any foreign particles from liquids, i.e. milk, wine, cream, water etc. Before modern methods everything was boiled or scalded.
St.Cloud Landing	Harbour in Minnesota
Stone boat	A flat platform built with planks to haul brush and rocks from a field, hooked onto a team of horses
Suet	The fat from an animal, it had many uses: to melt and put in bread or bannock dough, to fry or deep-fry. To put on a rag

	and use for polishing, (particularly stove, kept up in the warming oven above the stove.), also handy to rub on the axles of the Red River carts, saddles, chaps, tack in general, harnesses, etc.
Surrey	Fancy buggy with a fringed roof.-English
Squaw	An extremely derogatory term used when addressing an Indian woman. 'Esquau', the correct term means 'Indian Lady'.
Tack	Equipment used on horses, ie: harness, halters, bridles, saddles, etc.
Tallow	Hardened beef fat with a variety of uses in barnyard; also good for deep frying.
Tamarack	Hard muskeg trees.
Tapway	"That's right" -Cree
Teddered	'Tethered', a short rope to anchor a horse to a tree or peg in the ground, long enough for him to eat.
Tic-a-tom, tic-a-tom	Traditional Metis river music
Town Crier	Long before Television and Radio, villages were built around a Town Centre where an appointed 'gentleman' would be called in to announce any notable news. He would use an early version of the 'megaphone' and yell in a loud voice, standing under a flag that waved out next to the Town Hall.
Travois	A triangular cart made from two small trees joined at the top with a 3 foot brace that is hitched to a dog or horse for transporting the 'sick', etc.-French
Tres bien	"Very well!" –French
Tres difficile	Very difficult-French
Tripe	A fancy delicacy made from the intestine of an animal by cleaning well, then cooking over an open fire. It is turned

	inside out and stretched on a green poplar stick; turn until the fat drips and it toasts to a golden brown.
Trough	A wooden watering vessel for animals.
Udder	Pierre's Red River patois, meaning 'other'
Uppercuts	A hit under the chin.
Vous etes tres gentil	"You are very kind."-French
Vous satisfaire, oui?	"You are satisfied, yes?"-French
Wah Wah!	An expression of 'amazement' -Cree
Wampam belt	Small money bag held at the waist by a belt.-Cree
Wash-tub	A large metal tub, (galvanized to prevent rust) 2 1/2 to 3 feet in diameter, many uses: carrying meat, keeping fish in water for easy scaling, filling with berries for canning. Scrub-board was set into the soapy water and clothes were scrubbed thoroughly until clean. Saturday night, tub was set on two chairs, curtained with a sheet; fresh water from the reservoir was added after each child, smallest to biggest...everyone was scrubbed clean, including hair, ready for church in the morning.
Wunskah!	"Get up!" -Cree
Wapoose	Rabbit-Cree
WPR	Western Pacific Railway
Z'ere	'Their', as pronounced by the Catholic Sisters-English

Photos

Mother of author, Mae Bouvette, and Suzanne Coutu, wife of Hector Coutu, (a descendant of the Lagimodiere Clan.)

Hector Coutu- A descendant of the Julie Lagimodiere clan. Also, he is the author of "Lagimodiere and Their Descendants 1635-1885".

I have been supported with prayer and guidance by these ladies through-out my journey in spreading hope to our people. Our hope is to bring Healing and Reconciliation to all who have been suffering from the injustices arising from colonialism in North America.

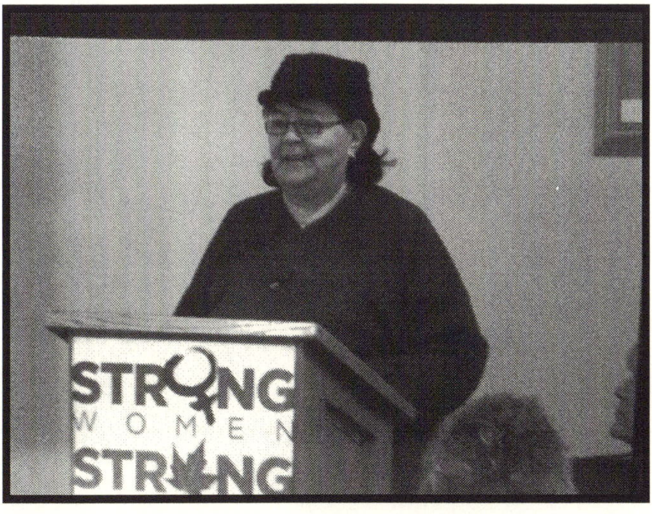

Author addressing a group of women.

Edwards Brothers Malloy
Oxnard, CA USA
November 24, 2014